The Second Catherine Aird Collection

Catherine Aird has served both as Vice-Chairman and as Chairman of the Crime Writers' Association and is the author of some sixteen detective novels. She has also written a *son et lumière* and has edited a number of parish histories. In recognition of her work she was awarded an honorary MA degree from the University of Kent and was made an MBE for her services to the Girl Guide Association. In October 1992 she was the first recipient of the CWA/Hertfordshire Libraries Golden Handcuffs Award for her outstanding contribution to detective fiction. Though she has lived in Kent for many years, she was brought up in Huddersfield.

Her new collection of short stories, *Injury Time*, is available in hardback from Macmillan.

Also by Catherine Aird in Pan Books

The Catherine Aird Collection
The Body Politic
A Going Concern

The Second
Catherine Aird
Collection

An Omnibus of Crime

Pan Books
London, Sydney and Auckland

The Religious Body first published 1966

Henrietta Who? first published 1968

The Complete Steel first published 1969

This combined edition published 1994 by Pan Books
an imprint of Macmillan General Books
Cavaye Place London SW10 9PG
and Basingstoke

Associated companies throughout the world

ISBN 0 330 33840 4

A CIP catalogue record for this book is available from
the British Library

Phototypeset by Intype, London
Printed by Cox & Wyman

Contents

The Religious Body

For my parents, with love

'What I want to know is:
One – who is the criminal?
Two – how did he (or she) do it?'

Ernest the Policeman,
in *The Toytown Mystery*
by S. G. Hulme Beaman

1

Sister Mary St Gertrude put out a hand and stilled the tiny alarm clock long before it got into its stride. It was five o'clock and quite dark. She slipped quickly out of bed, shivering a little. The Convent of St Anselm wasn't completely unheated but at five o'clock on a November morning it felt as if it was.

She dressed very quietly, splashing some cold water on her face from a basin in the corner of the little room. The water was really chilled and she dressed even more quickly afterwards. Her habit complete, she knelt at the *prie-dieu* in front of the window and made her first private devotions of the day. Then she drew back the curtains of the window and stripped off her bed.

It was then twenty-five minutes past five. Utterly used to a day ordained by a combination of tradition and the clock, she picked up her breviary and read therein for exactly five minutes. As the hands of the clock crept round to the half-hour she closed the book and slipped out of the door. It was Sister Gertrude's duty this month to awake the convent.

She herself slept on the top landing of the house and she went first of all to pull back those landing curtains. Half a mile away the village of Cullingoak still slept on in darkness. There was just one light visible from where she stood and that was in the bakery. It would be another half an hour before the next light appeared – in the newspaper shop, where the day's complement of disaster and gossip arrived from Berebury by van. Sister Gertrude arranged the drawn curtains neatly at the sides of the window and turned away. Newspapers had not been one of the things she had regretted when she left the world.

She descended to the landing below and drew back another set of curtains on the other side of the house. In this direction, a couple of fields away, lay Cullingoak Agricultural Institute. It, too, was invisible in the darkness, but presently the boy who was duty herdsman for the week would start the milking. Occasionally in the convent they could hear the lowing of the cattle as they moved slowly across the fields. Sister Gertrude turned down a corridor, counting the doors as she passed them. Six, five, fo . . . four. At four doors away there was no mistaking Sister Mary St Hilda's snore.

It rose to an amazing crescendo and then stopped with disturbing suddenness – only to start seconds later working its way up to a new climax. Sister Bonaventure called it the convent's answer to the Institute's cows, but then Sister Bonaventure declared the snore could be heard six doors away on a good day.

She may well have been right. It was true that the only person in the Convent of St Anselm who didn't know about Sister Hilda's snore was Sister Hilda. It was, thought Sister Gertrude wryly, a true test of religious behaviour to sleep uncomplainingly up to four – or even five – doors away from her, and greet the cheerful unknowing Sister Hilda with true Christian charity each morning. She had had to do it herself and she knew. But how she had longed to be able to go in and turn her over on to her other side.

She wished now that she could wake her first but there was a prescribed order for this as there was for everything else in convent life. It was decreed that the first door on which she had to knock every morning was that of the Reverend Mother. Why this was so, she did not know. It may have been because it was unthinkable that the Mother Superior should sleep while any of her daughters in religion were awake. It may have been one of the things – one of the many things – whose origin was lost in the dim antiquity when their order was founded.

She had to go round two more corners before she came to the Reverend Mother's door. She tapped gently.

'I ask your blessing, Mother.'

'God bless you, my daughter.' The answer came swiftly through the door in a deep, calm voice. She never had to knock twice to wake the Reverend Mother.

The next door on which she had to knock was that of the Sacrist. She must always be up betimes.

'God bless you, Sister.'

'God bless *you*, Sister,' responded the Sacrist promptly.

Then the Cellarer. She, too, had early work to do.

'God bless you, Sister.'

And the Novice Mistress.

No response.

Another knock, louder.

'God bless you, Sister,' sleepily. The Novice Mistress sounded as if she had been hauled back from a pleasant dream.

The Bursar and Procuratrix, the Mother Superior's right-hand woman Sister Lucy.

'God bless you, Sister.' No delay here. She sounded very wide awake.

Then she could start on the ordinary doors, one after the other. There were still fifty to go.

Knock.

'God bless you, Sister,' tentatively.

The unmistakable sound of dentures being seized from a tin mug.

Pause.

Then, triumphantly, 'God bless *you*, Sister.'

Knock, blessing, response. Knock, blessing, response.

In a way the formula made the job easier. 'Half-past five on a November morning and all's well' doubtless would have its uses, but hardly in a convent. She drew back yet another set of landing curtains and was glad she didn't have to say something about the weather fifty-five times every morning. It wasn't a particularly nice morning but not bad for November, not bad at all. It looked as if it would stay fine for tonight, which was Bonfire Night. Sister Gertrude had not been so long out of the world that she couldn't remember the importance to children of having a fine night for their fires. Besides, a damp November Fifth was a sore trial to everyone – then you never knew when they would let their fireworks off. She wondered what the students at the Agricultural Institute were planning. Last year they had burnt down the old bus shelter in the centre of the village. Not before time, she had been told, and now there was a brand new one there.

Knock, blessing, response. Knock, blessing, response.

The older the Sister, the quicker the response. Sister Gertrude had worked that out long ago. She called the older ones first – partly because they slept on the lower floors, partly because she could still remember how much those extra minutes' sleep had meant when she was a young nun. Sleep had been a most precious commodity then.

Knock, blessing, unintelligible response. That was old Mother Mary St Thérèse, aged goodness knows what, professed long before Sister Gertrude was born, with a memory like a set of archives. Woe betide any Reverend Mother with an eye for innovation. Mother Thérèse had outlived a string of Prioresses, each of whom, she managed to imply (without any apparent lapse of Christian charity), was not a patch on their predecessor. There were days now when she was not able to leave her room. The Reverend Mother would visit her then, and listen patiently to interminable recitations of virtues of Mother Helena of blessed memory, in whose time it seemed life in the Convent of St Anselm had been perfect.

Knock, blessing, response.

She turned back into the corridor where Sister Hilda was the soundest sleeper. The snore was still rising and falling 'like all the trumpets', thought Sister Gertrude, before she realized that it was an irreverent simile, and that custody of the mind was just as important as custody of the eyes even if it was half-past five in the morning and she was all alone in the dim corridor.

Knock, blessing, response.

That was the door next to Sister Hilda, Sister Jerome. Sister Gertrude wondered what sort of a night she had had. Perhaps the snore didn't bother her, but if it did, she couldn't very well say, not after solemnly undertaking to live at peace for ever with her Sisters in religion.

Knock, blessing, response.

Sister Hilda's door.

The snore ground to a halt, there were a couple of choking snorts, and then the pleasant voice of Sister Hilda sang out warmly, 'God bless *you*, Sister.'

It was strange but true that Sister Hilda had one of the most mellifluous speaking voices in the Convent. Sister Gertrude shook her head at this phenomenon and passed on to the next door.

Knock, blessing . . . no response.

Knock (louder), blessing (more insistently) . . . still no response.

Sister Anne's teeth were her own. She could think of no other reason for delay in answering and put her hand on the door: the room was empty, the bed made. A very human grin spread over Sister Gertrude's face. Sister Anne hadn't been able to stick another minute of that snore and had crept down early. Strictly forbidden, of course. So was making your bed to save dashing up before Sext. She made a mental note to pull her leg about that later, and, taking a look at her watch, hurried along to the next door. There was still the entire novitiate to be woken, to say nothing of a row of postulants – and *they* never wanted to get up.

At ten minutes to six Sister Gertrude slipped into her stall in the quiet chapel and went down on her knees until the service began. There was no formal procession into the chapel for this service. Each Sister came to her own stall and knelt until the stroke of six. She heard the crunch of car wheels on the gravel outside. That was Father MacAuley come to take the service. She lowered her head. She was glad enough to kneel peacefully, her first task of the day completed. Gradually in the few minutes before the service she emptied her mind of all but prayer and worship, and as the ancient ritual proceeded she was oblivious of everything save the proper order of bidding and response.

Until Sister Peter moved forward.

Sister Peter was Chantress, which office weighed heavily on her slight shoulders. She was young still and inclined to start nervously when spoken to.

After the Epistle she stepped into the aisle and walked up to the altar steps for an antiphon. Her music manuscript – hand-illuminated and old – was there, ready open on its stand.

The Sisters rose, their eyes on the Chantress, waiting for her to start the Gradual.

Sister Peter's voice gave them the note, and the antiphon began. The Sisters sang their way through the time-honoured phrases. On the steps of the altar, Sister Peter put out her right hand to turn the music manuscript over, touched it – and shot back as if she had been stung.

The nuns sang on.

Sister Peter's face paled visibly. She stared first at the manuscript and then at her own hand. It was as if she could not believe what she saw there. She went on staring at the manuscript. She made no attempt to turn the page over but stood there in front of the stand, an incredulous expression on her face, until the nuns had sung their own way to the end of the Gradual.

Then she genuflected deeply and turned and walked back to her stall, her face a troubled, tragic white, her hands clasped together in front of her but nevertheless visibly trembling.

The congregation settled themselves for the Gospel.

Convent life, reflected Sister Gertrude, was never without interest.

They filed out of the chapel in twos, hands clasped together in front, bowing to the altar. They proceeded to the refectory where they bowed to the Abbatial chair and then stood, backs to their own benches, while grace was said.

'Amen,' said the community in unison.

There was a rustle of habits and then the nuns were seated. One sat apart on a little dais, a reading desk in front of her. When all was still she began to read aloud from the Martyrology. The Refectarian stood by the serving hatch, her eye on the Reverend Mother. The Reader started to retail the sufferings of the early Christian martyrs. At the end of the first page she paused. The Reverend Mother knocked once on the table. The serving hatch flew up and the Refectarian seized an enormous teapot, set it down at a table and went back for another. A younger Sister appeared with the first of several baskets of bread. This was passed rapidly down one of the long tables.

The incredible tortures inflicted on the martyrs were obscured by the crunching of crusts and the sipping of hot tea. The Reader raised her voice to tell of boiling oil and decapitation. The teapot went on its second round, the bread baskets emptied. Only little Sister Peter seemed to be with the Reader completely. Her expression would have brought satisfaction to any torturer.

It was at this point that Sister Gertrude noticed the empty place. It was between Sister Damien, angular, intense and exceedingly devout, and Sister Michael, plumpish, placid and more than a little deaf. Sister Anne's place. She must have been taken ill in the night and whisked off to the convent's tiny sick bay. Sister Gertrude's glance slid along the bench to where the austere figure of Sister Radigund, the Infirmarium, was sitting. She would ask her at the end of the General Silence.

The morning's quota of bread and tea came to an end. The Reader was tidying up the remains of the dismembered martyrs in a general 'And in other places and at other times of many other martyrs, confessors and holy virgins to whose prayers and merits we humbly commend ourselves.'

'*Deo gratias*,' responded the community.

At this moment Sister Peter rose, bowed to the Mother Superior and went slowly round the table to stand in front of the Abbatial chair. The Mother Superior looked up at her and nodded. Sister Peter went down on her knees and clasped her hands together in front of her.

'I confess my fault,' began Sister Peter in a voice that was far from steady, 'to God and to you, Mother Abbess, and to all the Sisters that I have committed the great sin of damaging the Gradual . . .' There was an indrawing of breaths that would have done credit to a chorus in their unity. '. . . by placing a thumb mark on it,' went on Sister Peter bravely. 'For this and all my other faults and those I have occasioned in others, I humbly ask pardon of God and penance of you, Mother Abbess, for the love of God.' She finished in a rush and knelt there, eyes cast down.

The Reverend Mother considered the kneeling figure. 'May the Lord forgive you your faults, my dear child, and give you grace to be faithful to grace. Say a *Miserere* and . . .' she paused and looked across the room, '. . . and ask Sister Jerome if she will take a look at the mark quickly. It may be possible to remove it without lasting damage.'

In the general bustle and end of silence after breakfast, Sister Gertrude sought out Sister Radigund.

'Sister Anne? She's not ill that I know of. She might have gone to the sick bay on her own, of course, though it's not usual . . .'

It was expressly forbidden as it happened, but it would have been uncharitable of Sister Radigund to have said so.

'. . . I'll go up after Office if you like, to make sure.'

'Thank you,' said Sister Gertrude gratefully. She wondered now if she should have reported the empty bedroom. Her mind was more on that than on Sext, and afterwards she waited anxiously at the bottom of the staircase for Sister Radigund.

'She's not in the sick bay,' said the Infirmarium, 'nor back in her own cell either. I've just checked.'

'I think,' said Sister Gertrude, 'that we'd better go to the parlour, don't you?'

They were not the only sisters waiting at the Reverend Mother's door. Sister Jerome, the convent's most skilled authority on manuscript illumination, and Sister Peter were both there too. They knocked and a little bell rang. Sister Gertrude sighed. That was where the world and the convent differed so. In the convent to every sound and every speech there was a response. In the world – well . . .

The four Sisters trooped in. The Mother Superior was working on the morning's post with Sister Lucy, the Bursar. There were several neat piles of paper on the table, and Sister Lucy was bending over a note-book.

The Mother Superior looked up briskly.

'Ah, yes, Sister Peter. The mark on the Gradual. I'm sure that Sister Jerome will be able to remove it, whatever it is. These culpable faults are all very well but we can't have you – er – making a meal of them, can we? Otherwise they become an indulgence in themselves and that would never do.' She gave a quick smile. 'Isn't that so, Sister Jerome? Now, stop looking like a Tragedy Queen and go back to . . .'

Sister Peter burst into tears. 'That's just it, Mother,' she wailed. 'Sister Jerome says . . .' She became quite incoherent in a fresh paroxysm of tears.

'What does Sister Jerome say?' asked the Reverend Mother mildly.

Sister Jerome cleared her throat. 'That mark, Mother. I think it's blood.'

Sister Gertrude's knees felt quite wobbly. She gulped, 'And we can't find Sister Anne anywhere.'

2

Inspector C. D. Sloan had never been inside a convent before.

He had, he reckoned, been inside most places of female confinement in his working life – hospitals, prisons, orphanages, offices, and even – once – a girls' boarding school. (That had been in pursuit of a Ward in Chancery whom a great many other people had been pursuing at the same time. Sloan had got there first, though it had been a near thing.)

But never so much as a monastery, let alone a convent.

The call came into Berebury Police Station just before ten in the morning. The Criminal Investigation Department of the Berebury Division of the Calleshire Constabulary was not large, and as his sergeant was checking up on the overactivities of a bigamist, he had no choice at all about whom he took with him to the convent: Crosby, Detective Constable, William. Raw, perky and consciously representing the younger generation in the force, he was one of those who provoked Superintendent Leeyes into observing (at least once every day) that these young constables weren't what they were.

'You'll do, I suppose,' said Sloan resignedly. 'Let's go.' He stepped into the police car and Crosby drove the five and a half miles to Cullingoak village. He slowed down at the entrance to a gaunt red-brick building just outside Cullingoak proper and prepared to turn into the drive. Sloan looked up.

'Not here. Farther on.'

Crosby changed gear. 'Sorry, sir, I thought . . .'

'That's the agricultural institute. Where young gentlemen learn to be farmers. Or young farmers learn to be gentlemen.' He grunted. 'I forget which. The convent is the next turning on the right.'

It wasn't exactly plain sailing when they did find the entrance.

There was a high, close-boarded fence running alongside the road and the convent was invisible behind it. The double doors set in it were high and locked. Crosby rattled the handle unsuccessfully.

'Doesn't look as if they're expecting us.'

'From what I've heard,' said Sloan drily, 'they should be.'

Eventually Crosby found his way in through a little door set in the big one.

'I'll open it from the inside for the car,' he called over, but a minute or two later he reappeared baffled. 'I can't, Inspector. There's some sort of complicated gadget here . . .'

'A mantrap?' suggested Sloan heavily.

'Could be. It won't open, anyway.'

His superintendent didn't like his wit and his constables didn't appreciate it: which was, if anything, worse.

'Then we'll have to walk,' he said.

'Walk?'

'Walk, Crosby. Like you did in the happy days of yore before they put you in the CID. In fact, you can count yourself lucky you don't have to take your shoes off.'

Crosby looked down at his regulation issues.

'Barefoot,' amplified Sloan.

Crosby's brow cleared. 'Like that chap in history who had to walk through the snow?'

'Henry Two.'

'He'd upset somebody, hadn't he?'

'The Pope.'

Crosby grinned at last. 'I get you, sir. Pilgrimage or something, wasn't it?'

'Penance, actually.'

Crosby didn't seem interested in the difference, and they plodded up the drive together between banks of rhododendrons. It wasn't wet, but an unpleasant early morning dampness dripped from the dank leaves. Nothing grew under the bushes. The drive twisted and turned, and at first they could see nothing but the bushes and trees.

Sloan glanced about him professionally. 'Pretty well cared for really. Verges neat. No weeds. That box hedge over there was clipped properly.'

'Slave labour,' said Crosby, crunching along the drive beside him. 'Don't these women have to do as they're told? Vow of obedience or something?' He kicked at a stone, sending it expertly between two bushes. 'Anyone can get their gardening done that way.'

'Anyone can tell you're still single, Crosby. Let me tell you that a vow of obedience won't get your gardening done for you. My wife promised to obey – got the vicar to leave it in the marriage service on purpose – but it doesn't signify. And,' he added dispassionately, 'if you think that shot would have got past the Calleford goal-keeper next Saturday afternoon, you're mistaken. He's got feet.'

They rounded a bend and the convent came into view, the drive opening out as they approached, finishing in a broad sweep in front of an imposing porch.

'Cor,' said Crosby expressively.

'Nice, isn't it?' agreed Inspector Sloan. 'Almost a young stately home, you might say. The Faine family used to live here and then one of them – the grandfather I suppose he would be – took to horses or it may have been cards. Something expensive anyway and they had to sell out.' Sloan was a Calleshire man, born and bred. 'The family's still around somewhere.'

There were wide shallow steps in front of the porch, flanked by a pair of stone lions. And a large crest over the door.

Crosby spelled out the letters: ' "*Pax Intrantibus, Salus Exeuntibus*" – that'll be the family motto, I suppose.'

'More likely to be the good Sisters', Crosby. *Pax* means peace, and I don't think the Faines were a particularly peaceful lot in the old days.'

'Yes, sir, but what about the rest of it?'

He wasn't catching Sloan out that easily.

'Look it up, Constable,' he said unfairly, 'then you'll remember it better, won't you?'

'Yes, sir.'

Sloan climbed the last step and advanced to the door.

'Sir . . .'

'Yes, Crosby?'

'Er, what gives?'

'Didn't you get the message?' Sloan pressed the bell. 'Something nasty has happened to a nun.'

Unexpectedly a little light flashed on at the side of the door. Crosby peered forward and read aloud the notice underneath it: ' "Open the door and enter the hall".'

'Advance and be recognized,' interpreted Sloan, who had done his time in the Army.

They pushed open the outer door and stood inside a brightly lit vestibule. The next pair of doors was of glass. There was another notice attached to these: 'When the buzzer sounds push these doors.' Beyond them was a small hall, and at the other side of this was a screen stretching from floor to ceiling. In the centre of the screen was a grille.

Sloan was suddenly aware of a face looking at them through it. The two policemen were standing in the light, and beyond the grille was shadow, so they could see little of the face except that it was there – watching them. The scrutiny ended with a buzzer sounding loudly – and the lock on the glass door fell open.

Sloan pushed the doors and walked forward into the hall.

The face behind the grille retreated a fraction into the dark background and he saw it no better.

Sloan cleared his throat. 'I am Detective Inspector Sloan from Berebury CID.'

'Yes?' The voice was uninviting.

'I understand that one of the nuns—'

'Sister Anne.'

Behind his right ear he heard Crosby struggling to strangle a snort at birth.

'Sister Anne,' continued Sloan hastily, 'I am told has had . . . has unfortunately met with an . . .'

'She's dead,' said the face.

'Just so,' said Sloan, who was finding it downright disconcerting talking to someone he could not see.

'She's in the cellar,' volunteered the speaker.

'That's what I had heard.'

The voice attached to the face was Irish and that was about all Sloan could tell.

'I think you had better see the Mother Superior,' she said.

'So do I,' said Sloan.

There was a faint click and a shutter came down over the grille. The two policemen waited.

There were two doors leading out of the hall but both were locked. Crosby turned his attention to the lock on the glass doors.

'Electricity, sir. That's how it works.'

'I didn't suppose it was magic,' said Sloan irritably. 'Did you?'

This wasn't the sort of delay he liked when there was a body about. Superintendent Leeyes wasn't going to like it either. He would be sitting in his office, waiting – and wondering why he hadn't heard from them already.

They went on waiting. The hall was quite silent. There were two chairs there and, on one wall, a little plaster Madonna with a red lamp burning before it. Nothing else. Crosby finished his prowling and came back to stand restively beside Sloan.

'At this rate, sir, it doesn't look as if they're going to let the dog get a look at the rabbit at all . . .'

There was the mildest of deprecating coughs behind his right ear and Crosby spun round. Somewhere, somehow, a door must have opened and two nuns come through it, but neither policeman had heard it happen.

'Forgive us, gentlemen, if we startled you . . .'

Sloan had an impression of immense authority – something rare in a woman – and the calm that went with it. She was standing quite still, dignity incarnate, her hands folded loosely together in front of her black habit, her expression perfectly composed.

'Not at all,' he said, discomfited.

'I am the Mother Superior . . .'

'How do you do . . .' The conventional police 'madam' hung unspoken, inappropriate in the air. Sloan's own mother was a vigorous woman in her early seventies. He struggled to use the word and failed.

'. . . Marm,' he finished, inspired.

'And this is Sister Mary St Lucy.'

That was easier. He could call the whole world 'Sister'.

'Sister Lucy is our Bursar and Procuratrix . . .'

Sloan saw Crosby's startled glance and shot him a look calculated to wither him into silence.

The Mother Superior glanced briefly round the hall. 'I am sorry that Sister Porteress kept you waiting here. She should have shown you to the parlour.' She smiled faintly. 'She interprets her watchdog duties very seriously. Besides which . . .' again the faint smile '. . . she has a rooted objection to policemen.'

It was Sloan's experience that a lot of people had, but they didn't usually say so straight out.

'Not shared, I hope, marm, by all your Sisters . . .'

'I couldn't tell you, Inspector,' she said simply. 'This is the first time one has ever crossed our threshold.' She turned to one of the doors. 'I therefore know very little about your routine but I dare say you would like to see Sister Anne . . .'

'Not half,' whispered Crosby to her back.

'And Sister Peter, too, though I fear she won't be of much immediate help to you. She's quite overcome, so I've sent her to the kitchen. They're always glad of an extra pair of hands there at this time of the day. This way please.'

She led them through the nearer of the two doors into what had been the original entrance hall of the old house. It was two storeys high, with a short landing across one end. A pair of double doors led through into the chapel at the other end, but the centre of attraction was the great carved black oak staircase. Its only carpet was polish, and it descended in a series of stately treads from the balustraded gallery at the top to a magnificent newel post at the bottom, elaborately carved, with an orb sitting on the top.

The Mother Superior did not spare it a glance but, closely

followed by Sister Lucy, led them off behind the staircase through a dim corridor smelling of beeswax. Sloan followed, guided as much by the sound of the long rosaries which hung from their waists as by sight. Once they passed another nun coming the opposite way. Sloan tried to get a good look at her face, but when she saw the Reverend Mother and her party, she drew quietly to one side and stood, eyes cast down, until they had all passed. Then they heard the slight clink of her rosary as she walked on.

'Inspector,' Crosby hissed in his ear, 'they're all wearing wedding rings.'

'Brides of Christ,' Sloan hissed back.

'What's that?'

'I'll tell you later.'

The Reverend Mother had halted in front of one of the several doors leading off the corridor.

'This is the way to the cellar, Inspector. Sister Anne, God rest her soul, is at the foot of the steps.'

So she was.

Sister Lucy opened the door and Sloan saw a figure lying on the floor. Two nuns were kneeling beside it in an attitude of prayer. He went down the steps carefully. They were steep, and the lighting was not of the brightest.

When they saw the new arrivals, the two nuns who had been keeping vigil by the body rose quietly and melted into the background.

The body of the nun was spread-eagled on the stone floor, face downwards, her habit caught up, her veil knocked askew. The white bloodless hands were all he could see of death at first. There was a plain broad silver ring on the third finger of this left hand too.

The Reverend Mother and Sister Lucy crossed themselves and then drew back a little, watching him.

He couldn't tell in the bad light where the blood on her black habit began and ended, but there was no doubt from where it had come. The back of her head. Even in this light he could see there was something wrong with its shape. There was a hollow where no hollow should be.

He knelt beside her and bent to see her face. There was blood there, too, but he couldn't see any . . .

'We would have liked to have moved her,' said the Reverend Mother, 'or at least have covered her up, but Dr Carret said on no account to touch anything until you came.'

'Quite right,' he said absently. 'Crosby, have you a torch there?'

He shone it on the dead Sister's face. Blood from the back of her skull had trickled forward round the sides of the white linen cloth she wore under her cowl and round her head and cheeks. There was a word for it that he had heard somewhere once . . . w . . . w . . . wimple . . . that was it. Well, her wimple had held a lot of the blood back, but quite a bit had got through to run down her face and then – surely – to drip on the floor. Only that was the funny thing. It hadn't reached the floor. He swept the beam from the torch on it again. There was no blood on the floor. That on the face was congealed and dry, but there was enough of it for some to have dripped down on the floor.

And it hadn't.

'So, of course, we didn't touch anything until you saw her.' The quiet voice of the Reverend Mother obtruded into his thoughts. 'But now that you have seen her, will it be all right for us to . . .'

'No,' said Sloan heavily. 'It won't be all right for you to do anything at all.' He got to his feet again. 'I want a police photographer down here first, and any moving that's to be done will be done by the police surgeon's men.'

'Perhaps then Sister Lucy might just have her keys back, Inspector?'

'Keys?'

Sister Lucy flushed. 'I lent them to poor Sister Anne late yesterday afternoon. She was going to go through our store cupboards to make up some parcels for Christmas. We have Sisters in the mission field, you know, and they are very glad of things for their people at this time. She did it every year.' She hesitated. 'You can just see the edges of them under her habit there . . .'

'No.'

'You must forgive us,' interposed the Mother Superior gently. 'We are sometimes a little out of touch here with civil procedure, and we have never had a fatal accident here before. We have no wish to transgress any law.'

He stared at her. 'It isn't a question of the infringement of any rule, marm. It is simply that I am not satisfied that I know exactly how Sister Anne died. Moreover, you also have a nun here with blood on her hands which you say she is unable to explain . . .'

'Just,' apologetically, 'on one thumb.'

'And,' continued Sloan majestically, 'you want me to allow you to move a body and remove from it evidence which may or may not be material. No, marm, I'm afraid the keys will have to wait until the police surgeon has been. Have you a telephone here?'

The Mother Superior smiled her faint smile. 'In that sense at least, Inspector, we are in touch with the world.'

3

'Wait a minute, wait a minute,' grumbled Sister Polycarp. 'I'm coming as fast as I can.' She stumped towards the front door. 'Ringing the bell like that! It's enough to waken the dead.' She stopped abruptly. 'No, it's not, you know. It won't wake poor Sister Anne, not now.' She drew the grille back. 'Oh, it's you, Father. Come in. They're waiting for you in the parlour. It's about poor Sister Anne. She, poor soul, has gone to her reward and we've got the police here.'

'A nice juxtaposition of clauses,' said Father MacAuley.

'What's that?'

'Nothing, Sister, nothing.' Father MacAuley stepped inside. 'Just an observation . . .'

'Oh, I see. I should have kept them out myself, but Mother said that wouldn't help. Can't abide the police.'

'You're prejudiced, Polycarp. Nobody worries about the Troubles any more. You won't believe this but the Irish Question is no longer a burning matter of moment. You're out of touch.'

Sister Polycarp sniffed again. 'That's as may be. You're too young to remember, Father. But I never thought to have the police trampling about again, that I can tell you. Arrest poor Sister Peter, that's what they'll do.'

'Will they indeed?' Father MacAuley looked thoughtfully at the nun. 'That's the little one that squeaks when you speak to her, isn't it? Now why should they arrest her?'

'Oh, you know what they're like. She's got some blood on her hand and she doesn't know how it got there.'

'Tiresome,' agreed Father MacAuley.

'Otherwise it would have been a straightforward fall down the cellar steps and that would have been an end to it. Unfortunate of course' – Sister Polycarp recollected that not only was she speaking about the dead, but the newly dead, and crossed herself – 'but we could have sent the police packing. As it is they look like being underfoot for a long time.'

'Do they now?' Father MacAuley took off his coat. 'In that case . . .'

'It wouldn't matter so much,' burst out Sister Polycarp, 'if everyone didn't know.'

Father MacAuley wagged a reproving finger. 'Polycarp, I do believe that you're worried about what the neighbours will think.'

She bridled. 'It's not very nice, now, is it, for people to be seeing the police at a convent?'

Where a lesser woman might have bustled into the Parlour, the Reverend Mother contrived to arrive there ahead of her own habit, rosary and rather breathless attendant Sister Lucy.

'Father – thank you for coming so quickly. Poor Sister Anne's lying dead at the bottom of the cellar steps and we do seem to be in a rather delicate position . . .'

'Sister Peter want bailing out?'

'Not yet, thank you. No, I fancy it's not the presence of blood on the Gradual so much as the absence of blood elsewhere that's going to be the trouble. Don't you agree, Sister?'

Sister Lucy nodded intelligently. 'Yes, Mother.'

Father MacAuley sat down. 'Sister Anne, now she was the one with the glasses, wasn't she?'

'That's right,' agreed Sister Lucy. 'She couldn't see without them. Missions were her great interest, you know.'

He frowned. 'Fairly tall?'

'About my height, I suppose,' said Sister Lucy.

'But older?'

'That's right. She was professed before I joined the Order.

Perhaps Mother can tell you when that would have been . . .'

'No, no, I can't off-hand. But I do know how she would have hated having been the cause of all this trouble. She wasn't a fusser, you know. In fact,' she paused, 'she wasn't the sort of Sister whom anything happened to at all.'

'Until now,' pointed out Father MacAuley.

'Until now,' agreed the Mother Superior sombrely.

There was a light tap on the parlour door. Sister Lucy opened it to a very young nun.

'Please, Mother, Sister Cellarer says if she can't get into any of the store cupboards we'll have to have parkin for afters because she made that yesterday.'

'Thank you, Sister, and say to Sister Cellarer that that will be very nice, thank you.' The door shut after the nun and the Reverend Mother turned to Sister Lucy. 'What is parkin?'

'A north country gingerbread dish, Mother.'

'Eaten especially on Guy Fawkes' Night,' added MacAuley. 'A clear instance, if I may say so, of tradition overtaking theology.'

'It often does,' observed the Mother Prioress placidly, 'but this is not the moment to go into that with a cook who can't get to her food cupboards.' She told him about the keys. 'However, Inspector Sloan is telephoning his headquarters now. Perhaps after that we shall be allowed to have them back.'

The convent keys did not, in fact, figure in the conversation Inspector Sloan had with his superior.

'Speak up, Sloan, I can't hear you.'

'Sorry, sir, I'm speaking from the convent. The telephone here is a bit public.'

There was a grunt at the other end of the line. 'Like that, is it? Devil of a long time you've been coming through. What happened?'

'This nun is dead all right. Has been for quite a few hours, I should say. The body's cold, though the cellar's pretty perishing anyway and that may not be much to go on. I'd like a few photographs and Dr Dabbe, too . . .'

'The whole box of tricks?'

'Yes, please, sir – she's lying at the foot of a flight of stairs with a nasty hole in the back of her head.'

'All right, Sloan, I'll buy it. Did she fall or was she pushed?'

'That's the interesting thing, Superintendent. I don't think it was either.'

'Not like the moon and green cheese?'

'I beg your pardon, sir?'

'Either it is made of green cheese or it isn't.'

'N – no, sir, I don't think so.'

'If it's not one of the two possible alternatives then it must be the other, always provided, of course, that . . .'

Sloan sighed. Superintendent Leeyes had started going to an Adult Education Class on Logic this autumn and it was playing havoc with his powers of reasoning.

'I've left Crosby down in the cellar with the body, sir, until Dr Dabbe gets here.'

'All right, Sloan, I know when I'm being deflected. But remember – failure to carry a line of thought through to its logical conclusion means confusion.'

'Yes, sir.'

'Now, what was this woman called?'

'Sister Anne,' said Sloan cautiously.

'Ha!' The Superintendent ran true to form. 'Perhaps she *didn't* see anyone coming, eh?'

'No, sir.'

'And her real name?'

'I don't know yet. The Reverend Mother has gone to look it up.'

'Right. Keep me informed. By the way, Sloan, who found her in the cellar?'

'I was afraid you were going to ask me that, sir.'

'Why?'

'You're not going to like it, sir.'

'No?'

'No, sir.' Unhappily. 'It was Sister St Bernard.'

The telephone gave an angry snarl. 'I don't like it, Sloan. If I find you've been taking the mickey, there's going to be trouble, understand?'

'Yes, sir.'

'And Sloan . . .'

'Sir?'

'If you expect that to go in the official report, you had better bring that little barrel of brandy back with you.'

Sloan waited for Dr Dabbe at the top of the cellar steps and wished on the whole that he was back at the girls' boarding school. He could understand their rules. Not long afterwards the police surgeon appeared in the dim corridor, ushered along by a new Sister.

'Morning, Sloan. Something for me, I understand, in the cellar.'

'A nun, doctor. At the bottom of this flight of stairs.'

'Aha,' said Dr Dabbe alertly. 'And she hasn't been moved?'

'Not by us,' said Sloan.

'Like that, is it? Right.'

Sloan opened the door inwards, disclosing a scene that, but for the stolid Crosby, could have come – almost – from an artist's illustration for an historical novel. The two attendant Sisters were still there, kneeling, and the dead Sister lying on the floor. The solitary, unshaded electric light reflected their shadows grotesquely against the whitewashed walls.

'Quite medieval,' observed Dabbe. 'Shall we look at the steps as we go down?'

'There's not a lot to see,' said Sloan. 'Several of the nuns and the local GP, Dr Carret, went up and down before we got here, but there is one mark at the side of the seventh step that could be from her foot, and there is some dust on the right shoe that could be from the step. On the top of the shoe.'

'Just so,' agreed Dabbe, following the direction of the beam from Sloan's torch. 'Steps dusted recently but not very recently.'

The Sister with them coughed. 'Probably about once a week, doctor.'

'Thank you.' He glanced from the step to the body. 'Head first, Sloan, would you say?'

'Perhaps.'

'I see.' The pathologist reached the bottom step, nodded to Crosby, bowed gravely in the direction of the two kneeling nuns and turned his attention to the body. He looked at it for a long time from several angles and then said conversationally, 'Interesting.'

'Yes,' said Sloan.

'Plenty of blood.'

'Yes.'

'Except in the one place where you'd expect it.'

Sloan nodded obliquely. 'The photograph boys are on their way.'

'I know,' Dabbe said blandly. 'I overtook them.' The pathologist was reckoned to be the fastest driver in Calleshire. 'Notwithstanding any pretty pictures they may take, you can take it from me that whatever this woman died from, she didn't die in the spot where she is now lying.'

'That,' said Sloan, 'is what I thought.'

If anything Sloan appeared relieved to see another man in the parlour.

'Our priest, Inspector – Father Benedict MacAuley.' The Reverend Mother's rosary clinked as she moved forward. 'I asked him to come here as I felt in need of some assistance in dealing with – er – external matters. Do you mind if he is present?'

'Not at all, marm. I have left the police surgeon in the cellar. In the mean time, perhaps you would tell us a little about the . . . Sister Anne.'

Sloan wouldn't have chosen the convent parlour for an interview with anyone. It was the reverse of cosy. The Reverend Mother and Sister Lucy disposed themselves on hard, stiff-backed chairs and offered two others to the two policemen. Father MacAuley was settled in the only one that looked remotely comfortable. Sloan noticed that it was the policemen who were in the light, the Reverend Mother who was in the shadow, from the window. Vague thoughts about the Inquisition flitted through his mind and were gone again. The room was bare as the entrance hall had been bare, the floor of highly polished wood. In most rooms there was enough to give a good policeman an idea of the type of person he was interviewing – age, sex, standards, status. Here there was nothing at all. The overriding impression was still beeswax.

The Reverend Mother folded her hands together in her lap and said quietly, 'The name of Sister Anne was Josephine Mary Cartwright. That is all that I can tell you about her life before she came to the convent. We have a mother house, you understand, in London, and our records are kept there. I would have to telephone there, for her last address and date of profession. I'm sorry – that seems very little . . .'

Sister Lucy lifted her head slightly and said to the Reverend Mother: 'She was English.'

'As opposed to what?' asked Sloan quickly.

'Irish or French.'

'Frequently opposed to both,' said the Reverend Mother unexpectedly. 'When all else is submerged, that sort of nationality remains. It is a curious feature of convent life.'

'Indeed? Now we had a message this morning . . .'

'That would be from Dr Carret. He is so kind to us always. We sent for him at once.'

'When would that have been, marm?'

'After Office this morning. We didn't know about last night.'

'What about last night?'

'That she might have been lying there since then.'

'What makes you think that?'

'Dr Carret, Inspector. He said that was what had probably happened.'

'I see. But you didn't miss her?'

'Not until this morning.'

'When?'

'The Caller, Sister Gertrude, found her cell empty this morning. She thought first of all that she had merely risen early, but as she was not at breakfast either she mentioned it to the Infirmarium.'

'Then what happened?'

'After Office the Sister Infirmarium went to her cell to see if she was unwell.'

'And?'

'She reported to me that her cell was empty.'

'Had her bed been slept in?'

'I do not think Sister Infirmarium would have been in a position to know that. All the beds are made by the Sisters themselves . . .'

'It might have been warm.' Sloan shifted his weight on the hard chair. 'You can usually tell with your hand even if the bed has been aired – especially in winter.'

The Mother Superior's manner stiffened perceptibly. 'I do not suppose such a procedure occurred to Sister Infirmarium.'

'Of course not,' appeased Sloan hastily. Did he imagine the priest's sympathetic glance? For all he knew 'bed' might be a taboo word in this convent – in any convent. Probably was. He took refuge in a formula. 'I should like to see Sister Inf . . . Infirmarium presently. And this Sister Peter.'

'Ah, yes, Sister Peter.' The Reverend Mother's eyes rested reflectively on the inspector. 'The blood seems to have appeared on her thumb before Mass, and some of it was transferred to the Gradual during the service—'

'You left it?' interrupted Sloan.

'Yes, Inspector,' she said gently, 'we left it for you.'

'What did you do when you were told about the blood and that Sister Anne was missing?'

'I asked Sister Lucy here to help look for her.'

'Just Sister Lucy?'

'At first. A convent is a busy place, Inspector.'

'Yes, marm, I'm sure—' untruthfully.

'When their search failed to reveal her in any of the places where she might have been expected to have been taken ill, I asked other Sisters to go over the house and grounds very carefully.'

'I see.'

'This is a big house and it took some time, but, as you know, Sister St Bernard opened the cellar door and put the light on . . . you will want to see her, too, I take it?'

'Yes, please, marm.'

'We telephoned Dr Carret and he came at once. It was he who was so insistent on our leaving her lying on that cold floor.'

'Very right, marm.' He answered the unspoken reproach as best he could. 'I'm afraid this will be a police matter until we find out exactly what happened. Tell me, marm, at what time would everyone have gone to bed last night?'

At the boarding school it had been 'lights out'.

'Nine o'clock.'

'And after that no one would have gone into anyone else's bedroom . . .'

'No one is allowed in anyone else's cell at any time except the Caller, who is Sister Gertrude, the Infirmarium and myself.'

'I see. Presumably no one checks that the Sisters are in their cells?'

'No.'

This was not, after all, a boarding school.

'I am seeking, marm, to establish when Sister Anne was last seen alive.'

'At Vespers at half-past eight.'

'By whom?'

'Sister Michael and Sister Damien. Their stalls are on either side of Sister Anne's.'

'And you can tell me of nothing that might have caused Sister Anne to leave her cell last night?'

'Nothing. In fact, it is forbidden.'

That, decided Sloan, settled that. For the time being.

'I see, marm, thank you.' He stood up. 'Now, if you would be so kind as to get in touch with your – er – head office . . .'

'Inspector . . .'

'Yes, marm?' Sloan was ready with a handful of routine phrases about inquests, post-mortems and the like.

The Mother Prioress's rosary clinked. 'It is one of the privileges of convent life that strangers do not perform the Last Office. We always do that for our own Sisters ourselves.'

It was something that he had never considered.

4

The cellar was quite crowded by the time Sloan and Crosby got back there. Two police photographers had joined the unmerry throng and were heaving heavy cameras about. Dr Dabbe was still contemplating the body from all angles. The two Sisters were still praying – and the photographers didn't like it.

'Hey, Inspector,' whispered one of them. 'Call your dogs off, can't you? Giving us the creeps kneeling there. And getting in the way. I want some pictures from over that side but I'm blowed if I'm going on my knees beside them.'

'It might give them the wrong idea, Dyson,' agreed Sloan softly. 'They don't know you as well as I do.' He glanced across the cellar. 'They're not upsetting the doctor.'

'He's a born exhibitionist. All pathologists are and nothing upsets him. Nothing at all. I sometimes wonder if he's human.' Dyson screwed a new flash bulb into its socket. 'Besides, I don't want those two figuring in any pix I do take. Or I'll be spending the rest of my life explaining that they're not ravens from the Tower of London or the Ku Klux Klan or something.'

'Too much imagination, Dyson, that's your trouble.'

Nevertheless, he went back upstairs and found Sister Lucy.

'Certainly, Inspector,' she said, when he explained. 'I will ask the Sisters to continue their prayers and vigil in the chapel.'

Sloan murmured that that would do very nicely, thank you.

At a word from her the two Sisters in the cellar rose from

their knees in one economical movement, crossed themselves and withdrew.

'That's better,' said Dyson, changing plates rapidly. 'It's our artistic temperaments, you know, Inspector. Very sensitive to atmosphere.'

'Get on with it,' growled Sloan.

Dyson jerked a finger at his assistant and crouched on his knees in a manner surprisingly reminiscent of that of the two nuns. Instead of having his hands clasped in front of him they held a heavy camera. He pressed a button and, for a moment, the whole cellar became illuminated in a harsh, bright light.

A moment later the pathologist came up to him.

'I don't know about Mr Fox over there,' said Dr Dabbe, 'but I've finished down here for the time being. I've got the temperature readings – did you notice she was in a draught, by the way? – and all I need about the position of the body. It's cold down here but not damp. At the moment I can't tell you much more than Carret – a good chap, incidentally – that she died yesterday evening sometime. The body is quite cold. You'll have to wait for more exact details – which is a pity because I dare say it's important . . .'

'Yes,' said Sloan.

'I'll be as quick as I can.' He paused. 'From what I can see from here there's a fair bit of post-mortem injury – I think she was dead before she was put in this cellar and then damaged by the fall and so forth.'

'Nice,' said Sloan shortly.

'Very,' agreed the pathologist. 'Especially here.'

'Cause of death?'

'Depressed fracture of skull.'

'Can I quote you?'

'Lord, yes. I don't need her on the table for that. You can see it from here. That's not to say she hasn't other injuries as well, but that'll do for a start, won't it?'

Sloan nodded gloomily.

Dabbe picked up his hat. 'I've got a sample of the dust from that step and the shoe – I can tell you a bit more about that later. And the time of death . . .'

The quiet of the cellar was shattered suddenly by a bell ringing. No sooner had it stopped than they could hear the reverberations of many feet moving about above them.

'In some ways,' observed Sloan sententiously, 'this place has much in common with a girls' boarding school.'

'You don't say?' Dabbe cast a long, raking glance over the body on the floor. 'Of course, I don't get about as much as you chaps . . . What's the bell for? Physical jerks?'

'Meditation.'

'They could start on one or two little matters down here. I shall give my attention to a thumb print on a manuscript, and I'll get my chap to begin on the blood grouping.'

Sloan saw him out and then came back to the cellar. 'Dyson . . .'

'Inspector?'

'The name of your assistant?'

'Williams.'

'I thought so. Who is Mr Fox?'

Dyson hitched his camera over his shoulder and prepared to depart. 'One of the inventors of photography, blast him.'

The cellar door banged behind the two photographers, leaving Sloan and Crosby alone with Sister Anne at last.

'Now then, Crosby, where are we?'

Crosby pulled out his notebook. 'We have one female body – of a nun – said to be Sister Anne alias Josephine . . .'

'Not alias, Crosby.'

'Maiden name of – no, that doesn't sound right either. They're all maidens, aren't they?'

'So I understand.'

'Well, then . . .'

'Secular.'

'Oh, really? Secular name of Josephine Mary Cartwright. Medium to tall in height, age uncertain . . .'

'Unknown.'

'Unknown, suffering from a fractured skull . . .'

'At least . . .'

'At least – sustained we know not how but somewhere else.'

'Not well put but I am with you.'

'As I see it, sir, that's the lot.'

'See again, Crosby, because it isn't.'

'No?' Crosby looked injured.

'No,' said Sloan.

They waited in the cellar until two men appeared with a stretcher and then gave them a hand with the ticklish job of getting their burden up the stairs. Then . . .

'Inspector, I've been thinking . . .'

'Good. I thought you would get there in the end.'

'If that was the top of her shoe that hit the seventh step, then she didn't even die somewhere else in the cellar.'

'Granted.'

'Someone threw her down those steps after she was dead?'

'That's what Dr Dabbe thinks.'

'That's a nasty way to carry on in a convent.'

'Barbarous,' agreed Sloan, and waited.

Crosby, untrammelled by classes on Logic, should be able to get further than that on his own.

'The fall didn't kill her?' he suggested tentatively.

'Not this fall anyway.' He looked at the steep stairs. 'A weapon more like.'

'A weapon seems sort of out of place here.'

'So does a body in a cellar,' said Sloan crisply. 'Especially one that didn't die there.'

Crosby took that point too. 'You mean,' he said slowly, 'that they parked her somewhere else before they chucked her down?'

'I do. For how long?'

He was quicker this time. 'For long enough for the blood on her head to dry because it didn't drip on the floor?'

'You're doing nicely, Crosby.'

Crosby grinned. 'So we look for somewhere where someone stashed away a bleeding nun and/or whatever it was they hit her with?'

'If we have to tear the place apart,' agreed Sloan gravely.

In the event they didn't.

Prowling about in the dim corridor at the top of the cellar steps was Father MacAuley. He was on his hands and knees when Sloan almost fell over him.

'Ah, Inspector,' he said unnecessarily, 'there you are.'

'Yes, sir, and there you are, too, so to speak.' He regarded the kneeling figure expressionlessly. 'If it will save you any trouble, sir, I have already ascertained that this corridor was swept and polished early this morning.'

'Really?' He got to his feet. 'Good. Then we can get on with the next thing, can't we?'

'What's that, sir?'

'Finding where they left her until they pushed her down the steps, of course. It must be off this corridor somewhere.'

'Why is that, sir?'

'Too risky to drag a body across that enormous hall, don't you think? Someone might have come out of the chapel at any moment and there's that gallery at the top of the stairs. Anyone might be watching from there. No, I think she was – er – done to death round about here, or perhaps through in the kitchens somewhere.'

'We'll see, sir, shall we?'

Sloan opened the nearest door, but the priest shook his head.

'No, Inspector, it won't be there. That's the – er – necessarium. It's hardly big enough. Besides, the door only locks on the inside and there would always be the risk of someone wanting to use it, wouldn't there?'

The second and third doors revealed a small library, and a garden room with outside glass door, sink and vases.

They found what they were looking for behind the fourth door. It opened on to a large broom cupboard.

Crosby's torch played over the brown stain on the bare boards of the cupboard's floor.

MacAuley peered inquisitively over their shoulders. 'Someone kept their head – looks as if she was put in here head first so that the blood was as far away from the door as possible.'

Crosby shifted the angle of the torch's beam and said, 'Those nuns have been in here this morning for these brooms, I'll be bound.'

Sloan sniffed the polish in the air. 'I dare say. They wouldn't have noticed this blood though, not without a light. We'll see if the doctor has left.'

'Constable, if I might just borrow your torch . . .' MacAuley took it deftly from Crosby and began to cover the broom cupboard inch by inch in its beam.

Crosby stepped back into the corridor.

'Inspector . . .'

'Well?'

'What did whoever put her in here want to go and move her for?'

'Take a bit longer to find perhaps.'

'Would that matter?'

'I don't know yet, but even the most absent-minded of this crew would have noticed her when they came to do the cleaning this morning.'

Sloan was keeping a close eye on Father Benedict MacAuley withal. 'Besides, you do get a broken skull sometimes from falling down the cellar steps but very rarely from tripping over in a broom cupboard.'

'They hoped we would think she had fallen down those nasty steep stairs?'

'I shouldn't be at all surprised. Most people expect the police to jump to the wrong conclusions. And if you never do, Crosby, you will end up . . .' He paused. Father MacAuley was backing out of the cupboard.

'Where, Inspector?' Crosby was ambitious.

Sloan looked at him. 'Exactly where you are now – as a Detective Constable with the Berebury CID – because you wouldn't be human enough for promotion. Well, Father MacAuley, have you found what you were looking for?'

'No, I can't think what has happened to them.'

'Happened to what?' asked Sloan patiently.

'Sister Anne's glasses. She couldn't see without them, and yet they're nowhere to be found.'

5

Considering how little of the flesh of a nun could be seen, Sloan marvelled how much he was aware of the differing personalities of the Mother Prioress and Sister Lucy. In both cases good bone structure stood out beneath the tight white band across the forehead. There was self-control, too, in the line of both mouths, and, in Sister Lucy's case, more than a little beauty still. She must have been very good looking indeed once, and that not so very long ago.

He opened his notebook. 'Now, marm, with regard to comings and goings, so to speak – exactly how private are you here?'

That would be the first thing Superintendent Leeyes would want to know – an 'inside' job or an 'outside' one. On this hung a great many things.

'We are not a strictly enclosed order, Inspector. Sisters are allowed to leave the convent for works of necessity and mercy, and so forth. They have interviews here in the parlour unless it is a Clothing, when they come into the chapel. Our chapel was originally the Faine private one, and Mrs Faine and her daughter still attend services here, as do others in Cullingoak.' She smiled gently. 'We are, in fact, to have a rather special service here next month. Miss Faine is to be married to Mr Ranby, the Institute's Principal, and the Bishop has given his consent to our chapel being used – as it would have been had the Faines still lived here.'

'How do they get in?' enquired Sloan with interest.

'There is a door leading outside from the chapel. Sister Poly-carp unlocks it before the service.'

'Tradesmen?'

'We have everything delivered. Sister Cellarer deals with them at the back door, and Sister Lucy here pays them.'

'No one else?'

'Just Hobbett – he's our handyman. There are some tasks – just one or two, you understand – which are beyond our capacities.'

Sloan nodded. 'This Hobbett – does he have to run the gauntlet every day?'

'Past Sister Polycarp? No, his work is at the back. He has his own key to the boiler room and his own routine – dustbins, ladders, cleaning the upstairs outside windows and so forth. And the boiler for three-quarters of the time.'

'Three-quarters?'

'Sister Ignatius is the only person who can persuade it to function at all when the wind is in the east. Her devotions are frequently interrupted.'

They found Hobbett in a small, not uncosy room at the foot of a short flight of outside stairs descending to cellar level not far from the kitchen door. It was lined with logs, and a litter of chopped pieces of wood covered the floor. There was a chair with one arm broken and an old table. Hobbett was sitting at this having his midday break. There was a mug of steaming tea on the table. He was reading a popular daily newspaper with a tradition for the sensational.

'I am Inspector Sloan.'

The man took a noisy sip of tea and set the mug down carefully on the table. 'Hobbett.'

He hadn't shaved this morning.

'We are enquiring into the death of Sister Anne.'

Hobbett took another sip of tea. 'I heard one of 'em had fallen down the cellar steps.' He jerked his head towards the door in the corner. 'I don't go through that far meself or happen I might 'ave found her for you.'

'How far do you go through?'

'Just to the boiler – got to keep that going – and the coke place with kindling and that. Mostly I work in the grounds.'

To Sloan he hadn't the look of a man who worked anywhere.

'What were you doing yesterday?'

'Yesterday?' Hobbett looked surprised. 'I'd 'ave to think.' He took a long pull at his tea. 'I cleared out a drain first. The gutter from the chapel roof was blocked with leaves and I had to get my ladders out. Long job, that was. I'd just finished when Sister Lucy sent for me to shift a window that'd got stuck.'

'Upstairs or down?'

'Up. I'd just put my ladders away, too. She wouldn't have it left though. Said it was dangerous. One of 'em might have escaped through it, I suppose.' He sank the rest of his tea in one long swallow and licked his lips. 'Not that there's much for them to escape for, is there now?'

'This Sister Anne,' said Sloan sharply. 'Did you see her often?'

'Wouldn't know her if I did. Can't tell some of them from which, if you get me. There's about four of them that gives me orders. The rest don't bother me much.'

'When did you leave last night?'

'Short of five somewhere. Can't do much in the dark.'

'Nice type,' observed Crosby on their way back.

'And four doors,' said Sloan morosely, 'and about thirty windows.'

Sister Gertrude was having a bad day. First, though no one had mentioned it, she was deeply conscious of her neglect in ignoring Sister Anne's empty cell. And now she was troubled about something else. As a nervous postulant she had fondly imagined that there would be no worries in a convent, that the way would be clear and that obedience to the Rule would make following that way, if not easy, then at least straightforward.

It seemed she was wrong – or was she?

No nun was meant to carry worries that properly belonged to the Reverend Mother. Her instructions were simple. The Reverend Mother was to be told of them and her ruling was absolute. Then the Sister concerned need worry no longer.

What they had omitted to pontificate on, thought Sister

Gertrude, was at what point a worry became substantial enough for communicating to the Reverend Mother. What was bothering her was just an uneasy thought.

It had cropped up after luncheon. There was no proper recreation until the early evening, but after their meal there was a brief relaxation of the silence in which they worked. It lasted for about fifteen minutes until they resumed their duties for the afternoon. And the person who had been speaking to her in it was Sister Damien.

In the tradition of the convent an empty place was left at the refectory table where Sister Anne had always sat, her napkin laid alongside it. It would be so for seven days and then the ranks of nuns would close up as if she had never been. And Sister Damien and Sister Michael who had sat for several years on either side of Sister Anne would now for the rest of their mortal lives sit next to each other instead at meals, in chapel, and in everything else they did as a community.

'I think we will have our cloister now,' Sister Damien had remarked as they tidied up the refectory together.

'Our cloister? Now?' Sister Gertrude stopped and looked at her. The convent had always lacked a cloister but to build one as they would have liked by joining up two back wings of the house was well beyond their means. 'We shall need one very badly if they build next door, but where will the money come from?'

Sister Damien assiduously chased a few wayward crumbs along one of the tables. 'Sister Anne.'

'Sister Anne?'

Sister Damien pinned down another crumb with her thin hand. 'She knew we wanted a cloister.'

'We all knew we wanted a cloister,' said Sister Gertrude with some asperity. 'It's very difficult in winter without one, but that doesn't mean to say that . . .'

'Sister Anne was to come into some money and she's left it to us.'

'How do you know?'

'She told me,' said Sister Damien simply. 'She didn't have a dowry but she knew she was going to have this money some day.'

Sister Gertrude pursed her lips. Money was never mentioned in the ownership sense in the convent. In calculating wants and needs and ways and means, yes, but never relating to a particular Sister. And the size of a dowry was a matter between the Mother Superior and the novice.

'So we'll be able to have our cloister now and it won't matter about the building,' went on Sister Damien, oblivious of the effect she was creating. 'That's good, isn't it?'

Sister Gertrude busied herself straightening a chair. 'Yes,' she said in as neutral a voice as she could manage. 'Except for Sister Anne.'

Sister Damien wheeled round and caught her arm. 'But she is in heaven, Sister. You don't regret that, do you?'

But Sister Gertrude did not know what it was she regretted, and at the first sound of the convent bell she thankfully fled the refectory.

It was unfortunate for her peace of mind that the first person she bumped into was little Sister Peter. She was walking up the great staircase looking rather less cheerful than Mary Queen of Scots mounting the scaffold at Fotheringhay. She was holding her hand out in front of her with her thumb stuck out in odd disassociation from the rest of her body.

'Hasn't the Inspector finished with your thumb, Sister?' Sister Gertrude asked.

'Oh, yes,' she said mournfully. 'He's fingerprinted my hand, and confirmed that the blood did get on the Gradual from my thumb.'

'Well, then,' said Sister Gertrude a little testily, 'surely you can put it away now?'

Sister Peter regarded the offending member. 'He doesn't know how the blood got on it and neither do I. I've shown him everything I did this morning after you woke me – my own door, two flights of stairs to the long landing, the gallery, this staircase and straight into the chapel. The chapel door was open. Sister Polycarp does that. Sister Sacrist had got the Gradual ready like she always does. Besides everywhere's been cleaned by now. I just don't know . . .' This last was said *tremolo*.

'Neither do I,' said Sister Gertrude firmly. 'But you've helped all you can . . .'

'I can't think why anyone should want to harm poor Sister Anne.'

'Neither can I,' said Sister Gertrude somewhat less firmly. 'It might have been an accident, you know . . .'

Sister Peter looked unconvinced and continued on her way.

'Now, Sister St Bernard, I realize that this business must have given you an unpleasant shock, but I would like you to describe how you found Sister Anne.'

Sloan was back in the parlour with Crosby in attendance facing the Reverend Mother with Sister Lucy at her side. Sister St Bernard was standing between them. There would come a time when he would want to see a nun on her own but that time was not yet. Sister Lucy looked anxious and strained, but the Reverend Mother sat calm and dignified, an air of timelessness about her.

Sloan was being the perfect policeman talking to the nervous witness. There was no doubt that Sister St Bernard was nervous. Her damp palms trembled slightly until she hit on the idea of clasping them together in front of her, but she could not keep a faint quaver out of her voice so easily.

'We were asked to help look for Sister Anne about an hour after Mass this morning in case she had been taken ill anywhere. Sister Lucy and the others were going through the upstairs rooms and Sister Perpetua and I were doing the downstairs ones . . .'

Sloan was prepared to bet that Sister Perpetua was as young as Sister St Bernard and that no one had expected either of them to find the missing Sister.

'I don't know what made me open the cellar door . . . I had been in all the rooms along that corridor and—'

'Was it closed?'

'Yes.'

'Properly?'

'Yes.'

'Was it locked?'

'No.'

'Are you sure about that?'

'Oh, yes. It was because it was usually locked that I put the light on when I opened it. Otherwise I don't think I would have seen Sister Anne.'

'The door is normally kept locked, Inspector,' explained the Reverend Mother in a very dry voice, 'on account of the danger of falling down the steep steps in the dark.'

'I see, marm, thank you. Then what did you do, Sister?'

She had done very little, decided Sloan, except give the alarm and encourage the destruction of useful clues by opening and shutting the cellar door and fetching people who went up and down the steps.

And Sister Peter had been scarcely more helpful.

When she had gone the Reverend Mother beckoned Sister Lucy to her side. 'What was that address?'

'17 Strelitz Square, Mother.'

The Mother Prioress nodded. 'Inspector, that was the address from which Sister Anne came to us.'

'It's a very good one,' said Sloan involuntarily.

'She was a very good nun,' retorted the Reverend Mother drily. 'It was, of course, some time ago that she left home, but in the normal course of events I would telephone there to establish whether or not she still had relatives.'

Sloan took a quick look at his watch. 'Perhaps I'll telephone myself, marm.'

Standing in the dark corridor where the nuns kept their instrument he wondered if it wouldn't have been wiser to go to London. When he was connected to 17 Strelitz Square he was sure.

'Mrs Alfred Cartwright's residence,' said a female voice.

'May I speak to Mrs Cartwright, please?'

'Who shall I say is calling?'

'The Convent of St Anselm.' That would do to begin with.

'I will enquire if madam is at home.'

There was a pause. Sloan heard footsteps walking away. Parquet flooring. And then they came back.

'Madam,' said the female voice, 'is Not At Home.'

'It's about her daughter,' said Sloan easily. 'I think if she knew that she—'

'Madam has no daughter,' said the voice and rang off.

Sloan went back to the parlour. Only Crosby was there now.

'A bell rang, Inspector, and they both went – just like that. I didn't know if you wanted me to stop them.'

'You? Stop them?' said Sloan unkindly. 'You couldn't do it. Now, listen . . .'

There was a knock on the parlour door and Father MacAuley came in.

'Ah, Inspector, found the glasses?'

'Not yet, sir,' said Sloan shortly. It was bad enough investigating the death in the alien surroundings of a convent without having a priest pattering along behind him. And MacAuley wasn't the only one who wanted to know where Sister Anne's glasses were. Superintendent Leeyes would be on to their absence in a flash, and a fat lot of good it would be explaining to him that he and Crosby had looked everywhere for them.

'Did you get anything out of Lady Macbeth?' asked the priest.

'We confirmed all of Sister Peter's statements,' said Sloan stiffly.

'She's walking up and down the corridor muttering "What! Will these hands ne'er be clean?" ' He squinted at Sloan. 'All the perfumes of Arabia will not sweeten that little hand.'

'No, sir? The Mother Prioress tried an old Army remedy.'

'She did?'

'Spud bashing.'

'A fine leader of women, the Mother Prioress.' Father MacAuley grinned suddenly. 'I hear that the chap across the way – Ranby at the Agricultural Institute – he's gated his students for the evening. All to be in their own grounds by four o'clock this afternoon.'

'Can't say I blame him for that,' said Sloan. 'Last year they burnt down the bus shelter and there was hell to pay.'

'Nearly set the post office on fire, too,' contributed Crosby.

'Polycarp says all buildings burn well, but Government buildings burn better,' said the priest.

Sloan rose dismissively. 'I don't think Bonfire Night at the agricultural institute will concern us, sir.'

Wherein he was wrong.

6

It was still damp in the grounds, and for that Sloan was grateful. It meant that the footprints Crosby had found not far from the cellar door were perfectly preserved.

'Two sets, Inspector.' He straightened his back. They were in the shelter of one of the large rhododendron bushes. 'One of them stood for a while in the same place. The earth's quite soft here . . .' He slipped out a measure. 'Men's . . .'

'Perhaps.'

'It was a man's shoe, sir . . .'

'But was there a man inside it? Don't forget that this lot wear men's shoes – every one of them.'

Crosby measured the depth. 'If it was a woman, it was a heavy one.'

'Get a cast and we'll know for certain.' He looked round. 'It would be a good enough spot to watch the back of the place from.' From where he was standing he could see the kitchen door, the cellar steps, a splendid collection of dustbins and a small glass door which presumably led to the garden room. A broad path led round towards the front entrance of the house, and along this now was walking the Caller, Sister Gertrude.

'Inspector, Mother says will you come, please? She's had a letter.'

'It was handed to Sister Polycarp a few minutes ago,' said the Reverend Mother, 'by one of the village children from a gentleman who is staying at the Bull. He says in his letter that he proposes to call at the convent at four thirty this afternoon in the hopes of being able to see Sister Anne.'

'Does he?' said Sloan with interest. 'Who is he?'

The Mother Prioress handed over the letter. 'It's signed "Harold Cartwright". A relation, presumably.'

'Do you know him? Has he been here before?'

She shook her head. 'No. I do not recollect Sister Anne having any visitors. Do you, Sister?'

Sister Lucy looked up. 'Never, Mother.'

'Would she have seen this man in the ordinary way?'

'Not if she did not wish it, Inspector. Nor if I did not wish it. Sometimes visitors are no great help – especially to young postulants and novices – and are therefore not allowed.'

'He says here he hopes no objection will be raised to his visit, which is of considerable importance,' said Sloan, quoting the letter.

'To him,' said the Reverend Mother. 'Visitors are rarely important to us. Nevertheless, I think in this instance that we had better ask Sister Polycarp to show him to the parlour when he comes.'

He arrived promptly at four thirty, a man aged about fifty-five in a dark grey suit. He was heavily built and going grey. He wasted no time in getting to the point.

'I am Harold Cartwright, the cousin of Sister Anne, and I would very much like to see her for a few moments . . .'

'I am afraid,' said the Reverend Mother, 'that that will not be possible . . .'

'I know,' said the man quickly, 'that she probably does not wish to see me or any of her family, but it is on a matter of some importance. That is why I have travelled down here in person rather than written to her . . .'

'*When* did you travel down here?' asked Sloan.

Cartwright turned. 'Last night. I stayed at the Bull.'

'What time did you arrive?'

'Is that any concern of—'

'I am a police officer investigating a sudden death.'

'I see.' Again the man wasted no time in coming to the point. 'I got to the Bull about seven thirty, had a meal and a drink in the bar and went to bed.'

'Straight to bed?'

'No. If you're interested I went for a quick walk round the village to get a breath of air before going to my room.'

'I see, sir, thank you.'

'Mr Cartwright,' the Mother Prioress inclined her coif slightly, 'how long is it since you last saw Sister Anne?'

'Almost twenty years. I went to another convent to see her. Hersely, it was.'

'That would be so. We have a house there.'

'I went to ask if there was anything she wanted, anything we could do for her.' His mouth twisted. 'She said she had everything and I came away again.'

'Mr Cartwright, you must be prepared for a shock.'

He laughed shortly. 'I know she'll be a changed woman. No one's the same after twenty years. I'm not the same man myself if it comes to that.'

The Mother Prioress lowered her head. 'I have no doubt that great changes have been wrought by the passage of time in you both but that is not the point. I am sorry to have to tell you that the sudden death into which Inspector Sloan is enquiring is that of your cousin, Sister Anne.'

Harold Cartwright sat very still. 'You mean Josephine's dead?'

'Yes, Mr Cartwright.'

'When?'

'She died last night.'

'Why the police?'

'She was found dead at the foot of a flight of steps.'

'An accident, surely?'

'We hope so.'

'It couldn't be anything else here. I mean, not in a convent.'

'I would like to think not,' agreed the Mother Prioress, 'but that matter is not yet resolved.'

Cartwright turned to Sloan again. 'Why might it not be an accident? Would anyone want to harm my cousin?'

'I don't know, sir. I was hoping that you might be able to tell us.'

'Me? I haven't had sight nor sound of her for twenty years.'

'You're not her only relation?'

'No. Her father – my uncle – died years ago, but her mother's still alive . . .'

'Mrs Alfred Cartwright, 17 Strelitz Square?'

'That's right. How did you know?'

'The convent records,' said Sloan briefly.

'They didn't get on.'

'I inferred that.'

'My aunt is a very strong-minded woman. She greatly resented my cousin taking her vows. I don't think she has ever forgiven her.'

'I am sure *she* has been forgiven,' interposed the Reverend Mother.

'I beg your pardon?'

'By Sister Anne.'

'Oh, I see what you mean. Yes, of course.' It didn't seem as if Harold Cartwright had thought of this at all. He waved a hand vaguely. 'Before she died, you mean . . .'

'Many years ago,' said the Mother Prioress firmly. 'It would not be possible to live the life of a true religious and harbour that sort of unforgiveness.'

'No, no, I can see that.'

Sloan coughed. 'Now, sir, perhaps you'll tell us what it was that was so important that you had to see her about after all these years.'

But that was something Harold Cartwright obviously did not want to do. 'What? Oh, yes, of course. What I'd come to see her about?'

'Yes.'

'Well, it's not really relevant now she's dead. Just a family matter, that's all. Nothing that would concern anyone now, you understand.' He gave a quick smile. 'Death cancels all that sort of thing, doesn't it?'

'No,' said the Mother Prioress directly. 'Not in my experience.'

'No? Perhaps not, but it does alter them, and it has altered all I had come to see her about.'

Sloan let it ride. This was only the beginning. 'Will you be leaving Cullingoak tonight?' he asked him.

'No. Not now – I think I'd better stay on, don't you?' He frowned. 'Though there's my aunt. Perhaps I ought to go back to tell her . . .'

'I'll do that,' said Sloan suddenly.

Harold Cartwright said, 'Thank you.' He looked back to the Mother Superior and said diffidently: 'There'll be a funeral, I take it – would I be allowed to come to that?'

She nodded briskly. 'Of course, Mr Cartwright. But first there is, I understand, to be a post-mortem . . .'

Cartwright looked quickly at the Inspector.

'To establish the exact cause of death,' said Sloan.

It was dark when Sloan came out to Cullingoak for the second time that day. There were bonfires and fireworks all about as the police car slipped through the streets of Berebury and out into the open country towards Cullingoak.

'Get a move on, man,' he muttered irritably, as Crosby slowed down for a crossroads. He sat beside the Constable, his shoulders hunched up, hands sunk deep into his pockets, thinking hard.

As they swept into Cullingoak High Street he heard the clang of a fire engine's bell. He saw the engine careering along ahead of them, firemen pulling on their boots as they clung to the machine. It did a giant swerve and headed unerringly between the gates of the agricultural institute. Crosby followed suit and bumped up the drive after the fire engine.

The fire was over on their right, away from the institute's buildings. It was well alight, with flames leaping high into the air. Standing round it like a votive circle were the students. Their faces stood out in a white ring in the darkness, the dancing flames reflected in them.

Sloan burst from the car and ran over to the fire brigade.

'I want that fire out,' he shouted. 'Quickly.'

'Blimey,' said a Leading Fireman. 'It's only a bonfire.'

'I know it is,' snapped Sloan, 'but I want it out before the guy is burnt. This is a police matter, so look sharp. I want that guy in one piece whatever happens.'

'You'll be lucky,' said the man over his shoulder, and was gone.

Round the other side of the fire boys were still feeding the flames, and Sloan shouted at them too.

The fire brigade were running their hoses towards the fire, lacing them in and out of the spectators. The boys divided their attention between them and the fire. The latter was of magnificent proportions now, the flames licking their way to the figure lashed to the top.

There was a sigh from the crowd as the first flame lapped round the feet of the guy.

'Hurry,' urged Sloan.

He squinted up through the smoke and blackness. Impossible to tell if the material was alight or not. A tongue of flame ran up behind it towards the head. Sloan very nearly plunged into the flames himself to rescue it.

Suddenly some boys on his left moved quickly to one side and he saw the hose leap into life.

The noise of the bonfire gave way to the noise of water hissing upon flame, and the delectable smell of bonfire was succeeded by an acrid mixture of smoke and steam. The flames fell back.

'Don't hit the guy if you can help it,' said Sloan to the man struggling with the hose.

'You don't half want a lot, guv'nor,' retorted the man, continuing to play the hose where he wished. 'If it falls down in the middle of this you've had it. Besides, a drop of water won't do it no harm, will it? I reckon she was pretty warm where she was.'

Minutes later the Leading Fireman came up to him with the guy lying in his arms.

'Daftest rescue job I've ever done, but here you are.'

Sloan found himself nursing the damp, faintly charred effigy of a nun. There was a pair of spectacles tied ridiculously across the mock face.

A man came up to him. 'Inspector? I'm Marwin Ranby, the Principal of the Institute. I'm very sorry about all this. I feel I'm in some way to blame. You see, last year . . .'

'I know all about last year,' said Sloan grimly.

He had just seen a sight which made him feel very uneasy indeed: Harold Cartwright.

Marwin Ranby led the way into his study. He was hovering round the forty mark, Sloan decided, with a head of fair hair that made him seem younger than he probably was. The study was a pleasant room, with a fire burning at one end, a sofa and chairs round it. At the other end was a desk and bookshelves loaded with heavy agricultural tomes. Over the fireplace hung a Rowland Ward, and in one corner was a tray set with decanter and glasses.

Ranby waved Sloan to a chair and made for these.

'What will you have, Inspector? No? You don't mind if I do, do you?' He groaned. 'I don't know what's going to happen when Celia hears about this. Or the Mother Superior.'

Sloan laid his burden down on the sofa as tenderly as if she had been human. It wouldn't do the chintz much good, but Ranby wasn't in a position to complain.

'I blame myself,' went on the Principal. 'I gated them, you know, because of last year. I hoped that way we could minimize any damage done. You'd have thought that bus shelter was an ancient monument the way the bus company carried on. And look what happens.' He stared at the guy and shuddered. 'I'm to be married at the end of the month in the convent chapel by special permission of goodness knows who, and they go and burn a nun on Guy Fawkes' Night. What will Celia – Miss Faine, you know – say? And what will the Mother Prioress think?'

He started to pace up and down. Sloan examined the guy closely. The habit was genuine and it was the same as that worn by the nuns next door. The face had been made out of an old stocking, stuffed, with a couple of black buttons sewn on for eyes and the glasses kept on over these with a piece of string tying the ends together at the back. The rest of the habit was spread over a tightly stuffed large sack. No attempt had been made to make feet, and the figure – squat and dumpy – had a distinct resemblance to that of Queen Victoria towards the end of her Sixty Glorious Years.

'I suppose I should have expected something like this,' said Ranby after a minute or two. 'They are none of them old. Besides, they took the news of the gating too well.'

'When did you tell them, sir?'

'After supper on Sunday evening.' He laughed shortly. 'Gave them a day or so to hatch something up. She smells a bit, doesn't she?'

'The flames caught a little.'

'Inspector . . .'

'Sir?'

'Don't think me inquisitive but how did you come to hear about this? You're from Berebury, aren't you?'

'That's right, sir. Someone telephoned us.'

'The devil they did! Who on earth would do that? And why?'

'The caller didn't leave his name, sir. Just said he thought we'd be interested.'

'But why? It's not a crime, is it, to burn a guy? Or is it sedition? Or an anti-Popish Plot or something obscure like that?'

'No, sir, not that I know of.'

'Well, Inspector, while I don't blame you for rescuing it, I'm not sure that it might not have been better from my point of view if it had been burnt to cinders. Then there would have been no chance of either the Big House or the Dower House seeing it.' He finished his drink. 'But they'd have heard in the end, I suppose.'

'Do you know which of your students would have been responsible for this – the idea, getting the habit and so forth?'

'No.' The Principal frowned. 'We've got about a hundred and fifty men here with about a dozen natural leaders among them. They're here for three years, but the freshmen have only been in residence a month, so I would say a second- or third-year man for sure. That's a point. The habit . . . Don't say they took that from the convent!' He ran his hands through his hair. 'I'd never live that down. But they couldn't, Inspector. How would they get in or out?'

'I don't know if the habit came from there or not, sir, but I will find out presently.'

'And I'll find out the man responsible for the guy and take him round to the convent in the morning to apologize. I think I'd better tell Miss Faine myself. She's a very devout girl, you know.'

'She didn't come round this evening?'

'No, thank God. No, she's gone to London for the day to have a fitting for her dress.'

Sloan straightened up. 'Thank you, sir, you've been most helpful. There's just one thing. This ring-leader. I want to talk to him myself – before anyone on the staff, I mean. That's important.'

'I'm a bit bewildered, Inspector, but if that's how you want it, I'll track him down and send him to you.'

'If you would. My Constable's already seeing how far he can get tonight.'

'Is he?' Marwin Ranby looked momentarily annoyed, and then smiled again. 'Perhaps he'll be successful, though I fear we both represent authority. But, Inspector, why this interest in a guy? It's not usual for the police to—'

'Hadn't you heard, sir? One of the Sisters at the convent died last night from injuries that we can't immediately account for.'

'No!' He looked down at the travesty on the sofa. 'We are in trouble then. That makes this very much worse, doesn't it?'

'More interesting, too, sir, wouldn't you say? Now, if you would just hold the door open I'll put her in the car.'

The fire brigade had gone now and a few boys were trying to coax the damp fire back into life. Crosby loomed up out of the near darkness and helped Sloan lay the guy on the back seat of the police car.

'Watch her carefully, Crosby.'

'Inspector Bring-'em-back-alive,' murmured Crosby, but fortunately Sloan was out of earshot. He was stumbling among the trees looking for Harold Cartwright. He found him at the far corner of the reviving fire and drew him to one side.

'There's just one question I want to ask you, sir. Did you or did you not telephone us about this guy?'

'Me, Inspector? No. No, I heard about it in the Bull and came along to see what was going on. I would have rung you as soon as I saw the guy, of course, if I hadn't heard the fire siren.'

'Of course.'

Cartwright gave him a tight smile. 'I'm glad to see the Lady's Not for Burning. Funny thing for them to do, wasn't it?'

'Very.' Sloan stumped back to the car and climbed in beside Crosby. He sniffed. 'Something's burning – the guy . . .'

'No, sir, it's me.' Crosby flushed in the darkness. 'A jumping cracker. One of the little perishers tied it to my coat.'

'Get him?'

'No.'

'Let's hope it's not an augury, that's all.'

7

Back in Berebury Sloan dissected the guy with the same care that Dr Dabbe had gone about his post-mortem. He was joined by Superintendent Leeyes.

'Who is this man Cartwright?' he demanded.

'He says he's her cousin, sir.'

'And he just appears out of the blue asking to see her the afternoon after she's killed when he hasn't seen her for twenty years?'

'Yes, sir.'

'What does he want to do that for?'

'I don't know yet, sir.'

'Find out about him for a start. If he hadn't come to the convent this afternoon was there anything to connect him with this woman?'

'Only his name and address in the hotel register. It needn't have been the right one but it was.'

'So he has a reason – a good reason – for coming, Sloan, hasn't he? Otherwise he would have cleared off as soon as he could.' Leeyes grunted. 'Perhaps it was to make sure she was dead.'

'Or that he'd clobbered the right one.'

'If he'd waited to hear in the ordinary way about that death he might have waited quite a while, of course. There's no obligation on their part to tell anyone, I suppose.' He shrugged his shoulders. 'They call it a Living Death so perhaps there's not a lot of difference.'

'We've got a lead, anyway, which is something. I'll go to see the mother in the morning and also find out a bit more about this man. We've checked on the Bull already. He arrived at about seven thirty, spent an hour over his meal, had a couple of drinks in the bar and then went out for a stroll.'

The Superintendent's head went up. 'When did you say she was last seen alive?'

'About a quarter to nine – at the end of Vespers.'

'When did he get back?'

'The landlord didn't notice. Says he was busy with the usual crowd.'

'What's he like?'

'Not a fool.'

The Superintendent wasn't a fool either. 'What was he doing at this bonfire?'

Sloan shook his head. 'I don't know, sir.'

'And who rang here and told us about it?'

'A man's voice, it was, but that's all that switchboard can tell us.'

Leeyes indicated the guy. 'Someone wanted us to see this before it was burnt to a cinder. Why?'

'I don't know, sir. Not yet. There's one thing – the footprints we found weren't Cartwright's.'

'Those glasses – are they the missing ones?'

'I don't know that either, sir, yet.' Sloan undid them very carefully. 'We'll try them for fingerprints, but I doubt if we'll get anything worth while.' He undid the habit and coif and slipped them off, leaving a large stuffed farm sack lying on the bench. The habit, deeply scorched in places, was old and darned. He felt its thinness between his fingers.

Superintendent Leeyes grunted. 'I don't get it, Sloan. This woman, Sister Anne, she wasn't naked or anything?'

'Oh, no, sir,' said Sloan, deeply shocked. 'It's not that sort of place at all.'

'Perhaps she was killed in her Number Ones,' said Leeyes. 'Or perhaps this tomfoolery has got nothing whatsoever to do with it and you're wasting your time, Sloan. In that case,' he fingered the charred habit, 'it would seem that the wrong one's wearing the sackcloth and ashes – eh?'

'Yes, sir,' said Sloan dutifully.

Sloan had been married for fifteen years.

Long enough to view his wife's nightly ritual with face cream with patient indifference.

Long enough for her to be surprised as he slipped into bed beside her when he pulled the white sheet right round and across the top of her forehead.

'Denis, what on earth are you doing?'

He tucked the blanket as far under her chin as it would go and considered her.

'That's all you can see of a nun.'

'I should think so, too. What more do you want?'

'Funny what a good idea of a woman you can get from this bit.'

She shook her head. 'Don't you believe it, dear. Men always think that. It's not true.'

'No grey now.'

'Beast,' retorted his wife equably. 'On the other hand, you can't see my ankles.' Margaret Sloan had very good ankles and very little grey hair.

He relaxed his hold on the sheet and lay on his back.

'Margaret . . .'

'Well?'

'What would make a woman go into a convent?'

'Don't they call it having a vocation or something? Like nursing or teaching.'

'They can't all have felt a call, can they? There's over fifty of them there.'

'I don't know,' she said doubtfully. 'Perhaps they were religious-minded anyway and then something happened to drive them there.'

'Like what – as Crosby would say?'

'Being lonely, would you think, or jilted perhaps, or the man in their life loving another. That sort of thing.' She tugged at the pillow. 'Or not having any man there in the first place, of course.'

Sloan yawned. 'Escape, too, would you say? Not facing up to things. Running away from life.'

'There's always that, I suppose.'

'Not my idea of a life. The Superintendent called it a living death.' He pulled the eiderdown up. 'Can't see you going in one either, dear.'

'Oh, I don't know,' said his wife.

'What do you mean?'

'Suppose something had happened to you after we got engaged. What should I have done then, do you think? A living death wouldn't have mattered very much then, would it?'

He turned to face her, oddly disconcerted. 'I . . . I hadn't thought of that.'

She snuggled down in the bed. 'Mind you,' she said sleepily, 'I don't think I would have made a very good nun.'

Marwin Ranby's study at the agricultural institute looked almost as comfortable in daylight as it had done in the cosy, shaded light of last evening. There was a young woman with him. She had pale auburn hair and the delicate, almost translucent skin that often goes with it. The clothes she was wearing were deceptively, ridiculously simple, and Sloan was not at all surprised to find himself being introduced to Miss Celia Faine, the last of her line and Marwin Ranby's fiancée.

'I have been telling Miss Faine something of last night's excitement,' said the Principal.

'But, I suspect, not everything,' said Celia Faine with a smile. She had a pleasant unaffected voice. 'Marwin's being very discreet, Inspector.'

'I'm glad to hear it, miss,' responded Sloan.

'Or should I say "mysterious"? It's because he thinks I should mind. But I know his boys get up to all sorts of things. They wouldn't be boys if they didn't, would they? I don't think the Sisters would mind either if they did hear about it. They're perfectly sweet, you know, and so − sort of balanced, if you know what I mean. You feel they are finished with the petty, trivial things that don't matter. It isn't as if it was a demonstration against them or anything. Nobody minded them coming to Cullingoak, and we had to do something with the house. In fact, I think people are glad they're there in a way.'

'Celia thinks their sanctity balances out the devilment in my young men,' said Ranby lightly, matching her tone, 'but I'm not so sure myself. Until last night I wouldn't have thought they were even aware of them. We hear their bell on a clear day – that usually provokes a crack or two about getting the cows in – but nothing more.'

'What about last night?' asked Sloan.

'No news, Inspector. None of my staff knew anything about the guy.'

'You have other means of finding out?'

'Naturally. I can if necessary interview the whole lot, but that takes time. I was hoping to appeal to them at supper tonight – it's the first meal that they will all be at together. I have already checked that no one had a late pass on Wednesday night.'

'Is that infallible? My experience is that it isn't as a rule.'

'Rumour has it the biology laboratory window can be persuaded to open if pressure is judiciously applied in the right place.'

'I'll get my constable to fingerprint it straight away.'

'You really want this chap, don't you?'

'Yes,' said Sloan shortly. 'We do.'

Strelitz Square was still a square in the sense that its Georgian creator had intended, and there was still a garden in the middle. The houses were tall, dignified and – most significant of all – still lived in. Number Seventeen was on the north side, facing the thin November sun. Sloan and Crosby rang the bell at exactly ten thirty the next morning. An elderly, aproned maid answered the door.

He didn't mention the convent this time. 'Detective Inspector Sloan,' he said, 'would be obliged if Mrs Cartwright would spare him a moment or two.'

The woman looked them over appraisingly and then invited them in. She would enquire if Mrs Cartwright was at home.

'Funny way of carrying on,' said Crosby.

'You're in Society now, Constable, and don't you forget it. Plenty of money here.' Sloan looked quickly round the room into which they had been shown. 'Pictures, china, furniture – the lot.'

Crosby fingered a finely carved chair. 'Is this fashion, sir?'

'It was,' said Sloan, 'about two hundred years ago. It's antique, like everything else in the room.' He pointed to a set of Dresden shepherdesses. 'They'll be worth more than your pension. Don't suppose they picked up that walnut bureau for five bob either or those plates . . .'

'Good morning, Inspector.' An elderly figure appeared in the doorway. 'Admiring my Meissen? Charming, isn't it?'

'Good morning, madam,' said Sloan, not committing himself about the Meissen, whatever that was.

Mrs Cartwright was old, ramrod backed and thin. She rested a clawlike hand on the back of the chair just long enough for Sloan to see the battery of rings on it and then she sat down. She was dressed – and dressed very well indeed – in grey with touches of scarlet. Sloan searched her face for a likeness to Sister Anne but found only heavy make-up and the tiny suture marks of an old face-lift. Her hair was a deep mahogany colour and the total effect quite startling.

'You have something to say, Inspector.'

'Yes, madam.' Sloan jerked his mind back. She must be over eighty, and he thought he had bad news for her. 'I understand you had a telephone call yesterday afternoon from the Convent of St Anselm.'

Not a muscle on her face moved.

'And that you refused to take that call.'

'That is so.' Her voice was harsher than he expected.

'Why, madam?'

'Is it anything to do with you?'

'I'm afraid it is.'

'Really, Inspector, I can see no reason why . . .'

'You had a daughter there.'

Mrs Cartwright rose and walked towards a bell by the fireplace. 'I have no daughter.'

'One moment, madam. You are quite right . . .'

She stopped and looked at him.

'You have no daughter. But you had one.'

She stood rigidly in front of the fireplace and said again in a well-controlled voice, 'I have no daughter.' She put her finger towards the bell.

'Mrs Cartwright!'

'Well?' Her finger was poised.

'You had a daughter called Josephine Mary.'

A spasm of emotion passed across her face. 'Inspector, I lost my daughter thirty years ago.'

'Lost her?'

'Lost her. She left me, she left everything.' Mrs Cartwright waved a painted fingernail around the room. 'Abandoned. Moreover, Inspector, her name has not been mentioned in this house from that day to this. I see no reason to discontinue the habit. Now, if you will either state your business or leave.'

'When did you last see her, madam?'

'The day she left home.'

'Thirty years ago?'

'Thirty-one. She was eighteen and a half.'

So Sister Anne had been forty-nine. She hadn't looked as old as that.

'And you, madam, hadn't seen her yourself since then?' Sloan hoped he was keeping the wonder out of his voice.

'Not once. I told her that she needn't expect me to visit her. And I never did.'

'Had – have you any other children?'

'She was the only one, Inspector, and she left me. She was a convert, of course. Nothing would persuade her. Nothing.' The old eyes danced. 'She wanted to eschew the World, the Flesh and the Devil, Inspector, and she did. At eighteen and a half, without knowing anything about any of the three of them. I hope she's enjoyed it, that's all. Being walled up with a lot of other women praying all day long instead of getting married and having children. What's she done, Inspector? Run away after all these years?'

'No, madam.'

'Because if she has, you needn't come looking for her here.' There was a gleam of satisfaction in her voice. 'She wouldn't come back here, Inspector. I can tell you that. Not if it was the last place on earth.'

'No, madam, it's not that at all . . .'

'Don't say she's done something wrong! That I would find hard to believe. I shouldn't imagine you arrest many nuns, Inspector, but if she was one of them I must say I would derive a certain amount of amusement from the fact. She was so very pious.'

'I've come to tell you that she's dead.'

The old mouth tightened. 'She died as far as I'm concerned the day she left home.'

'And that she was probably murdered.'

'Poor Josephine,' she said grimly. 'She didn't escape the wicked world after all then, did she, Inspector?'

They were back in Berebury by lunchtime.

'Get anywhere?' asked Superintendent Leeyes.

'I don't know,' said Sloan. 'Can't say I blame her for leaving home. I'd have gone myself. Mother hasn't seen her for thirty years – or so she says anyway.'

'Check on that.'

'Lots and lots of money there.'

The superintendent's head came up. 'Is there now? Check on that, too, Sloan. Money is a factor in the crime equation.'

'Yes, sir.' Last winter the Superintendent had attended a course on 'Mathematics for the Average Adult'. It had left its mark.

'Who inherits?'

'I'll find out.'

Leeyes looked sharply across at him. 'It could be the convent, I suppose?'

'Not now she's dead, would you think?'

'Perhaps not. It would be interesting to know if she would have inherited had she lived. This mother – is she old?'

'Very. And she wouldn't have made her the sole heir – not from the way she was talking.'

'Cut off with the proverbial shilling, eh?'

'Yes, sir.'

Leeyes grunted. 'She mightn't have had any say. She a widow?'

'Yes.'

'Where does cousin Harold come in, then?'

'I don't know yet.'

'Find out then, man. It could be important.'

'Yes, sir.'

'And find out who gets it if the convent doesn't. That could be important, too.' He drummed his fingers on the desk. 'I don't suppose you'll get out of anyone at the convent what sort of dowry Sister Anne brought with her.'

'Dowry?'

'Gifts in money or kind brought to a marriage contract, Sloan. They have the same custom when a girl goes into a convent. In India it's a couple of cows or some sheep. My father-in-law gave me some dud shares.'

Sloan flushed. There had been a pair of brass candle-sticks that his wife had brought from her home, ugly as sin, that had dominated the mantelpiece of their best room all their married life. 'I know what you mean, sir. I'll try to find out.'

'Of course,' said Leeyes, off now on a different tack, 'this lot may have taken vows of perpetual poverty or something idiotic like that.'

'I hope not,' said Sloan piously. 'Upset all the usual motives too much, that would.'

'What's that? Yes, it would. We must hope that they haven't done anything so foolish.'

Sloan went back to his own room.

Crosby came in. 'Dr Dabbe wants to talk to you, sir, and there's a message from the convent.'

Sloan lifted his head. 'Well?'

'Please may they have their keys back?'

8

An unused knife, fork, spoon and table napkin marked the place at the refectory table where Sister Anne had sat for most of her religious life. Sister Michael and Sister Damien sat on either side of the gap – the one professed immediately before Sister Anne, and the other immediately after. It was the midday meal and the Reader was pursuing her way through the Martyrology.

The vicissitudes of the early faithful seemed to be as nothing compared with the trials of working through today's pudding. A reasonable stew had been eaten with the relish of those who have been up since very early morning, but today's pudding was obviously different.

Custom decreed that it should be eaten (many a martyr had died of starvation – or poison); their creed forbade criticism. So fifty-odd nuns struggled with a doughy indefinable mixture lacking the main ingredients of a sweet course.

Sister Cellarer was at the parlour door immediately the meal was finished.

'Mother, I hope I am lacking in neither ingenuity nor humility but I find it exceedingly difficult to cook without the basic essentials.'

'Not ingenuity, my child. No one could say that.'

Sister Cellarer flushed. 'It's quite impossible to—'

'Nothing is impossible, Sister. It may be difficult but impossible is a word no true religious should use lightly.'

'No, Mother.' Sister Cellarer lowered her eyes. 'I'm sorry . . .'

'As to humility, I'm not sure.' The Mother Prioress contemplated the hot and ruffled cook. 'Did you feel the community would blame you for the shortcomings of our dinner? If so, Sister, I suggest you examine your motives in complaining. I think if you look at them closely you will find an element of pride. Pride in personal skill is a dangerous matter in a convent. All work and skill here should be offered to our Lord from whom our strength to do it comes. The sin of pride is not one I should have to look for in you.'

A diminished Sister Cellarer was on her knees. 'I ask forgiveness, Mother. I should have thought.'

The Mother Prioress waved a hand. 'May God bless you, Sister. As it happens I have sent a message about the keys, but it may well be that we will not have them yet. I can see that the police would need to know if they had any significance.'

'They didn't have anything to do with Sister Anne at all,' said Sister Cellarer. 'Sister Lucy lent them to her just for the evening.'

'I have told them that,' said the Reverend Mother patiently, 'but until they know how it was that Sister Anne died I think they are justified in retaining them.'

Sister Cellarer rose. 'Of course,' she said soberly. 'That is what matters. Poor Sister Anne. It doesn't seem possible that only the day before yesterday none of this had happened at all.'

'The day before yesterday seems a very long time ago now.' The Mother Prioress gathered her habit up preparatory to going somewhere at her usual speed. 'Will you ask the Sacrist to come to see me in the chapel, and the Chantress, too, if she's about?'

Sloan got Dr Dabbe on the telephone.

'Sister Anne died from a depressed fracture of the skull,' said the doctor, 'caused by the application of the traditional blunt instrument. She had a post-mortem fracture of her right femur almost certainly caused by the fall down the cellar steps, and also sundry haematoma . . .'

'Heema what?'

'Bruises. Also mostly caused after death. You don't bleed much then, of course.'

'No.'

'I would say she was hit from behind and slightly above – perhaps by someone taller.'

'Man or woman?' asked Sloan eagerly, and got the usual medical prevarication.

'Difficult to say, Inspector. She wasn't hit so hard that only a man could have done it – on the other hand there were unusual features. The coif, for instance, and the complete absence of hair. It was a heavy blow, but in a good position with a wide swing it wouldn't have been out of the question for a woman – especially a tall one.'

'Weapon?'

'You want to look for something round and smooth and heavy.'

Sloan flipped over a page of his note-book. 'Time of death?'

'Between six and seven night before last.'

'*When?*'

'I can't tell you to the minute, you know. Let's put it this way – she had been dead approximately sixteen to seventeen hours when I saw her just after eleven o'clock yesterday morning.'

'But they have supper at quarter past six and—'

'She'd had supper,' said the pathologist laconically. 'She died on a full stomach, if that's any consolation to anybody. The meal was quite undigested. Shouldn't have fancied it myself. Too many peas.'

Sloan turned back to his note-book. 'But she was at some service or other – I've got it here – Vespers – at half past eight.'

'Not if she had steak and kidney pudding and peas at six fifteen,' said the pathologist. 'The process of digestion had barely started. I'll put it all in writing for you.'

'Thank you. This alters some of my ideas.'

'Post-mortems usually do.'

Sloan set down the telephone receiver very thoughtfully indeed.

*

Sister Polycarp satisfied herself with a quicker scrutiny this time. 'It's yourself, Inspector. And the Constable. Come in. You'll be wanting the Parlour, I suppose?' She shut the grille and appeared in person through one of the doors. 'This way. Mother Prioress is in the chapel but Sister Lucy will see you.'

They followed her through to the Parlour.

'I don't suppose you show many men through these doors,' ventured Sloan tentatively.

'The plumber,' said Polycarp tartly. 'Can't do without him, and the doctor. He comes to see old Mother Thérèse.'

'What about the agricultural institute? Do you have any visitors from there?'

She shook her head. 'That we do not. Young limbs of Satan, that's what students are.'

'What about Mr Ranby?'

'Oh, he came the other day to see about the wedding. I took him through to the parlour to talk to Reverend Mother and the Sacrist. We haven't had a wedding here before, you see. I think Mr Ranby comes to the chapel, too, but of course I hadn't seen him before.'

'Why "of course"?'

She stared at him. 'The grille. Across the chapel. Haven't you been in there?'

'Yes, I saw the grille.'

'Well, the community sits in front and then there's the screen and then the public.'

'So you can't see them?'

'Naturally not.'

'And they can't see you?'

'Of course not. That wouldn't be proper, would it?'

'Therefore you have no idea at all who comes in at the back?'

'Except that they are local people who always come – no. I open the side door before the service and lock it up afterwards.'

'Every time?'

She looked him straight in the eye. 'Every time, Inspector. And I do a round of doors and windows last thing at night.'

'When would that be?'

'Eight o'clock.'

Sloan reckoned he had been in short trousers when eight o'clock had been 'last thing at night'.

'And Hobbett?'

'He comes and goes according to his work and the weather. He has his own key to the boiler room.'

Polycarp shut the parlour door behind them.

Crosby tapped the bare, polished floor with his foot and pointed to the plain walls. 'Bit of a change from Strelitz Square for that Sister Anne.'

'I expect that's why she came.'

Sister Lucy came into the parlour with Sister Gertrude.

They bowed slightly, then sat down, hands clasped together in front, and looked at him expectantly.

Sloan undid a brown-paper parcel he had brought with him.

'This habit. Can you tell me anything about it?'

Sister Lucy leaned forward, and Sloan got a good look at her face for the first time. The bone structure was perfect. He didn't know about Sister Anne, but Sister Lucy would have cut quite a figure in a drawing-room. He tried to imagine hair where there was only a white coif now. With Sister Gertrude it was easier. Hers was the round jolly face of a 'good sort', the games mistress at a girls' school, the unmarried daughter . . .

'Yes, Inspector, I think I can.' Sister Lucy's voice was quiet and unaccented. 'This is the spare habit that we keep in the flower room. Should any Sister get wet while out in the grounds she can slip this on instead while she asks permission to dry her own habit in the laundry. It is kept behind the door on a hook.' She turned it round expertly. 'You see, here is the hook. It is very old and worn now, but none the less blessed for that.'

'Thank you, Sister. Now take a look at these.'

'Sister Anne's glasses!' Sister Lucy and Sister Gertrude crossed themselves in unison.

'You both confirm that?'

The two nuns nodded. Sister Lucy said, 'She wore particularly thick glasses, Inspector. I think she is the only member of the community with them as thick as that.' Her hand disappeared inside her habit and emerged again. 'Most of us wear glasses like these. For reading and sewing, you know, but Sister Anne had poor eyesight. She couldn't see anything at all without her glasses.'

'Thank you, Sisters. You have been very helpful.'

They acknowledged this with another slight bow. ('Like talking to a couple of Chinese mandarins,' said Sloan later.)

'Now I would like to tell the Mother Prioress where they were found.'

'She is in the chapel,' volunteered Sister Lucy, 'arranging the Requiem Mass for Sister Anne. And the Great Office of the Dead. When a Sister dies violently there are certain changes in the responses and so forth.'

Sloan permitted himself a bleak smile. 'That can't happen often.'

'On the contrary, Inspector. We sang just the same service at Midsummer.'

'You did? Who for?'

'Sister St John of the Cross.'

'Why?'

'She was hacked to death with a machete.'

'What! Where?'

'Unggadinna.'

Sloan breathed again. 'That's different.'

A faint chill came into the atmosphere. 'Not so very different, Inspector, for us.'

'There was Mother St Theobold, too, just after Easter,' put in Sister Gertrude diffidently. 'I was a novice when she was professed so I remember her well. She died in prison, you know, in Communist hands.'

'We assumed,' said Sister Lucy astringently, 'that she died violently, though we have had no exact details yet.'

'I'm sorry,' said Sloan awkwardly.

'And, of course,' persisted Sister Lucy, 'there are members of our order who *were* in China. We have no means of knowing whether or not they are accomplished among the elect.' They rose. 'We will see if Mother has finished in the chapel . . .'

Crosby stirred in his hard chair. 'Funny thing, sir. They don't ask any questions. Most people would have wanted to know where you got those glasses and that gown thing, wouldn't they?'

'Unless they knew.'

'I hadn't thought of that.'

The Mother Prioress came back with Sister Lucy. 'You have news for us, Inspector?'

'I don't know if it is news or not, marm, but we think Sister Anne was murdered.'

He was conscious of Sister Lucy's sharp indrawn breath, but the Reverend Mother only nodded.

'No, Inspector, that is not news. Father MacAuley had already intimated to me that Sister Anne died an unnatural death. He has also told me about last night's bonfire.'

'Sister Lucy has just identified the habit and Sister Anne's glasses.'

'How very curious that both should be found on a guy at the agricultural institute. Do you connect them with Sister Anne's death?'

'I can't say, marm, at this stage. The glasses were hers, she couldn't see without them; she was killed on Wednesday evening, and on Thursday evening they were found on this guy.'

'If,' said the Mother Prioress slowly, 'the whole episode of the guy had been an anti-Papist demonstration we, as a Community, would have been aware of feelings against us. After all, they are quite common. Sisters in our other houses have them to contend with – but not without knowing the feelings existed. Hate is so very communicable. Mr Ranby would have known, too, I think.'

'Granted, marm. But somebody took both the old habit and the glasses.'

She inclined her head. 'It would seem that the world has been to us or that one of us has been into the world.'

Sloan had reached this conclusion himself the evening before and turned to another matter.

'Going back to Sister Anne, herself, marm, can you tell me anything about her? As a person, I mean.'

The Mother Prioress smiled faintly. 'We try so very hard not to be persons here, you know. To conquer the self and to submerge the personality are part of our daily battle with ourselves in the quest for true humility. I would say that Sister Anne, God rest her soul, succeeded as well as any of us.'

'Er – yes, I see.' It was patent that he didn't. 'Now about her actual death. Did anyone stand to gain by that?'

'Just Sister Anne.'

'Sis . . .'

'It is part of our conviction, Inspector, that all true Christians stand to gain by death.'

He smiled weakly. 'Of course. But apart from Sister Anne herself?'

'I cannot conceive that anyone could gain from her death.'

'In the worldly sense, perhaps?'

'I take it that you mean financially? That is what people usually mean.'

'Yes.'

'The disposition of any material wealth would be entirely a matter for the Sister concerned.'

'Was Sister Anne wealthy?'

'I have no idea, Inspector.'

'She came from a wealthy home.'

'That is not always a measure.'

'Who would know?'

'Just the Mother Prioress at the time she took her vows.'

'And that was?'

'Mother Helena . . .'

'And she's dead?'

'. . . of blessed memory,' finished the Mother Prioress simultaneously.

That meant the same thing. Sloan was getting frustrated. 'Is there no way of finding out?'

Sister Lucy coughed. 'Mother, the Bursar's accounts. They might show something at the time. We know the date of profession. It would take a little while, but if a dowry had been received it would show in the figures.'

'Thank you,' said Sloan, taking the Mother Prioress's concurrence for granted. 'That would be a great help. Now, what about a will?'

'That,' said the Reverend Mother, 'would be at our mother house. It is no part of our intention not to conform to the common law of the land in which our house is situated.'

'Quite.'

'Sister Lucy shall telephone them for you presently.'

'Marm, there's another matter that has been troubling us. You told me that Sister Anne was at chapel on Wednesday evening and that that was the last time she was seen alive.'

'That is so. At Vespers by Sister Michael and Sister Damien.'

'Do you remember what you had for supper on Wednesday?'

It was clear that she didn't. She turned to Sister Lucy, who frowned. 'It wasn't a fast day, Mother. Was it steak and kidney pudding? I think it was. Yes, I'm sure. With peas and potatoes. And then a bread and butter pudding.'

'Thank you. Yes, I remember now. Is it important, Inspector?'

'What time did you have it?'

'At a quarter past six. That is when we always have it.'

'And then is when Sister Anne had hers?'

'Yes, naturally.'

'She couldn't have had hers later?'

'Not without my knowing.'

'What happens immediately after supper?'

'Recreation. From a quarter to seven to eight o'clock. Sisters bring any sewing or similar work to the old drawing-room and they are permitted to move about and talk there as they wish.'

'I see,' said Sloan. Nice for them, that was. 'And then?'

'They have various minor duties – preparing the refectory for breakfast, locking up the house, general tidying up at the end of the day and so forth. As they finish these the Sisters go into the chapel for private meditation until Vespers at eight thirty.'

'Thank you, marm, that is what I wanted to know. And Sister Damien and Sister Michael sat on either side of Sister Anne at Vespers?'

'That is so.'

'With the greatest respect, marm, that is not so. Dr Dabbe,

the pathologist, tells me that Sister Anne died immediately after supper. Her meal was quite undigested.'

There was a silence in the parlour, then. 'Someone sat between Sister Michael and Sister Damien.'

'So you tell us, marm.'

'So they told me, Inspector.'

'Where was Sister Anne's place in the chapel?'

'In the back row.'

'No one else need have noticed her, then?'

'No. No, I suppose not. As I said, the Sisters come in when they are ready and kneel until the service begins.'

'I think we should see the chapel and the two Sisters.'

'Certainly. Sister Lucy will take you there now.'

The Mother Prioress sat on in the empty parlour, deep in thought. She almost didn't hear the light tap on the door. She roused herself automatically. 'Come in.'

It was Sister Cellarer. 'Did he bring the keys, Mother?'

She stared at her. 'Do you know, Sister, I quite forgot to ask him.'

9

Father MacAuley was the next visitor to the parlour. Sister Gertrude brought him along.

'I had quite a job getting in. Polycarp thought I was the Press at first. I'll have to have a password. "Up the Irish" or some such phrase pleasing to her ear.'

'There were two reporters and a cameraman this morning,' said the Mother Prioress, 'but she sent them away.'

'So she told me. She didn't know if the photographer got his picture of her or not before she shut the grille. The flash, she said, reminded her of the dear old days in Ireland. Apparently the last really good flash she saw was the day the IRA blew up the bridge at—'

'I have warned the community,' continued the Mother Prioress, 'that they may have to go in the grounds in pairs as a precaution against their being – shall we say, surprised – by reporters. I feel there will be more of them.'

'They do hunt in packs as a rule.'

'Also there has been what I understand is called a new development in the case.'

'There has?'

'The pathologist has said that Sister Anne died immediately after supper which finishes at a quarter to seven. Sister Michael and Sister Damien say she sat between them at Vespers at eight thirty.'

The priest nodded sagely. 'The Press would like that.'

'I do not, Father. The implications are very disturbing. If Sister Anne was dead at half-past eight, who sat in her stall at Vespers?'

The priest sat down heavily. 'I don't know. The fact that we do not believe in – er – manifestations will scarcely influence the public – who don't know what they believe in. They, and therefore the Press, dearly love a ghost. Can't you see the headlines?'

The Mother Prioress winced.

In intervals between inspecting the convent chapel, Sloan took one telephone call and made another from the old-fashioned instrument in the corridor. Both were London calls, but neither would have conveyed very much to Mrs Briggs at the Cullingoak Post Office, who monitored all calls as a matter of course.

'With reference to your enquiry,' said the London voice, 'we have found a very interesting will in Somerset House, made by one Alfred Cartwright, father of Josephine Mary Cartwright. It was made a long time ago, and, in fact, several years before his death. Sounds as if he and his brother Joe were pretty cautious blokes. They'd got everything worked out carefully enough. If Alfred died first his widow was to have the income from his share of the Consolidated Carbons partnership for her lifetime. If he had children they were to get the share when their mother died. If he didn't have any children or if those children predeceased him *or* his brother, Joe, then the share in the Cartwright patent was to go to Joe and then his heirs and successors.'

'Keeping it in the family,' said Sloan.

'That's the spirit, old chap. Well, they seem to have gone along fairly slowly with the business – all this was just after the old Queen died, remember. Turn of the century and all that. Then suddenly – and without any warning either – Alfred ups and dies. Pneumonia, it was. We looked up the death certificate, too, while we were about it . . .'

'Thank you.'

'He doesn't leave very much but not to worry. Not many years afterwards along comes World War One and Cartwright's

Consolidated Carbons can't help making money. Lots and lots of it. Of course, our Alfred doesn't get the benefit being dead by now, but the stuff keeps on coming in. Must have been pretty well running out of their ears by 1918.'

'What about brother Joe?'

'There's no will registered of his, so presumably he's still alive. He probably made a reciprocal will at the same time as his brother, but of course he could have altered it since . . . By the way, we confirm Mrs Alfred Cartwright's statement that there was only one child of the marriage. This girl Josephine. Her husband died soon after the baby was born.'

'And brother Joe?'

'He had one son by the name of Harold. He must be all of fifty-five now.'

'We've met son Harold.' A thought struck Sloan. 'So Joe Cartwright will be quite an age.'

'Practically gaga, I should say,' said the voice helpfully.

'What about the firm now?'

'Ah, you want he whom we call our City editor. I'm only an historian. Fred Jenkins is the chap for the up-to-the-minute stuff. The only policeman who does his beat in striped pants and a bowler. No truncheon either. Says his umbrella's better. I'll give you his number.'

'Much obliged,' said Sloan. He rang it immediately.

'Cartwright's Consolidated Carbons? Very sound, Inspector. Good family firm. A bit old fashioned but most good old family firms are these days. Well run, all the same. Not closed minds, if you know what I mean. They're not entirely convinced that one computer will do the work of fifty men, but if you prove it to them they'll buy the computer and see the fifty men don't suffer for it.'

'The family still manage it?'

'Lord, yes. Harold Cartwright's the MD. Knows the business backwards. Learnt it the hard way, I should say. Let me see now, I think there are two sons and a daughter. That's right. The daughter married well. Iron ore, I think it was. The boys went to a good school and an even better university. The elder boy had a year at Harvard to see what our American cousins could teach him about business, and the younger one a year on the Rand.'

'You know a lot about them off the cuff.'

'One of the largest *private* companies in the country, Inspector, that's why,' retorted Jenkins promptly. 'They're always getting write-ups in the City pages suggesting they will be going public but they never do. They'd be quite a good buy when the time comes, of course, that's why there's the interest.'

'I think,' said Sloan slowly, 'I can tell you the reason why they've stayed private all these years.'

There was no mistaking the interest at the other end of the line. 'You can?'

'There was a residual legatee here in Calleshire in a convent.' There was a lot of satisfaction in being able to tell London something.

'That's it, then. What sort of share?'

'If she survived her uncle I'd say she was stuck in for half.'

Jenkins whistled. 'Buying her out would upset the applecart. I don't suppose they would have enough liquidity to do it. That's the trouble with that sort of heavy industry. On the other hand, if they go public and leave her in they could be in a mess. They might lose control, you see. Tricky.'

'Not quite so tricky now,' said Sloan. 'She was killed on Wednesday evening. I don't know how these things are managed, but I would like to know if this question of going public comes up again now.'

'I'll have a poke round the issuing houses. Might pick something up. Where can I get you?'

'Berebury Police Station.'

Sloan collected Crosby and Sister Lucy from the Chapel. She accepted the money he offered her for the telephone call without embarrassment or demur. 'Thank you, Inspector. Bills are quite a problem.'

All three of them went back to the parlour.

'It would seem, Mother,' said Sister Lucy carefully, 'that Sister Anne brought no dowry with her when she came. The Bursar's accounts for that year show no receipt that is likely to be hers.'

'Thank you, Sister.'

'I have had her will read to me over the telephone,' went on Sister Lucy. 'It was made at our mother house the year she took her vows. It bequeaths all of that of which she died possessed to our order.'

'How much is likely to be involved?' asked Sloan casually.

Sister Lucy looked at him. 'As far as I am aware, nothing at all. Sister Anne brought nothing with her and had no income of any sort while she was here.'

Father MacAuley coughed. 'Aren't we forgetting the potential?'

'What potential?' asked the Mother Prioress.

'Cartwright's Consolidated Carbons. That right, Inspector?'

'That's right, Father. I don't know where you get your information . . .'

'You don't live in Strelitz Square on twopence ha'penny a week.'

The Mother Prioress leaned forward enquiringly. 'Had Sister Anne something to do with – er – Cartwright's Consolidated Carbons?'

'She did, marm. They are a chemical company formed by her uncle and father to exploit an invention of theirs of a method of combining carbon with various compounds for industrial chemists.'

'I see.' The Mother Prioress nodded. 'That presumably was the source of the family income?'

'Yes, marm. You didn't know?'

'Not personally. My predecessor might have been told by Sister Anne. I do not think,' she added gently, 'that it would have concerned us in any way.'

'Yes,' interrupted Sister Gertrude unexpectedly. 'Yes, it would, Mother.'

Suddenly finding herself the object of every eye in the parlour, Sister Gertrude blushed and lowered her head.

'Pray explain, Sister.'

'This potential that you are talking about was some money that Sister Anne was to come into, wasn't it?'

Sloan nodded.

'Well, she knew about it. She told Sister Damien that the convent would have it one day and then we could have our cloister.'

There was silence.

Sister Gertrude looked from Inspector Sloan to Father Benedict MacAuley and back again. 'I don't know if there would have been enough for a cloister or not,' she said nervously, 'but Sister Damien thought so, and so did Sister Anne.'

'I think,' said the Mother Prioress heavily, 'that we had better see Sister Damien and Sister Michael now.'

Sister Damien came first. Tall, thin and stiff looking even in the soft folds of her habit, she swept the assembled company with a swift look and bowed to the Mother Prioress.

'The Inspector has some questions for you, Sister. Pray answer them to the best of your recollection.'

Sister Damien turned an expectant glance to Sloan.

'I want you to take your mind back to the events of Wednesday evening,' he began easily. 'Supper, for instance – what did you have?'

'Steak and kidney pie, and bread and butter pudding. The reading was of the martyrdom of Saint Denise.'

'And Sister Anne sat next to you?'

'Naturally.'

'Did you speak to her then?'

'Talking at meals is not permitted.'

There was an irritating glint of self-righteousness in her eye that Sloan would dearly love to have squashed. Instead he said, 'When did you see her again?'

'Not until Vespers.'

'What about Recreation?'

'I didn't see her then, I was talking to Sister Jerome about some lettering ink for prayer cards. We are,' she added insufferably, 'permitted to move about at Recreation.'

'When did you go into the Chapel?'

'About a quarter past eight.'

'Was Sister Anne there then?'

'No. She came much later. I thought she was going to be late.'

'But she wasn't?'

'No, not quite.'

'Did you speak to her?' asked Sloan – and wished he hadn't.

'Speaking in chapel is not permitted,' said Sister Damien inevitably.

'Did you notice anything about her particularly?'

'No, Inspector, but we practise custody of the eyes.'

'Custody of the eyes?'

The Mother Prioress leaned forward. 'You could call it the opposite of observation. It is the only way to acquire the true concentration of the religious.'

Sloan took a deep breath. Custody of the eyes didn't help him one little bit. 'I see.'

'There was just one thing, Inspector . . .'

'Well?'

'I think she may have been starting a cold. She did blow her nose several times.'

'About the cloister . . .'

An entirely different sort of gleam came into Sister Damien's eye. She smoothed away an invisible crease in her gown.

'Yes, Inspector, we shall be able to have that now. Sister Anne said that when she was dead we should have enough money to have our cloister. She told me so several times. And there would be some for the missions, too. She took a great interest in missionary work.'

'Did she tell you where the money was to come from?' asked Sloan.

'No. Just that it would be going back to those from whom it had been taken.' Sister Damien seemed able to invest every remark she made with sanctimoniousness. 'And that then restitution would have been made.'

Sister Michael was fat and breathless and older. She did not hear at all well. Panting a little she agreed that Sister Anne had been very nearly late. The last in the chapel, she thought. She hadn't noticed anything out of the ordinary but then she never did. She was a little deaf, you see, and had to concentrate hard on the service to make up for it.

But Sister Anne was there?

Sister Michael looked blank and panted a little more. One service was very like the next, Inspector, but she thought she would have remembered if Sister Anne hadn't been there, if he knew what she meant.

But she had just told him that Sister Anne was late.

Yes, well, Sister Damien had reminded her about that this morning.

What about yesterday morning when Sister Anne definitely wasn't there. Had she noticed then?

Well, actually, no. She wasn't ever very good in the mornings. It took her a little while to get going if he knew what she meant. Deafness, though she knew these minor disabilities were sent purely to test the weak on earth and were as nothing compared with the sufferings of saints and martyrs, was in fact very trying and led to a feeling of cut-offness. Of course, in some ways it made it easier to be properly recollected, if he knew what she meant.

He didn't. He gave up.

10

Harold Cartwright received them in his bedroom at the Bull. He appeared to have been working hard. The table was strewn with papers and there were more on the bed. There was a live tape-recorder on the dressing-table and he was talking into it when the two policemen arrived. He switched it off immediately.

'Sit down, gentlemen.' He cleared two chairs. 'It's not very comfortable but it's the best Cullingoak has to offer. I don't think they have many visitors at the Bull.'

'Thank you, sir.' Sloan took out a notebook. 'We're just checking up on a matter of timing and would like to run through your movements on Wednesday again.'

Cartwright looked at him sharply. 'As I told you before, I drove myself down here from London . . .'

'When exactly did you leave?'

'I don't know exactly. About half-past four. I wanted to miss the rush-hour traffic.'

'Can anyone confirm the time you left?'

'I expect so,' he said impatiently. 'My secretary for one. And my deputy director. I was in conference most of the afternoon and left as soon as I'd cleared up the matters arising from it. Is it important?'

'And how long did it take you to arrive here?'

He grimaced. 'Longer than I thought it would. Several hundred other motorists had the same idea about leaving London before the rush hour. I drove into the Bull yard a few minutes before half-past seven.'

'Three hours? That's a long time.'

'There was a lot of traffic.'

'Even so . . .'

'And I didn't know the way.'

'Ah,' said Sloan smoothly. 'There is that. Did you by any chance take a wrong turning?'

'No,' said Cartwright shortly. 'I did not. But I was in no hurry. I had planned to have the evening to myself and most of the following day. I don't know enough about the routine of convents to know the best time to call on them – but in the event that didn't matter, did it?'

'This business that you had come all this way to talk to your cousin about, sir, you wouldn't care to tell me what it was?'

'No, Inspector,' he said decisively. 'I should not. I cannot conceive of it having any bearing on her death. It was a family affair.'

'But you're staying on?'

'Yes, Inspector, I'm staying on.' He sat quite still, a figure not without dignity even in an hotel bedroom. 'The Mother Prioress has given me permission to attend Josephine's funeral but not – as you might have thought – to pay for it. Apparently a nun's burial is a very simple affair.'

Superintendent Leeyes was unsympathetic. 'You've had over twenty-four hours already, Sloan. The probability that a crime will be solved diminishes in direct proportion to the time that elapses afterwards, not, as you might think, in an inverse ratio.'

'No, sir.' Was that from 'Mathematics for the Average Adult' or 'Logic'?

'And Dabbe says that she died before seven and these women say they saw her after eight thirty?'

'Just one woman says so, sir.'

'What about the other fifty, then?'

'They'd got their heads down. Sister Anne sat in the back row always and apparently it isn't done to look up or around. Custody of the eyes, they call it.'

Leeyes growled. 'And this woman that did see her then, what was she doing? Peeping between her fingers?'

'She could be lying,' said Sloan cautiously. 'I'm not sure. She could be crackers if it came to that.'

'They can't any of them be completely normal, now can they?' retorted Leeyes robustly. 'Asking to be locked up for life like that. It isn't natural.'

'No, sir, but if there had been someone – not Sister Anne – at Vespers it would explain the glasses, wouldn't it?'

'It's better than "Sister Anne Walks Again" which is what I thought you were going to say.'

'No, sir, I don't believe in ghosts.'

'Neither do I, Sloan,' snapped Leeyes. 'I may be practically senile, too, but I don't see how it explains the glasses either.'

'Disguise,' said Sloan. For one wild moment he contemplated asking the Superintendent to cover his head with a large handkerchief to see if he would pass for a nun, but then he thought better of it. His pension was more important. 'I reckon, sir, that either there wasn't anyone at all in Sister Anne's stall at Vespers or else it was someone there in disguise.'

'Well done,' said Leeyes nastily. 'You should come with me on Mondays, Sloan. Learn a bit about logic. And was it Cousin Harold who was standing there?'

'I don't know, sir.'

'If it was, why the devil didn't he clear off? We didn't know he was there. We might never have found out.'

'Those footprints aren't his.'

'You're not making much headway, Sloan, are you?'

'Not since I've heard from Dr Dabbe, sir.'

For the first time he got some sympathy.

'It's usually the doctors,' grumbled Superintendent Leeyes. 'Try to pin them down on something and they'll qualify every single clause of every single sentence they utter. Then, when it's a blasted nuisance they'll be as dogmatic as . . . as' – he glared at his desk in his search for a comparative – 'as a lady magistrate.'

Sloan watched the Superintendent drive off towards his home and next meal, and went back to his own room. Crosby was there with two large cups of tea and some sandwiches.

'Well, Crosby, what did you make of Sister Damien's story?'

'Someone wanted us to think Sister Anne was still alive at eight thirty.'

'Ah, yes, but was it Sister Damien who wanted us to think that? Or was it someone else?'

Crosby took a sandwich but offered no opinion.

'And *why* did they want us to think that?'

'Alibi?' suggested Crosby.

'Perhaps. No one missed Sister Anne at Recreation so presumably they can move about then more or less as they like.'

'More or less, sir,' echoed Crosby darkly.

Sloan grinned. The man had a sense of humour after all. 'Did you give them back their keys?'

'Yes, sir. I went round all their cupboards with that Sister Lucy and opened them up. Nothing much there – food, stores and what have you. It was a hefty bunch of metal all right. Sister Lucy wears it round her waist all the time. They were certainly glad to have them back again.'

'What about their local standing?'

'High, sir. I checked with quite a few people in the village. They like them. They aren't any trouble. Their credit is good and they pay on the nail for everything. They live carefully, not wasting anything, and they do as much of their shopping as possible in Cullingoak.'

'That always goes down well.'

'I got on to Dr Carret, too. Only on the telephone though. He was out when I went there. He was called to the convent when Sister Anne was found, realized she hadn't fallen downstairs in the ordinary way and sent for us.'

'Very observant of him, that was. Is your standing with the canteen manageress good enough for another couple of cups?'

Apparently it was, for Crosby brought two refills back within minutes.

Sloan picked up a pencil. 'Now, Crosby, where are we now?'

'Well, sir, yesterday we had this body that we thought had been murdered. Today we know it has been. Weapon, something hard but blunt, probably touched by Sister Peter early yesterday morning.'

'And still to be found.'

'Yes, sir. We know that Sister Anne was also Josephine Mary Cartwright and that her mother said, "Never darken these doors again," a long time ago. And that when her mother dies she was due to come into a lot of money.'

'Only if she outlived her, Crosby. If she died first it reverts to Uncle Joe and his heirs, one of whom is camping at the Bull for some reason not yet revealed to us.'

'Well, there's money for someone in it somewhere, sir.'

'Show me the case where there isn't, Crosby, and I may not know how to solve it.'

'Sir, did that thin one, Damien, know that if Sister Anne died before her uncle, the uncle got the lot?'

Sloan nodded approvingly. 'That is something I should dearly like to know myself. You realize we have only got her word for it that Sister Anne – or someone she thought was Sister Anne – was at Vespers at eight thirty? The other one – Sister Michael – what she said wasn't evidence. More like hearsay.'

Crosby stopped, his cup halfway to his lips. 'You mean Sister Damien might be lying about that?' It was clearly a new idea to him.

'Don't look so shocked, Crosby.'

'I didn't think *they* would lie, sir.'

'Someone, somewhere,' he said sarcastically, 'is being untruthful with us, don't you think?'

'Oh, yes, sir, but I didn't think nuns would lie.'

'Not quite cricket, Crosby?'

'Yes, sir – I mean – no, sir.' Until he joined the Police Force, Crosby's ethics had been of a Sunday School variety – 'speak the truth and shame the devil'.

'If,' went on Sloan, 'Damien knew only that the convent was to come into a lot of money when Sister Anne died – or thought that was so – she could just have thought she was doing the convent a good turn – and Sister Anne, too, if it came to that – by hurrying things along.' He finished his tea and said profoundly: 'Who can tell what people will do if they are cooped up together like that for year upon year without any sort of outlet? What *do* you do, Crosby, when you start getting on each other's nerves? Say a few more prayers?'

'I saw a film about a prisoner-of-war camp once,' volunteered Crosby helpfully, 'where they killed a chap because he sniffed.'

Three loud knocks on the table at the end of a meal by the Mother Prioress indicated that she wished to speak to the community. Half a hundred female faces turned attentively towards the Abbatial chair. There were round faces, oval faces, faces of the shape known outside the convent (but never, never inside) as Madonna-type, fat faces, thin faces.

There were as many faces looking expectantly at the Reverend Mother as there were types of woman – almost – from the neat face of Sister Ignatius to the cheerful visage of Sister Hilda; from the calm features of Sister Jerome to the composed efficiency of Sister Radigund, the Infirmarium; from the still anxious look of Sister Peter to the intense concentration of Sister Damien.

'My daughters . . .' The Mother Prioress surveyed the dim refectory. It was long since dark outside, and the mock electric candles in their sconces on the wall provided only the minimum of light. 'My daughters, through the centuries those of our order have gone through many trials and tribulations, compared with which our present discomforts are as nothing. What we now endure is unfamiliar and distasteful to us – intrusion and enquiry are an anathema to the religious life – but it is not for us to complain now or at any time of what we suffer.' Her gaze travelled down the ranks of nuns. 'When we renounced the world we did not automatically leave doubt and sorrow behind. Nor are we immune from the physical laws of cause and effect. Nor should we wish to be.'

One of the novices, she who was sitting nearest to the pepper-pot, sneezed suddenly. The Novice-Mistress leaned forward slightly to identify the culprit.

'Sister Anne,' went on the Mother Prioress unperturbed, 'died on Wednesday evening some time after supper, probably in the corridor leading from the great hall to the kitchens. Her body was put into the broom cupboard and later thrown down the cellar steps. As you know, she was found there after a search on Thursday morning. It is now Friday evening. I should like you all to go back in your minds to Wednesday evening and consider if you saw or heard anything out of the ordinary pattern of religious behaviour.' She did not pause here as she might have done but went straight on to say, 'On Thursday evening, Guy Fawkes' Night, the effigy of a nun was burnt on the bonfire lit by the students of the agricultural institute. In the ordinary course of events I should not have troubled the community with this information, believing that the incident was more in the nature of high spirits than bigotry, but the guy was dressed in the habit that normally hangs behind the door of the garden room.'

It was evident that this was news to some of the nuns.

'Moreover, the guy was wearing Sister Anne's glasses.'

This was a bombshell. Heads went up. Grave glances were exchanged between the older Sisters. The younger ones looked excited or frightened, according to temperament.

'You will not, therefore, be surprised to know that the police require to know the exact whereabouts of every Sister from supper-time on Wednesday until they retired to their cells. If you spoke to Sister Anne after supper, or if you have any other information, it should be communicated to me, and only to me. I shall be in the parlour until Vespers.' She paused. 'The police also wish to be told the secular name of every member of the community, the date of her profession and the address from which she came to the Convent of St Anselm.'

The dining-room at the agricultural institute was also known as the refectory, but there the resemblance ended. It was brightly lit and very noisy indeed. One hundred and fifty healthy young men were just coming to the end of a substantial meal. Fourteen staff were having theirs at the high table on a dais at one end of the long room. Sundry maids were rattling dirty dishes through a hatch into the kitchen, and making it quite clear that they thought any meal which began at seven fifteen should end by eight o'clock.

Marwin Ranby, sitting in the centre of the high table, let the maids finish before he stood up. Students were easy to come by, maids much more difficult.

'Gentlemen, in its short life this institute has acquired a reputation for outrage on the night that commemorates the failure of the Gunpowder Plot . . .'

There were several cheers.

'Usually the damage can be repaired by the use of one simple commodity. Money.'

More cheers.

'And apologies, of course.'

'Good old Mr Ranby, sir,' called out a wit.

Ranby gave a thin smile. 'Well, it isn't good old anyone this time. Granted, in the ordinary run of events, we might have got by with a handsome apology to the Mother Prioress and an even more handsome contribution to the convent funds . . .'

Loud groans.

'This time it's much more serious . . .'

More groans.

'Yesterday, as you know full well, was November the Fifth. The evening before that – Wednesday – a nun died in the convent. The police, who, as you know, performed an excellent rescue job on the guy . . .'

Loud laughter, interspersed with more groans.

'The police,' said Ranby firmly, 'tell me that that habit came from the convent, probably the same day the nun died. Now, they're not accusing anyone of being implicated in this death but they do need to know who it was who was in the convent, how they got in and when. I think you can all understand that.' He looked quickly from face to face. 'Now, I'm asking those responsible – however many of you there are with a hand in this – to come to my study at nine o'clock tonight.'

11

Celia Faine was in the Principal's study with Marwin Ranby when Sloan and Crosby arrived. A maid had just deposited a tray of coffee on the table.

'Come in, Inspector, come in. How's the chase going?'

'Warming up nicely, sir, thank you.'

Ranby eyed him thoughtfully. 'I'm glad to hear it. I've got good news for you, too. We've got the culprits who made the guy.' He turned. 'Celia, my dear, will you be hostess while I tell the Inspector about Tewn and the others?'

Celia Faine smiled and took up the coffee pot. 'Don't be too hard on them, will you? They're nice lads and I'm sure they meant no harm.'

Ranby frowned. 'No, I don't think they did, but you can't be too sure. William Tewn is the chap you're looking for, Inspector. As far as I can make out, three of them initiated the scheme – a third-year man called Parker, and Tewn and Bullen, who are second year. Parker's the cleverest of the three – clever enough to organize the expedition without going to any risk himself, I should say. Bullen and Tewn went over the fence into the convent property on Wednesday night, while Parker kept watch. Bullen went as far as the outside wall, and Tewn went inside the building. He came out with the habit.'

'One moment, sir. How did you discover this?'

He gave a wry laugh. 'They – er – gave themselves up, so to

speak, in response to my appeal after supper this evening. I've just been speaking to them and they're waiting in my secretary's room for you.'

'Sugar?' Celia Faine handed round the coffee cups expertly. Sloan saw she would be a great asset to the rather too efficient Principal. 'Tell me, Inspector, where do you think they kept the guy until Thursday evening?'

'I know the answer to that one,' said Marwin Ranby rather shortly. 'In one of the cowsheds. That's where they made it up from the straw and the old sack. They had their firewood all ready. I hadn't raised any objection to a straightforward bonfire, you see . . .'

'No one thinks it's your fault, dear,' she said soothingly.

'Nevertheless,' went on Ranby, more philosophically, 'I suppose I should have thought something like this might happen . . . all the same, I don't like it. What I would like, Inspector, are those three men over at the convent first thing in the morning to apologize in person to the Mother Prioress and the community. It's the very least we can do . . .'

'Certainly, sir,' agreed Sloan peaceably. Ranby had good reason for wanting to keep on the right side of the Reverend Mother. 'If you want it that way. I don't see that it can do any harm.'

But once again he was wrong.

Messrs Parker, Bullen and Tewn were not too dismayed to find Sloan and Crosby taking an interest in their escapade.

'Just our bad luck that we chose a night when one of the nuns goes and gets herself killed,' grumbled Parker. 'Otherwise we stood a good chance of getting away with it.'

'You must admit it was a good joke, Inspector.' Tewn was a fresh-faced boy with curly hair and a few remaining infant freckles. 'Especially with old Namby-Pam – with the Principal going to be married at the convent at the end of the month. Sort of appropriate.'

It was a long, long time since Sloan's idea of a good joke had been anything so primitive.

'And?' he said dispassionately.

'Well,' said Town, 'it was a piece of cake, wasn't it?'

The other two nodded. Bullen, a slow-speaking, well-built boy, said, 'No trouble at all.'

'Come on, then,' snapped Sloan. 'How did you go about it? Ring the front door bell and ask for a spare habit?'

'No, we went to the back door,' said Town promptly. 'At least to the sort of cellar door.'

'And just opened it, I suppose. Without knocking.'

'Yes,' agreed Town blandly. 'Yes, that was exactly what we did.'

'At what time was this excursion?'

'About half past nine on Wednesday evening.'

'And you expect me to believe that this door was unlocked?'

'Oh, yes,' said Town. 'I just put my hand on the door and it opened.'

'And the habit?'

'That was there.'

'Waiting for you?'

Town's freckles coloured up. 'That's right.'

'And you just picked it up and came out again?'

'That's right.' Town poked a finger at Bullen. 'I was only inside half a minute, wasn't I?'

'Less if anything,' said Bullen. 'Like I said – no trouble at all.'

'No trouble!' echoed an exasperated Sloan. 'That's where you're wrong. There's lots of trouble.'

'But if Town was only inside half a minute and Bullen confirms it,' said the third young man, 'they can't have had anything to do with this nun, can they?'

Sloan turned towards him. 'You're Parker, I suppose? Well, there's just one flaw in your reasoning. How do I know that they're not both lying? Suppose you tell me where you were at the time?'

'Here in the Institute,' said Parker.

'In the biology lab, I suppose.'

Parker flushed. 'Yes, as it happens I was.'

'Any witnesses to prove it?'

'No . . . no. I don't think anyone saw me there.'

'Well, then . . .' Sloan let the sentence hang unfinished while he surveyed the three of them. 'So you three arranged the snaffling of the habit, did you? And you carried out the operation according to plan without any sort of hitch?'

'That's right,' said Town. 'We never saw a soul.'

'When you got the habit, what next?'

'Bullen and I brought it back with us. I kept it in my room until yesterday morning and then we made it up into a guy. It was easy,' said Town ingenuously, 'because nuns don't have much of a figure, do they?'

'And the glasses,' put in Sloan casually. 'Where did you pick them up?'

'What glasses?' asked Town.

'The guy that I rescued was wearing glasses,' said Sloan impatiently. 'Where did they come from?'

Parker nodded. 'Yes, it was. They were on her – it, I mean – when Bullen and I carried it out to the fire.'

'I didn't see any glasses,' said Town. 'We put a couple of buttons in for eyes.'

Bullen stirred. 'She was wearing glasses when Parker and I went to fetch her for the fire. We thought you'd put them on her, Town – they looked proper old fashioned.'

'Not me,' said Town. 'I didn't go back to the cowshed at all after we'd made her up in the morning. I was on the pig rota, remember? We had a farrowing at half-past six and I jolly nearly missed my supper.'

'I thought you'd cadged an old pair from Matron,' said Parker. 'She wears them just like that.'

Ranby was right: Parker was the most intelligent of the three. Sloan said, 'So you didn't take them from the convent with the habit?'

'Oh, no,' said Town quickly. 'Besides we wouldn't have known they weren't wanted, would we?'

'Like you knew the habit wasn't wanted?' suggested Sloan smoothly. 'Like you knew the door would be open for you . . .'

Town's colour flared up again, Parker looked sullen, Bullen quite impassive. All three remained silent.

'If, by any chance, any one of the three of you remembers how it came about that that cellar door was to be open to you on Wednesday evening, and that an old habit that nobody wanted just happened to be lying there for the taking, perhaps you'd be kind enough to let me know. It might, incidentally, just be in your own interests to do so, if you get me.'

Sloan and Crosby went back to the study. Celia Faine was sitting by the fire. She smiled at him. 'Here's the Inspector again. How did you find Marwin's little criminals?'

'Guilty, I hope,' said Ranby. 'I don't think there was any doubt, was there, that they got that habit?'

'None at all, sir. They admitted it.'

'Their idea of a good lark, I suppose.'

'That's right, sir, but they say they didn't take the glasses – the ones that the guy was wearing, remember?'

'Yes, Inspector, I remember. I'm not ever likely to forget, but I don't know who can help you there.'

'You can.'

'Me?' Ranby looked quite startled. 'How?'

'By telling me who could have had access to your cowsheds during the day.'

'Cowsheds?' His brow cleared. 'The guy – of course. Why, anyone, I suppose. There are all those who go in at milking and to clean and those who teach on milk handling and the Milk Marketing Board people. Any number in one day.'

'The sheds are never locked?'

'I doubt if there's even a key,' said Ranby. 'There's nothing to steal, you see.'

'So anyone could go in there at any time of the day without it occasioning any interest?'

'Anyone from the institute, of course. I don't know about outsiders. The vet's here often enough, and odd Inspectors – Ministry ones, I mean.'

'I see, sir. Thank you. I think that's all I need to know for the present. Goodnight, miss, goodnight, sir – sorry to have to disturb you so late . . .' At the door, he turned and looked back. 'These students of yours – are they allowed out into the village at all?'

'Oh, yes, Inspector, but they must be in by nine on a weekday and half-past ten at the weekend. That's early, I know, but we have an early start here. If they're going to be dairy farmers they might as well get used to it now, that's the way we look at it.'

Hobbett lived in a depressed-looking cottage just off Cullingoak High Street. Neither he nor his wife were noticeably welcoming to Sloan and Crosby. They were led through into the kitchen. It was not clean. A pile of dirty dishes had been taken as far as the sink but not washed. Parts of both an old loaf and a new one lay on the table with some more dirty cups. There were two chairs by the kitchen grate. Mrs Hobbett subsided into one of these which immediately demonstrated itself to be a rocking chair. She went backwards and forwards, never taking her eyes off the two policemen.

'Just a few more questions, Hobbett,' said Sloan mildly.

'Well?'

'We're interested in this key of yours to the convent.'

'What about it?'

'Where do you keep it, for a start?'

Hobbett jerked his thumb over towards the back door. 'There, on a hook.'

'Is it there now?'

'You've got eyes, haven't you? That's it, all right.'

'Is it always there?'

'Except when it's in my pocket.'

'You never lend it to anyone?'

'Me? What for? Catch people wanting to go in one of them places? Never. And it's my opinion that some of them that's inside would a lot rather be outside.'

'Nevertheless, you always lock up before you go every night?'

Hobbett scowled. 'Yes, I do, mate. Every night, like I said.'

Sloan was quite silent on the way back to Berebury, and Crosby couldn't decide whether he was brooding or dozing.

'Hobbett's the best bet,' said Sloan suddenly.

Brooding, after all. 'Yes, sir.'

'He could have got into that garden room without it seeming odd and taken the habit down to the cellar. Then all he has to do is to leave the door unlocked when he goes home.'

'Doesn't that dragon at the gate—'

'Polycarp.'

'Doesn't she check up on that door?'

'No need, Crosby. The door from the cellar to the convent proper is always kept locked. The Reverend Mother said so.'

'Why didn't he just take the habit, then?'

'Him? Catch him doing anything that'll lose him that nice soft number of a job he's got? Don't be daft. Look at it this way. All he had to do is to shift an old habit from that garden room – or whatever you call it – to his little lobby place. Nothing criminal in that.'

'Then give the keys to those lads?'

'Give nothing, man. He just forgets to lock the door, that's all. Nothing criminal in that, either. "Ever so sorry, Sister. It must have slipped my mind. Won't happen again." That's if they ever get to know, which they stood a good chance of not doing. Besides, that way Tewn, Parker and Whatshisname—'

'Bullen.'

' – Bullen have all the fun of going inside themselves. Much more daring, blast them. Heroes, that's probably what they think they are. Brave men. They've been inside a convent. Something to tell their grandchildren about. I wonder what Hobbett got out of it?'

'A few drinks?' suggested Crosby.

'And,' said Sloan, still pursuing his own train of thought, 'he didn't think he would be doing any harm because he knew they couldn't get any further.'

'Because the cellar door was always kept locked,' supplied Crosby. 'I say, sir, that's a point, isn't it? I mean, who opened the cellar door in the first place?'

Sloan grunted. 'We might make a detective out of you yet, Crosby. Who do you think opened it?'

Crosby subsided. 'I don't know, sir.'

'Neither do I,' retorted Sloan briefly. 'The important thing is that it was opened from the inside.'

'That narrows the field a bit, sir, doesn't it?'

'Does it, Crosby?'

'Well, you couldn't have just anybody walking about inside, could you?'

'No.'

'Well, then, sir . . .'

'You're forgetting Caesar's wife, Crosby.'

Crosby double-declutched to give himself time to think. 'Who, sir?'

'Caesar's wife. She was above suspicion.'

12

In the beginning Saturday morning resolved itself into routine.

Harold Cartwright had a large mail delivered to him at the Bull, and spent many more than the usual three minutes on the telephone to London. Mrs Briggs at the Cullingoak Post Office was hard put to it to keep up with his calls as well as serve her usual Saturday morning customers.

That part of the agricultural institute on early call got up and began to go about its business, regretting being born to the land and married to the land, wishing that it led urban lives when it wouldn't have had to get up early ever and not get up at all on Saturdays.

Life at the convent proceeded very much as usual. Sister Gertrude woke the community at the appointed time and they began to work their way through their immemorial, unchanging round. With one difference. Each Sister had to write on a piece of paper her secular name and address, date of profession and precise location immediately after supper on Wednesday evening. Only old Mother St Thérèse, to whom all days were the same, found this difficult.

It was routine, too, at the Berebury Police Station to begin with. Superintendent Leeyes sent for Sloan as soon as he got to his office. He was at his worst in the morning. That, too, was routine.

'Seen the papers?' Leeyes indicated a truly sepulchral photograph of Sister Polycarp behind the grille, caught in the camera flash with her eyes shut and mouth open. Under this was a much more sophisticated picture taken from a long distance with a telephoto lens of the outside of the convent through the trees. The effect was sinister in the extreme.

'Pursuing your enquiries, Sloan, that's what they say you're doing.'

'Yes, sir.' Sloan bent over to read the report. He was too good a policeman to scorn any facts newspaper reporters might dig out. Besides, they were free men by comparison – no Judges' Rules for them.

There wasn't very much in the paper. The brief news that a nun (unnamed) had died in the Convent of St Anselm at Cullingoak (short historical note on the order and its foundress – see any reference book), once the family seat of the Faines (three paragraphs on the Faine family straight from the nearest *Guide to the Landed Gentry*), and what they were pleased to call a startling coincidence – the burning of a nun as a guy the very next night – at the nearby agricultural institute (run by the Calleshire County Council, Principal, M. Ranby, B.Sc., formerly Deputy Head of West Laming School). Mr Ranby, said the report, was not available for comment at the institute yesterday. Wise man, thought Sloan. Then followed a highly circumstantial account of the burning of the guy by 'a student' who preferred not to give his name. The story wound up with a few generalizations about student rags and the information that an inquest was to be held on Monday morning next in the Guildhall, Berebury. Sloan straightened up.

'Could be worse.'

Leeyes grunted. He did not like the Press. 'Wait till you've seen the Sundays. Especially if they get hold of this time business.'

'Or the trio who got the habit. A pretty picture they would make. By the way, sir, it was Bullen and Tewn's footprints Crosby found. He's just checked. Bullen stood in one spot under the rhododendrons while Tewn went down in the cellar for the habit. That's what they told us, and the footprints tie up with that.'

'Not Harold Cartwright's?'

'No, sir.'

'Can't understand what the devil he's doing here, Sloan.'

'I don't know what he's doing, but he's working,' said Sloan. 'I've got a man keeping an eye on him. Lots and lots of paper work, telephone calls, tape-recorders, the lot.'

'He'll be lucky if he gets anything done that way. I never do. Quiet thinking is what gets things done, Sloan. More things are wrought by – er – quiet thought than you would believe.'

'Yes, sir.'

'Logical thought, of course, Sloan.'

'Of course, sir.'

'There's one aspect of this case I've been thinking about a lot . . .'

'Sir?'

'This weapon that Dabbe talks about . . .'

Sloan nodded. 'He said it was something smooth and round and heavy.'

'That describes a paperweight *and* a cannon ball,' said the Superintendent testily. 'We haven't found it yet, have we?'

'Not yet, sir.' Sloan liked the 'we'. 'We instituted a search on Thursday morning but found nothing. That Sister Peter wasn't what you could call a good witness. Too worked up for one thing. Swore she showed us everywhere she's been, and that wasn't very exciting, but no sign of any blunt instruments.'

'It must have been there, Sloan.'

'It must have been there when she touched it, sir. Crosby and I didn't see it. We went back for another look afterwards when she'd gone off to tell her troubles to somebody else, but we couldn't pick any lead up anywhere.'

'Narrows the field a bit, doesn't it?' said Superintendent Leeyes, just as Crosby had done.

'I don't see why,' said Sloan obstinately. 'Someone had only to know that it – whatever it was – was there, hadn't they? Comes to the same thing.'

Leeyes pounced. 'Ah, so you think it's an outside job, do you?'

Sloan shook his head. 'I don't know, sir. Not yet. I've an open mind.'

'Have you?' Leeyes glared at him. 'I hope that you don't mean an empty one.'

'No, sir. On the contrary, the possibilities are still infinite.'

The concept of infinity had already come up in the Superintendent's Logic course. It was now a word he treated with respect and no longer understood. He let the Inspector get as far as the door. 'Sloan . . .'

'Sir?'

'Do you know what they make nuns' habits from?'

'Wool, I suppose, sir.'

'Ah, but what sort of wool?'

'I couldn't say, sir.'

'From black sheep, Sloan.'

The day was still relatively young when Sloan and Crosby reached the convent. The Mother Superior and Sister Lucy received them as if it was already half over. The Mother Superior handed him a list of names.

'Thank you, marm. I feel we need all the information we can get in this matter.'

'Such knowledge as I have is, of course, at your disposal, Inspector.'

'First, marm, I have some news for you. Mr Ranby has traced the culprits of Thursday night's incident – three of his students were responsible for making the guy. He intends to bring them over this morning to apologize in person.'

She inclined her head graciously. 'There is no need for him to go to such trouble, but if he wishes it . . . Has their escapade any bearing on Sister Anne's death, would you say?'

'If,' countered Sloan carefully, 'she had happened upon them in the grounds or in the convent itself it might have – but I think it unlikely.'

'So do I,' said the Mother Superior firmly. 'Sister Anne – God rest her soul – would have reported such intruders to me immediately. I do not like to think that the students would have reacted to discovery with murder.'

'No, marm, nor do I.'

The faced each other in the small parlour. Irrelevantly it spun through Sloan's mind that he had never seen such fine skin on two women before. The older, more flaccid face of the Mother Superior reminded him of cream, the younger, firmer skin of Sister Lucy of the peaches that go with it. He remembered reading somewhere that good skin – like a good car – only needed washing with water. He must make a note to tell his wife about their complexions.

'Marm, there is a question that I must put to you.'

'Yes, Inspector?'

'Do you have anyone here who would rather not be here?'

'I do not think so.'

'No one who would – er – figuratively speaking, of course – like to leap over the wall?'

'No, Inspector. We are a community here in the true sense. I do not think any Sister could reach a state of wanting to be released from her vows without the community becoming aware of it. That is so, Sister Lucy, is it not?'

'Yes, Mother. It is something that cannot be hidden.'

'Likes and dislikes?' put in Sloan quickly.

The Mother Superior smiled faintly. 'Neither are permitted here.'

'You realize, marm,' he said more crisply, 'that any – shall we say, disaffection – would be pertinent to my inquiry, and that my inquiry must go on until it determines how Sister Anne died.'

She inclined her head. 'Certainly, Inspector, but if we had any disaffected Sister here, or even one unable to subdue her own strong likes or dislikes, she would have been sent away. There are fewer locks in a convent than the popular Press would have one believe.'

Sloan looked up suddenly. '*Has* anyone left recently?'

'Yes, as it happens they have.'

'Who?' He should have been told this before.

She looked at him. 'I cannot see that the departure of a Sister from the convent before the unhappy events of the past week can pertain to your enquiry.'

'I must be the judge of that.'

She gestured acquiescence. 'Sister Lucy shall find her secular name for you. It was Sister Bertha.'

'When did she leave?'

'About three weeks ago.'

'Where did she go?'

'I do not know.'

'You don't know?' echoed Sloan in spite of himself.

'It was not properly our concern to enquire,' said the Mother Superior. 'She felt that she could not continue in the religious life and asked to be released from her vows. This was done through the usual channels and she left.'

'Just like that?' asked Sloan stupidly.

'Just like that, Inspector.'

He pulled himself together. 'Had she any special connection with Sister Anne? Was she a friend of hers, for instance?'

'Friendship is not permitted in a convent. We are all Sisters here. She would have known Sister Anne to just the same extent as we all knew Sister Anne. No less and no more.'

'And you knew she wanted to leave – as a community, I mean?'

'Yes, we knew she wanted to leave.'

'If, marm,' he persisted, 'Sister Anne had been in a similar frame of mind, do you think you would have known?'

'Yes, Inspector,' she said with certainty. 'You probably do not realize how close are the lives we lead here. Private life, in the usual sense, does not exist. One therefore becomes very aware of the thoughts, not to say the spiritual condition, of one's Sisters. It is inevitable, and often does not even require formulation into words. Sister Anne, I do assure you, was not contemplating renouncing her vows.'

Sloan and Crosby went back to Berebury Police Station. Sloan spread out on his desk the list of names that the Reverend Mother had given him. They had barely sat down when the telephone beside Sloan rang.

'Yes. Speaking. Who?' It wasn't a local call.

'Jenkins,' said a voice. 'You rang me in London yesterday, remember? About a family called Cartwright. You still interested?'

'I am. Go on.'

'I think you're on to something, Inspector. Cartwright's Consolidated Carbons have made a move.'

'Have they?' asked Sloan cautiously. 'What sort of a move?'

'Towards going public. It seems, and I think this will interest you – that they have had everything prepared for some time.'

'Just waiting for someone to say the word?'

'So it would seem,' said the London man. 'These things take time, you know. Bankers to be instructed, brokers to be interested and so forth, to say nothing of organizing some useful advance publicity. Sounds as if they're going to chance their arm about the publicity build-up and go all out for speed. They'll get a good bit from the Sundays, of course. They'll be laying that on now.'

'How much speed do they want?'

'According to my informant, and he's usually reliable,' said Jenkins, 'applications will open at ten o'clock next Thursday morning and close at one minute past. I don't know at what sort of figure but I dare say they'll be over-subscribed. They're a well-organized firm.'

'You can say that again,' said Sloan drily.

'What's that? Oh, yes, I was forgetting your end.'

'So they'll be a public company at one minute past ten next Thursday morning?'

'That's it. Provided they deposit the necessary Articles of Association, seals and what-have-you with the Registrar and comply with all the rules and regulations and keep up with their paperwork.'

'Oh, they will,' Sloan assured him. 'They will. I don't think we need worry about that.'

'Going to put in for some?' asked Jenkins.

'Some what?'

'Shares.'

Sloan laughed. 'I'm not a betting man.'

'There's no risk,' said the other seriously. 'Cartwright's Consolidated Carbons must be one of the safest firms in the industry.'

'I wasn't thinking about their carbons.'

'No, no, of course not. There's just one thing, Inspector, though. If you've got any reservations about the company and the

City gets to hear about them before Thursday it'll cost someone a great deal of money.'

'And after Thursday?'

'It'll still cost a great deal of money but different people will lose.'

'And that's business?'

'That's business, Inspector.'

'I think I'll stick to police work.'

'I should,' agreed Jenkins. 'Much cleaner.'

Sloan put down the telephone. 'Curiouser and curiouser, Crosby. That needs a bit of thinking about.' He smoothed out the list of nuns for the second time. 'Have you got the name of the one that got away?'

Crosby produced his notebook. 'Miss Eileen Lome, no fixed address . . .'

'Surely . . .'

'Last known address, then, sir.'

'That's more like it.'

'144 Frederick Street, Luston. Sister Bertha that was.'

'We must see her, Crosby, just in case she can tell us anything.'

'Yes, sir.' The telephone rang again. Crosby answered it, and then handed over the receiver. 'For you, sir, I think. I can't quite hear who it is – it's a bit faint like.'

'Inspector Sloan here. Who is that?'

'The Convent of St Anselm, Inspector. It's Sister Gertrude speaking. Can you come quickly, Inspector, please? It's Sister Ninian. She was walking through the shrubbery . . .' The voice faded away.

'What happened to her?' asked Sloan urgently.

'Hallo, Inspector, are you there? This is Sister Gertrude from the convent. It's about Sister Ninian . . .'

'I heard that bit. What has happened to Sister Ninian?'

'Nothing, Inspector, not to her. To somebody else . . .'

'What has happened?' shouted Sloan.

'Another accident,' came the voice of Sister Gertrude distantly.

'Listen carefully, Sister. Keep the lower part of the telephone in front of your lips while you are talking and tell me who the accident has happened to.'

The answer came so loudly that he jumped.

'We don't know who he is.'

'He? You mean it's a man?'

'That's right, Inspector. He's dead in the shrubbery as I said. Sister Ninian found him.'

'This is very important, Sister. What sort of a man? Can you describe him?'

'Oh, yes, Inspector, easily. Young, with curly hair, oh – and a few freckles. Do you know him?'

Sloan groaned aloud.

13

It was a subdued Polycarp who opened the grille and then the parlour door, and a white and slightly shaking Sister Lucy who greeted them there. A young, silent Sister was with her.

'Mother said to take you straight to the shrubbery, Inspector, as soon as you arrived.' The religious decorum was still there but it was wavering a little in the interests of speed. 'It's quickest if you come through the house and out through the garden room.'

She led the way through the building, past the magnificent staircase, down the dim corridor where Sister Anne had died and through a door into the room of the flower vases.

She turned a drawn face to him. 'We don't know what happened at all, Inspector. Or when.'

He nodded without slackening his pace.

'You probably haven't met Sister Ninian, Inspector. She's one of our older Sisters. She is very fond of gardening and she often takes a turn through the grounds to keep an eye on things. She was just walking along this path when she turned down here.'

'Down here' turned out to be a narrow path running round the perimeter of the convent grounds. Sloan caught sight of black-habited figures among the bare winter trees. They were clustered round a still form lying awkwardly half in and half out of some bushes.

The Mother Superior turned when she heard him.

'I fear he's quite dead, Inspector.'

Sloan stepped beside her and looked down. There was no doubt about him being dead. The freckles that Sister Gertrude had described must have been those on his arms. She couldn't have seen them on his face. It was suffused with blood, a terrible mottled red and blue. A bloated tongue stuck out between lips parted in the mocking rictus of death.

'Strangulation,' he said briefly.

'Inspector . . .' It seemed suddenly as if it was a great effort for her to speak. 'Could this be William Tewn?'

'What makes you say that, marm? Have you ever seen this boy before?'

'No. No, never. Mr Rany came to see me this morning after you had gone. He brought two boys with him to apologize for the guy but he had been going to bring three. He said they couldn't find William Tewn.' She stared at the supine figure. 'He said he would send him over on his own whenever he turned up.'

Looking down at the dead youth, Sloan felt suddenly old and tired. 'Yes, marm, this is William Tewn. Now, could you all move away from here without disturbing the ground, please. It's very important . . .'

There was quite a gathering of nuns – Sister Gertrude, Sister Lucy, and three or four whom he did not know. He shepherded them gently back to the main path and left Crosby to rope off the area round the body.

'Now, if someone would tell me what happened . . .'

The story was Sister Ninian's to begin with. She was a neat, sensible woman of about sixty, and economical of speech. 'In winter, when it is fine, we all take some exercise before our midday meal. I do some of the gardening and make a practice of walking in a slightly different route each day. That way I can see things needing doing before they get out of hand. This path, as you can see, Inspector, runs round the entire convent property. The agricultural institute is the other side of that field. Cows have been known to stray, and the branches of trees to fall. That is the sort of thing I keep my eyes open for.'

Sloan nodded. Not, of course, for the bodies of dead men. That was chance.

'I had just turned down this portion of the path when I noticed a shoe sticking out . . .'

It was surprising, thought Sloan academically, how often it was a shoe that caught the attention. The soles of a pair of shoes were conspicuous in a horticultural setting.

'I approached it and found the body. I came back along this path until I found two other Sisters – Sister Gertrude and Sister Hilda here. They came back with me to the spot, and then Sister Gertrude went back to the convent to tell Mother.'

'And I,' said the Mother Superior, taking up the tale, 'asked Sister Gertrude to send for you while I came out here myself.'

'Bringing Sister Lucy with you?' asked Sloan suddenly.

She looked at him curiously. 'No, Inspector, as it happened I did not bring Sister Lucy out here with me. I left her waiting in the parlour to bring you here as soon as you arrived. Sister Gertrude came out here with the news that she had caught you at the police station and that you were on your way. We were exceedingly relieved to hear it.'

Sister Lucy, then, had been white and shaking without having seen the body? He cast back in his mind to Thursday morning. She hadn't reacted like that to the body of Sister Anne.

'Mr Ranby and the two students could scarcely have got back to the institute,' said the Mother Superior, 'before Sister Gertrude came in.'

Sloan looked at his watch. 'Were they with you long?'

'No. The two young men said they were very sorry for their intrusion; Mr Ranby apologized on behalf of the Institute and then they went. I had had to keep them waiting for a few moments because of Mr Cartwright.'

'He was here, too, this morning?'

'Yes, Inspector, he and Father MacAuley both came to see me after you left.'

Sloan sighed. 'I think we had all better go indoors, marm, and Crosby can take this all down. Besides, Dr Dabbe will be here again in a minute or two.'

*

'What?' howled Superintendent Leeyes. 'I don't believe it.'

'He's dead,' said Sloan flatly. 'Strangled and dragged off the path and half under some bushes.'

It seemed to Sloan that he had spent most of the last three days standing in the dark, draughty corridor where the convent kept their telephone.

'Tewn? Tewn?' said the Superintendent. 'That's the one of the three that actually went inside the convent for the habit, isn't it?'

'That's right, sir.'

Leeyes used an expression that would have surprised the watch committee.

'Yes, sir.' Sloan endorsed the sentiment, watch committee or no.

'It would have to be him.'

'Yes, sir.' Bitterly. 'It would.'

'How far did you get with him last night?'

'Just that it was child's play to walk in the cellar door and pick up the habit. No trouble they said.'

'He must have seen something,' said Leeyes.

'Yes, sir.'

'No hint of what it could have been when you spoke to him last night?'

'Not a clue, sir. I'm pretty sure that those three arranged with Hobbett – he's the handyman there – to leave the cellar door unlocked that night and the old habit inside. I don't see any other possibility – there was no sign of forced entry. And it sounded as if everything went according to plan. Parker kept watch on their return to the Institute, Bullen guarded the cellar door and line of retreat and Tewn went inside.'

'And so he dies.'

'Yes, sir.'

'Nasty, Sloan. I don't like it. Though tell me this – if he's going to be killed, why wait until today? It's Saturday now, it was Wednesday when they went into the convent . . .'

Sloan thought quickly. 'I didn't know who he was until after nine o'clock last night. Someone else might not have known either . . .'

'That's true. Sitting waiting for him to be identified, and then, when he is, killing him.'

'It would have been dark in that cellar on Wednesday night,' conceded Sloan. 'No one could have recognized him.'

'What about today?' asked the Superintendent heavily.

'I've only seen the Mother Superior so far. And the Sisters who were with the body when I got here. She says that the Principal had arranged for all three students to come across with him to say they were sorry for Wednesday's escapade but that Tewn just didn't turn up. Ranby was a bit put out apparently and said he would send Tewn over on his own later.'

'No wonder he didn't come.'

'Yes, sir. I'm going straight round there as soon as I've seen Dr Dabbe. I'm going to need all the information he can give me . . .'

It wasn't a great deal.

Sloan stood beside the pathologist out in the shrubbery.

'Strangulation,' agreed Dabbe. 'Not manual. I think it's a bit of fuse wire but I can't be sure. The skin's too engorged. Over your head in a flash, a quick jerk and that's that.'

'Vicious.'

'Neat and clean,' said Dabbe. 'And certain. Quiet, too. No time for a shout, you see. Not that there's anyone to hear out here, is there?'

They looked round the silent grounds.

'Convent, that way,' said Sloan. 'The institute, the other. Neither in earshot.'

'No nuns about at the time?'

'They're not let out until twelve. For their constitutional. There's Hobbett, their gardening factotum. He would have been out in the grounds somewhere . . .'

That wasn't the pathologist's concern and he was soon back with the body.

'Killed on this path, would you say, and dragged into the bushes by the armpits? You can still see where the jacket has been pulled up. His heels made a couple of scuff marks, too.'

Sloan peered down at the last pathetic imprints made by one William Tewn, student.

'A good place really,' went on the pathologist. 'He only had to be pulled a yard or two and he's practically invisible in all this growth. And whoever did it remembered to stand on that dead wood. Doubt if you'll find a footprint there, and the path's too hard.'

'Crosby's tried,' said Sloan, 'and he couldn't pick up anything. When did it all happen?'

The pathologist looked at his watch. 'Not more than two hours ago – say three at the very outside . . .'

'After half-past nine, then . . .'

'And not less than an hour ago – an hour and a half more likely.'

'It's not half-past twelve yet. That would make the outside limits somewhere between half-past nine and half-past eleven, only he wasn't available just after eleven when the institute party set out, so that makes it earlier than eleven, doesn't it?'

But abstract speculation wasn't of interest to the pathologist either. Of all men his work was to do with fact, with demonstrable fact.

'Perhaps I'll be able to narrow it down for you later,' he said cautiously.

Sloan nodded and asked the question on which everything hung. 'Any clue – any clue at all as to who could have done it?'

Dr Dabbe considered the body. 'He's not very big, is he? Anyone could have dragged him that short distance. As for whipping a length of fuse wire round someone's neck – that's not strength so much as strategy. You could only do it at all if it was totally unexpected. If you were to insist on some indication as to the person who could have done it' – Sloan remained silent, which was as good as insisting – 'then all I could tell you with any certainty,' offered the pathologist, 'was that they were probably as tall or taller than Tewn – and you could work that out for yourself. I can't tell you if it was a man or a woman but I can tell you that it wouldn't have been impossible for a woman – especially a tallish one. A quick flick of the wrist and it's all over.'

'And you wouldn't suspect a woman,' said Sloan slowly, 'would you? I mean your defences would be down, you would tend to trust her . . .'

Dr Dabbe gave a short, mirthless laugh. 'My dear chap, I've no doubt you would, but then we do do very different jobs, don't we?'

The news had gone before Sloan to the institute. There was that in the urgent way the porter hurried Sloan and Crosby to the Principal's room, in the curious stares of those students who had just happened to be hanging about the entrance hall and in the manner of Marwin Ranby himself that told the policemen that they knew.

The Principal was visibly distressed. 'I've just been trying to get in touch with the parents, Inspector, but I can't get a reply. It is Saturday lunch-time when not everyone's about – I was going away for the weekend myself as it happens – they may have done the same. They're farmers in the West Country, you know. Mr and Mrs Tewn, I mean, which is quite a way for them to come, I fear.'

'A shocking business, sir.'

'Terrible. This last few days have been quite bad enough, but this is a nightmare.'

'Perhaps if you can tell us what happened, sir . . .'

'That's just it, Inspector. Nothing happened. I'd arranged to go over this morning to call on the Mother Superior to make the three of them apologize for their incursion into the convent and for taking away the habit, which may have been old but which was doubtless of great significance to them. Celia – Miss Faine, you know – tells me that these garments are held to be very precious to the Sisters – they're handed down from one nun to another. I understand quite a number of them actually kiss each article of their habit before they put it on and so forth – and I felt it only right that these young men should say they were sorry in person. It's no use telling the young that these things don't matter, because they do.'

Sloan jerked his head in agreement.

'I thought eleven fifteen would do nicely. They only have two study periods on Saturday mornings and they finish at eleven and anyway that seemed to be as good a time as any for calling on the Mother Superior. I told them they were to present themselves here at five minutes past eleven to allow us time to walk over there . . .'

'One moment, sir. Whom did you tell to come then?'

Ranby frowned. 'Bullen, Parker and Tewn, of course.'

'Ah, I didn't mean quite that. To which one of the three did you give the message about the time?'

'Oh, I see. Bullen, it was. I told him to tell the other two. But only Bullen and Parker turned up. I must say, Inspector, I was more than a little cross at the time. And surprised. I wouldn't have said Tewn was the sort of man to back out of an interview like that, however unpleasant. It's horribly clear now, of course, why he didn't come.'

'You just went off to the convent without him?'

'Not at all. I sent Parker to his room to see if he was there and Bullen down to the common room. They both came back and said they couldn't find him and we then went off without him.'

'How long did it take, sir?'

'Saying we were sorry? About five minutes. The Mother Superior was very gracious, thanked them for coming and more or less wrote it off as high spirits which – if I remember correctly – Bullen said was "jolly decent of her in the circs".'

'The dead Sister – did she mention her?'

'Not at all.'

'She tells me she had to keep you waiting.'

'That's right. She was seeing another man. Largish with grey hair. Town clothes, too. He came out of the Parlour as we went in.'

Parker and Bullen were taking Tewn's death badly. They were sitting together at one end of the deserted common room. In the distance Sloan could hear luncheon being served, but it seemed Bullen and Parker were not hungry.

'I was sitting next to him at breakfast,' said Bullen in a bemused way. 'It doesn't seem possible, does it, that someone went and murdered him since?'

'When did you give him the message about going over to the convent?'

Bullen stirred slowly. 'I'd have to think. You know, I don't seem able to think straight, not now. Funny, isn't it?'

Sloan remembered the first sudden death that had come his way as a young constable. For years afterwards he had only had to shut his eyes for it all to come back to him. A road traffic accident that had been.

'You'll feel better in a day or so,' he said automatically, 'but you must try to think because we must know exactly what happened.'

'He thought he told him before the first study period – at least that's what he told me earlier on.' All the bounce had gone out of Parker, too. He was doing his utmost to be helpful. 'He didn't see Tewn after that.'

Sloan looked at Bullen. 'That right?'

'Yes, Inspector. He should have been with us for the second study period – we're . . .' He stopped and corrected himself. 'We were both in the second year, you see. But I didn't see him at all after we changed classrooms at ten o'clock. And neither did anyone else.'

14

'I expect,' observed Sloan to nobody in particular, 'that it seemed
a good idea to begin with, and the more you thought about it the
better you liked it. After all, you'd got the fire all laid on – got to
have a fire on Guy Fawkes' Night – you'd been gated too and
there was the convent practically next door, tempting Providence
you might say almost.' He paused. 'And an old habit wasn't much
compared with a bus shelter.'

Bullen stirred. 'We didn't think we were doing any harm. We
didn't think it would end like this.'

Parker retained more self-control. 'But why should Tewn get
killed? After all, we only swiped an old habit – there's no great
crime in that, is there?'

'I think,' said Sloan, 'Tewn's crime was that he saw something.'

'What?' asked Bullen dully.

'I don't know, but I'm hoping you two might. Listen – all three
of you plan to get inside the convent on Wednesday night to take
an old habit. Of the three of you only Tewn actually goes inside.
Of the three of you only Tewn gets killed.'

'And that's not coincidence, you mean?' said the slow-thinking
Bullen. He was paying more attention now, but he still looked
like someone who has been hit hard.

'The police don't like coincidence,' said Sloan. 'Tewn went
inside and Tewn was killed.'

'Tewn *and* a nun,' Parker reminded him. 'We have to go and

choose a night when a nun gets killed. There's a coincidence for you. I see what you're getting at, though, Inspector. You mean that . . .'

Sloan wasn't listening. A new and interesting thought had come to him. What had he just said himself? 'The police don't like coincidences.' There was one coincidence too many in what Parker had said.

'Listen both of you. I want you to go right back to the beginning and tell me where this idea about the habit came to you. And when.'

'I don't know about where,' said Bullen, 'but I know when. Sunday, after supper. The Principal said we were to be gated from four o'clock on Guy Fawkes' Night because of what happened last year.'

'Up till then what had you meant to do?'

Bullen looked a bit bashful. 'Do you know Cherry Tree Cottage? It's on the corner by the post office.'

'No.'

'It's a funny little place with a rather awful woman in it. I don't know the word that describes it best but—'

'Twee,' supplied Parker shortly.

'That's it. Well, she's got a garden full of those terrible things.'

'What terrible things?' Bullen was hardly articulate.

'Gnomes,' said Parker.

'And fairies,' said Bullen, 'and frogs and things. It's full of them. We thought – that is to say . . .'

'This year's good cause?' suggested Sloan.

'That's it,' said Bullen gratefully.

'I see. And when Mr Ranby forestalled you?'

'Then we had to think of something else quickly.'

'Whose idea was it to have a nun as a guy?'

Bullen shook his head. 'I can't remember. Not mine.'

'Nor mine,' said Parker quickly. Too quickly.

'Can you remember,' said Sloan sedulously, 'whereabouts it was that this idea didn't come to you?'

'Oh, yes,' said Bullen. 'In the Bull. That's where we . . .' He stopped.

'That's where you got on to Hobbett,' Sloan finished for him. Bullen flushed.

Sloan went on talking. 'That's where you two and Tewn settled that Hobbett was to take the old habit from the garden room to the cellar and to leave the cellar door – the only one to which he had a key – open on Wednesday night. You were to creep in and take it away and you presumably showed your appreciation of Hobbett's – er – kindness in the usual manner. I'm not concerned just now with the rights and wrongs of all that. What I want to know is: how many people knew you were going to be inside the convent that night?'

Parker looked up intently. 'I get you, Inspector. Quite a few, I should say, one way and another. Some of the men here for a start, the chap in charge of building the fire . . .'

'Anyone at the Bull?'

He frowned. 'I dare say there might have been one or two. Hobbett's not the sort of man you'd want to sit down and talk to in the ordinary way, is he? He's quarrelsome and people mostly keep away from him. We sat with him in a corner for a while and led him round to it. It's pretty crowded in there at weekends – it's the only place in Cullingoak, and all the institute men go there for a start. I reckon anyone seeing us could have put two and two together easily enough – we felt it was quite a good joke at the time.'

'I think it's quite possible,' said Sloan, 'that someone else thought so too.'

The day which had begun as routine continued that way, though in a different, more highly geared groove. Superintendent Leeyes cancelled his regular Saturday afternoon fourball the better to superintend what had quickly become known as the Convent case.

Mr Marwin Ranby cancelled his weekend away, spent the greater part of the afternoon on the telephone trying to get in touch with a remote farm in the West Country, and finally prevailed upon Miss Celia Faine to come round from the Dower

House to the institute for tea. That, at least, wasn't difficult.

For the Sisters it was perhaps a little easier. Saturday afternoon was for them a preparation for Sunday, a day without the significance of holiday or sport or relaxation. After Dr Dabbe had gone and his next mournful job of work had been carried away in a plain black van, the convent grille was closed and fifty women withdrew into their self-ordained silence. Not for them the endless unhappy speculation such as went round and round the institute, nor the wild rumour piled upon fantasy that was tossed rapidly round the village. (Of its two institutions, Cullingoak was quite happy to exaggerate what went on at the convent and to condemn out-of-hand the goings-on at the institute.)

All in fact that did go on at the convent was what anywhere else would have been termed a council of war. The Mother Prioress summoned those Sisters concerned in the finding of the dead William Tewn to the Parlour. They filed in silently, distributing themselves in an orderly circle – the neat Sister Ninian, the ebullient Sister Hilda, Sister Gertrude, Sister Lucy, a young Sister who had been with Sister Lucy when Sloan arrived, Sister Polycarp, the keeper of the gate who knew all comings and goings, and three others who had happened upon the scene of the crime. Lacking guidance about the correct religious behaviour in the unusual circumstances the three had stayed and moreover had failed lamentably to practise custody of the eyes. Now they wondered if having seen they should have moved immediately away . . . truly it was a difficult path they had chosen when they left the world.

The Mother Prioress began as she always did without preamble. 'There has been another murder. Not, as you know, a member of the community, but a student. He was killed in our grounds some time before Recreation this morning – at least that is the police view. The alternative is that he was killed somewhere else and brought to the convent grounds. Those of you who have seen him would agree it is very unlikely. No, I fear our connection with this particular student is closer than that. He is the one who came into the convent on Wednesday for the old habit which was subsequently rescued by Inspector

Sloan from the guy on the Institute bonfire. Do I make myself clear?'

It was an unnecessary question. The Mother Prioress always made herself clear.

'Therefore,' she continued lucidly, 'we still have a grave problem very near at hand. Sister Anne was killed here in the convent. This boy William Tewn – God rest his soul – who was the one to enter the convent on Wednesday has also been killed. Until both crimes have been solved completely we are none of us in a position to know that no member of the community is involved.'

She waited for this more oblique point to be appreciated.

'Moreover, we are bound by certain other considerations. Murder is not normally the action of a normal human being, still less that of a religious. But it can be the abnormal action of an abnormal person. That is the fact that we cannot overlook however much we might wish to.'

The cheerful face of Sister Hilda clouded over as the significance of this struck home.

'In the ordinary way,' went on the Mother Prioress, 'it would never be necessary for me to ask you to tell me of anything untoward in the behaviour of your Sisters, but we are not in the ordinary way. Far from it. We are somewhere now outside our experience, and there can be no peace of mind until the unhappy soul who has perpetrated these two crimes has been found and relieved of the terrible burden of their guilt.'

It wasn't how Sloan would have put it, but it came to the same thing.

'You mean, Mother, one of us might have done it?' Sister Hilda looked quite astounded.

'I trust not, but temporary – or permanent – aberration is never impossible.'

Sister Ninian nodded agreement. 'Any one of us could have slipped out into the grounds before Recreation and just stayed out and come in with the others afterwards . . .'

'Surely not!' exclaimed Sister Lucy.

Sister Polycarp looked down at her own strong hands. 'They say he wasn't very big.'

Sister Lucy shivered. 'But who – which one of us could possibly have wanted . . .'

'Have needed?'

'. . . have needed to do a terrible thing like that?'

'Two terrible things,' put in the Mother Prioress quietly.

Sister Ninian frowned. Her hair, if she had had any hair, would have been grey by now, turned by the passing years, as her eyebrows had been, to a pale greyish blur above her blue eyes. 'This means, Mother, doesn't it, that there is a connection between the two deaths?'

'A strong connection,' said the Mother Prioress. 'One so strong that the police feel they must interview every Sister today. They are particularly anxious that the details of the second crime of which you are already aware should not be communicated to the rest of the community. I have undertaken that you will not discuss it either with them or with anyone else. I do not need to remind you that you are under obedience in this respect.'

There was a series of assorted nods.

'The police,' said the Mother Prioress, 'have intimated to me that they consider it essential that these interviews are conducted by them with each Sister alone. It is not a procedure to which in the ordinary way I would have ever given my consent. As I have said before, we are no longer in the ordinary way. I have communicated with the Very Reverend Mother General at our mother house and with Father MacAuley. Both are of the opinion that this is not an unreasonable request. And Inspector Sloan has sent to Calleford for a – er – lady policewoman.'

'Luston?' barked Superintendent Leeyes. 'What the devil do you want to go to Luston for?'

'To see a Miss Eileen Lome, sir.'

'Are you going to tell me why, Sloan, or do I have to ask you?'

'She was a nun, sir, until about three weeks ago when she left the Convent of St Anselm.'

'Why?'

'I couldn't rightly say, sir. The Mother Prioress said she asked to be released from her vows and she was.'

Leeyes's head went up like a bloodhound getting a scent. 'Trouble in the camp?'

'Perhaps.'

'We should have been told before.'

'Yes, sir.'

'Luston's not very far.'

'No, sir. I thought I could go there while I wait for Sergeant Perkins to get over here from Calleford.'

The Superintendent gave a wolfish grin. 'Sent for Pretty Polly, have you?'

'Yes, sir. I can't make headway in an interview with the Mother Prioress supervising and a couple of others sitting around for good measure. I want them on their own.'

Leeyes nodded. 'What about the Institute?'

'No joy there, sir. Tewn's fellow conspirators can't or won't help much. Can't – I think. Bullen can't remember anything Tewn said about the inside of the convent that might give us any sort of lead. It might come to him, I suppose, though there's not much between his ears. Except bone. They're both trying to think hard of everything Tewn said or did since then.'

'Cartwright?'

'Gone into Berebury for the afternoon. Left the Bull as soon as he'd had his lunch.'

'Before you got there?'

'Yes, sir.' Sloan wasn't going to start apologizing at this stage. 'He says he'll be back, and he's left all his papers and clothes and so on. Besides, I've got a man at the London end checking up on Cartwright's Consolidated Carbons, and this business about their going public on Thursday. He wasn't all that pleased to be setting about it on a Saturday afternoon either.'

'Duty first,' said the Superintendent virtuously. He looked at the clock. His erstwhile golfing cronies would be at the seventh tee about now. Superintendent Leeyes had lost two balls there last Saturday afternoon – driven them straight into the rough. 'Cartwright will come back, I suppose? Because if not—'

'Our trouble has been surely that he's here in the first place,' objected Sloan. 'Practically underfoot, he's been. He's got motive, all right. But he's got brains too. Enough brains not to come knocking on the door out of the blue asking for Cousin Josephine if he dotted her on the head the night before.'

'It's very nice for him that she's dead,' said Leeyes. 'Very nice. Now he can go ahead and turn his private firm into a nice little public company with Heaven only knows what benefits to the principal shareholders.'

'Death duty,' said Sloan absently. 'From her father's will, Sister Anne's share reverts to her uncle on her death without issue, which is fair enough. If they turn it into a public company while she's alive she can have a say in everything because she's got a fifty per cent stake in the capital. And you can't run a chemical company from a convent. If they leave it alone then she and her uncle will each have to pay out a walloping proportion of the entire value of the firm in death duties sooner or later.'

'This way?' asked Leeyes silkily.

'This way they go public on Thursday and transfer large blocks of shares round the family – Harold's children – grandchildren for all I know – some for the trusty members of the Board – that sort of thing.'

'And I suppose you can also tell me why they didn't sell the whole boiling lot years ago?'

'Yes, sir. Then there wouldn't have been a job for our Harold Cartwright as Managing Director of Cartwright's Consolidated Carbons. Besides, Sister Anne's consent would have been necessary but not, I fancy, forthcoming.'

'Well then,' snapped Leeyes, rounding on him, 'why haven't you arrested Cartwright? You've got a case.'

'A case for arresting him,' conceded Sloan. 'Not much of a case against him.'

'Sloan.'

'Sir?'

'You aren't hatching a case against one of those nuns, are you? I don't fancy having the whole Force excommunicated.'

'I'm not hatching a case against anyone, sir. I don't think we can rule out anyone at all yet. The only apparent motive is Harold

Cartwright's, and it's a bit too apparent for my liking. Of course, it may not be the only one . . .'

'Hrrmph,' trumpeted Leeyes. 'There's still nothing to prove that the nuns *aren't* involved. One of them's dead inside their own convent, killed by a weapon that was left around for another of them to touch – haven't found that yet, have we, Sloan?'

'No, sir.'

'And then the student who goes inside goes and gets himself killed on eighteen inches of fuse wire – I suppose there's plenty of that in the convent?'

'Plenty, sir. A whole reel by the fusebox by the door out of Hobbett's little lodge . . .'

'Hobbett . . . there's always Hobbett, of course. What about Hobbett? You haven't missed him, too?'

'Not exactly missed him, sir. He went off into Berebury at lunchtime with his wife like he does every Saturday lunchtime.'

'Before they found Tewn?'

'He'd gone before we got there. I should say he knocks off sharpish.'

'So you don't know for sure?'

'No, sir. But we've got every man in Berebury looking out for him.'

'You've got a hope,' said Superintendent Leeyes, 'and on a Saturday afternoon, too.'

15

Ironically enough it was Harold Cartwright who turned up first.
At the police station. Crosby led him into Sloan's room.

'You've had another death,' he said abruptly.

'I fear so.'

'Where is this all going to end, Inspector?'

'I wish I knew, sir.'

'First my cousin Josephine and now this student. It doesn't
make sense.'

'Murder doesn't always. Not to begin with.'

'This boy – did my cousin know him?'

Usually it was Sloan who asked the questions, other people
who answered them. Clearly Harold Cartwright, too, was in the
habit of asking the questions that other people answered. Sloan
let him go on that way. Questions revealed quite as much as
answers; especially the ones that didn't get asked.

'William Tewn? No, sir, we have no reason to suppose that
Sister Anne knew him. Have you?'

'Me, Inspector? I told you I haven't had sight nor sound of
Josephine in twenty years.'

'So you did, sir. I was forgetting.'

Cartwright looked at him suspiciously. 'And it's true.'

'Yes, sir. We know that. Visitors and letters are both rationed
in a convent.'

'Like a prison,' said Cartwright mordantly. 'Poor Josephine.'

Sloan pushed a blotter away. Not tonight, Josephine. Nor any night, Josephine. Poor Josephine.

'And yet,' went on Cartwright, 'Josephine and this young man Tewn have both been killed this week.'

'That is so,' acknowledged Sloan.

'Tewn saw something that gave him a lead on Josephine's murder?'

'That's the obvious conclusion, isn't it, sir? We're working on that now.' So obvious that even the police couldn't miss it?

'So someone kills Tewn, too, to stop him talking?'

'Just so,' said Sloan. It could even be that way.

'This is Saturday. How did – er – whoever did it – know that Tewn hadn't talked about what he saw?'

'There are at least three answers to that, sir, aren't there?' Sloan was at his most judicial. 'One is that he didn't know if Tewn had talked or not, another is that Tewn saw something all right on Wednesday but that it didn't register as important until he heard that a nun had died that night . . .'

'And the third?'

'The third is that whoever killed Tewn might not have known until yesterday the name of the student who went inside the convent. He might not have known who it was he had to kill, just as we didn't know ourselves until yesterday evening. Just as you didn't know who it was either, sir.'

'But I did,' Cartwright said unexpectedly.

'You did? Who told you?' Sloan snapped into life.

'He did himself. At least I take it it was the same lad.'

'When?'

'On Thursday night at the fire. They were all standing round watching – like you do with a bonfire – waiting for the guy to catch alight. It was before you came along and did your brand-snatched-from-the-burning act.'

'Well?'

'I was standing with a bunch of 'em when I realized they'd got a nun up top as a guy. I made some damn silly remark about that being a path not leading to Rome and how had they managed to get the full rig. One of them said he and another chap had done it and it had been dead easy.'

'The vocabulary rings true,' said Sloan, leaning forward. 'Now what else did he say? Think very carefully, sir, this may be important.'

Cartwright frowned. 'Blessed if I can remember. No, wait a minute. There was something. The other chap with him made some sort of remark . . . "Easy as stealing milk from blind babies". That was it, and the first chap – the one who told me he'd got the habit—'

'Tewn.'

'He laughed and said he reckoned it was all a matter of getting the milk warm enough – if you did that everything else was all right.'

'Do you know what he meant?'

'No, Inspector, but the others all laughed at that. It sounded like some sort of institute joke. Or even an agricultural one.'

Sloan made a quick note. 'Now, about the fire, sir. You did tell me how it was you came to be there, didn't you?'

'I did, Inspector,' he said without rancour, 'but I will tell you again if you wish.'

Sloan inclined his head; and then regretted it. The eternal politeness of the nuns was quite infectious. He, a hardened police officer, would have to watch it.

'I was sitting in the bar of the Bull,' said Cartwright, 'on Thursday evening at something of a loose end. It is very unusual for me to have any free time, you understand. Also, I had only a few hours before being told by you of my cousin's premature death and I was not quite sure what was to be done about it. I meant to go out for a walk round the village to clear my thoughts a bit in any case, but when I heard some old man in a corner of the bar talking about a big bonfire at the institute I thought I might walk that way.'

'Substitute "dirty" for "old",' said Sloan, 'and you could be talking about a man I want to see.'

'Hobbett was the name,' said Cartwright. 'I found that out afterwards. Contentious fellow. He was sitting there dropping hints about fun and games at the institute. Apparently last year on Bonfire Night the students—'

'I know all about that,' said Sloan wearily.

'This man was saying more or less that for the price of a drink he could tell a tale, and I decided to take my walk.'

Sloan nodded. You could see why Cartwright was a captain of industry. He didn't waste words and he stuck to the point. He was giving just the right impression of anxious helpfulness, too, and so far had told Sloan just one thing that he didn't know already. Sloan eyed his visitor's figure. Business luncheons hadn't left too much of a mark there. He was only medium tall but strong enough to swing a weapon (somewhere between a paper-weight and a cannon-ball) down on the head of an unsuspecting woman. Not everyone's cup of tea, but then not everyone could run one of the largest private companies in the land either. You couldn't begin to work out where scruple and resolution came in – perhaps not too much of one and plenty of the other for both. He didn't know. He was only a policeman.

'But it really comes down,' Cartwright was saying, 'to asking who could possibly have wanted to kill my cousin Josephine.'

'Just you,' said Sloan pleasantly.

There was no spluttering expostulation. 'I didn't kill her,' said Harold Cartwright.

'Perhaps not,' said Sloan. 'But it's saved you a lot of trouble, hasn't it?'

The man eyed him thoughtfully. 'I'm not sure, yet. That's why I've come to see you. To ask for something.'

'You don't want,' said Sloan gently, 'the chairman of Cartwright's Consolidated Carbons to be publicly connected with the late Sister Anne of the Convent of St Anselm at Cullingoak who died in dubious circumstances on Wednesday – which is why you have stayed here in this village holding yourself ready for questioning rather than gone back to London where we should have had to come to see you.'

'Inspector, should you ever leave the police and want a job, come to see me.'

'Thank you, sir, but I feel I've earned my pension. And I'm going to enjoy it. This request for no publicity – I take it that you would like it to hold good until after one minute past ten on Thursday morning?'

Cartwright exhaled audibly. 'Just until then, Inspector. It's very important.'

'So,' said Sloan, 'is murder.'

Bullen came to the telephone readily enough.

'Warm milk?' he echoed stupidly.

'Something about milk,' said Sloan. 'Think, man, think. What exactly did Tewn say about warm milk?'

'Nothing,' said Bullen promptly.

Sloan sighed. 'A witness has told me that while you were watching the guy burn, Tewn made some remark about warm milk . . .'

'Oh, that,' said Bullen. 'I didn't know you meant that.'

'I do mean that.'

'I should have to think, Inspector.'

Sloan waited as patiently as he could while Bullen's thought processes ground their way through his memory.

'There was this man there . . .'

'What man where?'

'Some town fellow, a stranger, who came to see the fire. He made some sort of crack about the nun's habit and our getting hold of it. I said it was dead easy.'

'As easy as stealing milk from blind babies?'

'That's right, Inspector, and Tewn said it was all a matter of getting the milk warm enough.'

'What did he mean?'

'He was being funny, Inspector. We'd been having a study lesson on feeding calves that afternoon. We'd all been having a bash – all the second year that is – when the Principal came in and said it was all a matter of getting the milk warm enough and then everything else would be all right.'

'Oh, I see,' said Sloan.

'Jolly clever of poor old Tewn, wasn't it? Made us all laugh at the time. All the second year anyway. Was there anything else, Inspector, that you wanted to know?'

'What? No, no thank you, Bullen. That was all.'

*

Luston was the biggest town in Calleshire. Calleford had its Minster, its county administration, its history. Luston got on with the work.

Sloan and Crosby found Frederick Street in the decayed, once genteel, now shabby quarter of the town, by-passed alike by the glass self-service stores and the council's redevelopment schemes. They were there well before four o'clock, having fought their way through the crowded shopping centre into the suburbs. Most of the inhabitants of Luston seemed to be out shopping – but not the occupant of 144 Frederick Street. The lace curtain twitched as the car drew up at the door, but for all that it seemed an age before the door was opened. A woman stood there, ineffectually dressed in clothes off the peg, her hair combed oddly straight.

'Good afternoon?' she said uncertainly.

'Miss Eileen Lome?' It couldn't be anyone else, thought Sloan, not with that hair.

She nodded.

'I wonder if you could spare us a moment or two? We want to talk to you about the Convent of St Anselm.'

Her face lit up spontaneously and then darkened. 'You're not from the Press?'

'No, I'm Detective Inspector Sloan of the Berebury CID and this is Constable Crosby, my assistant.'

'That's different. Won't you come in?' She led the way through to the sitting-room. 'I don't want to talk to the Press. It wouldn't be right.'

'We quite understand.' Sloan was at his most soothing. 'We shan't keep you long.'

The sitting-room was aggressively tidy. Miss Lome ushered them into easy chairs and chose a wooden one for herself.

'I can't quite get used to soft chairs yet,' she said.

Sloan stirred uncomfortably in a chair he wouldn't have had inside his own home, let alone sat in. 'No, miss.'

'Can I make you some tea?' suggested Miss Lome. 'My sister's not back yet, but I think I know where everything is.'

'No, thank you, miss. We'd like to talk to you instead.'

She cocked her head a little to one side attentively. Sloan put her at forty-five, perhaps a trifle more. There was a youthful eagerness about her that made guessing difficult.

'When did you leave the convent?'

'Twenty-four days ago.'

'Why? I'm sorry – it's such a personal question, I know, but we have to . . .'

'I began to have doubts as to whether mine was a true vocation.'

'How long were you there?'

'Twenty-five years.'

'Twenty-five years?'

'Time has a different meaning there,' she said tonelessly.

'Nevertheless,' persisted Sloan, not unkindly, 'it's quite a while, isn't it? One would have thought . . .'

'It's different,' she said defensively, 'for those who come in later. They seem more – well – sure, somehow. They know that all they want then is to be there, and they've proved it to themselves, and in any case they're older.'

Sloan nodded. The word she was looking for was 'mature'. He did not supply it.

'But for the rest of us,' she said, 'who think we are sure at seventeen – you can't help but wonder, you know. And it grows and grows, the feeling that you aren't a true daughter of the Church.' She shook her head sadly. 'It is a terrible thing to lose your vocation.'

Crosby's face was a study.

'I'm sure it is, miss,' said Sloan hastily. And it was no use asking a policeman where to find one of them. They didn't deal in lost vocations. 'So they let you out, miss?'

'It wasn't quite as simple as that, but that's what happened in the end.' She brushed a hand across her straggly hair. She made it into a gauche, graceless gesture. 'It's getting a bit less strange now. My sister's taken me in, you know. She's being very kind though she doesn't understand how very different everything is. Every single thing.'

'Yes, miss, it must be.'

The disaffection of the former Sister Bertha, now restored to her old name of Eileen Lome, seemed unlikely to have any bearing on the death of Sister Anne. In that the Mother Superior appeared to be quite right. Sloan sighed. It had seemed such a good lead. Apart from making quite sure . . .

'I don't know if you've had any news from the convent lately,' he said.

'You mean about Sister Anne? My sister showed me the newspaper this morning.' She smiled wanly. 'She thought it would interest me.'

'You knew her well, of course?'

'Of course, Inspector. We had shared the same community life for over twenty-five years.'

'Tell me about her,' urged Sloan gently.

Miss Lome needed no persuading. 'She was professed about four years before me – the year I became a postulant, I think it was, though it's rather a long time ago for me to be sure. She had given up a very gay life in London, you know, to become a nun.' Miss Lome glanced round the modest sitting-room, economically furnished, plainly decorated. 'Dances, parties, the London Season – that sort of thing. Her family had money, I think . . .'

Sloan nodded.

'It used to worry Sister Anne a lot,' volunteered Miss Lome.

'What did?'

'All that money.'

Sloan read the look on Crosby's face as easily as if it had been the printed word. A lot of money wouldn't have worried him, it said. Just give him the chance and he'd prove it.

'In what way did it worry her?' asked Sloan.

'It was where it had all come from, Inspector, that was what she thought wrong. It was some sort of manufacturing process that was very valuable in making munitions in the First World War. But half the firm was to be hers one day, and then she intended to make restitution.'

Sloan felt a momentary pang of sympathy for Cousin Harold.

'She always took an interest in foreign missions,' continued Miss Lome. 'She thought it was a way in which she could atone.'

The look on Crosby's face, still easily readable, had changed to incredulity.

'She intended to sell out her interest in the firm?'

'That's right. As soon as it came to her.'

'And this was common knowledge?'

Miss Lome gave a quick jerk of her head. 'We knew it was something that worried her.'

'All those years?'

'Time,' said Miss Lome again, ruefully, 'has a different meaning in a religious house.'

She might have left the convent but she had brought with her the training of a lifetime. When not speaking her eyes dropped downwards, and her hands lay folded in her lap. In gawky, unsuitable clothes, face and figure innocent of make-up or artifice, the mannerisms of the nun bordered on the grotesque.

'Nevertheless,' said Sloan pedantically, 'you must have been very surprised and shocked to read about the murder . . .'

Another quick jerk of the head. 'I've been trying so hard not to think about the past – until today. Now, I can't think about anything else except poor Sister Anne.' She brightened with an effort. 'But one mustn't dwell on the bad things, must one? There were some very happy times, too.' She stared at him through a mist of tears and said wistfully, 'When everything seemed quite perfect.'

'Yes, miss, I'm sure there were. Tell me, have you been tempted to go back at all since you left?'

A curious colour crept over her face, and Crosby looked quite startled. Miss Lome was actually blushing.

'Just to the gate, Inspector. Not inside. There's a part of the convent you can see from the road if you know where to look . . .'

'The newspaper photographer found it.'

'That's right. I've been back as far as there – just to have a look, you understand. Silly and sentimental of me, I suppose.'

'When?'

'Funnily enough, it was this morning.'

16

'All right, all right,' challenged Superintendent Leeyes.

'You tell me of someone who wasn't at the convent this morning for a change. The whole bang shooting match were there if you ask me – Hobbett, Cartwright, MacAuley, Ranby, Bullen, Parker, fifty nuns and now this woman. Anyone could have killed Tewn. Anyone. It's a wonder he wasn't trampled to death in the crowd.'

'This woman says she just went as far as the gate, sir.'

'Tewn didn't go much farther himself, did he? And look what happened to him.'

'Yes, sir.'

'And as for her saying she just went as far as the gate, how do you know that? How do we know she didn't go farther than the gate on Wednesday? Suppose she's the answer to it being an inside job or an outside one – a bit of both, in fact? What's to stop her coming in on Wednesday, slipping into the back of the chapel for one of their eternal services and then waiting behind afterwards? You tell me the nuns don't know who comes into their chapel from the outside for services. Then all she has to do is to wait somewhere until just after supper. She knows where to find that old habit. And how to behave in it.'

'Yes, sir.'

'Then, after supper she waits in that corridor with a weapon that you've proved to me must have come from the convent though you can't find it.'

'No, sir.'

'Then she kills Sister Anne, hears someone coming and pushes her into the broom cupboard. Probably goes inside with her. And at half-past eight she creeps out for some service or other.'

'Vespers.'

'To stop the hue and cry being raised until the morning. She goes in last, knowing the others are too damn ladylike to look up, pretends she's got a cold and keeps her face buried in a handkerchief. Probably comes out last, too, then while the others go up to bed she sidles down the corridor and hides somewhere until it's all quiet.'

'The necessarium?' offered Sloan.

'The what?'

'The smallest room, sir.'

The Superintendent turned a dull shade of purple. 'Very probably, Sloan, very probably. I was forgetting,' he added savagely, 'that they aren't fairies. Then when all the others are tucked up in their nice warm cells, she comes out of there and pops into the broom cupboard, heaves Sister Anne's body down the cellar steps, and lets herself out through the cellar door and legs it back to Luston.'

Sloan studied the ceiling. 'Leaving the habit in the cellar for Tewn, who comes along ten minutes later and takes it away?'

Leeyes glared.

'Or alternatively,' went on Sloan, switching his gaze to the floor, 'she just happens to discard the habit there and Tewn just happens to come along and pick it up?'

'Tewn came there by arrangement, didn't he?' Leeyes shifted his ground with subtlety.

'With Hobbett, sir. He promised to have the habit there for the students and to leave the outside cellar door open.'

'Someone knew about that little conspiracy, Sloan.'

'Yes, sir, unless . . .'

'Unless what?'

'It was a totally inside job. Then it wouldn't have mattered what happened to the outside cellar door or the habit.'

'Who would have been lying?'

'Sister Damien.'

Leeyes shrugged. 'I don't like coincidence. Never have done.'

'Neither do I, sir, but you must allow for it happening.'

The Superintendent gave an indeterminate growl. 'What next?'

'Back to the convent with Sergeant Perkins, sir.'

'Have they brought Hobbett in yet?'

'Not yet, sir.'

'There's always the chance, I suppose,' said Leeyes hopefully, 'that he'll stand on one of them's toe . . .' The other three golfers would be coming up the eighteenth fairway by now – without him. 'Sloan . . .'

'Sir?'

'This woman, Eileen Lome – why did she leave the convent?'

'She lost her vocation,' said Sloan, shutting the door behind him very gently indeed.

Sergeant Perkins was in his room when he got back.

He nodded briskly. 'What do you know about convents, Sergeant?'

'That they're not allowed to have mirrors there,' she said. She was a good-looking girl herself.

'Poor things,' said Sloan unsympathetically. 'Now, about the case . . .'

She flung a smile at his assistant. 'Constable Crosby has been putting me in the picture, Inspector.'

Sloan grunted. 'It's not a pretty one. Two murders in four days. I don't know about your end of the county, but out of the ordinary run for us.'

'And us, sir. Just husband and wife stuff as a rule.'

Sloan picked up the sheets of paper the Mother Superior had sent him that morning. 'They've given us a list of every nun in the place, her – er – given name and her religious one, and what she said she was doing after supper on Wednesday. Now I suppose we shall need to know what they said they were doing this morning.'

'Never mind, sir, it's nearer than Wednesday. They're not as likely to have forgotten.'

'There is that,' admitted Sloan. He'd obviously got an optimist on his hands, which made a change from the Superintendent.

'How many are there of them, sir?'

'Just over fifty.' That should deaden anyone's enthusiasm for interviewing. 'And all falling over themselves backwards not to be too observant, inquisitive or whatever else you like to call it.'

She nodded.

'And,' he added for good measure, 'they don't seem to think it's right to have normal human feelings about people. Have you ever tried interviewing people without normal human feelings, Sergeant?'

'Often, Inspector. I get most of the teenage work in Calleford.'

He did not laugh. Nobody in the Calleshire Constabulary ever laughed at the word 'teenage'.

He turned to Crosby. 'Any luck with that list?'

'Yes, sir. There are four nuns who came into the Order late like Miss Lome said. Sister Margaret, Sister Lucy, Sister Agatha and Sister Philomena. Judging by all the other dates and ages the rest came in straight from school.'

'Poor things,' said Sergeant Perkins impulsively.

'And the other four?'

'Late twenties – one, early thirties – two, early forties – one.'

'Which one was that?'

'Sister Agatha. She came here from' – he flipped the sheets over – 'the Burrapurindi Mission Hospital.'

'It's a republic now,' said Sloan briefly. 'And the other late entries?'

'Sister Philomena and Sister Margaret seem to have been schoolteachers first.'

'The blackboard jungle.'

'And Sister Lucy' – he turned the pages back – 'there's no occupation down for her – just that she came from West Laming House, West Laming. It's not the best address though, sir.'

'No?'

'No, sir. One of them comes from a castle. Fancy leaving a castle to go and live in a convent.'

'Probably the only one who didn't notice the cold. Which one was that?'

'Sister Radigund.'

Sloan nodded. 'You might think Sister Agatha was the one to be in charge of the sick if she had been a nurse, but I suppose that would be too simple for them.'

'There's a Lady, too, sir.'

'They're all ladies, Crosby, that's their trouble.'

'No, sir. I mean a real one. It says so here. Lady Millicent.'

'And what's she now?'

'Mother Mary St Bridget.'

Sergeant Perkins leaned forward. 'Some are Mothers, are they then, Inspector?'

'A courtesy title, Sergeant, I assure you. For long service, I believe.'

Crosby made a noise that could have been a hiccup.

Sloan favoured him with a cold stare. 'Was there anything else, Crosby?'

'Just the Mother Superior, sir.'

'What about her?'

'Her name was Smith, sir. Mary Smith of Potter's Bar.'

The three of them stood on the convent doorstep and rang the bell. It was quite dark now. They could hear the bell echoing through the house, and then the slow footsteps of Sister Polycarp walking towards them.

Sergeant Perkins shivered. 'The only other thing I know about nuns is that they used to be walled up alive if they did anything wrong.'

Sloan was not interested. As a police officer he was concerned with crime, not punishment.

'There was the nun who was murdered in 1351,' proffered Crosby unexpectedly. 'By a crazy younger son.'

'And which was she?' demanded Sloan.

In the reflected light of the outer hall Crosby could be seen to be going a bit red. He gulped.

'The Police Concert,' he stammered hastily. 'We sang it – four of us – it's Noël Coward's.'

Sister Polycarp pulled the bolts of the door back. 'Sorry to keep you. I was in the kitchen.'

'That's all right,' said Sloan. 'Constable Crosby here has been entertaining us with recollections of a song of Mr Noël Coward's.'

'Coward?' Polycarp sniffed. 'Can't say I've heard the name. Ought I to have done?'

Sloan looked at her respectfully. 'Oh, Sister, you don't know what you gave up when you left the world.'

'Oh yes I do, young man. Believe you me I do.'

The former Mary Smith of Potter's Bar, now Mother Superior of the Convent of St Anselm, was in the parlour to greet them.

Sloan introduced Sergeant Perkins. 'I'm very sorry about this further intrusion, marm, but my superintendent insists . . .'

'But our bishop agrees, Inspector, so pray do not worry on that score. We appreciate your difficulties.'

An hour later he wondered if she did.

It was slow, painstaking work, seeing nun after nun, each with eyes demurely cast down, voices at low, unobtrusive pitch, each having to be asked specifically each question.

'What did you do immediately after supper on Wednesday evening, Sister?'

'The washing-up, Inspector.'

'The vegetables for the next day, Inspector.'

'Prepared the chapel, Inspector.'

'Swept the refectory, Inspector.'

'Some lettering on prayer cards, Inspector.'

'A little crochet, Inspector.'

'There was a letter I was permitted to write, Inspector.'

'Studied a book on the life of our Founder, Inspector.'

And to each one: 'When did you last see Sister Anne?'

As one woman they replied: 'At supper, Inspector.'

Someone had been in her stall at Vespers, they knew that now, but they had no suggestions to make. None had seen anything untoward then or at any other time. Or if they had they weren't telling Sloan and that good-looking young woman he had with him.

It was not noticeably different when he asked about that morning.

The same pattern of cleaning, cooking, praying emerged.

'Admin stuff,' he observed to Sergeant Perkins in between nuns.

'They don't look unhappy,' she said.

'I don't think they are. Once you've got used to it, I'm sure it's a great life.'

She grinned. 'Not for me, sir.'

'No,' said Sloan. 'I didn't think it would be. Next please, Crosby.'

There were faces he was beginning to know now. Characteristics were identifying themselves to him in spite of the strenuous efforts of their owners to suppress them.

Sister Hilda, whose lively, dancing eyes and harmonious voice belied her sombre habit. She had seen nothing on Wednesday or Saturday.

'But that's not surprising, Inspector, is it? That corridor is pretty dim in daylight, let alone in the evening. And we don't exactly go in for bright lights here, do we? As for this morning – once you're out of range of the windows practically anything can happen.'

'Could anyone leave the house unobserved?'

'Probably not, but,' she said frankly, 'anyone could go out into the grounds without anyone else asking why. It wouldn't be anything to do with them, you see, so they wouldn't notice properly if you know what I mean.'

Then there was the thin-lipped Sister Damien, who unbent not one fraction without the restraining presence of the Mother Superior.

'Had I seen anything suspicious I would have told Mother immediately,' she said.

'And this morning?'

'I was dusting the library. I saw and heard nothing out of the ordinary.'

'You know Miss Eileen Lome, of course?'

She shook her head. 'The name means nothing to me, Inspector.'

'Sister Bertha that was . . .'

'Ah, yes.' Her narrow features assumed a curious expression compounded of regret and disapproval. 'The former Sister Bertha.'

'Have you seen her since she left?'

'None of us have seen her, Inspector, since she renounced her vows. It would not have been proper.'

And, nearly the last, Sister Lucy.

She came in and sat down, hands folded serenely in her lap, waiting expectantly for Sloan to speak.

'It's a little strange, Sister, interviewing you in your own parlour, but – er – needs must. This is Sergeant Perkins who has come over from Calleford.'

Two women in two very different uniforms regarded each other across the room. It did something for each, decided Sloan, but then uniforms usually did.

'You've got your keys back, Sister, I see.'

She patted the huge bunch which hung from her girdle. 'Yes, indeed, Inspector, my badge of office. I was lost without them.'

'Sister, this dead boy, William Tewn, did you know him?'

'No, Inspector. I had never heard of him until this morning.'

'Nor seen him before?'

She shook her head. 'Never. Nor the two other boys who came over with Mr Ranby. The students can be seen from the convent grounds if they are working on their own land, but they're not usually near enough to identify and I'm sure no Sister would ever . . .'

'We have to ask any number of questions in our job,' he said placatingly. 'And they may seem irrelevant.' But they weren't, he thought to himself. She had been pale and shaking when she met him at the convent door this morning after the second murder.

He had seen that with his own two eyes, which made it cold, hard evidence.

'Sister, you came later than most to the convent . . .'

She bowed her head. 'That is so. I've been professed for only ten years now.'

It was quite comical to see Woman Sergeant Perkins doing a quick calculation of Sister Lucy's age on the material available to her.

'Happy years?' queried Sloan.

'Everything was very strange at first, Inspector, but it gradually becomes a very rewarding way of life.'

'Most of your – er – colleagues came here straight from school – it is permitted then to enter later?'

She nodded. 'It is permitted, Inspector. It does not happen very often. I had not intended to become a nun when I left school, you see, but my aunt – I was brought up by an aunt – she was able to get dispensation from the Very Reverend Mother General.'

'I see,' said Sloan. 'Thank you, Sister.'

He didn't see, but Sergeant Perkins did.

'What's a good-looking woman like that doing in a convent?' she asked shrewdly, when Sister Lucy had retired. 'There's waste for you. Put her into a decent frock and she'll still stop the traffic. I'll bet she's got good legs, too . . .'

'We shall never know,' said Sloan. 'Shall we?'

'Of course,' went on Sergeant Perkins, 'all that shy stuff that they play at – eyebrow-fluttering, not looking at you and that sort of thing – that's all very fetching anyway, but she's a real good looker, isn't she?'

'It's double murder we're investigating,' said Sloan drily. 'Not abduction. And it wasn't the good-looking one that bought it either. It was the one with the fifty per cent holding in Cartwright's Consolidated Carbons.'

'And she was plain?'

'Not as bad as some we've seen this afternoon,' said Sloan fairly, 'but plain enough.'

Sergeant Perkins sighed. 'So it wasn't her Sir Galahad at Vespers, disguised as a nun and come to rescue her?'

'If it was anyone at all,' said Sloan, 'it was the murderer.'

'Like the joke says?'

'What joke?'

Sergeant Perkins opened her eyes wide. 'Haven't you heard it, sir?'

'Not yet,' said Sloan grimly, 'but I'm going to. Now,' he looked from one to the other, 'Crosby, have you heard it?'

'Yes sir. Often.' He coughed bashfully. 'They sing it every time I go into the canteen.'

'Do they indeed? Suppose you sing it to me now . . .'

'Not sing it, sir. I can't sing.'

'I want to hear it, Crosby, and fast.'

Crosby cleared his throat and managed a sort of chant:

> 'You may kiss a nun once,
> You may kiss a nun twice,
> But you mustn't get into the habit.'

17

'That you, Sloan?'

Sloan held the convent telephone receiver at a distance suitable for the Superintendent's bellow.

'Leeyes here,' said the voice unnecessarily.

'Evening, sir.'

'Just to let you know,' trumpeted the Superintendent, 'that the rest of the Force haven't been idle while you've been sitting around in that parlour with Sergeant Perkins.'

'And fifty nuns, sir.'

Leeyes chose not to hear this. 'We've got Hobbett for you.'

'Good,' said Sloan warmly. 'I want a few words with him.'

'They picked him up in the Dog and Duck just after opening time.

'Keep him, sir, I'll be back.'

'I wasn't proposing to let him go, Sloan, though he's invoking everyone you've ever heard of. And then some. They tell me he'd hardly had time to sink his first pint and he's very cross.'

'That suits us nicely, sir. Can you leave him to cool off while I go on from here to the institute? There's something I want to ask them there.'

'I don't mind, Sloan, though I dare say the Station Sergeant might. However, you can make your own peace with him later. Talking of Sergeants, Sloan . . .'

'Sir . . .'

'Sergeant Gelden's turned up at last. With that bigamist. Silly fool.'

It was only fairly safe to assume he meant the bigamist.

'Do you want him back instead of Crosby?'

Sloan sighed. 'No, sir. Not at this stage. I'll keep Crosby now I've got him, but if you can spare Gelden I'd very much like him to go to West Laming for me.'

'Tonight?' They would have finished the nineteenth hole too before the Superintendent got to the golf club. 'Funny place to send a man on a Saturday night.'

'Yes, sir.' Sloan turned through the pages of his notebook, peering at his own handwriting. The electric light bulbs in this corridor couldn't be a watt over twenty-five. 'I want him to find out all he can about a Miss Felicity Ferling, who left there about ten years ago.'

'I suppose you know what you're doing, Sloan.'

'Yes, sir.' Someone had once said, 'Never apologize, never explain.' Someone with more self-confidence than he had. Disraeli, was it? 'And tell him,' added Sloan boldly, 'to ring me from there. Not to wait until he gets back.'

'He won't get back, not tonight anyway. It must be the best part of ninety miles away.'

'Yes, sir, but if he starts now I should hear from him before ten.'

The Superintendent came in on another tack. 'Getting anywhere with all those women?'

'I'm not sure, sir,' parried Sloan. 'They're a strange crew. Not like ordinary witnesses at all. They don't wonder about anything because they don't think it's right.'

'Theirs not to reason why . . .' Leeyes didn't seem to see where the rest of that quotation was going to lead him. 'Theirs but to do . . . and . . . er . . . die.'

'Just so, sir,' said Sloan.

Sergeant Perkins went with them to the institute.

'I may need you,' said Sloan. 'I expect Ranby's fiancée will be there. She's got good legs and you can at least see 'em.'

'No uniform?'

'I wouldn't say that. Classic wool twin-set, single string of pearls, quiet tweed skirt . . .'

'One of those,' said Sergeant Perkins feelingly.

'Nice girl all the same, I should say. She won't have abandoned Ranby at a time like this.'

They found not only Celia Faine with Ranby in the Principal's room but Father MacAuley too.

'A sad, sad business,' said the priest.

'Terrible,' endorsed Ranby. 'A young life like that just cut off. It doesn't make sense. Do you – may one ask – are you making any headway, Inspector?'

'In some ways,' said Sloan ambiguously.

'His people will be here by midday tomorrow. Not that that's any help. We know who he is.' The Principal looked older now.

'We don't know very much about him though,' commented Sloan mildly.

'I can't say that we do either. One tends to know best those who come up against authority – sad but true – and Tewn wasn't one of those. He seemed a likeable lad; not an outstanding student, mark you, but a trier.'

'He'd remembered one of the things you'd taught him,' said Sloan.

Ranby twisted his lips wryly. 'I'm glad to hear it. What was that?'

'Something about feeding the calves. All a matter of getting the milk warm enough.'

The Principal's face stiffened. 'Getting the milk warm enough?'

'That's right, sir. When you feed calves by hand, you taught them – on Thursday afternoon, was it? – that getting the calves to take the milk was all a matter of getting the milk warm enough.'

'So I did,' said Ranby warily, 'but what's it got to do with Tewn's death?'

'I couldn't say,' murmured Sloan equivocally. 'I couldn't say at all. Now, sir, would you say this lad had any enemies?'

'Just the one,' said Ranby drily.

'What? Oh, yes, sir, I see what you mean. Very funny.' Sloan sounded quite unamused.

'Poor lad,' said Celia Faine. 'At least he couldn't have known very much about it. Strangling's very quick, isn't it?'

'So I'm told, miss.' He looked at her. 'Sister Anne wouldn't have known all that much either, come to that. Just the one heavy blow.'

The girl shivered. 'It doesn't seem possible. Cullingoak's always been such a peaceful, happy village. And now . . .' She made a gesture of helplessness. 'Two innocent, harmless people are killed.'

'Innocent,' said Sloan sharply, 'but not harmless. That's the trouble, isn't it?'

Father MacAuley nodded. 'The boy was harmless until he got inside the convent. Sister Anne – we may have thought she was harmless but someone wanted her dead. It wasn't an accident. It couldn't have been.'

'Murder,' said Sloan tersely. 'Well planned and carried out.' There was a small silence. 'However, no doubt we shall find out in due course the person responsible and thence the murderer of this lad Tewn.'

The priest nodded. 'In due course, I'm sure you will. I've just left the convent – they're not altogether happy about being left alone tonight without any male protector but they tell me you can't spare a man.'

Sloan shook his head. 'Sorry. Not on a Saturday evening. Any chance of your going back there, Father, for a while?'

'Me? Certainly, Inspector. I quite understand how they feel. Their experiences of the past four days are enough to make anyone feel apprehensive.'

Ranby nodded. 'I don't blame them either. I'll come across with you, Father, and see if we can't arrange something for tonight. What about their gardener fellow?'

'Hobbett? No,' said Sloan regretfully. 'You can't have him. We're keeping him at the station this evening for questioning. I shouldn't care to have the responsibility of leaving him as protector.'

'Ranby and I will go across when they've had supper and Vespers then,' said the priest, 'and fix things so that they feel safer.'

'So that they are safer,' said the Principal.

'Thank you.' Sloane rose to go. 'There was just one thing I wanted to ask Miss Faine . . .'

Celia Faine lifted her eyebrows enquiringly.

'You know the house better than anyone, miss?'

'Perhaps I do,' she agreed. 'I was a child there and children do explore.'

'Tell me – it's an old house, I know – is there any place there that someone could hide? A priest's hole or anything like that?'

She smiled. 'Not that I know of, Inspector. Nothing so romantic. Or exciting.' She frowned. 'It's large, I know, as houses go, but straightforward – the hall, the chapel, the dining-room – that's the refectory now, of course – one or two smaller rooms – the drawing-room was upstairs. I expect it's a dormitory now, and then the long gallery. I can't think what they'll have used that for. Nothing else. No mysteries.' She smiled again. 'The only thing I ever discovered as a child was the newel post at the bottom of the great staircase. My cousin and I were playing one day and we found the orb at the top lifted out. It's on a sort of stalk and it slides in and out quite easily. We used to play with that a lot.'

'Round and smooth and heavy and staring you in the face,' snapped Superintendent Leeyes. 'Well, is there blood on it?'

'Dr Dabbe's examining it now,' said Sloan. 'But it's been cleaned three times since Wednesday night, and when these nuns say clean they mean clean.'

'Did the Sister with the blood on her hand . . .'

'Peter.'

'Did she touch it that morning?'

'She thinks she did. She won't swear to it, but she thinks she sometimes touches it.'

'She thinks she sometimes touches it,' mimicked the Superintendent. 'What a crowd! And did she sometimes touch it on Thursday morning?'

'She can't remember for certain. She might have done.'

'When was it cleaned?'

'First thing after breakfast. Before Terce and Sext.'

'What are . . .?'

'Their Office, sir.'

'Before they'd realized it was blood on that book?'

'The Gradual? Yes, sir. They didn't examine the book until afterwards. The staircase, landings and hall are always cleaned immediately after breakfast each day.'

Leeyes drummed his fingers on the desk. 'So it could still be anyone, Sloan.'

'Anyone, sir, who knew that part of the newel post came out and would constitute a nice heavy weapon, ideal for murder.'

Hobbett was easy meat really.

'You can't keep me here, Inspector. I haven't done nothing wrong and I can prove it. I wasn't running away neither. I allus come into Berebury Sat'day afternoons.'

'What you did wrong, Hobbett, was agreeing to let those young gentlemen into the convent. I know an old habit isn't worth much, but look at the trouble you've caused. And now you're involved in a double murder case whether you like it or not, aren't you?'

'I didn't 'ave nothing to do with no murder. I just fergot to lock up Wednesday night, that's all. Clean went out of my mind.'

'You arranged – for a small consideration,' said Sloan in a steely voice, 'to leave the old habit in your wood store in the cellar and to forget to lock up. And three students named Parker, Bullen and Tewn were to creep in and collect it. Tewn did the creeping and Tewn's dead.'

'It weren't nothing to do with me,' protested Hobbett. 'I only did like you said. Moving an old piece of cloth from one place to another and forgetting to lock up – that's not a crime, is it? What's that got to do with murder?'

'Everything,' said Sloan sadly. 'It provided the opportunity.'

*

The telephone was ringing as Sloan got back to his room.

Crosby handed over the receiver. 'For you, sir. London.'

'Inspector Sloan? Good. About our friends the Cartwrights and their Consolidated Carbons . . .'

'Yes?'

'Something I think will interest you, Inspector.'

Yes?'

'Harold – the principal subject of our enquiry – highly respected, highly respectable businessman. Hard but straight.'

'Well?'

'His father – Joe – not such a good businessman but quite a fellow with the chemicals in his day. Past it now, of course.'

'Of course. He must be about eighty-five.'

'That's just it. He is. And he had a stroke on Tuesday night. He's still alive but not expected to recover.'

Sloan whistled. 'So that's what upset the applecart!'

'At a guess – yes.'

'Thank you,' said Sloan. 'Thank you very much.'

'I'm glad it was useful information,' said the voice plaintively, 'because I should have been at Twickenham this afternoon.'

Sloan pushed the telephone away from him.

'So, Crosby, if Sister Anne died before Uncle Joe all was well. If she consented to the firm going public all was not well but better than it might have been. If she neither died nor consented, Cousin Harold inherited his father's half minus death duties leaving Sister Anne with her half intact and a strong leaning to the Mission field and making restitution.'

'Tricky,' said Crosby.

'Tricky? Cousin Harold must have been in a cold sweat in case his father died before he got to Cullingoak and Sister Anne.'

'Sir, what about that awful old woman we saw in London, Sister Anne's mother – doesn't she come into this?'

Sloan shook his head. 'No. She's only got a life interest that reverts to either her daughter, brother-in-law or nephew according to the order in which they survive. We can leave her out of this. Give me that telephone back, will you? I'm going to ask Cousin Harold to go up to the convent.'

'Tonight?'

'Tonight, Crosby. After the good Sisters have had supper and Vespers.'

Crosby started to thumb through the telephone directory.

'Crosby, where's Sergeant Perkins?'

'In the canteen, sir.'

'Get them to save me something, and then tell her I want to see her. I'm going back to see the Superintendent when I've spoken to Cousin Harold.'

'It was blood then, Sloan.'

'Yes, sir. Dr Dabbe's just sent along his report. Minute traces, dried now and mixed with polish, but indubitably blood.'

'Group?'

'The same as Sister Anne's, the same as on the Gradual.'

'And as a possible weapon?'

'Ideal.' Sloan tapped the pathologist's report. 'He won't swear to it being the exact one . . .'

'Of course not,' said Leeyes sarcastically. 'They never will.'

'But it fits in every particular.'

'Good enough for the jury, but not the lawyers?'

'Yes, sir.'

'And what do you propose to do now?'

Sloan told him.

18

Neither the Mother Superior nor Sister Lucy were present at Vespers that Saturday evening. If any member of the community so far forgot herself as to notice the fact, they took good care not to look a second time at the two empty stalls. The welfare of the Convent of St Anselm sometimes necessitated their presence in the parlour with visitors. So it was this evening.

There were three of them, and a grumbling Sister Polycarp had let them in and taken them to the parlour. The Convent of St Anselm did not usually have visitors at the late hour of eight thirty in the evening and she resented the interruption of her routine. She would have resented still further – had she known about it – two other visitors who had come privily to another door a little earlier. They had tapped quietly on the garden-room door that Sister Polycarp had so carefully locked and bolted only an hour before that. But it was mysteriously opened for them and they stepped inside, a man and a woman, locking it as carefully behind them as Sister Polycarp had done so that should she chance to check again there was nothing to show that it had been opened and closed again in the mean time.

The Mother Superior greeted those who had come by the front door, keeping Sister Polycarp by her side.

'Father, how kind of you to come back, and Mr Ranby, too.'

'We don't like to think of you alone here all night with a murderer at large.'

She bowed. 'It is indeed difficult to sleep with that thought. We have been more than a little perplexed.' She lowered her voice. 'You see we cannot exclude the possibility that the – er – perpetrator of these outrages is within our own house.'

Both men nodded.

'Especially,' went on the Mother Superior, 'now that the police have discovered the murder weapon was here all the time.'

'They have?' said Ranby.

'The orb on the top of the newel post. Inspector Sloan has taken it away.'

'Now, about tonight . . .' said the priest.

'Mr Cartwright has come up from the village, too.' said the Mother Superior. 'He is just looking through the cellars for us now. We felt a little uneasy about the cellars.'

'Yes, indeed,' said Father MacAuley soothingly. 'I think it would be as well if Cartwright, Ranby and I worked out some scheme for patrolling the building, cellars and all.'

'We had already decided to do that ourselves,' said the Mother Superior, 'but if you would be so kind as to augment our – rather feminine efforts it would be a great kindness.'

'An hour each on,' suggested Ranby, 'and two off. That is if Cartwright agrees?'

'Right,' said MacAuley.

'With one Sister . . .'

'With two Sisters,' said the Mother Superior firmly.

'With two Sisters in the gallery at the top of the stairs.'

'Thank you, gentlemen. That should keep us safe through the night. I will detail the Sisters immediately. They are quite used to night vigils, you know. In Lent we keep them between the Offices of Compline and Lauds.'

Sergeant Gelden rang Sloan at Berebury Police Station at a quarter to ten.

'That you, Inspector? About a Miss Felicity Ferling of West Laming House.'

'I'm listening, Sergeant.'

'It's like this, sir . . .'

Sloan listened and he wrote, and he thanked Sergeant Gelden. Then he drove out to Cullingoak. He parked his car at the Bull and walked to the convent from there, timing the walk. Then he, too, went round to the garden door and tapped very quietly. He was admitted by no less a personage than the Mother Superior herself.

She produced a list for him. 'From ten to eleven, Father MacAuley and Sisters Ninian and Fidelia; from eleven to twelve Mr Cartwright and Sisters Damien and Perpetua and from twelve to one Mr Ranby and Sisters Lucy and Gertrude.'

'And so on through the night?'

'Yes, Inspector, unless anything untoward happens. Sister Cellarer has sent a supply of hot coffee and sandwiches to the parlour for those not actually watching.'

'Any difficulties?'

'None. All three gentlemen were quite agreeable to my suggestions.'

'Let's hope they've swallowed everything. And the rest of the Community?'

'Gone to bed, Inspector, as usual.'

'Good. And the arrangements for changing over the watch so to speak?'

'The retiring Sisters will knock on their successors' doors ten minutes before the hour.'

'Excellent. Is Sister Lucy in bed?'

'Sister Lucy has perforce been in bed for some time, now, Inspector.'

He gave her a quick smile. 'We're nearly there, marm.'

'Pray God that you are,' she said soberly.

Sloan made himself as comfortable as he could in the flower room and settled down to wait. And to wonder.

If he opened the door the minutest fraction he could see the hall and its sentinel. First it was Father MacAuley who paced up and down the hall and then did a methodical round of doors and windows. Sloan had to retreat behind a curtain for that. And then Harold Cartwright, noisier than the priest, conscientiously poking about along the corridor and talking quietly up the stairs to Sister Damien and Sister Perpetua.

He heard them at about quarter-past twelve and again at a quarter to one.

'Everything all right up there with you?'

'Yes, thank you, Mr Cartwright. It's all quiet, thank God.' Sister Damien's thin whisper came floating down the stairs in reply. 'We're just going along to wake the others. We'll see you at two o'clock again.'

'Right you are.'

Sloan heard him do one last quick round and then nip back towards the parlour. Then the parlour door opened and Ranby came out. He came straight to the garden room, and Sloan was hard put to it to get behind his curtain in time. Ranby pulled back the bolts and left the door slightly ajar and then went back to the hall.

Sloan came out from behind his curtain and held the door open. Ranby was standing at the foot of the stairs, calling softly upwards.

'Are you there, Sister Lucy?'

Sister Gertrude came to the balustrade and leaned over. 'We're both here, Mr Ranby. Is there something wrong?'

'No. I just wanted a word with Sister Lucy about Tewn. It's something she said earlier this morning. It's just occurred to me it might be important.'

Sister Gertrude withdrew and Sister Lucy appeared in her stead on the landing and began walking slowly down the polished treads, her head bent well down, her massive bunch of keys swinging from her girdle.

Ranby retreated a little as she descended, backing away from the small well of light in the hall, away from the gaze of Sister Gertrude. He came, as Sloan thought he would, towards the dark corridor where Sister Anne had died, the corridor where Sloan stood waiting and watching.

'Felicity,' Ranby whispered urgently to her, 'come this way. I must talk to you.'

The nun turned obediently in his direction and walked exactly where he said.

'This way,' he urged. 'So that the others don't hear us.'

She was almost level with him now, his eyes watching her every movement, not seeing at all the dim shadowy figure that was following her down the stairs, pressed against the furthest wall.

As she drew abreast of him he put up an arm as if to embrace her. It quickly changed to a savage grasp, his other hand coming up in front of her neck searching for soft, vulnerable cartilage and vital windpipe.

The eager questing fingers were destined to be disappointed in their prey.

The nun did a quick shrug and twist and Ranby let out a yelp of pain. The arm fell back, but he came in with the other. That did him no good at all. The nun caught it and flung herself forward against it. Ranby fell heavily, her weight on top of him.

And then Sloan was there and the dark shadow on the wall was translated into Detective Constable Crosby with handcuffs at the ready. Along the corridor the parlour door opened and Father MacAuley and Harold Cartwright came hurrying out.

The nun clambered off Ranby, hitching up her habit in an un-nun-like way. 'These blasted skirts,' she said, 'certainly hamper a girl.' She struggled out of the headdress and shook her hair loose. 'But this is worse. Fancy having to live in one of these.'

'That's not Sister Lucy,' gasped Ranby.

'No,' agreed Sloan. 'That's Police Sergeant Perkins in Sister Lucy's habit.'

19

'I didn't think it would come off a second time,' said Sloan modestly.

The Superintendent grunted. He didn't usually reckon to come in to the station on a Sunday morning, but then his Criminal Investigation Department didn't arrest a double murderer every day of the week. Sloan, Perkins, Gelden and Crosby were all present – and looking regrettably pleased with themselves.

'No snags at all?' asked Leeyes.

'Worked like a charm,' said Sloan cheerfully. 'He was quite taken in by Sergeant Perkins. So was I, sir. Anyone would have been.'

'Would they indeed?' said Leeyes. 'Sergeant Perkins makes a good nun, does she?'

Sergeant Perkins flushed. 'That headdress thing . . .'

'Coif,' supplied Sloan, now the expert.

'Coif is about the most uncomfortable thing I've ever worn.'

'You didn't wear her hair shirt then,' said Leeyes acidly.

'No, sir. On the other hand, sir, you can't blame Ranby for making a mistake that first time. You can't see a nun's face unless you get a straightforward front view, you know, and I don't suppose he wanted to do that anyway.'

'Don't forget either, sir,' put in Sloan, 'that nuns don't age as quickly as we do. I don't know why. But Sister Anne looked the sort of age he expected Sister Lucy to look by now.'

'And,' went on Sergeant Perkins, 'it's about the darkest corridor I've ever been in.'

'That's their subconscious harking back to candle–power,' said Sloan *sotto voce*.

Leeyes ignored this. 'So Ranby killed Sister Anne on Wednesday in error?'

'Pure and simple case of mistaken identity, sir. It all fits. He was out to kill Sister Lucy, the Bursar and Procuratrix, who always wears the great big heavy bunch of keys hanging from her girdle. Always.'

'Except on Wednesday evenings?'

'No, just this one Wednesday so that Sister Anne could look out some gifts to send to the Missions in time for Christmas. I gather in the ordinary way she would have come with her, but she was busy on Wednesday evening.'

'What's she got to be busy about?'

Sloan didn't know. He didn't think he would ever know what made them busy in a convent. 'Anyway, sir, she handed over her badge of office – a very conspicuous one – to Sister Anne, and so Ranby thinks it's her. He picks up the orb on the newel post . . .'

'He knew all about that, did he?'

'Oh, yes, sir, from Celia Faine. He hits Sister Anne very hard indeed on the back of the head and puts it back. Not even bothering to wipe it very clean. If it's found it's a pointer to an inside job, isn't it?'

'It wasn't found,' pointed out the Superintendent unkindly. 'Not until someone laid it out on a plate for you.'

'No, sir,' said Sloan. 'On the other hand it didn't mislead us about its being an inside job either, did it? And then, sir,' he went on hurriedly, not liking the Superintendent's expression, 'he bundles the body into the broom cupboard and takes the glasses off. It's quite dark in there too and so he still doesn't know he's nobbled the wrong horse.'

'And then what?'

'He goes back to the institute for supper.'

'He does what?'

'Goes back to the institute for supper.'

'Who threw her down the stairs, then?'

'He did.'

'When?'

'After supper.'

'Why?'

'Delay her being found, upset the timing, make us think she'd fallen – that sort of thing. Implicating Tewn, too, if necessary. It wouldn't have been any bother to drag her along the corridor and shove her down the steps as he was there anyway.'

'How do you mean he was there anyway?'

'He came back after his own supper at the institute,' said Sloan, 'to attend Vespers. He didn't want her found before the boys got to the convent. He hadn't an alibi for a quarter to seven or thereabouts when he killed her, but if she was thought to be alive at nine when they went off to bed it would throw a spanner in the calculations.'

'Are you trying to tell me, Sloan – not very clearly if I may say so – that Ranby came twice to the convent on Wednesday night?'

'Yes, sir, I am. He came to the service that they have just before their supper as an ordinary worshipper – Benediction I think it's called – and probably waited behind afterwards. The nuns all go into the refectory at a quarter past six for their supper and he goes along the corridor, opens the cellar door, nips down for the habit, puts it on and comes back up into that corridor. Then comes the tricky bit. He has to wait for Sister Lucy to come along. He takes the orb down.'

'Didn't anyone notice it had gone?'

'I doubt if they'd have missed anything, not even the kitchen stove, until the time came to use it. No, I think he just stood inside the broom cupboard until he saw her come along.'

'She'd have to be alone,' objected Leeyes doubtfully.

'Yes, she would, but don't forget that after supper they have their recreation. They're allowed to potter about a little at will. It was the only chance he took really – her not happening to come his way. But if she didn't he could always go looking for her.'

'In the convent?'

'It's not difficult to pass as a nun if you're in the habit. He's fair-skinned anyway, they can't see his hair, he's got his own black shoes and socks on, trousers wouldn't show and believe you me, sir, nuns are the least observant crowd of witnesses it has been my unfortunate lot to encounter. They seem to think it's a sin to notice anything. And the light's so bad you never get a really clear view of anything after daylight. Ranby never saw Sister Anne's face sufficiently well at any time to know it wasn't Sister Lucy. There's no light to speak of in the corridor itself, and he wouldn't dare shine a torch. That would be asking for trouble.'

'So he kills Sister Anne, goes back to the institute for supper . . .'

'That's right, sir. They would notice if he weren't there anyway, but particularly at the institute supper.'

'Why?'

'There are fourteen resident staff all told, including Ranby, so if one is missing there are—'

'I can do *simple* arithmetic, Sloan.'

'Yes, sir.' Sloan coughed. 'As soon as the supper at the institute was finished I reckon he came back, put on the habit and Sister Anne's glasses. He only had to be last in to the chapel to know which was her stall.' He took a breath. 'And he was – Sister Damien said so. Then he waits until the nuns have gone to bed, drags the body to the top of the cellar steps, throws it down, leaves the habit ready for Tewn, puts the glasses in his pocket and goes back to his quarters in the institute. I expect he rang for the maid to take away his coffee cup or sent for one of the staff or students – something like that to imply that he'd been there all the time. Nobody's likely to ask him any questions, though, because he thought there was nothing to connect him with the convent at all.'

'But there was?'

'There must have been something or he wouldn't have had to kill Tewn.'

'Ah, Tewn. I was forgetting Tewn.' The Superintendent never forgot anything.

'I think Tewn had to die because he saw something which connected Ranby with the convent.'

'What?'

Sloan tapped his notebook. 'I'm not absolutely certain but I think I can guess.'

'Well?'

'Ranby stepped out of that habit somewhere around nine fifteen or nine twenty after being inside it for nearly an hour. Tewn picked it up at nine thirty.'

'Well?'

'It would still be warm, sir. I think Tewn noticed.'

'That crack about warm milk,' burst out Crosby involuntarily.

Sloan nodded. 'Ranby must have had good reason for thinking Tewn knew or guessed something. It would be easy enough for him to catch Tewn in between the study periods yesterday morning and tell him they were walking over to the convent without the others.' He shrugged his shoulders. 'We'll never know what it was Tewn knew. Unless Ranby tells us. Mind you, sir, I don't think he will. The only thing he's said so far is "Get me my solicitor." '

'Much good that'll do him,' said the Superintendent. 'You've got him cold, I hope.'

'I hope so,' echoed Sloan piously, 'but it's a long story.'

The Superintendent sighed audibly. 'Suppose you go back to the beginning . . .'

'There are really two beginnings, sir.'

'One will do very nicely, Sloan. Let's have the earliest first.'

'That was twelve years ago, sir, in West Laming. Where Sergeant Gelden went last night.'

Sergeant Gelden nodded corroboratively.

'It concerns two people,' said Sloan, 'Mr Marwin Ranby, then Deputy Headmaster of West Laming School, and a Miss Felicity Ferling, niece of Miss Dora Ferling of West Laming House. It was their both having come from West Laming that put me on to Ranby. This pair became very friendly indeed – Miss Ferling was a very charming, good-looking girl, greatly loved by her aunt who had brought her up. She became engaged to be married to this promising young school-master and everything was arranged for the wedding. Two weeks before it Miss Dora Ferling had a visitor – Mr Ranby's wife. He was already married. The wedding was abandoned, and Miss Felicity Ferling broken-hearted.'

'So she took her broken heart to the convent?'

'Not at first. They don't like women there for that reason, but apparently she'd always been very devout and interested in the life.'

'He seems to like 'em that way,' observed the Superintendent. 'Some men do. And the second beginning?'

'Ten days ago. At a public inquiry into the planning application to develop the land in between the convent property and the institute. Both sent representatives to it. The institute sent Mr Ranby and someone from the County Education Department. The convent sent the Mother Superior and—'

'Don't tell me,' said the Superintendent. 'I can guess.'

'Sister Lucy – their Bursar. Just the worst possible time for her to turn up from Ranby's point of view. He's engaged again – this time to Miss Celia Faine, who stands a good chance of being wealthy if this development is allowed.'

'Nasty shock for him – seeing his old flame sitting there.'

'Very. And in nun's veiling too. Pretty impregnable places, convents.'

'Ahah, I see where you're getting, Sloan.'

'Exactly, sir. Ranby goes home to brood on ways and means.'

'And his own students provide the answer?'

'That's right, sir. Plot Night in more ways than one. I think we shall find that Ranby either overheard or got to hear of the arrangement with Hobbett and seized his chance that night. The only other thing he needed to know was how to identify Sister Lucy without looking each nun in the face. A little judicious pumping of Hobbett would give him the answer to that, too – she always wore a great big bunch of keys. You'll have spotted the other misleading fact yourself, I'm sure, sir.'

Leeyes growled noncommittally.

'Hobbett,' went on Sloan, 'doesn't know Sister Lucy doesn't wear glasses all the time. Any more than Ranby does. She would have been wearing them at the inquiry and when she paid Hobbett.'

'You make it sound very simple,' complained the Super-intendent.

'It was, sir. Motive, means and opportunity, the lot. He can't risk failure of a second attempt to marry a well-to-do unprotected girl – so there's the motive. The means are at hand – even down to the weapon – and his own students presented him with opportunity.'

'Are you trying to tell me, Sloan, that Ranby can have gone to that chapel with his future intended and those nuns not have known him from Adam?'

'Yes, sir. The Sisters sit in front of a grille, and the congregation would only ever see their backs. And,' he added under his breath, 'they none of them know Adam.'

'What's that, Sloan?'

'Nothing, sir.'

'I don't want any of your case based on false premises.'

'No, sir.' That was the course on Logic rearing its head again.

Leeyes turned to Crosby. 'None of this "when did you stop beating your wife" stuff, eh, Constable?'

Crosby looked pained. 'I'm not married, sir.'

Harold Cartwright was still at the Bull.

'Fine woman, the Mother Superior. Makes me realize some of my ideas were a bit Maria Monk – you know, the Awful Disclosures thereof.'

Sloan did not know, and said instead, 'Any news of your father, sir?'

Cartwright shot him a sharp glance. 'You knew, didn't you?'

'Yes, sir.'

'He's much the same, Inspector, thank you. I'm going back home today but I'm coming back . . . Inspector Sloan?'

'Sir?'

'It was Ranby who sent for the police on Bonfire Night, wasn't it?'

'Yes, sir. I think he wanted us to see the habit and glasses just in case he had to pin something on someone else. After all, it wasn't very likely one nun would kill another really.'

'And safer than throwing the glasses away.'

'He was a bit too anxious to implicate the students. He suggested they might have got out of the biology laboratory window long before he was supposed to know what time they had gone to the convent.'

Cartwright gave his quick smile. 'That job's still open for you, Inspector.'

'No, thank you, sir, but there is one – what you might call – lost soul in need of one rather badly. A defector from St Anselm's. I doubt if she's really employable myself.'

'I could see,' offered Cartwright.

'The name is Lome, Miss Eileen Lome. I'll give you her address.'

'And I'll give you my London one.'

Sloan coughed. 'I have it, sir, thank you.'

Cartwright nodded gravely. 'I was forgetting. But I'll be coming back to the Bull. Funny thing you know, the Bull doesn't mean the animal at all.'

'No, sir?'

'No. It means the Papal Bull. Isn't that odd? The Mother Superior told me.'

Sloan went back to the car and tapped Crosby on the shoulder. 'Get thee to a nunnery.'

Sister Gertrude set off in the direction of the parlour. There must be visitors there again. Usually Sister Lucy was sent for, but today Sister Lucy was being kept very busy by the Mother Superior on the question of the costs of a cloister. And this time they knew where the money was coming from. Mr Harold Cartwright. Usually, when the Convent of St Anselm spent some money, they had no idea from whence the wherewithal would appear. It always came, of course, but that was not easy to explain to a builder.

She hurried down the great staircase and wondered how long it would be before she could look at the newel post without a shudder. There was a portrait at the bottom of the stairs, framed and glass covered. If you stood in a certain way you could catch sight of your own reflection. Sister Gertrude paused, squinted up at herself and pulled her coif quite straight. Very wrong of her, of course. She would try not to do it again. But it was a temptation.

She joined the Mother Superior and went into the parlour.

'So it was Mr Ranby all the time,' said the Mother Superior directly.

'Yes, marm,' said Sloan. 'He swallowed the bait – Sergeant Perkins – hook, line and sinker. If I may say so, Father MacAuley has a real talent for dissembling. Ranby never guessed the idea of the night watch was all a put-up job.'

'Inspector, there is no doubt, is there?'

'No, marm, we've found out other things too. He shaved twice that day and so on.'

'Poor soul,' she said compassionately, 'to be so concerned with the passing things of the world.'

'Yes, marm.' He coughed. 'Miss Faine . . . how . . .'

'Father MacAuley went to see her this morning after Mass. We must pray for her.'

Sloan shifted uncomfortably in his chair. 'Of course.'

'The two boys from the institute?' she enquired.

Sloan brightened. 'They're taking it very well. It's quite taken their minds off Tewn.'

'Inspector, when did you first suspect . . .?'

'Sister Lucy was white and shaking when I got here yesterday after you'd found Tewn's body. It wasn't that that had upset her because she hadn't seen it. What she had seen, of course, was Ranby. And Ranby had seen her and realized he'd killed the wrong Sister.'

'He must have been a desperate man by last night.'

'He was, marm. He tried to kill Sergeant Perkins. There was no doubt about that.'

The Mother Superior inclined her head. 'Sergeant Perkins is a courageous woman.'

'In the course of duty, marm,' he said hastily. It was a different discipline, a different dedication from that of the Sisters, but for all that it was still an equally dedicated way. 'About Hobbett . . .'

'In future,' she said drily, 'he can ring for Sister Polycarp.'

A bell suddenly echoed through the convent. Both nuns rose, Sister Gertrude with a perceptible start. She had been wondering who it could be among the community who would be bidden to move into the cell that had been Sister Anne's, the cell next to Sister Hilda the snorer. Was it wrong to pray God it wouldn't be her?

Sister Polycarp stumped to the door with the two policemen. 'Good day, gentlemen . . .'

Was it Sloan's imagination or did she slam the grille behind them?

Crosby looked back at the convent. 'You wouldn't have thought, sir, would you, that after all that, it would turn out to be a *crime passionnel*?' He pronounced it 'cream'. 'Not here.'

'No,' said Sloan shortly, 'you wouldn't.'

'That motto on the door, Inspector . . .'

'Well?'

'Do we really know what it means?'

Sloan turned on his heel and stared at the writing. '*Pax Intrantibus, Salus Exeuntibus*. Didn't you look it up, Crosby? You should have done. Very enlightening.'

'Please, sir . . .'

'Peace to those who enter,' translated Sloan. 'Salvation to those who leave.'

Henrietta
Who?

For All My Eleven o'Clock Friends,
with Love.

1

Harry Ford was a postman. He was a postman of a vintage that is fast disappearing – that is to say he still did his delivery round on a bicycle. The little red vans had reached the large village of Down Martin but his own round of the smaller ones like Larking and Belling St Peter was just as quick on two wheels as on four.

And he, for one, wasn't sorry. Gave you time to think, did a bicycle, even if it was a bit chilly at six o'clock of a dank morning in March. He was well muffled up against the cold though and he didn't mind the half dark. Besides, there were compensations. Another few weeks and he'd be abroad in that glorious early morning light that did something for the soul.

He braked gently as he coasted round the corner into Larking. He knew exactly where to brake on this road. In fact, there wasn't much of the village he didn't know after delivering its mail all these years.

An outsider would have said Larking was typical of a thousand other English villages. And, as it happened, this was true, though the people of Larking wouldn't have liked it. It had all the appurtenances of a normal village and the usual complement of important – and self-important – people: two different groups.

Spiritual leadership was provided by the Reverend Edward Bouverie Meyton (his father had been an admirer of Pusey). He lived at the Rectory on the green by the church (one Diocesan leaflet, three appeals, a Missionary newsletter, the quarterly report of the Additional Curates' Society and an interesting letter from the Calleshire Historical Association).

Secular leadership came from James Augustus Heber Hibbs, Esquire, at The Hall (an assortment of bills, two closely typed pages of good advice from his stockbroker, a wine list, a picture postcard from his cousin Maude and a letter from Scotland about a grouse moor).

Harry Ford, postman, was not deceived. He knew as well as anyone else that real power – as opposed to leadership – was vested behind the counter at the post office cum general store in the vast person of Mrs Ricks (one seed catalogue: Mrs Ricks rarely committed herself to paper).

Larking shared a branch of the Women's Institute with the neighbouring hamlet of Belling St Peter (Mrs Hibbs was president) and a doctor with a cluster of small communities round about.

And everyone thought they knew everything about everyone else.

In which they were very mistaken.

Harry Ford looked at the post office clock, dimly visible through the uncurtained window – though only from habit. He had done the round so often that he didn't need a clock to know that – saving Christmas and a General Election – he would finish his Larking delivery at a quarter to eight in the farthest farmhouse, where – letters or not – he would fetch up in the kitchen with a cup of scalding tea.

Only it didn't work out that way this morning.

For ever afterwards he was thankful that he had been on his bicycle and not in a little red van. If he had been in a van, as he frequently reiterated in the days that followed, he couldn't possibly have avoided the huddled figure that was lying in the road.

'Right on the corner at the far end of the village,' he said breathlessly into the telephone after he had taken one quick look and pedalled furiously back to the telephone kiosk outside the post office. 'Lying in the road. Do come quickly,' he implored the ambulance. 'If anything else comes round that bend they won't be able to avoid her either.'

That word 'either' was full of profound significance.

'Where exactly?' demanded the man at the ambulance station. Larking was deep in rural Calleshire and the whole of that part of the county was an intricate network of minor roads. And it wasn't really light yet.

'Through Larking village proper,' said Ford, 'and out on the other road to Belling St Peter.'

'The other road?' countered the man on the telephone, who had been caught out by bad directions before.

'Not the main road to Belling. The back road. Come to Larking Post Office and then fork left and she's about a quarter of a mile down the road on the bad bend.'

'Right you are. You get back to her, then.' The duty man on the Berebury Ambulance Station switchboard flipped a lever which connected him with the crew room. 'Emergency just come in, Fred. Back of beyond, I'm afraid. Woman lying in the road.'

'Dead?'

'Caller didn't say she was alive,' he said reasonably, 'and he didn't mention injuries. Just that she was lying in the road.'

'Dead, then,' said the experienced Fred.

'Or drunk,' said the man in charge, who had been at the game even longer.

She wasn't drunk.

Harry Ford, going back to have a second, more considered look, decided that beyond any doubt at all she was dead. He had been almost sure the first time by the inadequate gleam of his bicycle lamp but now with the sky growing lighter every minute he was absolutely certain.

Her Majesty's Mails being his prime concern he propped his bicycle safely in the deep hedge, that same deep hedge that made this a blind corner, then he came back and stood squarely in the middle of the road. He would be seen by anyone coming now. Not, he decided, that there was ever likely to be much traffic on this road – still less so early in the morning.

This line of thought proved productive.

Not only, now he came to think of it, would there be almost no vehicles using this road first thing in the morning but it was equally unlikely that anyone would be walking along it either.

Still less a woman.

A man, perhaps, walking up to one of the farms to do the milking, but not a woman.

He considered in his mind the houses beyond. There were about six of them before you could say you were really out of Larking and then there was a two-mile stretch with just three big farms, then Belling St Peter.

Harry Ford advanced a little.

He might know her himself, come to that – he knew most Larking people.

But he hadn't taken more than a step when he heard something coming. It was too soon for the ambulance; besides the direction was wrong. He cocked his head, listening. It wasn't a car either, he decided, getting out into the middle of the road ready to wave anything on wheels to a standstill. Quite suddenly the oncoming noise resolved itself into a tractor which pulled up to a quick halt as the driver saw him.

'Accident?' shouted the man at the wheel above the engine noise.

''Fraid so,' shouted back Ford.

The tractor engine spluttered and died and there was a sudden silence.

'She's dead,' said Ford.

The young man got down from his high seat. It was one of the sons of the farmer from farther down the road, by the name of Bill Thorpe.

'I found her,' said Ford.

Not that it looked as if she'd been hit by a bicycle.

'She's from one of the cottages, isn't she?' said Thorpe, peering down. 'You know, Harry, I think I know who she is.'

Ford, who to tell the truth hadn't been all that keen on having a really close look on his own, was emboldened by the presence of the young man and bent down towards the cold white face. 'Why, it's Mrs Jenkins.'

'That's right,' said Thorpe.

'Boundary Cottage,' responded the postman automatically. (The odd letter, no circulars, very few bills.)

Thorpe looked round. 'Hit and run,' he said bitterly. 'Not even a ruddy skid mark.'

'It's a nasty corner,' offered Ford.

Thorpe was still looking at the road. 'You can see where he hit the verge a bit afterwards and straightened up again.'

Ford didn't know much about cars. 'Too fast?'

'Too careless.'

'You'd have thought anyone would have seen her,' agreed Ford.

'Walking on the wrong side, though.'

'Depends whether she was coming or going,' said Ford, who was the slower thinker of the two.

'I should have said she was walking home myself,' pronounced Thorpe carefully. 'Last night.'

'Last night?' Ford looked shocked.

'If that mark on the grass is his front tyre after he hit her when she was walking along the left-hand side of the road towards her home.'

'But last night,' insisted Ford. 'You mean she's been here all night?'

Thorpe scratched an intelligent forehead. 'I don't know, Harry, but she isn't likely to have been walking home this morning in the dark, is she?'

Harry Ford shook his head. 'A very quiet lady, I'd have said.'

'And,' continued Thorpe, pursuing his theory, 'if she'd been going anywhere very early she'd have been walking the other way. No, I'd say myself she was going home last night.'

'Off the last bus, perhaps,' suggested the postman.

'Perhaps.'

'Her daughter's not at home then,' said Ford firmly. 'Otherwise she'd have been out looking for her.'

'No, she's away still. Back at the end of term.' He looked down at the still figure in the road and said, 'Sooner now.'

'I rang the ambulance,' said Ford, for want of something to say.

Thorpe moved with sudden resolution. 'Well, then, I'll go and ring the police. Don't you let them move her until they come.'

'Right.'

Thorpe paused, one foot on the tractor. 'Poor Henrietta. No father and now no mother either.'

Police Constable Hepple came over from Down Martin on his motorcycle and measured the road and drew chalk lines round the body and finally allowed the ambulance men to take it away. He, too, knew Mrs Jenkins by sight.

'Widow, isn't she, Harry?' he said to the postman.

'That's right. Just the one girl.'

He got out his notebook. 'Does she know about this?'

'She's away,' volunteered young Thorpe. 'At college.'

'Do you know her exact address?'

But young Thorpe went a bit pink and said rather distantly that he did not. So PC Hepple made another note and then measured the tyre mark on the grass verge.

'I'd say a 590 × 14 myself,' offered Thorpe, who was keen on cars. 'That's a big tyre on a big car.' Now that the body had gone he could talk about that more freely too. 'Those were big-car injuries she had.'

PC Hepple, who had reached much the same conclusions himself, nodded.

''Tisn't what you'd call a busy road,' went on Thorpe.

'Busy!' snorted Harry Ford. 'I shouldn't think it gets more than a dozen cars a day.'

'Even the milk lorries all go the other way,' said Thorpe, 'because it's a better road.'

'Did you have any visitors at the farm last night?' Hepple asked Thorpe.

'Not a soul.'

'Perhaps it was someone who'd taken the wrong turning at the post office.' That was the postman.

'Wrong turning or not,' said Hepple severely, 'there was no call to be knocking Mrs Jenkins down.'

'And,' said Thorpe pertinently, 'having knocked her down to have driven on.'

*

It seemed to Henrietta Jenkins that she would never again be quite the same person as she had been before she stepped into the cold, bare police mortuary.

A sad message, telephoned through a series of offices, had snatched her from the Greatorex Library where she had been working. A succession of kind hands had steered her into the hastily summoned taxi and put her on to the Berebury train. She had been barely aware of them. She vaguely remembered getting out at Berebury more from force of habit than anything else. A police car had met her – she remembered that – and brought her to the police station.

Voices had indicated that there was no need for her to identify the body just now. Perhaps there were some other relatives?

No, Henrietta had told them. There was no one else. She was an only child and her father had been killed in the war.

Perhaps, then, there was someone close in Larking who would . . .'

Henrietta had shaken her head.

Tomorrow, then?

She had shaken her head again. Now.

Something like this was only possible if you didn't think about it. She heard herself say – very politely: 'Now or never.'

She had followed a policeman down a long corridor. She didn't think she had ever seen a policeman without a helmet on – absurd the tricks one's mind played at a time like this.

He drew back a white sheet. Briefly. And looked not at the still face lying there but at Henrietta's own live one.

She nodded speechlessly.

He laid the sheet back gently and led the way back to the world of the living. Henrietta was shivering now but not from cold. The policeman – she noticed for the first time that he was a sergeant – brought her a cup of tea. It was steaming hot and almost burnt her mouth but Henrietta drank it thirstily, gladly giving the hot liquid all her attention.

Even the sensation of pain, though, could not drive away the memory of the mortuary.

'It's the smell that upsets people,' said the Police Sergeant kindly. 'All that antiseptic.'

'It is a bit dank,' admitted Henrietta shakily. The detached, educated half of her mind noted how primitive it was of her to be so grateful for human company; but nothing would have taken her back into that other room again. Only if the body had been that of a stranger could she have borne that.

The Sergeant busied himself about some papers on his desk while she drank. Presently she said, 'Sergeant, what happened?'

'The Larking postman found her lying in the road, miss. She'd been run over by a car on that last bad bend as you leave Larking village.'

'I know the place. Why?'

'Why was she knocked down? That we don't rightly know, miss. You see, the car didn't stop.'

Henrietta stifled a rising wave of nausea.

'We'll pick him up, sooner or later, you'll see,' said the Sergeant. 'Someone will have seen his number.'

Henrietta said dully, 'The number doesn't really matter to my mother or me now.'

'No, miss.' It seemed for a moment as if he was going to explain that it mattered to the police but instead he said carefully, 'Constable Hepple found her handbag – afterwards – and there was a letter from you inside it.'

'I always wrote on Sundays.'

'Yes, miss. People do that are away. Sunday's the day for that sort of thing . . .'

'I wish I'd had time to say something before . . .'

The Sergeant offered what comfort he could. 'There's not a lot really needs saying, miss, not when it comes to the point. Families have said everything long ago, or else it's something that doesn't need saying.' He paused. 'What about tonight, miss?'

'I shall be all right.'

'We'll run you home to Larking, of course, but . . .'

'It's something I've got to get used to, isn't it?' she said. 'Being alone from now on.'

2

Police Constable Hepple of Down Martin was a conscientious man. First of all he measured the tyre mark in the grass and drew a plan. Then he borrowed an old sack from Bill Thorpe's tractor and covered the imprint against damage. After that he began a systematic search of the area.

He was rewarded with the discovery of Mrs Jenkins's handbag, knocked out of her hand and flung into the long grass by the roadside. He took charge of this and continued his search but found nothing else. The letter inside from Henrietta having given her address he telephoned this and his report to his headquarters at Berebury, leaving to them the business of finding her and telling her the bad news.

He himself went back to the scene of the accident and took a plaster cast of the tyre mark. He then proceeded – as he would have said himself – to Boundary Cottage. He checked that it was safely locked – it was – and then went on to visit the other five cottages. Three of these were in a short row and two others and Boundary Cottage were detached, standing in their own not inconsiderable gardens.

There was no reply from Mulberry Cottage, which was Boundary Cottage's nearest neighbour – some people called Carter lived there – but all the occupants of the others and of the two other farms besides the Thorpes said the same thing. They had had no visitors the previous evening. They had heard and seen nothing.

Hepple went home and wrote out a second, slightly fuller report, and spent part of his afternoon in Larking village trying to establish who had been the last person to see Mrs Jenkins alive.

It was because of his careful checking-over of Boundary Cottage that he was so surprised to have a telephone call from Henrietta the next morning.

'Someone's been in the house,' she said flatly.

'Have they, miss? What makes you think that?'

'In the front room . . .'

'Yes?' He had his notebook ready.

'There's a bureau. You know the sort of thing – you can write at it but it's not exactly a desk . . .'

'I know.'

'It's been broken into. Someone's prised the flap part open – they've damaged the wood.'

'When did you discover this, miss?'

Henrietta looked at her watch. It was just after ten o'clock in the morning. 'About ten minutes ago. I came straight out to ring you.'

'This damage, miss, you'd say it was someone trying to get inside without a key?'

'That's right.'

He hesitated. 'It couldn't have been your mother, miss? I mean, if she had lost her own key and needed to get in there quickly for something . . .'

'She'd never have spoilt it like this,' retorted Henrietta quickly. 'Besides she wasn't the sort of person who lost keys.'

'Yes.' Hepple knew what she meant. His own impression of Mrs Jenkins was of a neat quiet lady. Law abiding to a degree.

'Moreover,' went on Henrietta, 'if she had had to do something like that I'm sure she'd have told me in her letter.'

PC Hepple came back to the question of time.

'When?' repeated Henrietta vaguely. 'I don't know when.'

'Yesterday, miss. You came back yesterday.'

'That's right. They brought me home from Berebury in a police car afterwards . . .'

'About what time would that have been, miss?'

But time hadn't meant anything to Henrietta yesterday.

'It was dark. I don't know when exactly.'

'Was the bureau damaged then?' persisted Hepple.

'I don't know. I didn't go into the front room at all last night. I've just been in there now . . .'

'The cottage was all locked up just gone twelve o'clock yesterday morning,' said Hepple, 'because I went along myself then to check. There were no signs of breaking and entering then, miss.'

'There aren't any now,' said Henrietta tersely. 'Just the bureau. That's the only thing that's wrong.'

With which, when he got there, PC Hepple was forced to agree.

'Windows and doors all all right,' he said. 'Unless they had a key, no one came in after I checked up yesterday morning.'

They went back to the front room and considered the bureau again. Henrietta pointed to a deep score in the old wood.

'My mother never did that. She'd have sent for a locksmith first.'

'Yes.' Now he could see the bureau, that was patently true. No one who owned a nice walnut piece like this would ever spoil it in that way just to get inside. 'What did she keep in there, miss, do you know?'

'All her papers,' said Henrietta promptly. 'Receipts, wireless licence – that sort of thing . . .'

'Money?'

'No, never. She didn't believe in keeping it in the house – especially a rather isolated one like this.'

'Jewellery?'

Henrietta shook her head. 'She didn't go in for that either – she never wore anything that you could call jewellery. My father's medals, though. They were in there.'

Henrietta's gaze travelled from the bureau to the mantelpiece and a silver framed photograph of an Army sergeant – and back to the bureau. 'They're in a little drawer at the side. I'll show you them if you like . . .'

'No,' said Hepple quickly. 'Don't touch it, miss.'

She dropped her hands to her sides.

'Fingerprints,' said Hepple. 'It may not be worthwhile but you can't be sure until you've tried.'

'I hadn't thought of that . . .' Her voice trailed away.

'Now, miss, about last night.' Constable Hepple was nothing if not persistent.

'They brought me home in a police car, sometime in the early evening I think it was. I didn't hear . . . about Mother until nearly lunch time and it took me a while to get back to Berebury. Then I was there for quite a bit . . .'

'Yes, miss.'

'They didn't want to leave me here alone the first night but I promised I'd go across to Mrs Carter if I wanted anything.'

'But,' argued Hepple gently, 'the Carters are away. I called there this morning.'

'That's right. Only I didn't know that until I banged on her door and didn't get an answer. So I came back here.'

'Alone?'

'Yes.'

'You're sure you didn't come into this room?'

'Not until this morning.'

'You heard nothing in the night?'

'I didn't hear anyone levering the bureau open if that's what you mean. And I'm sure I would have done.'

They both regarded the splintered lock.

'Yes,' said Hepple, 'you would.'

'Besides which,' said Henrietta, heavy eyed, 'I can't say that I slept much last night anyway.'

'No, miss,' the policeman was sympathetic, 'I don't suppose you did.'

'And this couldn't have been done quietly.'

'So,' said Hepple practically, 'that means that this was done before you got back yesterday evening, which was Wednesday, and after your mother left home for the last time – which was presumably some time on Tuesday.'

'That's right,' agreed Henrietta. 'If she'd had to do it, she'd have told me in a letter – and if she'd found it done I'm sure she would have told the police.'

*

'Can't understand it at all, sir.' Police Constable Hepple rang his headquarters at Berebury Police Station as soon as he left Boundary Cottage. He was put on to the Criminal Investigation Department. 'Mind you, we don't know what's gone from the bureau – if anything. The young lady isn't familiar with its contents. Her mother always kept it locked.'

'Did she indeed?' said Detective Inspector Sloan.

'And there's no sign of forced entry anywhere.'

'Except the bureau.'

'That's right, sir.' Hepple paused significantly. 'I shouldn't have said myself it was the sort of place worth a burglary.'

'Really?' Sloan always listened to opinions of this sort.

'It's just one of Mr Hibbs's old cottages. Mind you, they keep it very nice. Always have done.'

'Who do?'

'Mrs Jenkins and Henrietta – that's the daughter. Of course, coming on top of the accident like this I thought I'd better report it special.'

'Quite right, Constable.'

'Seems a funny thing to happen.'

'It is,' said Sloan briefly. 'How far have they got with the accident?'

'Usual procedure with a fatal, sir. Traffic Division have asked all their cars to keep a lookout for a damaged vehicle, and all garages to report anything coming in for accident repair. I've got a decent cast of a nearside front tyre . . .'

'Size?'

'590 × 14.'

'Big,' said Sloan, just as Bill Thorpe had done.

'Yes, sir. They're asking for witnesses but they can't be sure of their timing until after the post-mortem. The local doctor put the time of death between six and nine o'clock on Tuesday evening, but I understand the pathologist is doing a post-mortem this morning.'

'We'll know a bit more after that,' agreed Sloan.

Wherein he was speaking more truthfully than he realized.

'Yes, sir,' said Hepple. 'They'll be able to fix an inquest date after that. I've warned the girl about it. But as to this other matter, sir . . .'

'The bureau?'

'It doesn't make sense to me. That house was all locked up when I went round it at twelve yesterday. I could swear no one broke in before then.'

Sloan twiddled a pencil. 'She could have gone out on Tuesday and forgotten to shut the door properly.'

'Ye-es,' said Hepple uneasily, 'but I don't think so. Careful sort of woman, I'd have said. Very.'

'When did she go out on Tuesday? Do we know that? And where had she been?'

'We don't know where she'd been, sir. No one seems to know that. Her daughter certainly doesn't. As to when, she caught the first bus into Berebury and came back on the last.'

'Not much help. She could have gone anywhere.'

'Yes, sir. And it meant the house was empty all day.'

'And all night.'

'All night?'

'She was lying in the road all night.'

'So she was,' said Hepple. 'I was forgetting. In fact, you could say the house was empty from first thing Tuesday morning until they brought the daughter from Berebury on Wednesday evening.'

'I wonder what was in the bureau?'

'I couldn't say, sir. She didn't keep money in there, nor jewellery. Nothing like that. Just papers, her daughter said.'

Detective Constable Crosby was young and brash and consciously represented the new element in the police force. The younger generation. He didn't usually volunteer to do anything. Which was why when Detective Inspector Sloan heard him offering to take a set of papers back to Traffic Division he sat up and took notice.

'Nothing to do with us, sir,' the constable said virtuously. 'Road traffic accident. Come to the CID by mistake, I reckon.'

'Then,' said Sloan pleasantly, 'you can reckon again.'

Crosby stared at the report. 'Woman, name of Grace Jenkins, run down by a car on a bad bend far end of Larking village.'

'That's right.'

'But Larking's miles away.'

'In the country,' agreed Sloan. 'Let's hope the natives are friendly.'

Sarcasm was wasted on Crosby. He continued reading aloud. 'Found by H. Ford, postman, believed to have been dead between ten and twelve hours, injuries consistent with vehicular impact?'

'That's the case. Read on. Especially PC Hepple's report of this morning.'

'Bureau in deceased's front room broken open. No signs of forced entry to the house.' Crosby sounded disappointed. 'That's not even breaking and entering, sir.'

'True.'

'I still don't see,' objected Crosby, 'what it's got to do with her being knocked down and killed.'

'Frankly, Crosby, neither do I.' Sloan put out his hand for the file. 'In fact there may be no connection whatsoever. In which case some of your valuable time will have been wasted.'

'Yes, sir.' Woodenly.

'That is,' he added gravely, 'a risk we shall have to take.'

Detective Inspector Sloan read the accident report again and thanked his lucky stars – not for the first time – that he didn't work in Traffic Division.

'Of all the nasty messes,' he mused aloud, 'I think a hit-and-run driver leaves the worst behind. No medical attention. No ambulance. No insurance.'

'And no prosecution,' said Crosby mordantly. He pointed to the report. 'Perhaps this character who hit her was drunk.'

'Perhaps.' Sloan got up from his desk. 'Though it was a bit early in the evening for that.'

'Perhaps *she* was drunk then,' suggested Crosby, undaunted.

Sloan shook his head. 'Hepple didn't suggest she was that sort of woman – quite the reverse in fact . . . A car, please, Crosby, and we shall venture into the outback at once.'

They didn't go quite straight away because the telephone on Sloan's desk started to ring.

'Berebury Hospital,' said a girl's voice. 'Can Inspector Sloan take a call from the Pathologist's Department, please?'

Crosby handed the receiver over to Sloan, who said, 'Speaking.'

'Dabbe here,' boomed a voice.

'Good morning, doctor,' said Sloan cautiously.

'I've been trying to talk to your Traffic Division about a woman I'm doing a PM on.'

'Yes?'

'They say she's your case now and you've got all the papers . . .'

'In a way,' agreed Sloan guardedly. He'd sort that out with Traffic afterwards.

'I've got her down,' said the pathologist, 'as Grace Edith Jenkins.'

'That's right. We're treating it as an RTA, doctor.'

'Road traffic accident she may be,' said the pathologist equably. 'I'll tell you about that later. That's not what I'm ringing about. The notes that came in with her say she was identified by her daughter.'

'That's right.'

'No, it isn't.'

Sloan picked up the file. 'Miss Henrietta Eleanor Leslie Jenkins said it was her mother.'

'Any doubt about the identification?'

'None that I've heard about, doctor.'

The pathologist grunted. 'She wasn't disfigured at all – there were no facial injuries to speak of.'

'No? Is it important, sir?'

'Either, Inspector, this girl . . .'

'Miss Jenkins.'

'Miss Jenkins has identified the wrong woman . . .'

'I don't think so,' objected Sloan, glancing swiftly through the notes in the file. 'The village postman and a neighbouring farmer's son called Thorpe put us on to her – to say nothing of Constable Hepple. They all said it was Mrs Jenkins well before we got hold of the daughter.'

'That's just it,' said the pathologist.

'What is, sir?'

'She wasn't the daughter.'

'But . . .'

'This woman you've sent me may be Mrs Grace Edith Jenkins,' said Dabbe.

'She is.'

'I don't know about that,' went on the pathologist, 'but I can tell you one thing for certain and that's that she's never ever had any children.'

'Her daughter, doctor, said . . .'

'Not her daughter . . .'

Sloan paused and said carefully, 'Someone who told us she was Miss Henrietta Eleanor Leslie Jenkins then . . .'

'Ah,' said Dabbe, 'that's different.'

'She said she was prepared to swear in a Coroner's Court that this was the body of her mother, Mrs Grace Edith Jenkins, widow of Sergeant Cyril Jenkins of the East Calleshires.'

The pathologist sounded quite unimpressed.

'Very possibly,' he said. 'That's not really my concern, but . . .'

'Yes?'

'You might take a note, Inspector, to the effect that I shall have to go to the same Coroner's Court and swear that, in my opinion, she – whoever she is – had certainly never had any children and had very probably never been married either.'

3

'Have you turned over two pages or something, Sloan?'

The Superintendent of Police in Berebury glared across his desk at the Head of his Criminal Investigation Department. It was a very small department, all matters of great moment being referred to the Calleshire County Constabulary Headquarters in Calleford.

'No, sir. The girl positively identified the woman as her mother and Dr Dabbe, the pathologist, says the woman had never had any children.'

'How does he know?' Truculently.

'I couldn't begin to say, sir,' said Sloan faintly. The Superintendent's first reaction was always the true English one of challenging the expert. 'But he was quite definite about it.'

'He always is.'

'Yes, sir.' Sloan coughed. 'There are really three matters . . .'

Superintendent Leeyes grunted discouragingly.

'First of all a woman is knocked down and killed on Tuesday evening not far from her home.' Sloan stopped and amended this. 'Not far from what we believe is her home. At some stage before or after this but before Wednesday evening someone lets himself into her house with a key but doesn't have a key to the bureau so breaks it open . . .'

'Why?'

'We don't know yet, sir. Thirdly . . .'

'Well?'

'The woman isn't the mother of the girl who identified her as her mother.'

'It's not difficult,' said Leeyes loftily. 'She's probably the father's bastard.'

Sloan ignored this and said conversationally, 'Mrs Jenkins seems to have been a very unusual woman, sir.'

'You can say that again,' said the Superintendent. 'I've never heard of unnatural childbirth before.'

'She managed' – Sloan was still struggling to keep the tone at an academic level – 'she managed to keep her private affairs private in a small village like Larking.'

'I'll admit that takes some doing. Did she have a record, then?'

'I don't know, sir, yet, but that's not quite the same thing as a secret.'

'No? Perhaps, Sloan, I've been in the Force too long . . .'

'I think this secret must have been of a matrimonial nature.'

The Superintendent brightened at once. 'Then perhaps it was Mr Jenkins who had the record.'

'I'll check on that naturally, sir, but there is another possibility.'

'There are lots of possibilities.'

'Yes, sir.'

'Not all of them to do with us.'

'No, sir. This could well be just a family matter.'

'Most of our cases,' the Superintendent reminded him tartly, doing one of his famous smart verbal about-turns, 'are family matters.'

'Yes, sir.' He paused. 'Constable Hepple doesn't know anything about them not being mother and daughter and he's been living out that way for donkey's years.'

'A good man, Hepple,' conceded Leeyes. 'Knows all the gossip. If there's much crime in the south of Calleshire he never tells us.'

This might not have been Her Majesty's Inspector of Constabulary's view of what constituted a good policeman but the Superintendent was not a man who looked for work.

'What are you going to do about it?' he asked Sloan.

'See the girl for a start – and the bureau.'

'She could be lying.' Leeyes tapped Traffic Division's file. 'According to Dr Dabbe she is.'

'Her mother could have lied to her . . .'

'A by-blow of the father's,' repeated the Superintendent firmly, 'for sure, brought up as her own. Some women will swallow anything.'

'Perhaps,' said Sloan cautiously. 'But just suppose she isn't Grace Edith Jenkins?'

Superintendent Leeyes looked quite attentive at last. 'I don't believe we've had a case of personation in the county for all of twenty years.'

Young Thorpe had called at Boundary Cottage to see if Henrietta needed anything, and to say how sorry he was.

'It is nice of you, Bill,' she said sincerely, 'but I'm quite all right.'

He stood awkwardly in the doorway, almost filling it with his square shoulders. He wasn't all that young either but being Mr Thorpe of Shire Oak Farm's son he was destined to be known as young Thorpe for many years yet.

'I liked your mother, you know,' he said, 'in spite of everything.'

'I know you did, Bill,' Henrietta said quickly.

'She was probably right to make us wait. First I was away at the agricultural college and then with her being so keen on your going away too.'

Henrietta nodded. 'She really minded about that, didn't she?'

'Some people just feel that way about education,' said Bill Thorpe seriously. 'My father's the same. He couldn't go to college himself but he made me. He's right, I suppose. You learn – well, it's not exactly how much you learn but the reasons behind things.'

'And it wasn't very long, was it?'

He smiled wanly. 'It seemed a long time.'

'You never wrote.'

'Neither did you,' returned Bill.

'We promised not to. I thought it might make things easier.'

'Did it?'

Henrietta shook her head. 'No.'

'Nor for me.' He looked at her for a minute, then, 'Mother said to come to the farm to sleep if you wanted.'

'Will you say thank you? There's nothing I'd like more but,' she grimaced, 'I think if I once didn't stay here on my own I'd never get back to doing it again. She'll understand, I know.'

Thorpe nodded. 'We're a bit out of the way, too, at the farm. There'll be a lot to be done here I expect.'

'It's not that but' – she pushed her hair back vaguely – 'there seem to be people coming all the time. The Rector's coming down to talk to me about the funeral and Mr Hepple said he'd be back again about the inquest.' She gave a shaky half-laugh. 'I'd no idea dying was such a – well – complicated business.'

'No,' agreed Thorpe soberly. He allowed a decent interval to elapse before he said, 'Any news of the car?'

'What car – oh, that car? No, Bill, they haven't said anything to me about it yet.'

Henrietta thought that Inspector Sloan and Constable Crosby had come from the Berebury CID solely to examine her mother's bureau for fingerprints.

'It's in the front room,' she said, leading the way. 'I haven't touched it.'

Sloan obligingly directed Crosby to perform this routine procedure while he talked to Henrietta.

'Nothing missing from the rest of the house, miss?'

'Not that I know of, Inspector. It all looks all right to me.' She paused. 'It's such an odd thing to happen, isn't it?'

'Yes,' said Sloan simply.

'I mean, why should someone want to break in here . . .'

'Not break in, miss. PC Hepple said all the doors and windows were intact. He found the place quite well locked up really. Whoever got in here came in by the door. The front door.'

('The back one's bolted as well as the Tower of London,' was what Hepple had said.)

'The front door,' he repeated.

'That's worse,' said Henrietta.

'Your mother, miss, would she have left a key with anyone?'

'No.' Henrietta considered this. 'I'm sure she wouldn't. Besides there were only two keys. There was one in her handbag and one hanging on a hook in the kitchen. That's the one I use when I'm at home.'

'I see.'

Henrietta shivered suddenly. 'I don't like to think of someone coming in here . . .'

'No, miss.'

'. . . with a key.'

Sloan wasn't exactly enamoured of the idea either. It left the girl in the state the insurance companies called being 'at risk'.

'Now, miss, I think we can open the bureau.'

Crosby had finished his dusting operations. He stood back and said briefly, 'Gloves.'

Sloan was not surprised.

'Was it usually kept locked?' he asked Henrietta.

'Always.'

'Are you familiar with its contents?'

'Not really. My mother kept her papers there. I couldn't say if they are all there or not.'

Sloan eased back the flap. Everything was neatly pigeonholed. Either no one had been through the bureau or they had done it conscious that they would be undisturbed. Sloan pulled out the first bundle of papers.

'Housekeeping accounts,' he said, glancing rapidly through them. Grace Jenkins and her alleged daughter had lived modestly enough.

'That's right,' said Henrietta. 'You'll find her cheque book there too.'

Sloan took a quick look at the bank's name for future reference. It was at a Berebury branch. He put the tidily docketed receipts back and took out the next bundle. It brought an immediate flush to Henrietta's cheeks.

'I'd no idea she kept those.'

Sloan looked down at a schoolgirl's writing.

'My letters to her,' she said in a choked voice, 'and my school reports.'

If this was acting, thought Sloan, it was good acting.

'Mothers do.' He chose his words carefully. 'Part of the treasury of parenthood, you might say. By the way, where did you go to school?'

'Here in the village first, then Berebury High.'

Sloan put the infant Henrietta's literary efforts back in their place and took out the next bundle.

'These seem to be about the cottage.' He turned over a number of letters. 'Fire insurance, rating assessment and so forth.'

Sloan put them back but not before noting that all were quite definitely in the name of Mrs G. E. Jenkins.

'Boundary Cottage,' he said. 'Did it belong to your mo– to Mrs Jenkins?'

'No.' Henrietta shook her head. 'To Mr Hibbs at The Hall. It's the last of the cottages on his estate. That's why it's called Boundary Cottage.'

'Can you think of any reason why anyone would want to break in here?'

She shook her head again. 'I don't think she kept anything valuable there. That's why I can't understand anyone wanting to go through it. There wasn't anything to steal . . .'

'It doesn't look,' he said cautiously, 'as if, in fact, anything has been stolen.'

She reached over and pointed out a little drawer. 'If you would just look inside that, Inspector . . . thank you. Ah, they're all right. My father's medals.'

It was the opening Sloan was looking for.

'I'll need a note of his full name, miss, for the inquest.'

'Sergeant Cyril Edgar Jenkins.'

'And your mother's maiden name?'

'Wright,' said Henrietta unhesitatingly.

'Thank you. That's his photograph, I take it?'

'It is.' Henrietta handed it down from the mantelpiece and gave it to Sloan. 'He was in the East Calleshires.'

'That's unusual, isn't it, miss? I mean, they're mostly West Calleshires in these parts.'

'He came from East Calleshire,' she said.

'I see.' Sloan studied the picture of a fair-haired man in soldier's uniform and glanced back at Henrietta's darker colouring.

'I was more like my mother to look at,' she said, correctly interpreting his glance. 'The same colour hair . . .'

But Mrs Jenkins was not her mother. Dr Dabbe had said so.

'Really, miss?' said Sloan aloud. 'Now, you wouldn't have a photograph of her by any chance?'

'In my bedroom. I'll fetch it.'

'A pretty kettle of fish,' observed Sloan morbidly to Crosby the minute she was out of earshot.

'Someone's been through that bureau with a toothcomb, sir,' said Crosby. 'Glove prints everywhere.'

'Wonder what they wanted?'

'Search me.' Crosby ran his fingers in behind pigeonholes, pressing here and pulling there. 'Nothing to suggest a secret drawer.'

'That's something to be thankful for, anyway . . . Ah, there you are, miss, thank you.'

Henrietta handed him a snapshot in a leather frame – quite a different matter from the studio portrait that had stood on the mantelpiece.

'It's not a very good one but it's the only one I've got.'

Sloan held the snap in front of him. It was of an ordinary middle-aged woman, taken standing outside the back door of the cottage. She had on a simple cotton frock and had obviously been prevailed upon to come out of the kitchen to be photographed. She was smiling in a protesting sort of way at the camera.

'I was lucky to have one of her to show you,' said Henrietta. The sight of the picture had brought a quaver into her voice which she strove to conceal from the two policemen. 'She didn't like having her photograph taken.'

'Didn't she indeed?'

'But I had a college friend to stay for a few days the summer before last and she had a camera with her.'

'Do you mean to say, miss, that this is the only photograph of your mother extant?'

She frowned. 'I think so. Angela – that was her name – sent it to us when she got home.'

Inspector Sloan stood the two photographs side by side, the formal silver-framed studio study and the quick amateur snapshot.

'On my left, a sergeant in the East Calleshire Regiment called Cyril Edgar Jenkins . . .'

'My father,' said Henrietta.

'Aged about – what would you say?'

'He was thirty-one,' supplied Henrietta. 'Is it important?'

'And on my right a middle-aged woman called Grace Edith Jenkins . . .'

'My mother,' said Henrietta.

There was a short silence. Henrietta looked first at one policeman and then at the other.

Sloan avoided her clear gaze and said, 'Can you remember anything before Larking?'

'No, I can't.' She looked at him curiously but she answered his question. 'I've lived here ever since I can remember. In Boundary Cottage. With my mother.'

'And you don't remember your father at all?'

'No. He was killed soon after I was born.'

'What do you know about him?'

'Him?'

'Yes, miss. I'll explain in a minute.'

She hesitated. She had an image of her father in her mind, always had had and it was compounded of many things: the words of her mother, the photograph in the drawing-room, the conception of any soldier, of all soldiers, killed in battle – but it wasn't something easily put into words.

'He wasn't afraid,' she said awkwardly.

'I realize that.' They didn't award medals for cowardice. 'But what do you know about him as a person? What was his occupation, for instance?'

'He worked on a farm.'

'Did he own it?' Property owners as a class of person were easy to trace, popular with the police.

'I don't think so. He was the farm bailiff for someone.' She frowned. 'His father had a small farm, though. It wasn't really big enough for my father to work as well – that's why he worked for someone else.'

'Whereabouts?'

'Somewhere on the other side of Calleshire. I'm not sure exactly where.'

'So that is where your mother came from to Larking?'

'From that direction somewhere, I suppose. I don't know exactly. She said he – my father, that is – had moved about a bit getting experience. He would have had to run his father's farm one day on his own and he needed to learn.'

'I see.' He gave her a quick grin. 'So on Saturday nights, miss, you – er – support the East Callies?'

She responded with a faint smile. The regimental rivalry between the East and West Calleshires was famous. 'They get on very well without my help. The West Callies have lost their mascot twice already this year.'

'Have they, indeed? Vulnerable things, mascots. Now this farm of your – er – grandfather's – do you know where that was?'

'It was called Holly Tree Farm, I know,' said Henrietta promptly, 'because I remember my mother telling me there was a very old holly tree there that my grandfather wouldn't have cut down even though it was just in front of the house and made the rooms very dark. He used to say you can't have a Holly Tree Farm without a holly tree.'

'A very proper attitude,' agreed Sloan stoutly. 'Did you ever go there?'

'Not that I can remember. I think he died when I was quite young.'

'But your mother used to talk about the farm?'

'Oh, yes, a lot. She grew up near there too.'

'And so she had known your father all her life?'

Henrietta nodded. 'Certainly since they were children. She used to tell me a lot about him when he was a little boy. But, Inspector, I don't see what this has got to do with my mother's death.'

'No, miss, I don't suppose you do.' Sloan paused judiciously. 'It's not easy to say this, miss, and if it weren't a matter of you having to give formal evidence of identification at the inquest it might not even be something we need to take cognizance of.'

'What might not be?' Henrietta looked quite mystified.

'This Cyril Jenkins . . .'

'My father?'

'Had he been married twice by any chance?'

'Not that I know of. Why?'

'Or Grace Jenkins? Had she been married to anyone else besides Cyril Jenkins?'

A slow flush mounted Henrietta's cheeks. 'No, Inspector, not to my knowledge.'

Like a cat picking its way over a wet path Sloan said delicately, 'There is a possibility that your name may not be Jenkins.'

'Not Jenkins?'

'Not Jenkins.'

'I may be being very stupid,' said Henrietta, 'but I don't see why not.'

'It was Dr Dabbe.'

'Dr Dabbe?'

'The pathologist, miss, from the hospital. He conducted a post-mortem examination on the body of the woman who was knocked down.'

'That's right.' She nodded. 'My mother.'

'No, miss.'

Henrietta sat down suddenly. 'I came into the police station on Wednesday – yesterday, that was – when I got back. They asked me to look at her. I signed something. There was a sergeant there – he'll tell you.' She screwed up her face at the recollection. 'There wasn't any doubt. I wish there had been. It was her. Her face, her clothes, her handbag. I've never seen anyone dead before but I was absolutely certain . . .'

Sloan put up a hand to stem the memory. 'It's not quite that, miss . . .' He couldn't tell if she knew nothing at all or if she knew a great deal more than he did. It was impossible to know.

She pushed a strand of hair away from her face and said very quietly, 'Well, what exactly is it, then?'

'This woman who you identified yesterday as Mrs Grace Edith Jenkins . . .'

'Yes?'

Sloan didn't hurry to go on. He felt oddly embarrassed. This wasn't the sort of subject you discussed with young girls. He didn't often wish work on to the women members of the Force but perhaps this might have been one of the times when . . .

'I'm sorry to have to tell you, miss, that the pathologist says she's never had any children.'

A blush flamed up Henrietta's pale face. She tried to speak but for a moment no sound came. Then she managed a shaky little laugh. 'I'm afraid there must have been some terrible mistake, Inspector . . .'

Sloan shook his head.

'A mix-up at the hospital, perhaps,' she went on, heedless of his denial. 'It happens with babies sometimes, doesn't it? Perhaps it's the same sometimes in – in other places . . .'

'No, miss . . .'

She took a deep breath. 'That was my mother I saw yesterday. Beyond any doubt.'

The doubt in Sloan's mind, because he was a policeman paid to doubt, was whether the girl was party to this knowledge about Grace Jenkins. He didn't let it alter his behaviour.

'I fear,' gently, 'that the pathologist is equally adamant that the subject of his examination had never borne children.'

He saw the blush on the face of the girl in front of him fade away to nothing as she suddenly went very very pale.

'But . . .' Henrietta's world seemed suddenly to have no fixed points at all. She struggled to think and to speak logically. 'But who am I, then?'

4

'Where do we go from here, sir?'

'That you may well ask, Crosby.' Sloan was irritable and preoccupied as they walked away from Boundary Cottage. 'All we've got so far is a girl who isn't who she thinks she is, the body of a woman who probably wasn't what she said she was and two photographs.'

'Yes, sir.' Crosby closed the gate behind them.

'Added to which we're leaving an unprotected girl, who has just been subjected to a great emotional shock, alone in a relatively isolated house to which we strongly suspect someone has already gained admittance with a key.'

'She could go to friends. There must be someone near who would have her.'

'I don't doubt that, but it would be most unwise of her to go to them.'

'Unwise, sir?'

'Unwise, Crosby. If we advise it and she goes she might have difficulty in regaining possession of her mother's – of Mrs Jenkins's – belongings.'

'I hadn't thought about that, sir.' There was a distinct pause while Crosby did think about it, then, 'From whom, sir?'

'I don't know.'

'I see, sir.' He didn't, in fact, see anything at all but thought it prudent not to say so.

'Have you thought that after this she may well not be in a position to prove her title to the cottage tenancy?'

'No, sir.' Crosby digested this in silence. Then, 'A sort of Tichborne Claimant in reverse, you might say, sir.'

'That's it,' agreed Sloan. Crosby, who was ambitious for promotion, had recently taken to looking up old cases. He stood for a moment beside the police car and then said, 'A landlord usually knows a tenant as well as anyone after a while. Drive to The Hall, Crosby.'

It lay between the village and Boundary Cottage, to the south of the church. Whereas the Rectory was Georgian, The Hall was older. It was quite small but perfectly proportioned.

'That's it,' observed Sloan with satisfaction. 'They had a bit about it in one of those magazines last year. My wife showed it to me. Late Tudor.'

'Make a nice rest home for tired constables,' said Crosby.

James Hibbs saw them in his study. He was a well-built man in well-built tweeds. His hair was black running to grey and Sloan put his age at about fifty-five. As they went in two aristocratic gun dogs looked the two policemen over, decided they were not fair game and settled back disdainfully on the hearth.

'Shocking business,' agreed Hibbs. 'Don't like to think of something like that happening on your own doorstep, do you?'

'No, sir.'

'Any news of the fellow who did it?'

'Not yet, sir.'

'All in good time, I suppose.' He sighed. 'A good woman. Brought that girl up very well considering.'

'Considering what, sir?'

Hibbs waved a hand. 'That she'd had to do it on her own. No father, you know. Just her pension.'

'Had you known her long?'

'Couldn't say I really knew her at all. She wasn't that sort of a woman. But she'd been here quite a while.' He looked curiously at Sloan. 'She came to Larking in the war. Couldn't tell you exactly when. Is it important?'

'No, sir. What we're trying to trace are some other relatives besides the girl.'

'Oh, I see. Yes, I suppose she's still under age. Must be, of course, now I come to think of it.'

'Why?'

'The Thorpe boy wanted to marry Henrietta and Mrs Jenkins said no.'

'Really, sir? On what grounds?'

'Age. The girl wasn't twenty-one at the time and still at university. Another year to go, then.'

Sloan's gaze travelled upwards over the fireplace. An old oar, smoke darkened, rested above it. A long time ago James Hibbs had rowed for his college.

'Nice lad,' remarked Hibbs inconsequentially. 'Can't think why she opposed it.'

'To go back a bit further, sir . . .'

'Yes?'

'When she came here. Do you know where it was from?'

Hibbs frowned. 'I had an idea it was East Calleshire somewhere but I couldn't be certain. I'd plenty of empty cottages on my hands at the time and old White would have been glad enough to get a tenant of any sort.'

'Old White?'

'My agent at the time. Dead now, of course. He fixed it all up. I was only here intermittently. On leave.'

'I see.'

'Never thought we'd get anyone to live in Boundary Cottage after old Miss Potter died. Too far out.'

'And how did you get Mrs Jenkins?'

Hibbs shrugged his shoulders. 'I couldn't tell you, Inspector, not at this distance of time. White might have advertised it but I doubt it. Sending good money after bad in those days.'

'Not now, sir.'

'Good Lord, no. I could have sold it a dozen times since then if it had been empty. Sort of place people see on a Sunday afternoon drive in summer time and think they'd like to live in.'

'Yes.' Sloan looked reflectively round the study. 'You wouldn't happen to have any records about this tenancy still, would you, sir?'

Hibbs considered this. 'It's worth a look, I suppose. Old White was one of the old school. Neatest man I ever knew. Care to walk across to the Estate Office?'

Hibbs introduced them to the young man who was working there, called Threlkeld.

'Boundary Cottage, Mr Hibbs?' Threlkeld stepped across to a filing cabinet. In the background Sloan could hear the low hum of a milking machine plant. The Hall was being run on very business-like lines. A file was produced. 'What was it you wished to see?'

'The tenancy agreement, please.'

Sloan watched him turn back the contents of the file. On top were details of the Rural District Council's Main Drainage connections, then, under a date for a few years earlier an estimate for repairs to the roof, Schedule 'A' forms galore, more estimates, much smaller ones as they went back through the years. Nothing recorded the falling value of the pound like labour costs.

And rent.

Sloan almost – but not quite – whistled aloud when he saw the figure.

'Not a lot, is it?' said Hibbs ruefully. 'That's the Rent Restriction Act for you.'

Threlkeld went on turning back the pages. Everything was in date order. Suddenly the handwriting changed to an old-fashioned copperplate.

'Old White,' said Hibbs. 'Wrote a beautiful fist.'

Threlkeld paused. 'Here we are, Mr Hibbs. Miss Potter died in December.'

'Pneumonia,' said Hibbs. 'I can remember that much.'

'The new tenant,' went on Threlkeld, 'took possession at the end of May. It was empty in between. You apparently signed an all-repairs lease . . .'

'For my sins,' groaned Hibbs.

'. . . and it was accepted by her solicitors on behalf of their client in this letter, dated May 28th.'

'Oh,' said Sloan.

'It *was* East Calleshire then,' said Hibbs. 'I had an idea it was. Look, they were Calleford solicitors.'

Sloan leaned over and read the address aloud. 'Waind, Arbi-can & Waind, Ox Lane, Calleford.'

Acting on behalf of their client, Mrs G. E. Jenkins, they had advised her to accept Mr Hibbs's offer of Boundary Cottage, Larking, at the rent as stated.

'You don't remember her at all before this date, sir?'

Hibbs shook his head. 'No. She came quite out of the blue. Old White probably thought that was a fair enough rent at the time and better than nothing.'

'He was wrong,' said Threlkeld unwisely. 'No rent at all would have been better.'

Hibbs turned. 'It's easy to be wise after the event, Threlkeld. Besides, in those days one did give some consideration to widows and orphans.'

Hibbs agreed readily enough to Sloan borrowing the letter and they took it back to Berebury with them.

Henrietta waited until Sloan and Crosby had gone.

She made herself stay sitting down in the front room until she heard the police car draw away. Then she slipped on a coat and left the house.

It was fresher outside. There was a March wind blowing and she felt more free than in the confined atmosphere of the house. Boundary Cottage had suddenly become much too small for her – there hardly seemed air enough inside for her to breathe.

She didn't go along the road but through the orchard behind the cottage and then along the old footpath. It brought her out near the church. Across the green from the church was the Rectory.

She went up to the door. It was half open. Somewhere beyond in the wide hall someone was counting aloud.

'Four, five . . .'

She knocked on the door.

'Who is it?' called a woman's voice.

'I'd . . . don't know,' said Henrietta miserably.

'Well, come in whoever it is – oh, it's you, Henrietta. Come in, dear, and just hold that for me, will you, while I finish these. I won't be a minute.' A short, stout woman pushed a pile of freshly laundered surplices into Henrietta's hands. 'Now, where was I?'

'Five.'

'Six, seven, eight – what that Callows boy does with his, I can't think – nine, ten. That's the lot, thank goodness.' She took the bundle back again. 'Edward can take them across with him later. Now, come along in by the fire. You look frozen.'

'I'm not cold. Just a bit shaky, that's all.'

'I'm not surprised,' retorted Mrs Meyton. 'Losing your poor mother like that. A terrible shock. The Rector was coming down to see you this afternoon – didn't you get his message?'

'Yes. Yes, I did.' Henrietta drew in a deep breath. 'Mrs Meyton . . .'

'Yes, dear?'

'I want you to tell me something.'

'What's that?'

'Do you remember my mother and me coming here?'

Mrs Meyton nodded vigorously. 'Yes, dear. It was just before the war ended.'

'Did we come together?'

'Did we come together?' She smiled. 'Of course you did. You were only a very tiny baby, you know. I remember it quite well. Such a sad little family.'

'My father . . .'

Here Mrs Meyton shook her head. 'No, it was just after he was killed. I never met him.'

'But,' urgently, 'you do remember us coming together?'

'Certainly. Boundary Cottage had been empty for a long time – since old Miss Potter died, in fact – and I remember how glad we were that someone was going to live in it after all.' Mrs Meyton raised her eyebrows heavenwards. 'A rare old state it was in, I can tell you, but your mother soon got to work on it and she had it as right as ninepence in next to no time – garden and all.'

'She liked things just so . . .'

Mrs Meyton wasn't listening. 'How the years do go by. It hardly seems the other day but it must be all of twenty years . . .'

'Twenty-one,' said Henrietta. 'I'll be twenty-one next month.'

'I suppose you will.' Mrs Meyton regarded the passing years with disfavour. 'I don't know where the time goes. And the older you get the more quickly it passes.'

'Baptism,' said Henrietta suddenly.

'What about it, dear?'

'Was I christened here in Larking?'

But here Mrs Meyton's parochial memory failed her. She frowned hard. 'Now, I would have to think about that. Is it important? Edward would know. At least,' she added loyally, 'he could look it up in the Register.'

Memory was not one of the Rector's strong points.

'Do you think he would? You see' – she swallowed hard – 'you see, the police have just told me that Grace Jenkins wasn't my mother after all.'

Mrs Meyton looked disbelieving. 'Not your mother?'

'That's what they said.'

'But,' said Mrs Meyton in a perplexed voice, 'if she wasn't, who was?'

'That's what I'd like to know.' There was a catch in her voice as she said, 'I expect I'm illegitimate.'

'Nonsense.' Mrs Meyton shook her head. There were thirty years of being a clergy wife behind her when she said, 'Your mother wasn't the sort of woman to have an illegitimate baby.'

'She hadn't ever had any children,' said Henrietta bleakly, 'and she wasn't my mother, so it doesn't apply.'

'I shouldn't have said myself,' went on Mrs Meyton, 'that she was the sort of woman either to say she'd had a baby if it wasn't hers.'

'Neither would I,' agreed Henrietta promptly. 'That's the funny thing . . .'

'But if she did,' sensibly, 'I expect she had a good reason. They must have adopted you.'

'I hadn't thought of that.'

'A cup of tea,' said Mrs Meyton decisively, 'that's what we both need.'

Ten minutes later Henrietta put her cup down with a clatter. 'I've just thought of something . . .'

'What's that, dear?'

'How do I know I'll be twenty-one in April?'

'Because . . .' Mrs Meyton's voice trailed away. 'Oh, I see what you mean.' Then, 'A birth certificate, dear. You must have a birth certificate. Everyone does.'

'Do they? I've never seen mine.'

'You'll have one somewhere. You'll see. Your mother will have kept it in a safe place for sure.'

'The bureau . . .' cried Henrietta.

'That's right,' said Mrs Meyton comfortably.

'It's not right,' retorted Henrietta. 'Someone broke into the bureau on Tuesday.'

'Oh, dear.'

'And there's certainly no birth certificate in there now . . .'

'A copy,' said Mrs Meyton gamely. 'You can send for one from Somerset House.'

'But don't you see,' cried Henrietta in despair, 'if she wasn't my mother I don't know what name to ask for.'

5

'Crosby . . .'

'Sir?' Crosby had one ear glued to the telephone receiver but he listened to Sloan with the other.

'You tell me why a woman brings up a child as her own when it isn't.'

'Adopted, sir, that's all.'

'Why?'

'Why adopt, sir? I couldn't say, sir. Seems quite unnecessary to me. Asking for trouble.' His early years on the beat had made a child-hater out of Crosby.

'Why adopt when she did,' said Sloan. 'That's what I want to know.'

'When?' echoed Crosby.

'The middle of a war, that's when. With her husband on active service.'

'Do we know that, sir, for sure?'

'We don't know anything for sure,' Sloan reminded him with some acerbity, 'except that Dr Dabbe swears that this Grace Edith Jenkins never had any children.' He paused. 'We know a thing or two that are odd, of course.'

'The bureau?'

'The bureau. Someone broke into that for a reason.'

'They found what they were looking for . . .'

'Yes, I think they did. Something else that's odd, Crosby . . .'

Crosby thought for a moment. 'Odd that they didn't have to break into the house. Just the bureau.'

'Very odd, that.'

'Yes, sir.' Crosby waved his free hand. 'Dr Dabbe is coming on the line from the hospital now, sir.'

Sloan took the receiver.

'This road traffic accident you sent me, Sloan, one Grace Edith Jenkins . . .'

'Yes, doctor?'

'I confirm the time of death. Between six and nine o'clock on Tuesday evening. Nearer nine than six.'

'Thank you.' Sloan started to write.

'She was aged about fifty-five,' continued the pathologist.

'Forty-five, I think it was, doctor.' Sloan turned back the pages of the file. 'Yes. Her daughter said she was forty-five. Forty-six next birthday.'

'And I,' said Dr Dabbe mildly, 'said she was about fifty-five.'

Sloan made his first significant note.

'She had also had her hair dyed fairly recently.'

'Oh?' said Sloan.

'From – er – blonde to brunette.'

'Had she indeed?' The pathologist never missed anything.

'I should say she had been hit from behind by a car which was travelling pretty fast. The main injury was a ruptured aorta and she would have died very quickly from it.'

'Outright?'

'In my opinion, yes.'

That, at least, was something to be thankful for.

'I should say the car wheel went right over her, also rupturing the spleen. There are plenty of surface abrasions . . .'

'I'm not surprised.'

'Both ante-mortem and post-mortem.'

'Post-mortem?'

'There was also a post-mortem fracture of the right femur,' said the pathologist.

Sloan said, 'I'm sorry to hear that.'

'I fear,' said Dr Dabbe, 'that these injuries are consistent with her having been run over by a heavy vehicle twice.'

'Two successive cars?' asked Sloan hopefully.

The pathologist sounded cautious. 'I'd have to see the plan of how she was lying but I'd have said she was definitely hit from behind the first time.'

'That's what the Constable in attendance thought.'

'And from the opposite direction the second time.'

'Nasty.'

'Yes . . .'

Sloan replaced the receiver and looked out of the window. 'A car, Crosby, and quickly. I want to get back to Larking before the light goes. And get on to Hepple and tell him to meet us at the scene of the accident.'

Henrietta was still at the Rectory when the Rector returned.

He was undismayed when his wife told him that Henrietta was not Grace Jenkins's daughter.

'That explains something that always puzzled me,' he said.

Henrietta looked up quickly. 'What was that?'

'Why she came to Larking in the first place. As far as I could discover she had no links here at all. None whatsoever.' Mr Meyton was a spare, grey-haired scholarly man, a keen student of military history and the direct opposite of his tubby, cheerful wife. 'If I remember correctly you both arrived out of the blue so to speak. And no one could call Boundary Cottage the ideal situation for an unprotected woman and child in wartime.'

Henrietta blinked. 'I hadn't thought of that . . .'

'If she was deliberately looking for somewhere lonely . . .'

'Nowhere better,' agreed Henrietta. 'I just thought she liked the country.'

'It occurred to me at the time she had set out to cut herself off,' said Mr Meyton. 'Some people do. A great mistake, of course, and I always advise against it.'

'Now we know why,' said Henrietta.

'Perhaps.'

'She wanted everyone to think I was hers.'

'She probably didn't want you to know you weren't,' said Mr Meyton mildly. 'Which is something quite different.'

'But why on earth not?' demanded Henrietta. 'Lots of children are adopted these days.'

'True.' The Rector hesitated. 'There are other possibilities, of course.'

'I'm just beginning to work them out,' drily.

'She might have had you by a previous marriage . . .'

'No. It wasn't that.'

'Or even – er – outside marriage.'

'Nor that,' said Henrietta tonelessly. 'The police said so. She wasn't anybody's mother – ever.'

'I see. There will be reasons, you know.'

She sighed. 'I could have understood any of those things but this just doesn't make sense.'

'It is an unusual situation.' Mr Meyton gave the impression of choosing his words with care.

'Grace Jenkins brought me up as a daughter,' said Henrietta defiantly, 'whatever anyone says.'

'Quite so.'

'And I swear no one could have been kinder . . .'

'No.' He said tentatively, 'Perhaps – had you thought – most likely of all, I suppose – that you were a child of your father's by a previous marriage.'

Mrs Meyton who had been sitting by, worried and concerned, put in anxiously, 'That would explain everything, dear, wouldn't it?'

'I had wondered about that,' said Henrietta.

The Rector stirred his tea. 'It is a distinct possibility.'

Henrietta stared into the fire. 'That would make me her step-daughter.'

'Yes.' He coughed. 'It might also account for the strange fact that following his death she didn't tell you.'

'She didn't,' said Henrietta vigorously, 'behave like a stepmother.'

'That's a fiction, you know,' retorted the Rector. 'You've been reading too many books.'

Henrietta managed a tremulous smile, and said again, 'Grace Jenkins brought me up as a daughter. I know she loved me . . .'

'Of course she did,' insisted Mrs Meyton.

'Perhaps that's the wrong word,' said Henrietta slowly. 'It was more than that. I always felt' – she looked from one of them to the other struggling to find a word that would convey intangible meaning – 'well, cherished, if you know what I mean.'

'Of course, I do,' said Mrs Meyton briskly. 'And you were. Always.'

'It wasn't only that. She made great sacrifices so that I could go away to university. We had to be very careful, you know, with money.' She pushed her hair back from her face and said, 'She wouldn't have done that for just anybody, would she?'

What could have been a small smile twitched at the corners of the Rector's lips but he said gravely enough, 'I think we can accept that – whoever you are – you aren't – er – just anybody.'

'But am I even Henrietta?'

'Henrietta?'

'Henrietta Eleanor Leslie – those are my Christian names . . .'

'Well?'

'I thought I was my mother's daughter until this morning.'

'You're looking for proof that . . .'

'That at least I'm Henrietta.'

'If you had been baptized here . . .'

'I wasn't, then?'

The Rector shook his head. 'No. Your mother . . .'

'She wasn't my mother.'

'I'm sorry.' He bowed his head. 'I was forgetting. It isn't easy to remember . . .'

'No.' Very ironically.

'Mrs Jenkins told me you were already baptized.'

He did remember then. Aloud Henrietta said, 'That's why the bureau was broken into, then. I can see that now.'

'You think there must have been something there?'

'I do.'

The Rector frowned. 'It does rather look as if steps have been taken to conceal certain – er – facts.'

Henrietta tightened her lips. 'It's not going to be easy, is it?'
'What isn't?'
'Finding out who I am.'

Sloan and Crosby saw Constable Hepple soon after they had
forked left at the post office. He had brought a plan with him.

'You can't see the chalk lines any more, sir,' he said, 'but the
deceased was lying roughly here.'

'I see.'

'Walking home and hit from behind, I'd say,' went on Hepple.
'People never will walk towards oncoming traffic like they
should.'

'No.'

'His front wheel caught that bit of grass verge afterwards,
deflected a bit by the impact, I'd say.'

Sloan nodded.

'I've got a good cast of that,' said Hepple.

Sloan stood in the middle of the bend and looked in both
directions. It was a bad bend but with due care and attention
there was no need to kill a pedestrian on it.

Hepple was still theorizing. 'I reckon he didn't see her at all,
sir. There's not a suspicion of a skid mark on the road. Dare
say he didn't realize what he'd done till afterwards and then
he panicked.'

That was the neat and tidy explanation. And but for Dr Dabbe
it would probably have been the one that went down on the
record. Pathology was like that.

'Where exactly did you say she was lying?' asked Inspector
Sloan.

Constable Hepple stood squarely on the spot where he had
seen the body.

'That,' pronounced Sloan sombrely, 'fits in very well with the
first set of injuries . . .'

'The first, sir?' Hepple looked shocked. 'You mean . . .'

'Run over twice,' said Sloan succinctly.

'Once each way,' amplified Crosby for good measure.

'But . . .' Hepple pointed to the patch of road where he was standing. 'But, sir, someone coming the other way – from Belling St Peter – would have had to come on to quite the wrong side of his road to hit her.'

'Yes.'

'But . . .' said Hepple again.

'I am beginning to think someone did come on to quite the wrong side of his road to hit her,' said Sloan, still sombre. 'The pathologist reports that a second car went over her after she was dead.'

'After she was dead?'

'Broke her femur.'

'A second car?' echoed Hepple wonderingly. 'Two cars ran over Mrs Jenkins on this road . . .'

'Yes.'

'And neither of them stopped?' That was the enormity to PC Hepple. A new crime in an irresponsible society, that's what that was, something they'd have been ashamed to put on the Newgate Calendar.

'Two cars,' said Sloan ominously, 'or the first one on its way back.'

Constable Hepple looked really worried. 'I don't like the sound of this at all, sir.'

'No.' Sloan looked at the village constable. 'I don't think I do either.' He examined the road again. 'Now, tell me this – just supposing that it was the same car that hit her both times . . .'

'Yes, sir?' Clearly Hepple didn't like considering anything of the sort.

'Where would he have been able to turn?'

This was where really detailed local knowledge came into its own.

'If he'd wanted to stay on the metalled road, sir, he'd have had to go quite a way. There's no road junction before Belling and this road is too narrow for a really big car to turn in. But if he'd settled for a gateway or the like . . .'

'Yes?'

'Then Shire Oak Farm is the first one you'd come to beyond

the houses. The Thorpes'. After that there's Peterson's and then Smith's . . .'

Inspector Sloan sent Crosby off to search for tyre prints. 'It's probably too late, but it's worth a look.' Then he asked Constable Hepple to tell him what he knew about the late Mrs Grace Jenkins of Boundary Cottage.

'Known her for a long time, sir, and always very pleasant when we met.' Thinking this might be misconstrued he added hastily, 'Never in the course of duty, mind you, sir. I never had occasion to speak to her in the course of duty. A quiet lady. Kept herself to herself, if you know what I mean.'

Sloan knew and wasn't pleased with the knowledge. Not the easiest sort of person to find out about.

'Tuesday,' he said. 'Did you find out anything about what she'd been doing on Tuesday?'

'She was away from Larking all day,' replied Hepple promptly, 'that's all I know. She went off on the early bus – the one that gets people into Berebury in time for work. And she came back on the last one. Two Larking people got off at the same time. Mrs Perkins and Mrs Callows.'

'Do we – does anyone – know how she spent the day?'

'Not yet, sir. They – Mrs Perkins and Mrs Callows – had been shopping but if Mrs Jenkins had, I don't know what she'd done with her basket because it wasn't here when I searched yesterday morning.'

'I see.'

'Must have been all of eight o'clock when she was killed,' went on Hepple. 'Allowing for the walk from the post office.'

Sloan stroked his chin. 'Eight o'clock fits in with what the pathologist says.'

'Sir.' The conscientious Hepple was still worried about something.

'Yes?'

'This second accident – was it straight after the first?'

'I don't know. Nobody knows.'

'Oh, I see, sir, thank you.'

'We only know,' said Sloan, 'that she was killed outright by the first one, and that after it another car ran over her.'

Hepple had scarcely finished shaking his head over this before Crosby was back.

'Didn't have to go very far, sir.'

'How far?'

'He – whoever he was – turned in the first farm gateway . . .'

'Shire Oak Farm,' said Hepple. 'The Thorpes'.'

'He was fairly big,' went on Constable Crosby. 'He had to have two goes at it to get round.'

'Yes.' That was what Sloan would have expected.

'The offside rear tyre print's nearly gone – had some big stuff through that gate since then I should think . . .'

'Tractors,' supplied Hepple, 'and the milk lorry.'

'But there's a good one of a nearside rear.'

Sloan pointed to the grass verge. 'So we've got a nearside front tyre print there . . .'

'A good clear one,' contributed Hepple professionally.

'And a same sized nearside rear tyre print turning in the Thorpe entrance about – how far away would you say, Crosby?'

'About half a mile.'

Hepple didn't like the sound of that at all. 'So you think he came back this way, sir?'

'I do.'

'He must have seen her the second time,' persisted Hepple. 'The road isn't wide enough for him not to have seen her lying across it the second time even if he didn't the first.'

'I am beginning to think,' said Sloan grimly, 'that he saw her quite well both times.'

'You mean, sir . . .'

'I mean, Hepple, that I think we're dealing with a case of murder by motorcar.'

6

The offices of Waind, Arbican & Waind were still in Ox Lane, Calleford.

Inspector Sloan telephoned from the kiosk outside Larking Post Office. There were, it seemed, now no Mr Wainds left in the firm but Mr Arbican was there, and would certainly see Inspector Sloan if he came to Calleford. Sloan looked at his watch and said they might make it by six o'clock. Cross country it must be all of forty miles from Larking to the county town.

They got there at ten minutes to the hour, running in on the road alongside the Minster as most of the population were making their way home. Crosby wove in and out of the crowded streets until he got to Ox Lane.

The solicitor's office was coming to the end of its working day too. In the outer office a very junior clerk was making up the post book and two other girls were covering over their typewriters. One of them received the two policemen and showed them into Mr Arbican's room. The solicitor got to his feet as they entered. He was in his early fifties, going a little bald on top, and every inch the prosperous country solicitor. The room was pleasantly furnished, if a little on the formal side.

'Good afternoon, gentlemen. Do sit down.' He waved them to two chairs, and said to the girl who had shown them in, 'Don't go yet, Miss Chilvers, will you? I may need you.'

Miss Chilvers looked resigned and returned to the outer office.

Arbican looked expectantly across his desk. It had a red leather top and was in rather sharp contrast to the wooden one at which Sloan worked.

'It's like this, sir,' began Sloan. 'We're in the process of making enquiries about a client of yours . . .'

Arbican raised an eyebrow but said nothing.

'Or it might be more correct,' went on Sloan fairly, 'to say a former client.'

Arbican cleared his throat encouragingly but still did not speak.

'A Mrs Jenkins,' said Sloan.

'Jenkins?' Arbican frowned. 'Jenkins. It's a common enough name, but I don't think I know of a client called Jenkins.'

'Jenkins from Larking,' said Sloan.

'Larking? That's a fair way from here, Inspector. I shouldn't imagine we would have many clients in that direction. You're sure there's no mistake?'

'We are working, sir, on the supposition that she came from East Calleshire before she went to Larking.'

'Ah, yes, I see. Quite possibly. Though I can't say offhand that the name alone means anything to me.' He raised his eyebrows again. 'Should it?'

'We have a letter you wrote.. . .'

Arbican's voice was very dry. 'I write a great many letters.'

'To a Mr James Heber Hibbs of The Hall, Larking.'

Arbican shook his head. 'I'm very sorry, Inspector. Neither name conveys anything.'

'That could be so, sir. It was all a long time ago.'

'You're being quite puzzling, Inspector . . .'

'Yes, sir,' said Sloan stolidly. He took out the letter James Hibbs had given him and handed it across the desk to the solicitor. 'Perhaps you'd care to take a look at it.'

Arbican took the letter and read it through quickly. 'I'm sorry I couldn't remember the name but I must have written hundreds of letters like this. In fact, Inspector, it's neither an uncommon name nor an uncommon letter.'

'I suppose not, sir.'

'It was – er – as you say quite a long time ago, too.'

'Over twenty years.'

'Then you can't really have expected me to remember.' He smiled for the first time. A quick professional smile. 'I was a comparative youngster then, cutting my legal teeth on routine where I couldn't do any harm.'

'But you did write it?'

He scanned the letter again. 'I must have done. These are certainly my initials at the top – F.F.A. Therefore' – he frowned – 'therefore we must have done business with this Mrs G. E. Jenkins.' He looked curiously across at Sloan. 'And so?'

'And so you might have some records, sir,' responded Sloan promptly.

'I very much doubt it at this distance of time. We destroy most records after twelve years except conveyances and wills. However, we can soon see.' He rang for Miss Chilvers whose look of patient resignation had changed with the passage of time to one of plain resentment. 'Miss Chilvers, will you please see if we have any records of a Mrs G. E. Jenkins of . . .' he looked down at the letter, 'Boundary Cottage, Larking.'

Miss Chilvers withdrew but her unforthcoming expression started a new train of thought in Sloan's mind. He waved vaguely towards the outer office. 'Perhaps, sir, whoever actually typed the letter might remember. Not Miss Chilvers naturally . . .'

Arbican looked at the letter again and shook his head.

'No?' said Sloan.

'I'm afraid not. I should say that our Miss Lendry typed this letter. Her initials are there after mine – W.B.L.'

'Couldn't she help?'

'No. She isn't with us any more.'

'Perhaps we could find her,' suggested Sloan. 'Do you know her address?'

'I'm sorry. I was using a euphemism.' He sighed. 'Miss Lendry's dead. About six months ago.' He tapped the letter. 'She wouldn't have been all that young when this was written, but she'd have remembered all right.'

'I see.'

'Been with the firm for years,' said Arbican. 'Knew everything . . .'

'Right-hand woman?' suggested Sloan helpfully.

They could hear Miss Chilvers bumping her way round the filing cabinets in the outer office.

Arbican sighed. 'It's not the same without her.'

Sloan knew what he meant. Miss Chilvers returned with little ceremony to announce that she couldn't find anything about a Mrs G. E. Jenkins at all anywhere.

'Thank you,' said Arbican. He turned to Sloan. 'I'm sorry, Inspector, it doesn't look as if we're to help you with this Mrs Grace Jenkins but if we do come across anything . . .'

Sloan got to his feet. 'Thank you, sir. I'd be much obliged if you'd let me know.'

Arbican handed the letter back. 'Whoever she was, it looks as if she got her settlement all right.'

'Settlement?' said Sloan sharply.

The solicitor pointed to the letter. 'Isn't that what that was?'

'Was it?' countered Sloan.

'I can't remember,' said Arbican cautiously, 'but it reads to me now as if it could have been. We advised her to accept the man's offer – that phrasing sounds like a settlement to me but I may be wrong. It's all a long time ago, now, Inspector, and I certainly can't remember.'

'Murder by motorcar!' exploded Superintendent Leeyes. 'Are you sure, Sloan?'

'No, sir.' Sloan was both tired and hungry. 'Not yet.'

It was nearly eight o'clock in the evening and they had just got back to Berebury Police Station after an hour's driving along the main road from Calleford.

'But Crosby found some tyre prints in a gateway where the car turned and came back, and Dr Dabbe says she was run over twice.'

'Twice?' said the Superintendent, just as Hepple had done.

'Twice. Once alive, once dead.'

'Macabre chap, Dabbe.'

'Yes, sir.' Sloan paused. 'It's not exactly the sort of road where you could miss seeing someone lying in it.'

'So that makes you think that . . .'

'I think,' said Sloan heavily, 'that she was knocked down from behind on that bend on purpose by someone who afterwards turned in the entrance to Shire Oak Farm and who came back and deliberately hit her again.'

Leeyes grunted.

'Only he had a bit of bad luck.'

'It sounds to me,' said the Superintendent sarcastically, 'as if he wasn't the only one who had a bit of bad luck.'

'No, sir.'

'Well, in what way was he unlucky?'

'He happened to kill her outright the first time he went over her which meant the pathologist knew he'd gone over her twice.'

'How?'

'Because the second lot of injuries were post-mortem ones. They don't – bleed,' he added elliptically.

'You wouldn't convince a jury on that alone, Sloan.'

'I shouldn't try,' retorted Sloan spiritedly. 'But it's not alone. Put it together with the breaking into of the bureau and the fact that whoever Grace Jenkins was she wasn't the mother of the girl.'

'Ah, yes. I was forgetting the daughter had been smuggled in in a warming pan.'

'That's about the only explanation that fits at the moment,' agreed Sloan gloomily. 'There's something else, too, sir.'

'What's that?'

'This woman – Grace Jenkins – was having her daughter on about something else. Her age.'

'Her age?'

'Yes, sir. She told the girl she would be forty-six next birthday. Dr Dabbe says she was older than that.'

'He should know, I suppose.'

'Yes, sir.'

'Anything else?'

'She'd had her hair dyed.'

'Who hasn't?' said Leeyes cynically.

'From blonde to brunette.'

'It's usually the other way,' agreed the Superintendent.

'The girl's hair is dark,' said Sloan, 'but the father's is fair – noticeably fair – even in a photograph. Grace Jenkins was fair too – before she had her hair dyed.'

'A pretty puzzle,' Leeyes said unhelpfully.

'Yes, sir. So far we've confirmed that the woman went to Larking when the girl was a small infant and passed her off to everyone as her own.'

'It's been done before.'

'Yes, sir. They rented a small cottage in the grounds of The Hall estate.'

'Buried in the country.'

'Exactly, sir. The rent is very low indeed. Seems almost nominal now but it may have been fair enough at the time. Landlord says he isn't allowed to put it up.'

'He may not have wanted to,' observed Leeyes.

'That thought had occurred to me, sir.'

'That's been done before too,' said the Superintendent emphatically.

'What has, sir?'

'Parking an infant in a corner like that. Where you can keep an eye on it.'

'Without acknowledging anything,' Leeyes grunted. 'What's he like?'

'Hibbs? Dark. But it's not a father we're short of, sir, it's a mother.'

'Someone who couldn't acknowledge it either, I dare say,' said the Superintendent.

'Perhaps. Then who is Grace Jenkins?'

'And why kill her?'

'Aunt?' said Sloan as if he had not spoken. 'Nanny? Or grandmother?'

'Wet nurse, more like,' growled Leeyes.

Sloan told him about the letter and the interview with Arbican.

'He thought the wording read like the outcome of a settlement rather than straightforward renting.'

'There's nothing straightforward about this case,' said the Superintendent irritably. 'Nothing at all.'

'No, sir.'

'We don't even know for a start that the deceased has been correctly identified.'

'We've no evidence either way about that,' said Sloan carefully. 'The only actual evidence we've got that will stand up in a Coroner's Court is that she was childless. We've got none as to who she is.'

'Then,' said the Superintendent irritably, 'you'd better get some, hadn't you, Sloan . . .'

'Yes, sir.'

'. . . And quickly.'

Henrietta refused to stay the night at the Rectory.

'It's very kind of you,' she said awkwardly. 'Mrs Thorpe asked me to go to Shire Oak as well but I don't think I will, all the same. I feel – well – I feel I ought to begin as I mean to go on.'

'You may be right there,' conceded the Rector, though the kindhearted Mrs Meyton was all protestation. 'I'll just walk back with you, though, and see you safely home.'

'Is it?'

'Is it what?'

'Home,' said Henrietta.

He took the question very seriously. 'You know, what you need is a good solicitor.'

'I feel,' she said fervently, 'as if I need more than that. A magician, at least.'

But she was grateful to him for escorting her home and said so.

He came indoors with her and checked that Boundary Cottage was secure for the night.

Henrietta pointed to the photograph on the mantelpiece. 'Now I know why the police were so interested in my father.'

'Yes.'

'I wasn't able to tell them much.'

The Rector nodded slowly. 'Your mother never spoke about him to me.'

'She did to me – but mostly about the sort of person he was. Not,' bitterly, 'concrete facts for policemen.'

'No.'

'And she wasn't my mother.'

'I was forgetting,' he apologized obliquely.

'It's made me realize how little I really know about him too.'

'A sergeant in the East Calleshires,' said Mr Meyton, moving towards the photograph. 'That's definite enough.'

'Yes.'

'And he saw a fair bit of action.'

'Yes.'

'The DCM and the Military Medal, I think,' said the Rector, taking a closer look still. 'Yes, that's right.'

Henrietta opened the bureau drawer. 'They're in here so that's another thing that's definite.'

She pulled open the little drawer inside the bureau and got out the two medal cases. 'Here they are.'

She handed them to the Rector. He flicked them open.

'Henrietta,' he said.

'Yes?'

'These medals . . .'

'Don't tell me,' she said in a voice that was almost harsh, 'that there's something wrong with those too.'

'That chap in the photograph . . .'

'My father.'

'He had the DCM and the Military Medal.'

'I know.'

'These,' the Rector indicated the two in his hand, 'these are the DSO and the MC.'

7

'Who?' asked Sloan into the telephone.

'A Mr Meyton, sir,' said the Station Sergeant. 'The Rector of Larking.'

'Do you know him, Sergeant?'

'Not to say know him exactly,' replied the Sergeant carefully. 'Not him, himself, if you know what I mean. But we know his hat and his gloves and his umbrella – particularly his umbrella. It comes in here practically every time he comes into Berebury. Very clearly marked, though, I will say that for them.'

'Put him through,' said Sloan resignedly.

He listened. Then in a quite different voice, 'Are you sure, sir?'

'Oh, yes, Inspector.' Mr Meyton might forget his hat, gloves and umbrella but not his military history. 'Henrietta showed them to me last night and I took the liberty of taking them home with me for – er – safe keeping.'

'Thank you, sir.'

'And they're quite different. This one was a white enamelled cross pattée with a slightly convexed face. The edge of the cross was gold.'

'And the DCM?'

'Circular and made of silver,' replied the Rector promptly. 'It's connected to a curved scroll clasp, too. The one that was in the bureau has a ring which fits on to a straight clasp.'

'You saw the ribbons on the photograph?' said Sloan, thinking quickly.

'I did indeed. And they're not even similar . . .'

'Oh?'

'The DSO ribbon,' said the Rector, warming to his theme, 'is red with an edging of blue. The DCM one is crimson, dark blue and crimson in equal widths.'

'Yes,' said Sloan thoughtfully, 'there's all the difference in the world, I can see that. What about the other two?'

'The MC and the MM, Inspector? The MC ribbon is white, a sort of purply blue and white in three equal stripes.' The Rector paused. 'I think I'm right in saying the Military Medal has a narrow white centre stripe with narrow red, then I think it's narrow white, and then two edging stripes of rather wider dark blue on each side.'

'Six – no seven stripes,' said Sloan.

'That's right.'

'Not easily confused even on a photograph.'

'No. It's not the different colours then, of course, it's the widths which you can see.'

'And you can't very well confuse three broad stripes with a ribbon with seven small ones on.'

'No,' agreed the Rector. 'Not easily.'

'I see,' said Sloan slowly.

'The other one was a cross, too,' went on the Rector. 'Whereas the Military Medal is round and attached to a curved scroll clasp.'

'Didn't they have any names on?' asked Sloan. 'I thought they sometimes did.'

'Sometimes,' said the Rector. 'The owner's name, rank and date are usually engraved on the reverse of the MC.'

'Usually?' No one could have called Sloan slow.

'Yes, Inspector. Not on this one. I'm no expert, of course, but I should say . . .'

'Yes, sir?'

'I should say that – er – steps have been taken to remove the owner's name from this one.'

'Would you, sir?' Sloan became extremely alert.

'The back is almost smooth – but not quite.'

'I understand, sir. You've been most helpful. There'll be an explanation, of course, but in the mean time perhaps you would be kind enough to keep them under lock and key until I get to you. I dare say,' he added heavily, 'there will be rhyme to it as well as reason. If you know what I mean, sir.'

'Indeed, yes,' affirmed Mr Meyton. 'There are, of course, matters which are properly mysterious to us in the religious sense but – er – finite matters are always . . .'

'No, Inspector,' Henrietta shook her head. 'I can't tell you anything more than that because I don't know anything more.'

'I see, miss. Thank you.' Sloan and Crosby were back in the parlour of Boundary Cottage, sitting where they had been sitting the day before. Then, Henrietta had looked as if she hadn't slept much the previous night.

Now she looked as if she hadn't slept at all.

'The Rector,' she went on wearily, 'just said that they weren't the right medals for the photograph.'

'Yes, miss. He rang me.'

'He took them away.'

'Yes.'

'Inspector . . .'

'Yes, miss?'

'Why weren't they taken on Tuesday?'

'On Tuesday, miss?'

'By whoever broke into the bureau.'

'I couldn't say, miss.'

'They must have seen them. They weren't locked up in their cases or anything.'

'No.' He cleared his throat and said cautiously, 'If they'd gone then, of course, you would have missed them.'

'Naturally.'

'Well, that – their absence – might have served to call your – call our attention to – er – any irregularities in the situation between you and your – er – parents.' Sloan felt himself going a bit hot under the collar. It wasn't a sensation he was accustomed to. 'I don't think it is generally appreciated that the – er – fact of childlessness is – er – established at a routine post-mortem.'

He hadn't appreciated it himself, actually.

Until yesterday.

To his relief Henrietta smiled wanly and said, 'I see.'

'I mean,' expanded Sloan, 'the chances of your discovering that they were the wrong medals . . .'

'Wrong?' she said swiftly.

'Wrong for the photograph.'

'Go on, Inspector.' Warily.

'The chances of them being handled by anyone knowing quite as much about the subject as Mr Meyton were really very slight.'

Since putting down the telephone Sloan had sent Crosby to check up on the Rector's standing as an historian and found it high. Particularly in the field of military history.

'Inspector, are you trying to tell me that someone has been unlucky?'

'That's one way of looking at it, miss. But for the accident of the Rector seeing them you might never have known.'

'Known what?' she said with a sigh. 'What exactly does it mean we know now that we didn't know before?'

'That the medals are significant,' said Sloan promptly.

She looked up. 'Do you think so, Inspector?'

'I do, miss, though I don't know what of just yet. Give us a little time.' He hesitated and then said, 'I think we may be going to find the answer to a lot of questions in the past.'

She nodded. 'Twenty-one years ago.'

'Why then?'

'I'll be twenty-one next month. At least I think I will be if my mother . . .' she corrected herself painfully, 'if what I've been told is correct.'

'Twenty-one?' Sloan frowned. 'That could be important.'

'To me, Inspector.' Her voice had an ironic ring. 'The key of the door perhaps. But not to anyone else.'

'I shouldn't be too sure about that, miss. Not just yet.'

'And it rather looks,' she went on as if she hadn't heard him, 'as if I'm not the only one to have a key to the front door of Boundary Cottage, doesn't it?'

'True.' He paused. 'Yesterday you told me as much as you could remember being told about your father.'

'Yes?'

'What all do you know about your . . . about Grace Jenkins?'

It was pitifully little in terms of verifiable fact – if she was telling him the truth. Her mother had been a children's nurse for a family called Hocklington-Garwell, somewhere over the other side of the county. Henrietta didn't know the exact address but she had been brought up on stories of the Hocklington-Garwell children. There had been two of them – both boys. Master Hugo and Master Michael. Then Grace Wright had met Cyril Jenkins, and married him.

'After that,' concluded Henrietta tightly, 'I understood they had had me.'

'I see,' said Sloan.

'And that very soon afterwards my father had been killed.'

'I see,' said Sloan again.

'But they didn't have me,' observed Henrietta astringently.

'She didn't,' agreed Sloan. 'The chances of your being your father's child – so to speak – are high.'

'Thank you,' she said gravely. 'I'll remember that.'

'And the chances of her having come from East Calleshire are higher still.' He told her about Messrs Waind, Arbican & Waind in Calleford. 'So, miss, I think we can take it that the mystery originates that way somewhere.'

He did not mention murder.

'What I want to know,' said the Superintendent testily, 'is not who got which going but what you're doing about it, Sloan.' The Inspector was speaking from the call box in Larking village.

'Yes, sir. In the first instance we are looking for a car which hit a woman . . .'

'An unknown woman,' pointed out Leeyes.

'A woman who may or may not be unknown,' agreed Sloan

more moderately, 'which hit her on a bad bend outside Larking village on Tuesday evening sometime between say six and nine o'clock.'

'And have you got anywhere?'

'No, sir.'

'There's an inquest coming along on Saturday morning,' said Leeyes very gently. 'It's the law, Sloan, and the first thing the Coroner does is to take evidence of identification.'

'Yes, sir.' He hesitated. 'We've no reason to suppose she isn't Grace Jenkins . . .'

Superintendent Leeyes gave an intimidating grunt.

'But,' went on Sloan hastily, 'I'm going to make some enquiries about her pension now, and see the two people who came back on the bus with her on Tuesday night. And I've got a man checking up now on the marriage register in Somerset House . . .'

'What's that going to prove?'

'Whether or not this Grace Edith Wright did, in fact, marry one Cyril Edgar Jenkins. That should give us a lead.'

'One way or the other,' said Leeyes pointedly.

'Exactly, sir. We've got the experts working on those tyre casts too, and we're putting out a general call for witnesses. We're also trying to establish how she spent Tuesday – that may have some bearing on the case . . .'

Leeyes grunted again.

'It's a bit difficult,' said Sloan, 'because the girl has no idea . . .'

'It strikes me that the girl has no idea about too many things . . .'

'She was away at college at the time.'

'Check up on that, too, Sloan.'

'Yes, sir. This man Hibbs . . .'

'Ah, yes,' ruminatively. 'Hibbs. That solicitor fellow you were talking to yesterday . . .'

'Arbican.'

'He mentioned a settlement, didn't he?'

'Yes, sir.'

'It could have been with Hibbs.'

'Yes, sir. That had already occurred to me.'

'Could he have killed Grace Jenkins?'

'It strikes me,' said Sloan pessimistically, 'that anyone could have killed her. Anyone at all.'

'He's a local,' said Leeyes.

'Yes, sir.'

'He would know about the bend . . .'

'And the last bus.'

'So you see . . .'

'And that it's a deserted road at the best of times, but especially at night.'

'I don't like the country,' declared Leeyes. 'There are never any witnesses.'

'No, sir.'

'Find out what Hibbs was doing on Tuesday night.'

'Yes, sir.'

'What sort of a car has he got?'

'The right sort,' said Sloan cautiously.

'What?'

'That size tyre fits half a dozen cars. He happens to have one of them. A Riley.'

'Was it damaged?'

'I only saw the back.'

'Then take a look at the front, Sloan, somehow. I don't care how.'

'Yes, sir.'

'Bill, will you do something for me?'

Bill Thorpe throttled back the tractor to silence point and started to climb down from his high seat. 'Not something.' He grinned. 'Anything.'

In spite of all that had happened, Henrietta smiled.

'Changed your mind about coming to the farm to sleep?' asked Bill. 'Mother'll be pleased. She's been worried about you down here on your own these last two nights.'

'No, Bill, it's not that.' Henrietta pulled her coat round her shoulders. 'I'm not leaving Boundary Cottage even for one night.'

'It was just that . . .'

'I feel it's the only link I've got now with things like they used to be.'

'I expect you're bound to feel like that for a bit,' he said awkwardly. 'I dare say it'll wear off after a while.'

'No, it won't . . .'

'I see.'

She shook her head. 'No, you don't, Bill. But – it's difficult to explain – but the cottage and the things in it are the only things that seem real to me somehow.'

'I'm real,' said Bill Thorpe. And indeed he looked it, foursquare against the spring sky.

'I know you are. It's not that.'

'Well, what is it, then?'

She shivered, 'I feel I need to actually see the things I know there. Otherwise . . .'

'Otherwise what?'

'Otherwise,' she said soberly, 'I think I shall go out of my mind.'

'Here,' protested Bill. 'Take it easy. No one can make you leave if you don't want to.'

'Can't they just!' retorted Henrietta. 'That's what you think, Bill.'

'You're a protected tenant,' insisted Bill firmly. 'No one can make you leave. I'll see to that. Besides, Mr Hibbs would never turn you out. He's not that sort of man.'

'I don't think he would either,' said Henrietta slowly. 'He's always been very kind.' She looked at Bill and opened her eyes wide. 'He's always been very kind.'

'Yes, yes,' said Thorpe impatiently. 'I know. I think you're worrying about nothing.'

'I'm not.' She paused, then: 'Bill . . .'

'Yes?'

'I've got something to tell you.' She swallowed twice in quick succession. 'You're not going to like it.'

'Try me,' he said evenly.

'The police say Grace Jenkins wasn't my mother.' Now it was out she felt better. 'And,' she added defiantly, 'I don't know who was.'

In the event his reaction was surprising.

He kissed her.

And then:

'You don't know how glad I am to hear you say that.'

Henrietta looked up at him in astonishment – he was half a head taller than she was – and said, 'Why?'

'I thought it was me.'

'You thought what was you?'

'The reason why your mother wouldn't let us get married.'

'She wasn't my mother,' said Henrietta automatically.

'Exactly.' Bill Thorpe was beaming all over his face.

'I don't see what that's got to do with us not getting married.'

'Don't you?'

'No.'

'Silly.' He looked down at her affectionately. 'We couldn't get married without her permission because you weren't twenty-one.'

'I know that . . .'

'She couldn't give it.'

'Why not?'

'Because she wasn't your mother. You've just said so.'

'I never thought of that,' said Henrietta wonderingly. 'I thought it was only because she wanted me to finish my three years at university.'

'And I thought it was because she didn't like Bill Thorpe,' said Bill Thorpe ruefully.

'And all the time,' whispered Henrietta, 'it was because she didn't want me to know I wasn't hers.'

'Until you were twenty-one,' concluded Thorpe. 'I reckon you were to be told then.'

She shivered. 'Now we may never know.'

'Don't you believe it.'

'Bill . . .' tentatively.

'Yes?'

'There must be some . . . some reason why she didn't want me to know.'

He nodded. 'Knowing your mother I should say a good reason.' He hesitated. 'She'd got all this worked out, hadn't she?'

'It rather looks like it. I . . . I don't know what to think.'

Bill Thorpe looked at the sky. It was the subconscious glance of a farmer. 'What was it you wanted me to do, then?'

'Take me to Calleford this afternoon.'

8

'Where are we now, Crosby?'

It was a rhetorical question. Inspector Sloan and Detective Constable Crosby were, in fact, walking from Boundary Cottage towards Larking Post Office.

'We thought we didn't know about the mother,' responded Crosby. 'Now we don't know about the father either.'

'Not well put, but I am with you.'

'In fact,' went on Crosby morosely, 'we hardly know anything.' He did not like walking.

'We know a woman was killed by a motor vehicle in – er – unusual circumstances.'

They were not far now from the fatal bend in the road. Crosby looked up and down. 'You couldn't *not* see someone on a road as narrow as this.'

'No.' Sloan reverted to Grace Jenkins. 'We know that she was childless.'

'But,' put in Crosby, 'that she pretended not to be.'

'Just so,' said Sloan. 'An interesting situation.'

'And that's all we do know,' concluded Crosby flatly.

'Try again,' advised Sloan, 'because it isn't.'

Crosby's brow became as furrowed as one of the Thorpes' ploughed fields.

'There's something fishy about the photograph and the medals?'

'There is.' Sloan was already listing in his own mind the inquiries which would have to be made about the photograph and the medals. 'But go back to the woman for a moment . . .'

Crosby's brow resumed its furrows.

'Why,' asked Sloan helpfully, 'was she killed?'

There was a long pause. 'Search me,' said Detective Constable Crosby at long last.

'If Sergeant Gelven wasn't on annual leave, Constable, I wouldn't have to,' said Sloan crisply.

'No, sir.'

They had passed the bad bend now and were walking towards the centre of the village. The Hall lay over on their right, nestled into the folding countryside in the sheltered site selected in their wisdom by its Tudor builders. It would be in the best situation for several miles around and there would have been a spring or a good well near by.

They walked past the gates. They were well hung and newly painted. Nothing, thought Sloan, gave you as good a view of the state of a property as the gates. Mr James Hibbs was clearly a man of means who was prepared to pay attention to detail.

'I think we know why she was killed,' said Sloan.

The church had come into view now. It, too, was on the right of the road. If Sloan knew anything about landowners there would be a gate through into the churchyard from the grounds of The Hall. The ultimate in status symbols.

'Do we?' said Crosby cautiously.

'You mentioned adoption . . .'

'Yes, sir.'

'There comes a point when – like it or not – it is customary to tell the adopted child the – er – truth about its parents or lack of them.'

'Twenty-one,' said Crosby.

'Just so. All wrong, of course. The right time is before they can understand.'

'Yes, sir. The psychologists say . . .'

'I understand,' said Sloan coldly, not liking the word, 'that you should stress that they are chosen.' He looked Crosby up and down. 'Not an unhappy accident of fate like everyone else's children.'

'No, sir.'

They could see beyond the church now to the Rectory and the patch of grass that presumably did duty as a village green. No one could have called Larking picturesque – which probably meant it was spared a good deal – but it was by no means unattractive.

'I think she was killed because the girl is going to be twenty-one next month.'

'And someone doesn't want Henrietta to know who she is?' responded Crosby brightly.

'Don't strain yourself thinking too hard, Constable, will you?'

'No, sir.'

'She tells us she is going to be twenty-one in April,' continued Sloan, 'and I think she has been correctly informed on this point, but April would be too late for the killing of Grace Jenkins for two reasons . . .'

He waited hopefully for Crosby to enumerate them.

Crosby said nothing.

'Two reasons,' went on Sloan in a resigned way. When he got back to Berebury he would look up the leave schedules to see when Sergeant Gelven was coming back. They weren't going to solve anything at all at this rate. 'One of them is that the girl would have been back from college by then.'

Crosby nodded in agreement.

'The other is . . .'

'Daylight,' said Crosby unexpectedly.

'Exactly. By April the last bus would be getting to Larking in the twilight rather than the sort of darkness you can easily run someone down in. There's another thing . . .'

Crosby cocked his head like a spaniel.

'This wedding . . .'

'She wouldn't let them get married,' said Crosby. 'That chap Hibbs told us that.'

'Have you thought why not? Thorpe's a nice enough lad by all accounts . . .'

They were right in the centre of the village now and he and

Crosby knocked on the door of the house of the last person known to have seen the late Grace Edith Jenkins alive.

'That's right,' said Mrs Martha Callows, not without relish. 'I reckon me and Mrs Perkins was the last to see her. On the last bus, she was, same as we were.'

She admitted the policemen into an untidy house, knocked a cat off one chair, scooped a child out of another and invited them to sit down.

'The last bus from Berebury?' asked Sloan with the air of one anxious to get everything clear.

'There aren't any other buses from anywhere else,' Mrs Callows said, 'and there aren't all that many from Berebury. If you miss the seven five you walk.'

'Quite so. Was it crowded?'

'Not after Cullingoak. Most people get out there. Get down, you.' This last was said to the cat, which, thwarted of the chair, was settling on the table.

'Where did you get out?'

'The post office. That's the only stop in Larking. We all got out there. Me and Mrs Perkins and her.'

'About what time would that have been?'

'Something short of eight o'clock.'

The cat had not, in fact, troubled to get down and was now investigating some dirty plates which were still on the table.

'You'd been shopping?' said Sloan generally.

'Sort of. Mrs Perkins – that's who I was with – her husband's in hospital. That's why we was on the late bus. Visiting hours. Course, we'd been round the shops first . . . Berebury's a long way to go for nothing.'

'Quite so. Had Mrs Jenkins got a shopping basket?'

'Now I come to think of it,' said Mrs Callows, screwing up her face in recollection, 'I don't know she had.' Her face cleared suddenly. 'But then she wouldn't have, would she?'

'Why not?' enquired Sloan with interest.

'Friday's her day for Berebury. Not Toosday. She goes in Fridays, regular as clockwork. Always has done.'

'Not Tuesdays?'

Mrs Callows shook her head. 'Not shopping.'

'I see. Tell me' – Sloan was at his most confidential – 'tell me, was she her usual self otherwise?'

A wary look came into Mrs Callows's eye. 'Yes, I suppose you could say she was.'

Sloan tried another tack. 'Cheerful?'

'I wouldn't say cheerful meself. Polite, of course, hoh yes, always very polite was Mrs Jenkins, but not what you'd call cheerful.'

'Talkative sort?'

Mrs Callows shook her head. 'Not her. Never much to say for herself at the best of times but take Toosday f'rinstance. "Good evening," she says. "We could do with a bit better weather than this, couldn't we? Too windy." And passes right down the bus to the front and sits there by herself.'

'Kept herself to herself?'

'That's right. She did.' Mrs Callows reached out absently and gave the cat a cuff. It retreated but only momentarily.

'She didn't tell you how she'd spent the day?' asked Sloan.

Mrs Callows sniffed. 'She wouldn't tell us a thing like that. She wasn't the sort.'

'I see.' Sloan reverted to officialese. 'We are naturally anxious to trace Mrs Jenkins's movements on Tuesday . . .'

'There I cannot help,' said Mrs Callows frankly. 'Neither of us set eyes on her until we got to the bus station.'

'What about afterwards?'

'When we got back to Larking, you mean?'

'That's right.' Sloan waved an arm. 'Other people, for instance. Was there anyone about?'

She shook her head. 'We didn't see anybody else, but then we wouldn't, would we?'

'Why not?'

'Because it was Toosday, like I said.'

'Tuesday?'

'The first Toosday,' amplified Mrs Callows. 'Institoot night.'

'I see. So what happened when you all got off the bus?'

'She turned down the lane towards her house. Mrs Perkins and me – we went the other way. That was the last we saw of her.'

'I see,' said Sloan. 'Thank you.'

'It's a nasty bend,' volunteered Mrs Callows suddenly.

'Indeed, yes. By the way, did you see any vehicular traffic?'

Mrs Callows looked blank. 'Oh, you mean cars? No, none at all.'

Sloan and Crosby rose to go.

'Except,' she added, 'the ones parked outside the King's Head.'

Sloan and Crosby took a look at the King's Head car park on their way from Mrs Callows's house to the post office.

It was an asphalt affair and disappointing.

'We won't get a tyre print on this.' Crosby stood in the middle of it and stamped his foot. 'Hard as iron.'

Inspector Sloan didn't appear to be interested in the surface of the car park. He was moving about and looking down the road to his right.

'Anyway,' went on Crosby, 'she was killed on Tuesday. Today's Friday. Other vehicles would have come in here since then and rubbed them out.'

'What exactly can you see from here, Constable?'

Crosby looked down the road. 'The post office, sir, and a telephone kiosk, the fork in the road to Belling St Peter, the signpost and so forth.' He paused, then, 'A woman pushing a pram, a delivery van, a row of horse chestnuts . . .'

'This is not a nature ramble, Crosby.'

'No, sir.'

'Anything else?'

'There's the church, sir, beyond the bus stop.'

'Precisely.'

Crosby looked puzzled. 'Is the church important, sir?'

'No.'

'The bus stop?'

'Don't overdo it, Crosby, will you?'

'No, sir.' He turned back to Sloan. 'Where to, now, sir?'

'The post office. To see a Mrs Ricks. The admirable Hepple says she knows everything.'

But this was not quite true.

While confirming that the late Grace Jenkins always went into Berebury on Fridays, and seldom, if ever, on Tuesdays, Mrs Ricks was unable to say why she had left on the early bus and come back on the late one. Sloan squeezed alongside a sack of corn while the tall Crosby ducked out of the way of a vicious-looking billhook which was suspended from the ceiling. It was above his head – but only just.

'I don't know,' she wheezed regretfully. It was an admission she rarely had to make. 'She wouldn't have said. She wasn't a talker.'

'So I heard,' said Sloan.

'I saw her leave in the morning,' offered Mrs Ricks. 'In her best, she was.'

'Was she?' said Sloan, interested.

'And she was gone all day. At least I never saw her get off a bus before I closed.' Mrs Ricks apparently monitored the bus stop outside the post office window as a matter of course.

'Nasty things, car accidents,' observed Sloan to nobody in particular.

'You needn't think, officer,' said Mrs Ricks, divining his intentions with uncanny accuracy, 'that you'll find anyone to say a word against Mrs Jenkins, because you won't.'

'Madam, I assure you . . .'

'She didn't,' went on Mrs Ricks with the insight born of years of small shopkeeping, 'mix with people enough to upset them, if you see what I mean.'

Sloan saw what she meant.

'Difficult job, all the same,' he said diffidently, 'bringing up a child without a father.'

Mrs Ricks gave a crowing laugh. 'She brought her up all right. She never did anything else all day but look after that child. And that house of hers.'

'Devoted?' suggested Sloan.

Mrs Ricks gave a powerful nod. 'It was always "Henrietta this" and "Henrietta that" with Mrs Jenkins,' she said a trifle spitefully. 'A rare old job it was to get her to take an interest in anything else.'

'I see.'

Mrs Ricks gave a sigh and said sententiously, 'Here today, gone tomorrow. We none of us know, do we, when we shall be called . . .'

Sloan got her back to the point with an effort. 'Do you happen to know which is her pension day?'

'That I do not,' declared Mrs Ricks. 'But I can tell you one thing . . .'

'What's that?'

'That she never got it here.'

'Oh?'

'There's some that don't.' She looked round the crowded little store, saleable goods protruding from every square inch of wall and ceiling space, and lining most of the floor too. 'They like somewhere bigger.'

Sloan saw what she meant. The sales point of the billhook was practically making itself felt.

'Especially,' said Mrs Ricks in her infinite wisdom, 'if it isn't as much as they'd like you to think. Sergeant, wasn't he?'

Sloan nodded.

Mrs Ricks sniffed. 'Sometimes they were. Sometimes they weren't.'

Calleford Minster rose like an *éminence grise* above and behind the clustered shops at the end of Petergate. Mr Arbican of Messrs Waind, Arbican & Waind would be very happy to see Henrietta but her appointment with him was not until a quarter to three. Farmers as a race lunch early and Henrietta and Bill Thorpe had time to spare.

Henrietta turned towards the Minster. 'It's lovely, isn't it?'

Bill Thorpe turned an eye on the towering stone. 'It's more than lovely. Do you realize it could be useful to you?'

'To me?'

He nodded. 'That chap in the photograph . . .'

'My father,' responded Henrietta a little distantly.

'He was – what did you say? – a sergeant in the East Calleshires?'

'That's right. What about it?'

'He was killed, wasn't he?'

She flushed. 'So I understand.'

'Well, then . . .'

'Well then what?'

'Calleford's their town, isn't it?'

Henrietta sighed. 'Whose town?'

'The East Calleshires,' explained Bill Thorpe patiently. 'The Regiment. They've got their barracks here. Like the West Calleshires have theirs in Berebury.'

'What if they have?'

He pointed to the minster. 'If this is their home town then I think we might find their memorial in the minster here, don't you?'

'I hadn't thought of that,' she said slowly. 'He – my father –'ll be there, won't he?'

Bill Thorpe led the way towards the minster gate. 'We can soon see.'

The East Calleshires did have their memorial in the minster. Henrietta followed Bill Thorpe into the minster and down the nave. She lagged behind slightly as if she did not want to be there, glancing occasionally at the memorials to eighteenth-century noblemen and nineteenth-century soldiers.

An elderly verger led them to the East Calleshire memorial on the north wall of the north transept.

'It catches the afternoon light just here, you know,' he said. 'Nice piece of marble, isn't it?'

'Very,' said Bill Thorpe politely.

'They couldn't get no more like it,' the man said. 'Not when they came to try. Still, they weren't to know they were going to need a whole lot more less than twenty years later, were they?'

Bill Thorpe nodded in agreement. 'Indeed not. That knowledge was spared them.'

'So that,' went on the man, 'come 1945 they decided they would put those new names on these pillars that were there already. Quite a saving, really, though the money didn't matter, as it happened.' He sighed. 'Funny how often it works out like that, isn't it?'

'Very,' said Bill Thorpe.

'The same crest did, too.' It was obvious that the man spent his days showing people around the minster. His voice had a sort of hushed monotone suitable to the surroundings. 'That's a nice bit of work, though they tell me it's tricky to dust. They don't think of that sort of thing when they design a monument.'

'I suppose not.'

The verger hitched his gown over his shoulders. 'You two come to look somebody up?'

'Yes,' said Bill. 'Yes, we have.'

'Thought so. People never ask unless they particularly want to see someone they was related to.' He looked them up and down and said tersely, 'First lot or second?'

'Second.'

He sucked his breath in through gaps in his teeth. 'It'll be easier to find them.'

' "An epitaph on an army of mercenaries," ' said Bill Thorpe sadly as the old man wandered off.

Henrietta wasn't listening.

'Bill,' she tugged his sleeve urgently. 'Look.'

'Where?'

She pointed. 'There . . .'

'It goes,' agreed Bill Thorpe slowly, 'from Inkpen, T. H. to Jennings, C. R.'

'There's no one called Jenkins there at all,' whispered Henrietta.

9

Bill Thorpe shifted his weight from one foot to the other and considered the matter.

'He should have been here, shouldn't he?'

'He was in the East Calleshires,' insisted Henrietta. 'My mother always said he . . . I was told he was but there's the photograph too.'

'The man in the photograph was wearing their uniform.'

'Exactly,' said Henrietta.

'But that's all.'

'All?'

'All you know for sure,' said Thorpe flatly.

Henrietta turned a bewildered face back to the memorial. 'Do you mean the man in the photograph wasn't killed?'

Bill ran his eye down the names. 'He may have been killed and not called Jenkins.'

'Or,' retorted Henrietta astringently, 'I suppose he may have been called Jenkins and not been killed.'

'That is the most probable explanation,' agreed Thorpe calmly.

'How – how am I going to find out?'

'Did you ever see your mother's pension book?'

'She didn't cash her pension at the post office,' she said quickly. 'She took it to the bank. She told me that. Then she used to cash a cheque.'

'I see.'

There was a long pause and then Henrietta said, 'So that, whether or not he was my father, he wasn't killed in the war, was he?'

'Not if he was in the East Calleshires and was also called Jenkins,' agreed Bill Thorpe, pointing to the memorial. 'Of course there is another possibility.'

Henrietta sighed but said nothing.

'He might not have been killed on active service,' went on Thorpe.

'You mean he might have died a natural death?'

'People do, you know,' said Thorpe mildly. 'Even in wartime.'

She was silent for a moment. Then, 'Nothing seems to make sense any more.'

'Everything has an explanation.'

'This must sound very silly,' she said, choosing her words carefully, 'but let me say what I know for certain. There is a photograph . . .'

'The photograph is a fact,' acknowledged Bill Thorpe.

'Which you have seen.'

'Then the photograph is doubly a fact,' he murmured ironically.

'There is a photograph of a man in the uniform of this regiment in the drawing-room at home, and . . .'

'And that,' said Bill Thorpe, 'is all you know for certain.'

She stared at him. 'A man who I thought was my father.'

'Ah, that's different.'

'Who I thought was called Jenkins.'

'Who may or may not be called Jenkins.'

'And who I thought was killed in the war.'

Bill Thorpe pointed to the memorial again. 'Don't you see that he might be called Jenkins or he might have been killed in the war – but not both. The facts are mutually exclusive – unless he changed regiments halfway through or something out of the ordinary like that.'

'Or died a natural death,' persisted the girl.

'Or a very unnatural one,' retorted Thorpe.

Henrietta waited.

'Well,' said Thorpe defensively, 'if he'd been shot as a spy or a deserter or something like that . . .'

'I hadn't thought of that.'

'. . . We're hardly likely to find his name here, are we?' Bill waved a hand which took in all the hallowed thirteenth–century stone about them.

'That means,' decided Henrietta logically, 'that you don't think the man in the photograph is . . .' she hesitated, 'or was my father.'

'There is something wrong with the medals . . .'

'There's something wrong with everything so far,' rejoined Henrietta. 'We're collecting quite a bit of negative evidence.'

'Just as useful as the other sort,' declared Thorpe.

'I'm glad to hear it,' she said rather tartly. 'At the moment the only thing we seem to be absolutely sure about is that there is a photograph of a sergeant in the East Calleshires which has been standing in Boundary Cottage ever since I can remember.'

'The photograph is a fact,' agreed Bill Thorpe with undiminished amiability.

'And so is the name of Jenkins not being on this memorial.'

'The evidence is before our very eyes, as the conjurors say.'

'And the police say Grace Jenkins wasn't my mother.'

Bill Thorpe looked down at her affectionately. 'I reckon that makes you utterly orphan, don't you?'

She nodded.

'Quite a good thing, really,' said Thorpe easily.

Henrietta's head came up with a jerk. 'Why?'

'I don't have to ask anyone's permission to marry you.'

She didn't respond. 'I'm worse than just orphan. I don't even know who I am or who my parents were.'

'Does it matter?'

'Matter?' Henrietta opened her eyes very wide.

'Well, I can see it's important with – say – Shire Oak Majestic. A bull's got to have a good pedigree to be worth anything.'

'I fail to see any connection,' said Henrietta icily.

'I'm not in love with your ancestors . . .'

The verger ambled up behind them. 'Found what you were looking for, sir, on that memorial?'

'What's that? Oh, yes, thank you, Verger,' said Thorpe. 'We found what we were looking for all right.'

'That's good, sir. Good afternoon to you both.'

Not unexpectedly, Mr Felix Arbican of Messrs Waind, Arbican & Waind, Solicitors, shared Henrietta's view rather than Bill Thorpe's on the importance of parentage. He heard her story out and then said, 'Tricky.'

'Yes,' agreed Henrietta politely. She regarded that as a gross understatement.

'It raises several – er – legal points.'

'Not only legal ones,' said Henrietta.

'What's that? Oh, yes, quite so. The accident, for instance.' Arbican made a gesture of sympathy. 'I'm sorry. There are so many cars on the road these days.' He brought his hands up to form a pyramid under his chin. 'She was walking, you say . . .'

'She was.'

'Then there should be less question of liability.'

'There is no question of where the blame for the accident lies,' said Henrietta slowly. 'Only the driver still has to be found.'

'He didn't stop?'

She shook her head.

'Nor report it to the police?'

'Not that I've heard.'

'That's a great pity. If he had done, there would have been little more to do – little more from a professional point of view, that is, than to settle the question of responsibility with the insurance company, and agree damages.'

Henrietta inclined her head in silence.

'And they usually settle out of court.'

Henrietta moistened her lips. 'There is to be an inquest . . . on Saturday morning.'

'Naturally.'

'Is Berebury too far for you to come?'

'You want me to represent you? If your – er – mother was a client of mine at one time – and it seems very much as if she must have been, then I will certainly do that.'

'The Inspector told me she came to you once . . .'

'A long time ago.'

'You don't recall her?'

Arbican shook his head.

Henrietta lapsed back in her chair in disappointment. 'I was so hoping you would. I need someone who knew her before very badly . . .'

'Quite so.' The solicitor coughed. 'I think in these – er – somewhat unusual circumstances my advice would be that you should first establish if a legal adoption has taken place. That would put a different complexion on the whole affair. You say there are no papers in the house whatsoever?'

'None. There was this burglary, you see . . .'

Arbican nodded. 'It doesn't make matters easier.'

'No.'

'In the absence of any written evidence we could begin a search of the court adoption registers . . .'

Henrietta looked up eagerly.

'But it will necessarily be a slow business. There are about forty County Courts, you see, and – er – several hundred Magistrates' Courts.'

'I see.'

'A will,' said Arbican cautiously, 'might clarify matters.'

'In what way?'

'It would perhaps refer to the relationship between you and Grace Jenkins. Whilst not being her – er – child of the body you could still stand in a legal relationship to her.'

'I don't see how.'

'Have you thought that you could be a child of an earlier marriage of one of the two parties?'

She sighed. 'I don't know what to think.'

'If that were so then you must have been the child of one of them . . .'

'Not Grace Jenkins,' reiterated Henrietta.

'If you aren't,' went on the solicitor, 'and the fact of this in each case can be proved, then you could be a child of a marriage, the surviving partner of which subsequently married one of the two persons whom you had hitherto considered your parents . . .'

She put her hands up to her head. 'You're going too quickly.'

'That would entail a third marriage on someone's part – but three marriages are not out of the place these days.'

'It – it's very complicated, isn't it?'

'The law,' said Arbican cheerfully, 'is.'

She hesitated. 'Mr Arbican, if I were illegitimate?'

The fingers came up under his chin again while the solicitor pontificated. 'The law is much kinder than it used to be, and if your – the person whom you thought to be your mother has made a will in your favour it is of little consequence.'

'It isn't that,' said Henrietta quickly. 'Besides we – she had no money. I know that.'

Arbican looked as if he was about to say that that was of no consequence either.

'In any case,' went on Henrietta, 'I wouldn't want to claim anything I wasn't entitled to, and if she wasn't my mother, I don't see how I can be.'

'A will,' began Arbican, 'would . . .'

'She may not have made one,' countered Henrietta. 'She wasn't expecting to die.'

'Everyone should make a will,' said the solicitor sententiously.

While farmers lunch early, and clergy at exactly one fifteen, policemen on duty lunch not at all. Inspector Sloan and Constable Crosby found themselves back in the Berebury Police Station after two thirty with the canteen offering nothing more substantial than tea and sandwiches. Crosby laid the tray on Sloan's desk.

'It's all they had left,' he said briefly.

'Somerset House didn't have anything either,' Sloan told him, pushing a message pad across the desk. 'No record of any Grace Edith Wright marrying any Cyril Edgar Jenkins within five years of either side of when the girl thought they did.'

Crosby took another sandwich and thought about this for the length of it. Then, 'Grace Jenkins must have had a birth certificate.'

'Wright,' said Sloan automatically.

Crosby, who thought Sloan had said 'Right,' looked pleased and took another sandwich.

'Though,' continued Sloan, 'if she's Wright, why bring Jenkins in at all, especially if she's not married to him.'

Crosby offered no opinion on this.

'Moreover, where do you begin to look?'

'Where, sir?' he echoed.

'Where in time,' explained Sloan kindly. 'Not where in space. It'll all be in Somerset House. It's a question of knowing where to look. The girl tells us Grace Jenkins was forty-five years old. The pathologist says she was fifty-five or thereabouts.'

'Yes,' agreed Crosby helpfully.

'And that's not the only thing. The girl says she was married to one Jenkins, deceased, and her maiden name was Wright. Somerset House can't trace the marriage and Dr Dabbe thinks she was both unmarried and childless.'

'More tea?' suggested Crosby constructively.

'Thank you.' Sloan reached for his notebook. 'We can't very well expect the General Register Officer to give us the birth certificate of someone whose age we don't know and whose name we aren't sure about. So, instead . . .'

'Yes, sir?'

'You will start looking for a family called – what was it? – ah, yes: a family called Hocklington-Garwell. And a farm.'

'A farm, sir?'

'A Holly Tree Farm, Crosby.'

'Somewhere in England, sir?'

'Somewhere in Calleshire,' snapped Sloan.

Crosby swallowed. 'Yes, sir.'

Sloan read through the notes of the interview with Mrs Callows. 'Then there's the bus station. Grace Jenkins arrived there on Tuesday morning and left there on the seven five in the evening. See if you can find any lead on where she went in between.'

'Yes, sir.'

'Do you remember what it was that was unusual about her on Tuesday?'

'She was killed?'

'Try again, Constable . . .' dangerously.

Crosby frowned. 'She was dressed in her best . . .'

'Anything else?'

'It wasn't her day for shopping in Berebury.'

'Exactly.'

'You could just say it wasn't her day,' murmured Crosby, but fortunately Inspector Sloan didn't hear him.

Henrietta came out of the office of Waind, Arbican & Waind, and stood on the Calleford pavement. Bill Thorpe was a little way down the road and she waved. He turned and came towards her asking, 'Any luck?'

'None,' Henrietta said despondently. 'He doesn't remember her at all.'

'What about the legal side?' He fell in step beside her. 'I've found a tea shop down this lane.'

'The legal side!' echoed Henrietta indignantly. 'I'd no idea adoption was so easy. And there's no central register of adoption either.' There was quite a catch in her voice as she said, 'I could be anybody.'

'We'll have to get the vet to you after all. Turn left at this corner.'

Her face lightened momentarily. 'Strangles or spavin?'

'To look at your back teeth,' said Bill Thorpe. He pushed open the door of the tea shop and led the way to the table. They were early and the place was not full. He chose the one in the window and they settled into chairs facing each other.

Henrietta was not to be diverted. 'I am a person . . .'

'Undoubtedly. If I may say so, quite one of the . . .'

'You may not,' she said repressively.

'Tea, I think, for two,' he said to the waitress. 'And toast.'

'When I was a little girl,' said Henrietta, 'I used to ask myself, "Why am I me?" Now I'm grown up I seem to be asking myself, "Who am I?" '

'Philosophy is so egocentric,' complained Bill Thorpe, 'and everyone thinks it isn't. I'm not at all sure I like the idea of your studying it.'

'I'm me,' declared Henrietta.

'And very nice, too, especially your . . .'

'I know I'm me, but where do we go from here?'

Bill Thorpe stirred. 'Your existence isn't in doubt, you know. Only your identity.'

'Then who on earth am I?'

'I don't know,' he said placidly, 'and I don't really care.'

Henrietta did. 'At this rate I could be anybody at all.'

'Not just anybody.'

'There are over fifty million people in this country and if I'm not called . . .'

'We can narrow the field a bit.'

'You're sure?'

'Unless I'm very much mistaken,' he underlined the words, 'you're female. That brings it down to twenty-five million for a start.'

'Bill, be serious. This is important.'

'Not to me, it isn't. But if you insist . . .'

'I do.'

'Then you're a leucodermii.' He grinned. 'That's silenced you. I did anthropology for a year. Enjoyed it, too.'

She smiled for the first time that day. It altered her appearance beyond measure. 'Science succeeding where philosophy has failed, Bill?'

'Well you're the one who wants to find out who you are. Not me.'

She lowered her eyes meekly. 'And you tell me I'm a leucodermii.'

He waved a hand. 'So you are. If I said, "Come hither, my dusky maiden," you needn't come.'

That startled her. 'I'm English.'

It was his turn for irony. 'White, through and through?'

She flushed. 'Not that, but surely . . . I never thought I could be anything but English. Oh, I am. Bill, I must be.'

'Indo-European anyway.' He moved his chair back while the waitress set the tea in front of them. 'Thank you.' While Henrietta poured out, he squinted speculatively at her. 'Your head's all right.'

'Thank you.'

'Mesocephalic. Not long, not broad, but medium.'

'That sounds English if anything does.'

'The lady mocks me.' He held up a hand and ticked off the fingers one by one. 'You're not Slav, nor Mongol . . .'

'Thank you.'

'. . . nor Mediterranean type. If your cheek bones had been a fraction higher, you could have been Scandinavian . . .'

'I feel English.'

'Nurture, not nature.'

'I hadn't thought of that.'

'Unless you believe in all this inherited race consciousness theory.'

She shook her head. 'I don't know enough about it.'

'Nobody does. Have some toast. Then I think all we can conclude is that you are free, white and nearly twenty-one.'

'Free?' echoed Henrietta.

'Remarkably so. No attachments whatsoever. Except to me, of course.'

She wouldn't be drawn but sat with her head turned away towards the window, staring at the street.

' "Free as nature first made man," ' quoted Bill.

'You'll be talking of noble savages in a minute, I suppose.'

'Never!'

'Tell me this,' she said. 'Do vets still go in for branding?'

'Sometimes,' he said cautiously. 'Why?'

'Because a few marks on my ear at birth would have saved a lot of trouble all round, that's why.'

'You'd better have another cup of tea,' he said. 'And some more toast.'

She refilled her cup and his, and sat gazing through the teashop window at the passers-by.

Suddenly she let her cup fall back into her saucer with an uncontrolled clatter. 'Bill, look. Out there.'

'Where?'

'That man.' She started to struggle to her feet, her face quite white.

'What about him?'

She was pointing agitatedly towards the back of a man walking down the street. 'It . . . it's the man in the photograph . . . Oh, quickly. I'm sure it is.'

'You mean your father?' He pushed his chair back.

'Cyril Jenkins,' she said urgently. 'I swear it is. It was exactly like the man in the photograph but older.' She started to push her way out of the tea shop. 'Come on, Bill, quickly. We must catch him whatever happens.'

10

It was well after four o'clock before Inspector Sloan and Constable Crosby met again. Crosby went into Sloan's room at the Berebury Police Station waving a list.

'Nearly as long as my arm, sir, this.'

'It can't be as long as your face, Crosby. What is it?'

'The Holly Tree Farms in Calleshire.'

'Routine is the foundation of all police work, Constable. You should know that.'

'Yes, sir. Records have come through on the phone, too, sir. They've got nothing against any Cyril Edgar Jenkins or Grace Edith Wright.'

'Or Jenkins.'

'Or Jenkins.'

'That doesn't get us very far then.'

'No, sir.' Crosby still sounded gloomy. 'And I can't get anywhere either with this family that the girl says her mother used to work for.'

'Hocklington-Garwell?' Inspector Sloan frowned. 'I was afraid of that. They may not have lived in Calleshire, of course . . .'

'No, sir. I'd thought of that.' Crosby looked as if he might have to take on the world.

'And there is always the possibility that the girl may be having us on.'

'You mean they might not exist?' If Crosby's expression was anything to go by, this was not quite cricket.

'I do.'

Crosby looked gloomier still. 'It's a funny name to be having us on with, sir, if you know what I mean.'

'That, Constable, is the most sensible remark you've made for a long time.'

'Thank you, sir.'

'Therefore I am inclined to think that the Hocklington-Garwells do exist.'

'Not in Calleshire, sir,' said Crosby firmly. 'Several Garwells but no Hocklingtons and not a sniff of a Hocklington-Garwell.'

'Give me the Garwellses' addresses then,' said Sloan. 'We've got to start somewhere and we're getting nowhere fast at the moment.'

'It would have been a lot simpler,' said Crosby plaintively, 'if she had had the baby and we were looking for the father.'

Superintendent Leeyes said much the same thing in different words a few minutes later in his office in the same corridor.

'I've dealt with a few paternity orders in my time, Sloan, but I'm damned if I've met a maternity one yet.'

'No, sir.' He coughed. 'This case has several unusual features.'

'You can say that again,' said his superior encouragingly. 'Found out whose the medals were?'

'Not yet, sir. The old boy at the Rectory's quite right. Knows his stuff. They're the wrong ones for the photograph quite apart from the fact that the DSO and MC are never awarded to sergeants.'

'Officers, medals for the use of.'

'Yes, sir.'

'This man Hibbs at The Hall. He an officer type?'

'Yes, sir.'

'Hrrrmph.'

'I've had a look at his car,' said Sloan hastily. 'It looks all right to me. It's not all that new and I don't know how much damage to expect to the car from her injuries. I'll have a word with Traffic about that. And Dr Dabbe.'

'And check,' growled Leeyes, 'that he hasn't had them repaired. Plenty of time for that since Tuesday.'

'Yes, sir.'

'What was he doing on Tuesday evening anyway?'

'Nothing,' said Sloan cautiously.

'Nothing?'

'He was alone at home.'

'Was he indeed? Interesting.'

'You see, sir, it was the first Tuesday in the month.'

'I am aware of that, Sloan, but the significance eludes me . . .'

'That's Institoot – I mean, Institute night.'

'You don't say.'

'Mrs Hibbs,' said Sloan hurriedly, 'is branch president. So she was out.'

'No servants?'

'A daily. A real one.'

'A real one?'

'Comes every day. Daily.'

'There's no need to spell it out for me, man.'

'No, sir.'

'What you are trying to tell me – and taking the devil of a long time about it, if I may say so – is that James Heber Hibbs was alone all evening at The Hall, he has a car whose tyre marks correspond with those found at the scene of the accident and you aren't yet sure if he killed Grace Whatever-her-name-is.'

'Yes, sir.'

'Anything else?'

'There may well be something odd about this chap Jenkins, sir, apart from the medals.'

'You can say that again,' responded Leeyes generously.

'I've been making a few enquiries about his pension.'

'Oh?'

'And I can't trace it. It wasn't paid out via the local village post office which is not all that surprising, but it didn't go into her bank account either. I've just seen the manager. No pension voucher record there. Her account was kept going with a small regular monthly cash payment over the counter.'

'Who by?' sharply.

'Grace Jenkins herself to all intent and purposes,' sighed Sloan. 'According to the paying-in slips, she always handed it over herself.'

'Maintenance,' concluded Leeyes.

'Yes, sir, with any clue to its source carefully concealed.'

'And anything not concealed equally carefully removed from the bureau on Tuesday.'

'Just so,' agreed Sloan.

'From what you've said so far,' said the Superintendent, 'she doesn't strike one as having been a kept woman.'

'Only literally, sir, if you follow me. I think it was the child who was kept. I've got in touch with the pension authorities and they're doing a bit of checking up now but it'll take time. It's not as if it were an uncommon name even.'

'No.' The Superintendent thought for a moment and then said, 'The most interesting question from our point of view is who was keeping both of them.'

'Yes, sir.'

'And why.' The Superintendent sat silent, thinking. Sloan knew better than to interrupt his thoughts. 'If,' said Leeyes at last, 'we knew why they were being kept I dare say we'd know who killed the woman.'

'Whatever the story,' said Sloan, 'I think we can be fairly sure the situation changed when the girl reached twenty-one.'

'And someone didn't like it the new way.'

'No.'

'That means there's money somewhere, Sloan, or I'm a Dutchman.'

'Perhaps.' Sloan tapped his notebook. 'It could be a question of inheritance easily . . .'

'Or concealment of birth.'

'I'd thought of that, sir. I've been on to the General Register Office with the only reasonable thing I could think of to ask them.'

'What was that?'

'A list of the female children born about the same time as Henrietta Jenkins says she was and who have the same Christian names.'

'That's a tall order,' said the Superintendent.

'They said it would take time,' agreed Sloan dubiously. 'I don't suppose a Friday afternoon's the best moment to ask them either.'

'No.' Leeyes looked at his watch. 'Late on Friday afternoon at that.'

'She was called Henrietta Eleanor Leslie though.'

'That's better than Mary, I suppose.'

'But you don't have to register a birth for six weeks and . . .'

'And,' said the Superintendent grimly, 'we've only got her word for it that those are her names and that that is when she was born.'

'Just so,' said Sloan.

That was the moment when the telephone began to ring.

Leeyes picked it up, listened for a moment and then handed it over to Sloan. 'A call for Inspector Sloan from Calleford. Urgent and personal.'

Sloan took the receiver in one hand and a pencil in the other. 'Speaking . . .'

He listened attentively, then he asked two questions in quick succession, advised the speaker to go home and replaced the receiver.

'That was Bill Thorpe, sir.'

Leeyes nodded. 'That's the chap who helped find the body, isn't it? The one the girl wanted to marry . . .'

'Him,' said Sloan. 'He's with the girl in Calleford now and she's just seen Cyril Jenkins.'

'Who?' roared Leeyes.

'Cyril Jenkins.'

'He's dead.'

'Not if she's just seen him,' said Sloan reasonably.

'How does she know it's him?'

'Living image of the man in the photograph but older.'

'She's imagining it, then.'

'She swears not.'

'Wishful thinking.'

'A dead likeness,' said Sloan pithily. 'That's what Thorpe said.'

'Did he see him himself?'

'No. Not his face. Just his back.'

'I don't like it, Sloan.'

'No, sir.' He waited. 'There's something else.'

Leeyes' head came up with a jerk. 'What?'

'They've been in the minster looking at the East Calleshire Memorial there.'

'Well?'

'Jenkins's name isn't on it and he was supposed to have been killed in the war.'

'Well, if he's alive and kicking in Calleford this afternoon that's hardly surprising, is it? Be logical, Sloan.'

'Yes, sir.' You couldn't win. Not with Superintendent Leeyes.

'And I suppose they let him get away.'

'They were in a tea shop, sir. By the time they got out he'd disappeared.'

'So we don't know if the girl was right or wrong?'

'Strictly speaking, no.'

'And we don't know either, Sloan, if she is having us all on, the Thorpe boy included.'

'No, sir.'

'If she is, do you realize that nearly all the evidence we've got – if you can call it evidence – comes from her?'

'Yes, sir. Apart from Dr Dabbe, that is . . .'

'It's a lonely furrow,' agreed Leeyes sardonically, 'that the doctor's ploughing. What did you tell them to do?'

'Go home to Larking,' said Sloan. 'As the crow flies they're nearer there than they are to Berebury. I'll go down to Larking to see them later.'

Leeyes grunted.

'And,' continued Sloan, 'I'll get some copies of Jenkins's photograph blown up and rushed over to Calleford. No harm in looking for him . . .'

'No harm in finding him,' retorted Leeyes meaningfully. 'It'll be interesting to see if they can pick him up over there. I understand that they can do almost anything at Headquarters.'

'Yes, sir.' The Superintendent pursued his own private vendetta with County Constabulary Headquarters at Calleford.

'Of course,' blandly, 'he may not be called Jenkins.'

'No,' agreed Sloan dutifully.

'And that won't make it any easier for them.'

He did not sound particularly sorry about this.

Sloan went into Traffic Division on his way back from seeing the Superintendent. A lugubrious man called Harpe was in charge. He had a reputation for having never been known to smile, which reputation he hotly defended on the grounds that there had never been anything to smile about in Traffic Division. He was accordingly known as Happy Harry.

So it was now.

'Nothing's turned up, Sloan,' he said unsmiling. 'Not a thing. No witnesses. No damaged cars. Nobody reported knocking a woman down.'

'Where do you usually go from here?'

'Inquest. Newspaper publicity. Radio appeal for eyewitnesses to come forward.'

'Any response as a rule?'

'It all depends,' said Harpe cautiously. 'Usually someone comes forward. Not always.'

'They won't this time,' prophesied Sloan. Harpe's pessimism was infectious.

'Don't suppose they will. Lonely road. Unclassified, isn't it? Nobody about. Dark. Pubs open. Shops shut.'

'Institute night.'

'What's that?'

'Nothing.'

'Our chaps have been in all the local repair garages – no one's brought in anything suspicious, but then if they were bent on not coming forward they'd go as far afield as they conveniently could.'

'Or not repair at all.'

Harpe looked up. 'How do you mean?'

'If this was murder,' said Sloan, 'they'd be dead keen on not getting caught.'

'I'll say.'

'Well, I don't think they'd risk having telltale repairs done in Calleshire.'

'They might sell,' said Harpe doubtfully. 'We could get County Hall to tell us about ownership changes if you like.'

'I wasn't thinking of that, though it's a thought. No, if I'd done a murder with a motor car and got some damage to the front . . . how much damage would it be, by the way?'

Harpe shifted in his chair. 'Difficult to say. Varies a lot. Almost none sometimes. Another time it can chew up the front quite a lot. Especially if the windscreen goes.'

'It didn't,' said Sloan. 'There was no glass on the road at all. We looked.'

'That means his headlamps were all right then, too, doesn't it?'

Sloan nodded.

'Of course,' went on Harpe, with the expert's cold-blooded logic, 'if you're engineering your pedestrian stroke vehicle type of accident on purpose . . .'

'I think we were.'

Harpe shrugged. 'If you can afford to wait until you can see the whites of their eyes, then naturally you pick your spot.'

'How do you mean?'

'You hit them full on.'

'Amidships, so to speak?'

'Between the headlamps,' said Harpe seriously. 'You wouldn't break any glass then.'

'I see,' said Sloan.

'Of course, your "exchange principle" still applies.'

'What's that?'

'Car traces on the pedestrian. Pedestrian traces on the car. Paint, mostly, in the first case . . .'

'Dr Dabbe didn't say and he never misses anything.'

'Blood stains on the car,' went on Harpe cheerlessly, 'and hair and fibres of clothing – only you haven't got the car, have you?'

'No,' said Sloan. 'Then, to go back to concealing the damage . . .'

'If you didn't want to take it anywhere to repair . . .'

'I know what I'd do.'

Harpe looked at him uncompromisingly. 'Well, and what would you do?'

'Bash it into a brick wall,' said Sloan cheerfully. 'Or arrange another accident that would destroy all traces of the first. That would make him safe enough if they did find the car.'

Even then Harpe did not smile.

It was about a quarter to six when Henrietta and Bill Thorpe got back to Boundary Cottage, Larking.

Henrietta went straight through into the front room and halted in her tracks. Bill nearly bumped into her.

'Oh, I'd forgotten,' she said.

'What?'

'The police Inspector took the photograph away with him.'

'Why?'

'The medals,' said Henrietta vaguely. 'He was going to talk to the Rector about them.'

'There's a fair bit of talking needing doing,' said Bill, settling himself in a chair. 'Am I glad you're going to be twenty-one next month!'

'Why?' She hardly bothered to turn her head.

'Because if we've got to find this character Jenkins and ask his permission for you to marry me we're in real trouble.'

'He's not my father,' said Henrietta. 'My father's dead.'

'How do you know?'

'I don't,' she agreed miserably. 'I don't know anything. I don't even know what I know and what I don't know.'

Bill Thorpe nodded comprehendingly. 'I follow you – though thousands wouldn't. All the same, I'm glad that we'll be able to get to the altar without him. Shouldn't know where to begin to look.'

'It was him,' she said in the tone of one who has said the same thing many times before. 'I'd know him anywhere again. I knew that photograph like the back of my hand.'

'So you said before.'

'He was older, that's all.'

'Twenty years older?'

'About.' She sat down too. 'Men don't change all that much.'

'Sorry to hear you say that.' Bill Thorpe grinned and ran a hand over his face. 'There's room for improvement here. Or do you like me as I am?'

She made a gesture with her hand. 'I can't like you, Bill – I can't like anyone at the moment. Not until I know who I am. Oh, I can't put it into words but there just isn't any of me left over for things like that. Besides, you must know who it is you're marrying.'

'You,' said Bill Thorpe promptly. 'And very nice, too.'

'Bill, do be serious.'

'I am,' he said. 'Deadly. I want to marry you. You as you are now.'

She shook her head. 'I'm too confused. I don't know what I want.'

'I do,' he said simply. 'You.'

She turned away without speaking.

Bill Thorpe was not disconcerted. Instead he looked at his watch and then switched on the radio. It hummed and hawed for a bit and then presently the weather forecast came on. He listened intently until it was finished and was just leaning across to switch the radio off when the announcer said: 'The six o'clock news will follow in a minute and a quarter. Before the news there is a police message. There was an accident on the lower road to Belling St Peter in the village of Larking, Calleshire, on Tuesday evening when a woman was knocked down and fatally injured. Will the driver of the vehicle and anyone who witnessed the accident or who may be able to give any information please telephone the Chief Constable of Calleshire, telephone Calleford 2313, or any police station.'

Henrietta gave a sudden laugh. It was high-pitched and totally devoid of humour.

'Any information!' she cried. 'That's good, isn't it? If they only knew how much information we needed . . .'

11

'External examination,' Inspector Sloan began to read. 'The body was of a well-nourished female . . .'

Dr Dabbe's typewritten report of his post-mortem examination, addressed to H. M. Coroner for Calleshire and marked *Copy to Chief Constable*, lay on Inspector Sloan's desk. He got as far as 'aged about fifty-five' when Detective Constable Crosby came in.

'Everyone else seemed to be having tea, sir, so I brought some down. And the last of the cake.'

'Good,' said Sloan. 'I was beginning to feel the opposite of well nourished myself. How have you got on?'

Crosby carefully carried a cup of tea across the room and sat down. Then he opened his notebook. 'The hair, sir . . .'

'Ah, yes.' Sloan fingered Dr Dabbe's report. 'I've got the name of that dye down here. All twenty-five syllables of it.'

'I found the ladies' hairdressing saloon, sir . . .'

'They drop the second "o", Constable, nowadays.'

'Really, sir? Well, she had it done at a place called Marlene's in the High Street. I spoke to a young person there by the name of Sandra who – er – did her.'

'When?'

'Every second Friday at ten o'clock. Without fail.'

'Yes.' Sloan set his cup down. 'It would have to be without fail. Otherwise it would show.'

'What would, sir?'

'Her fair hair. According to Dr Dabbe she was fair haired.'

'And the girl was dark so she dyed hers dark, too,' concluded Crosby, 'so that the girl would think . . .'

'It's as good a disguise as any, too,' said Sloan. 'Especially if you don't expect it.' He paused. 'Cyril Jenkins was fair. You could see that much on the photograph.'

'Yes, sir.'

'That suggest anything to you?'

'No, sir.'

Sloan sighed. 'Constable, I agree the possibilities in this case are infinite. The murderer could be anyone, and as far as I am concerned the victim could be anyone and I am not altogether sure of the nature of the crime but there are just one or two clues worth considering.'

'Yes, sir,' said Crosby stolidly.

'The fact that Cyril Jenkins had . . .'

'Should it be "has", sir?'

Sloan glared. 'What's that? Oh, yes, that's a point.' He grunted and went on. 'Has – may have – fair hair and Grace Jenkins had fair hair which she took pains to dye the same colour as Henrietta's is interesting . . .'

'Yes, sir.'

'It's worse than drawing teeth, Crosby. Don't you have any ideas at all?'

'Yes, sir. But not about this,' he added hastily, not liking the look on Sloan's face.

'Has it occurred to you that there is one possibility that would account for it? That Cyril and Grace Jenkins were brother and sister . . .'

'No, sir,' replied Crosby truthfully. He thought for a minute and then said very, very cautiously, 'Where would the baby come in, then?'

'I don't know.' Sloan turned back to the report. 'How did you get on otherwise?'

'No joy about where she'd been all day except that it wasn't in Berebury.'

'What?'

'I showed her photograph to the Inspector at the bus station. He thinks he saw her at the incoming unloading point about half five. Doesn't know what bus she got off . . .'

'Wait a minute,' said Sloan suspiciously. 'How does he remember? That was Tuesday. Today's Friday.'

'I wondered about that, too, sir, but it seems as if an old lady tripped and fell and this Grace Jenkins helped her up and dusted her down. That sort of thing. And then handed her over to the bus people.'

Sloan nodded. 'Go on.'

'It appears she stayed in the bus station until the Larking bus left at seven five. In the cafeteria most of the time. The waitress remembered her. Says she served her with . . .'

'Baked beans,' interposed Sloan neatly.

Crosby looked startled. 'That's right. At about . . .'

'Six o'clock,' supplied Sloan.

'How do you know, sir?'

'Not me.' Laconically. 'The pathologist. He said so. She ate them about two hours before death. That ties up with her being killed as she walked home from the last bus.'

'Wonderful, sir, isn't it, what they can do when they cut you up?'

'Yes,' said Sloan shortly.

Crosby turned back to his notebook. 'Wherever she'd been she didn't get to the bus station until after the five fifteen to Larking had left, otherwise she'd presumably have caught that.'

'Fair enough,' agreed Sloan. 'What came in after five fifteen and before she went into the cafeteria?'

'A great many buses,' said Crosby with feeling. 'It's about their busiest time of the day. I've got a list but I wouldn't know where to begin if it's a case of talking to conductors.'

'Return tickets?' murmured Sloan. 'They might help.'

Crosby looked doubtful. Sloan went back to the post-mortem examination report.

'Was Happy Harry any help, sir?' ventured Crosby a little later.

'Inspector Harpe,' said Sloan distantly, 'has instigated the usual routine enquiries.'

'I see, sir. Thank you, sir.'

Suddenly Sloan tapped Dr Dabbe's report. 'Get me the hospital, will you, Crosby? There's one thing I can ask the pathologist . . .'

He was put through to Dr Dabbe's office without delay.

'About this Grace Jenkins, doctor . . .'

'Yes?'

'I notice you've made a note of her blood group.'

'Routine, Inspector.'

'I know that, doctor. What I was wondering is if the blood group could help us in other ways.'

'With the alleged daughter, you mean?' said Dabbe.

'Her alleged husband has turned up too,' said Sloan; and he explained about the sighting of Cyril Jenkins.

'Blood groups aren't a way of proving maternity or paternity. Only of disproving it.'

'I don't quite follow.'

'If the child has a different one then that is a factor in sustaining evidence that it is not the child of those particular people.'

'And if it is the same?'

'That narrows the field nicely.'

'How nicely?' guardedly.

'Usually to a round ten million or so people who could be its parents.'

'I see.' Sloan thought for a moment. 'We already know that Grace Jenkins is not the mother of Henrietta . . .'

'We do.'

'But if Cyril Jenkins is alive and is the father of Henrietta, then their blood groups would tie up, wouldn't they?'

A low rumble came down the telephone line. 'First, catch your hare . . .'

General Sir Eustace Garwell was at home and would see Inspector C. D. Sloan.

This news was conveyed to the waiting policemen by an elderly male retainer who had creaked to the door in answer to their ring. He was the fourth Garwell upon whom they had called since leaving the police station late that afternoon. The other three had numbered several Jenkinses among their acquaintance but not a Cyril Edgar nor a Grace and certainly not a Henrietta Eleanor Leslie. Nor did they look as if they could ever have had a hyphen in the family, let alone a Hocklington.

It was different at The Laurels, Cullingoak.

Sloan and Crosby had left it until the last because it was on the way to Larking. Both the hyphen and the Hocklington would have gone quite well with the Benares brass trays and the faded Indian carpets. There were a couple of potted palms in the hall and several fronds of dusty pampas grass brushed eerily against Crosby's cheek as he and Inspector Sloan followed the man down the corridor. He walked so slowly that the two policemen had the greatest difficulty in not treading on his heels. There was that in his walk though, together with the fact that he had referred to 'the General' and not 'Sir Eustace' that made Sloan say:

'You've seen service yourself.'

'Batman to the General, sir, since he was a subaltern.'

'The West Calleshires or the Cavalry?' hazarded Sloan.

The man stopped in his tracks and drew himself up to his full height. 'The East Calleshires, sir, not the West.'

Sloan began to feel hopeful.

'We only live in the western part of the county,' went on the man, 'because her ladyship was left this property, and though she's been dead some years, the General's too old to be making a change.'

'I'm sorry,' said Sloan, suitably abject.

A very old gentleman struggled out of a chair as they entered.

'Come in, gentlemen, come in. It's not often I have any callers in the evening. We live a very quiet life here, you know. Stopped going out when m'wife died. What'll you take to drink?'

Sloan declined port, madeira and brandy in that order.

'On duty, sir, I'm afraid.'

The General nodded sympathetically, and said they would

forgive him his brandy and soda because he wasn't on duty any more, in fact it was many a long year now since he had been.

'It's about the past we've come,' said Sloan by way of making a beginning.

'My memory's not what it used to be,' said the old man.

'Pity,' murmured Crosby *sotto voce*.

'What's that? I can't hear so well either. Damned MO fellow wants me to have a hearing aid thing. Can't be bothered.' The General indicated a chair on his left and said to Sloan, 'If you would sit here I shall hear you better.' He settled himself back in his own chair. 'Ah, that's more comfortable. Now, how far back in the past do you want to go? Ladysmith?'

'Ladysmith?' echoed Sloan, considerably startled.

'It was Mafeking they made all the fuss about – they forgot the siege of Ladysmith.' He fixed Sloan with a bleary eye. 'Do you want to know about Ladysmith?'

'You were there, sir?'

The General gave a deep chuckle. 'I was there. I was there for a long time. The whole siege. And I've never wasted a drop of drink or a morsel of food since.' He leant forward. 'Are you sure about that brandy?'

'Certainly, sir. Thank you.'

The General took another sip. 'Commissioned in '99. Went through the whole of the Boer War. Nearly died of fever more than once. Still' – he brightened – 'none of it seemed to do me any harm.'

This much, at least, was patently true. They were looking at a very old man indeed but he seemed to be in possession of all his faculties. Sloan thought back quickly, dredging through his schoolboy memory for names of battles.

'Were you at Omdurman, Sir Eustace?'

Sir Eustace Garwell waved the brandy glass under his nose with a thin hand, sniffing appreciatively. The veins on his hand stood out, hard and gnarled. 'No, sir, I was not at Omdurman. Incredible as it may seem now, I was too young for that episode in our military history. At the time I was very distressed about missing it by a year or so. I was foolish enough to fear that there

weren't going to be any more wars.' He gave a melancholy snort.
'I needn't have worried, need I?'

'No, sir . . .'

'Now, on the whole I'm rather glad. You realize, don't you,
that had I been born a couple of years earlier I should probably
be dead by now.'

Sloan took a moment or two to work this out and then he said,
'I see what you mean, sir.'

'The East Callies were there, of course. Battle honours and
all that . . .'

'Yes.' Sloan raised his voice a little. 'There is just one little
matter on which you may be able to help us by remembering.
After Ladysmith. Probably sometime between the wars.'

'I was in India from '04 to 1913,' said the General helpfully.
'In the Punjab.'

'Not those wars,' said Sloan hastily, hoping Sir Eustace was
too deaf to have heard Crosby's snort. 'Between the other two.'

'Ah. It wasn't the same, you know.'

'I dare say not,' said Sloan drily.

'Everything changed after 1914 but war most of all.'

'Do you recollect a Sergeant Jenkins in the regiment, sir?'

There was a row of ivory elephants on the mantelpiece, their
trunks properly facing the door. Sloan had time to count them
before the General replied.

'Jenkins, did you say? No, the name doesn't mean anything to
me. Known quite a few men of that name in m'time but not in the
regiment. Hirst might know. Ask him.'

'Thank you, sir, I will.'

'They put me on the Staff,' said the old voice querulously. 'You
never know anyone then.'

'Did you ever have a woman called Grace Jenkins working for
you either, sir?'

'Can't say that we did. We had a housekeeper but she's been
dead for years and her name wasn't Jenkins.'

'Or Wright?'

'No. One of the cleaning women might have been called that.
You'd have to ask Hirst. They come and go, you know.'

If the dust on the ivory elephants was any measure, this was one of the times when they had gone.

'No, not a cleaning woman,' said Sloan. 'A children's nurse, perhaps. A nanny?'

'Never had any children,' said the General firmly. 'No nannies about the place ever.'

'I see, sir. Thank you. Well, then, I must apologize for disturbing you. Routine enquiry, you understand.'

'Quite so.'

Sloan got up to go. 'About a woman who used to work as a children's nurse for a family called Hocklington-Garwell and we're trying to trace . . .'

Without any warning the whole atmosphere inside the drawing room of The Laurels, Cullingoak, changed.

Two beady eyes peered at Sloan over the top of the brandy glass. Just as quickly the old face became suffused with colour. A choleric General Sir Eustace Garwell put down his glass with shaking hands.

'Sir,' he said, quite outraged, 'is this a joke?'

He struggled to his feet, anger in every feature of his stiff and ancient frame. He tottered over to the wall and put his finger on a bell.

'If I were a younger man, sir,' he quavered, 'I would send for a horse whip. As it is, I shall just ask my man to show you the door. Goodnight, sir, goodnight.'

12

As always, Sloan was polite.

He had long ago learned that there were few situations where a police officer – or anyone else, for that matter – gained by not being.

Henrietta was sitting opposite him and Crosby in the little parlour of Boundary Cottage.

'Yes, Inspector, I'm certain it was Hocklington-Garwell. It's not really a name you could confuse, is it?'

'No, miss, that's very true.'

'Besides, why should I tell you a name like that if it isn't the one I was told?'

'That's not for me to say, miss.'

She stared at him. 'You do believe me, don't you?'

'The mention of the name certainly upset the old gentleman, miss. He ordered us out of the house.'

Henrietta just looked puzzled. 'I can't understand it at all. It was Hocklington-Garwell and they had two boys. Master Michael and Master Hugo. I've heard such a lot about them always . . .'

'The General said he hadn't had any children,' said Sloan.

'There you are, then. It must have been the wrong man . . .'

'But the merest mention of the name upset him, miss. There was no mistake about that.'

She subsided again, shaking her head. 'I can't begin to explain that. They're wrong, you know, when they say, "What's in a name?" There seems to be everything in it.'

'Just at the moment,' agreed Sloan. He coughed. 'About the other matter, miss . . .'

'My father?'

'The man in the photograph.'

'Cyril Jenkins . . .'

'Yes, miss. We've got a general call out for him now, starting in the Calleford area . . .'

'You'll find him, won't you?'

'I think we will,' said Sloan with a certain amount of reservation. 'Whether, if we do, we shall find he fulfils all three conditions of identity . . .'

'Three?'

'That your father, the man in the photograph and Cyril Edgar Jenkins are all one and the same.'

She nodded and said positively, 'I can only tell you one of them, that he was the man in the photograph.' She tightened her lips. 'You'll have to tell me the other two afterwards, won't you?'

Sloan frowned. There were quite a few little matters that Cyril Jenkins could inform them about and the first question they would ask him was where exactly he had been just before eight o'clock on Tuesday evening. Aloud he said, 'We'll tell you all we can, miss, though you realize someone might simply have borrowed his photograph to put on the mantelpiece here?'

She smiled wanly. 'Is that what they call a father figure, Inspector?'

'Something like that, miss.'

'Why should she have told me he was dead if he wasn't?'

'I don't know, miss.' Sloan couldn't remember a time when he had used the phrase so often. 'He might have left her, I suppose . . .' It wasn't a subject he was prepared to pursue at this moment, so he cleared his throat and said, 'In view of what you have told us about the war memorial and the Rector about the medals, we are in touch with the War Office but there will inevitably be a little delay.'

A brief smile flitted across her face and was gone. 'Friday afternoon's not the best time, is it?'

'No, miss, I doubt if we shall have anything in time for the inquest.'

'Mr Arbican's coming,' she said, 'and he's going to get someone to start going through the court adoption records.'

'That's a long job,' said Sloan, who had already taken advice on this point.

'Starting with the Calleshire County Court and the Berebury, Luston and Calleford Magistrates' ones. That's the most hopeful, isn't it?' she said. 'I expect you think I'm being unreasonable, Inspector, but I must know who I am – even if Bill Thorpe doesn't care.'

'Doesn't he?' said Sloan alertly.

She grimaced. 'He only thinks it's important if you happen to be an Aberdeen Angus bull.'

'Back to Berebury?' enquired Crosby hopefully, as they left Boundary Cottage. Breakfast was the only solid meal he had had so far that day and he was getting increasingly aware of the fact.

Sloan got into the car beside him. 'No.' He got out his notebook. 'So young Thorpe doesn't care who she is . . .'

'So she said.'

'But he still wants to marry her.'

'That's right,' said Crosby, who privately found it rather romantic.

'Has it occurred to you that that could be because he already knows who she is?'

'No,' responded Crosby simply.

'I think,' said Sloan, 'we shall have to look into the background of young Mr Thorpe. Just to be on the safe side, you might say.'

'Now?' Crosby started up the engine.

'No. Later. Just drive up the road. We're going to call at The Hall. To see what Mr James Hibbs knows.'

Mr and Mrs Hibbs were just finishing their evening meal. Enough of its aroma still hung about to tantalize Crosby's idle digestive juices, though there was no sign of food. The Hibbses were having coffee by a log fire in their hall, the two gun dogs supine before it. A bare wooden staircase clambered up to the first floor. The rest was dark panelling and the total effect was of great comfort.

Sloan declined coffee out of cups so tiny and fragile-looking that he could not bear to think of them in Constable Crosby's hands.

'You're quite sure?' said Mrs Hibbs. She was a tall, imposing woman with a deep voice. 'Or would you prefer some beer?'

Sloan – to say nothing of Crosby – would have greatly preferred some beer but he shook his head regretfully. 'Thank you, no, madam. We just want to ask a few more questions about the late Mrs Grace Jenkins.'

'A terrible business,' said Mrs Hibbs. 'To think of her lying there in the road all night, and nobody knew.'

'Except, I dare say,' put in Hibbs, 'the fellow who knocked her down. All my eye, you know, this business that you can say you didn't notice the bump. Any driver would notice.'

'Quite so, sir.'

'It's a wonder that James didn't find her himself,' went on Mrs Hibbs, placidly pouring out more coffee.

'Really, madam?'

'You sometimes take Richard and Berengaria that way, don't you, dear?'

'Yes,' said Hibbs rather shortly.

Sloan said, 'Who?'

'Richard and Berengaria.' She pointed to the dogs. 'We always call them after kings and queens, you know.'

'I see, madam.' Sloan, who thought dogs should be called Spot or Lassie, turned to James Hibbs. 'Did you happen to take them that way on Tuesday, sir?'

'No, Inspector.'

'Which way,' mildly, 'did you take them?'

'Towards the village. I had some letters to post.'

'About what time would that have been?'

'Half-past eightish.'

'And you saw nothing and nobody?' The answer to that anyway was a foregone conclusion.

'No.'

'I see, sir. Thank you.' Sloan changed his tone and said easily, 'We're running into a little difficulty in establishing the girl's antecedents . . . it wouldn't matter so much if Henrietta – Miss Jenkins – weren't under twenty-one.'

'Probate, I suppose,' said Hibbs wisely. 'And she was intestate, too, I dare say. I'm forever advising people to make their wills but they won't, you know. They think they're immortal.'

'Quite so, sir,' said Sloan, who hadn't made his own just yet.

'She needn't worry about the cottage, if that's on her mind. She's a protected tenant and anyway I can't see myself putting her on the street.'

This was obviously meant to be a mild joke for his wife smiled.

'Even if Threlkeld would advise it,' went on Hibbs heartily, 'and I expect he would. There's more to being an agent than that.'

'That letter he found for us,' said Sloan, 'which put us on to the Calleford solicitors . . .'

'Yes?'

'It didn't get us much further. They had no records of any dealings with her.'

'I'm not really surprised,' said Hibbs. 'It was a long time ago.'

'That's true.' Sloan, it seemed, was all affability and agreement. 'Actually, we have gone a bit further back than that. To some people Grace Jenkins used to work for . . .'

'Really?' Hibbs didn't sound unduly interested.

'They were called Hocklington-Garwell.'

'Yes?' His face was a mask of polite interest.

'Does the name convey anything to you?'

Hibbs frowned. 'Can't say it does, Inspector.'

But it did to Mrs Hibbs.

Sloan could see that from her face.

Superintendent Leeyes was never in a very good mood first thing in the morning. He sent for Inspector Sloan as soon as he got to the police station on the Saturday morning. The portents were not good.

'Well, Sloan, any news?'

'Not very much, sir. Inspector Harpe hasn't got anything for us at all on the Traffic side. No response at all to the radio appeal. Of course, it's early days yet – it only went out last night . . .'

Leeyes grunted. 'They either saw it or they didn't see it.'

'No witnesses,' went on Sloan hastily. 'No cars taken in for suspicious repairs anywhere in the county . . .'

'I don't know what we have a Traffic Division for,' grumbled Leeyes.

Sloan kept silent.

'What about Somerset House?'

'Still searching, sir.'

Leeyes grunted again. 'And the pensions people?'

'They've been on the phone. They say they're paying out a total disability pension to a Cyril Edgar Jenkins . . .'

'Oh?'

'Not him. This one was wounded on the Somme in July 1916.'

'That's not a lot of help.'

'No, sir.' He coughed. 'In view of the brief reappearance of Jenkins I've asked the War Office to turn up the Calleshire Regiment records. His discharge papers would be a help.'

'So would his appearance,' said Leeyes briskly. 'Calleford haven't found him yet, I take it?'

'I rang them this morning,' said Sloan obliquely. 'They'd visited all the people called Jenkins in the city itself without finding anyone corresponding to either the photograph or the girl's description – but there's a big hinterland to Calleford. And it was their market day yesterday too. He might have come in to that – or to shop or to work.'

'Or to see the minster,' suggested Leeyes sarcastically. 'What I don't like about it is the coincidence.'

'I suppose it is odd,' conceded Sloan. 'The one day the girl happens to go there she sees him.'

'She says she sees him,' snapped Leeyes.

'On the other hand he might be there every day. For all we know he is.'

'Get anywhere with the Garwells?' Superintendent Leeyes always changed his ground rather than be forced into a conclusion which might subsequently turn out to be incorrect. His subordinates rarely caught him out – even if they never realized why it was.

Sloan obediently told him how far he had got with the Garwells.

Leeyes sniffed. 'Funny, that.'

'Yes, sir. The General very nearly threw a fit and Mrs Hibbs knew something. I'm sure of that.'

'What about Hibbs himself?'

'Didn't move a muscle. If the name meant anything to him, it didn't show in his face like it did in hers.'

'Is he putting the girl out?' said Leeyes hopefully. 'That might mean something.'

'No.' Sloan shook his head. 'He says she's a protected tenant but in any case he wouldn't.'

'Why not?'

'It's still a bit feudal out there, sir.'

'They had this sort of trouble in feudal times.'

'Gave me the impression, sir, that he felt a bit responsible for his tenants.'

'Impression be blowed,' retorted Leeyes vigorously. 'What we want to know is whether he was literally responsible for the girl. Biologically speaking.'

'Quite so,' murmured Sloan weakly.

'It's all very well for him to be hinting that he couldn't put her on the street because it wasn't expected of a man in his position but,' Leeyes said glaring, 'that's as good a way of concealing a real stake in her welfare as any.'

'Sort of taking a fatherly interest?' suggested Sloan sedulously.

The Superintendent snorted. 'This village patriarch of yours – what's his wife like?'

'Tall, what you might call a commanding presence.'

Leeyes looked interested. He felt he had one of those himself.

'She didn't,' said Sloan cautiously, 'strike me as the sort of woman to overlook even one wild oat.'

'There you are then.' He veered away from the subject of the Hibbses as quickly as he had brought it up. 'What next?'

'The inquest is in an hour.' Sloan looked at his watch. 'And then a few enquiries about young Master Thorpe of Shire Oak Farm.'

'Oh?' Leeyes's head came up like a hound just offered a new scent.

'He,' said Sloan meaningfully, 'doesn't care who she is. He just wants to marry her as soon as possible. That may only be love's young dream . . .'

'Ahah.' The Superintendent leered at Sloan. 'From what you've said she's a mettlesome girl.'

'On the other hand,' said Sloan repressively, 'it may not.'

The Rector of Larking and Mrs Meyton and Bill Thorpe all went into Berebury with Henrietta for the inquest. It was to be held in the town hall and they met Felix Arbican, the solicitor, about half an hour beforehand in one of the numerous rooms leading off the main hall.

'I can't predict the outcome,' was the first thing he said to them after shaking hands gravely. 'You may get a verdict of death by misadventure. You may get an adjournment.'

'Oh, dear,' said Henrietta.

'The police may want more time to find the driver of the car . . .'

'And Cyril Jenkins.'

Arbican started. 'Who?'

Henrietta told him about the previous afternoon.

'I'm very glad to hear you've seen him,' responded the solicitor. 'It would seem at this juncture that a little light on the proceedings would be a great help.'

'No light was shed,' said Henrietta astringently.

'None?'

'We couldn't find him in the crowd,' said Bill Thorpe.

Arbican turned to Thorpe and asked shrewdly, 'Were you able to identify him?'

Bill Thorpe shook his head. 'I only saw his back.'

'I see. So Miss Jenkins is the only person who is certain who it was and the police haven't yet found him?'

'Yes,' intervened Henrietta tersely.

'Extraordinary business altogether.'

'More extraordinary than that,' said Mr Meyton, and told him about the medals.

Arbican's limpid gaze fell upon the Rector. 'Most peculiar. Let us hope that the police are able to find this man and that when they do some – er – satisfactory explanation is forthcoming.' He coughed. 'In the mean time I think we had better come back to the more immediate matter of the inquest.'

Henrietta lifted her face expectantly. The animation which had been there since she saw Cyril Jenkins had gone.

'Your part, Miss Jenkins, is quite simple. You have only to establish identity.'

'Quite simple!' she echoed bitterly. 'It's anything but simple.'

'To establish identity as you knew it,' amplified Arbican. 'If the police have evidence that Grace Jenkins was not – er – Grace Jenkins they will bring it. As far as you are concerned that has always been the name by which you knew her . . .'

'Yes.'

'Strong presumptive evidence. In any case . . .'

'Yes?'

'The Coroner holds an inquest on a body, not – so to speak – on a person. An unknown body sometimes.'

'I see.'

'His duty will be to establish the cause of death. If it was from other than natural causes, and it – um – appears to have been, then he has a parallel duty to enquire into the nature of the cause.'

'I see.' Henrietta wasn't really listening any more. For one thing, she found it difficult to concentrate now. Her mind wandered off so easily that she couldn't keep all her attention on what someone was saying. For another she didn't really want to hear a legal lecture from a prosperous-looking man in a black suit. He had never had cause to wonder who he was. He was too confident for that.

'The cause of death,' he was saying didactically, 'would appear to be obvious. The main point must be the identity of the driver. If the police found him we could try suing for damages.'

'Damages?'

'Substantial damages,' said Arbican.

'If no one else saw the car even, let alone the driver, I don't see how they'll ever find him.'

Bill Thorpe was getting restive too. 'And it was nearly a week ago already.'

'They'll go on trying,' said the solicitor. 'They're very persistent.'

'You say,' put in Mrs Meyton anxiously, 'that all Henrietta will have to do will be to give evidence of identification?'

'That's all, Mrs Meyton. It won't take very long. The Coroner may want to know if Mrs Jenkins's sight and hearing were normal. If it seems relevant her doctor could be called in as an expert witness on the point. Otherwise the Coroner will just note what she says.'

' " 'Write that down,' the King said," ' burbled Henrietta hysterically, ' " 'and reduce the answer to shillings and pence.' " '

Arbican looked bewildered.

'*Alice in Wonderland*,' said the Rector, as if that explained everything.

13

There was a sudden stir and a rustle of feet. Seven men filed into the room where the inquest was being held and sat together at one side of the dais. Henrietta looked at Arbican.

'The jury, Miss Jenkins.'

She hadn't known there would be a jury.

'There is always a jury when death is caused by a vehicle on a public highway.'

The Rector counted them. 'I thought juries were like apostles . . .'

Arbican frowned. 'I beg your pardon?'

'Twelve in number.'

'Not for a Coroner's Inquest.'

'So We Are Seven?'

Arbican frowned again. 'We are seven?'

'It's another quotation,' said Mr Meyton kindly.

Henrietta was the first person to be called. A man handed her a Bible and told her what to say.

'I hereby swear by Almighty God that the evidence I shall give touching the death of Grace Edith Jenkins shall be the truth, the whole truth and nothing but the truth.'

The Coroner picked up his pen. 'Your name?'

She swallowed visibly. 'Henrietta Eleanor Leslie Jenkins.'

'You have seen the body declared to be that of a woman found on the lower road to Belling St Peter in the village of Larking on Wednesday morning last?'

'Yes.'

'A little louder please, Miss Jenkins.'

'Yes.'

'And you identify it as that of the said Grace Edith Jenkins?'

'I do.'

'What was your relationship to the deceased?'

She stared at a spot on the wall above and behind the Coroner's head and said faintly. 'Adopted daughter.'

The Coroner twitched his papers. 'I must ask you to speak up. I am aware that this must perforce be a painful occasion to you but an inquest is a public inquiry, and the public have a right, if not a duty, to hear what is said.'

'Adopted daughter.' She said it more firmly this time, as if she herself were more sure.

'Thank you.' His courtesy was automatic, without sarcasm. 'When did you last see the deceased alive?'

'Early in January, before I went back to college.' She hesitated. 'I was due home at the end of this month but, of course . . .' her voice trailed away.

'Quite so.' The Coroner made a further note on his papers. 'That will be all for the time being, Miss Jenkins. I must ask you to remain in the building as you may be recalled later.'

Harry Ford, postman, came next, and deposed how he had come across the body early on Wednesday morning.

Graphically.

Mrs Callows described how Mrs Jenkins had got off the last bus with her and Mrs Perkins.

Melodramatically.

Then PC Hepple related that which he had found.

Technically.

The Coroner wrote down the width of the carriageway and said, 'And the length of the skid mark?'

Hepple cleared his throat. 'I'm sorry, sir, I'm afraid there wasn't one.'

The Coroner was rather like a rook. An elderly but still spry rook. And very alert. He didn't miss the fact that there was no evidence of the car's brakes being urgently applied. Nor did he comment on it. Henrietta moved a little forward on her chair as if she hadn't quite heard the Constable properly but otherwise his statement made no visible impact.

Then a tall thin man was taking the oath with practised ease. He identified himself – though the Coroner must have known him well – as Hector Smithson Dabbe, Bachelor of Medicine and Bachelor of Surgery, Consultant Pathologist to the Berebury Group Hospital Management Committee. Then he gave his evidence.

Impersonally.

Henrietta lowered her head as if in defence but she couldn't escape the pathologist's voice while he explained that, in his opinion, the injuries sustained by the body which he was given to understand was that of one Grace Edith Jenkins . . .

Henrietta noticed the word 'which'. Grace Jenkins was – had been – a person. She wasn't any longer. This man had said 'which' not 'who'.

'. . . were consistent,' said Dr Dabbe, 'with her having been run over by a heavy vehicle twice.'

Henrietta felt sick.

The Coroner thanked him and then shuffled his papers into order and looked at the jury. 'I am required by law to adjourn an inquest for fourteen days if I am requested to do so by the Chief Constable on the grounds that a person may be charged with murder, manslaughter or with causing death by reckless or dangerous driving.'

He paused. Someone in the room sneezed into the stillness.

'I have received such a request from the Chief Constable of Calleshire and this inquest is accordingly adjourned for two weeks. No doubt the Press will take cognizance of the fact that the police are appealing for witnesses.'

The press – in the person of a ginger-haired cub reporter from the *Berebury News* – obediently scribbled a note and suddenly it was all over.

*

Inspector Sloan came up to Henrietta. 'I won't keep you, miss. There's just one thing I must say to you.'

'Yes?'

'I know you weren't thinking of it but I must formally ask you not to go abroad before the inquest is resumed.'

She smiled wanly. 'I promise.'

He hesitated. 'May I hazard a guess, miss, that you've never been abroad at all?'

'Never, Inspector. How did you know?'

He didn't answer directly. 'Did you ever want to?'

'Yes, I did. Especially lately. Since I've been at university, I mean. Some friends went on a reading party to France last summer. They asked me to go with them and I should have liked to have gone . . .'

'But Grace Jenkins didn't want you to . . .' put in Sloan.

'That's right. How did you know?'

'Did she say why?'

'I thought it was because of the money.'

'It may have been, miss, but there could have been another reason too.'

'Could there?' It was impossible to tell if she was interested or not.

'To go abroad you need a passport.'

'Yes . . .'

'To get a passport you need a birth certificate.'

She was quicker to follow him than he had expected, swooping down on the point. 'That means I'm not Jenkins, doesn't it?'

'I think so.'

'Otherwise,' went on Henrietta slowly, 'she could have arranged it all without my actually seeing the birth certificate.'

'Probably.'

'But not if my surname wasn't Jenkins.'

'No.'

They stood a moment in silence then Henrietta said, 'I shall have to sign my name somewhere sometime . . .'

'I should stick to Jenkins for the time being,' advised Sloan.

'A living lie?'

'Call it a working compromise.'

'Or shall I just make my mark?'

'Your mark, miss?'

'I think an "X" would be most appropriate.' She gave him a wintry smile. 'After all, it does stand for the unknown quantity as well as the illiterate.'

He opened his mouth to answer but she forestalled him.

'There's one thing anyway . . .'

'Yes, miss?'

'I'm practically certain of a place in any college team you care to mention.'

'College team?' echoed Sloan, momentarily bewildered.

'There's always an A. N. Other there, you know,' she said swiftly. And was gone.

'That's that,' observed Crosby without enthusiasm as he and Inspector Sloan got back to the police station afterwards. 'We've only got two weeks and we still don't know what sort of a car or where to look for the driver.'

'One good thing, though,' said Sloan, determinedly cheerful. 'From what the Coroner said everyone will think we're looking for a dangerous driver.'

Crosby sniffed. 'Needle in a haystack, more like. PC Hepple said to tell you there's nothing new at his end. He can't find anyone who saw or heard a car on Tuesday evening.'

'No.' Sloan was not altogether surprised. 'No, I reckon whoever killed her sat and waited in the car park of the pub and then just timed her walk from the bus stop to the bad corner.'

'That's a bit chancy,' objected Crosby. 'She might not have been on that bus.'

'I think,' gently, 'that he knew she was on it. The only real risk was that someone else from down the lane might have been on it too. But now I've seen how few houses there are there, I don't think that was anything to worry about.' He pushed open his office door, and crossed over to his desk. There was a message lying there for him. 'Hullo, the Army have answered. Read this, Crosby.'

'Jenkins, C. E., Sergeant, the East Calleshires,' read Crosby aloud. 'Enlisted September, 1939, demobilized July, 1946. Address on enlistment . . .'

'Go on.'

'Holly Tree Farm,' said Crosby slowly, 'Rooden Parva, near Calleford.'

'The plot thickens,' said Sloan rubbing his hands.

'That's what the girl told us, wasn't it, sir? Holly Tree Farm.'

'That's right. She said she didn't know the second bit.' He paused. 'Get me the Calleford police . . .'

Sloan spoke to someone on duty there, waited an appreciable time while the listener looked something up and finally thanked him and replaced the receiver.

Crosby stood poised between the door and the desk. 'Are we going there, sir?'

'Not straight. We're calling somewhere on the way. They've looked up the address. There's no one called Jenkins there now. Walsh is the name of the occupier.' Sloan looked at his watch. 'It's nearly twelve. Do you suppose Hirst nips out for a quick one before lunch?'

'Hirst?' said Crosby blankly.

'The General's man. We must know what's so sinister about the magic words Hocklington-Garwell.'

Which was how Detective Inspector Sloan and Detective Constable Crosby came to be enjoying a pint of beer at the Bull in Cullingoak shortly after half-past twelve. The bar was comfortably full.

'He usually comes in for a few minutes,' agreed the landlord on enquiry. 'He's got the old gentleman, see. Got to give him his lunch at quarter past. Very particular about time, is the General. Same in the evening. He can't come out till he's got him settled for the night.' He swept the two plainclothesmen with an appraising glance. 'You friends of his?'

'Sort of,' agreed Sloan noncommittally.

The landlord leaned two massive elbows on the bar. 'If it's money you're after you can collect it somewhere else. I'm not having anyone dunned in my house.'

'No,' said Sloan distantly. 'We're not after money.'

'That's all right, then,' said the landlord.

Sloan allowed a suitable pause before asking, 'Horses or dogs?'

The landlord swept up a couple of empty glasses from the bar with arms too brawny for such light work. 'Horses. Nothing much – just the odd flutter – like they all do.'

'Did he come in last night?'

'Hirst?' The landlord frowned. 'Now you come to mention it, I don't think he did. Perhaps his old gentleman wanted him. He's not young, isn't the General.'

'Quite,' agreed Sloan. 'What'll you have?'

It was nearly ten to one before Hirst appeared. He came in quietly, a newspaper – open at the sporting page – tucked under his arm. He looked a little younger in the pub than he had done in the General's house but not much. His shoes were polished to perfection and his hair neatly plastered down but he, like his master, was showing signs of advancing age. Sloan let him get his pint and sit down before he looked in his direction.

'I fear, Hirst, that I upset the General last night,' he said.

Hirst looked up, recognized him and put down his glass with a hand that was not quite steady. 'Yes, sir. That you did.'

'It was quite accidental . . .'

'Proper upset, he was. I had quite a time with him last night after you'd gone, I can tell you.'

'You did?' enquired Sloan, even more interested.

'Carrying on alarming he was till I got him to bed.'

'Hirst, what was it we said that did it?'

'The General didn't say.' He lifted his glass. 'But he was upset all right.'

'I was asking him something about the past,' said Sloan carefully, watching Hirst's face. 'Something I wanted to know about a woman who – I think – was called Grace Jenkins.'

There was no reaction from Hirst.

'Do you know the name?' persisted Sloan.

'Can't say that I do.' Reassured, he took another pull at his beer. 'It's a common enough one.'

'That's part of the trouble.'

'I see.'

'Garwell's not a common name,' said Sloan conversationally.

'No,' agreed Hirst. 'There's not many of them about.'

'And Hocklington-Garwell isn't common at all.'

Hirst set his glass down with a clatter. 'You mentioned Hocklington-Garwell to the General?'

'I did.'

'You shouldn't have done that, sir,' said Hirst reproachfully.

'This woman Jenkins told her daughter that she used to be nursemaid to the family.'

'No wonder the General was so upset. In fact, what with her ladyship being dead, I should say it would have upset the General more than anything else would have done.'

'It did,' agreed Sloan briefly, 'but why?'

Hirst sucked his teeth. 'Begging your pardon, Mr Sloan, sir, I should have said it was all over and done with long before your time.'

'What,' cried Sloan in exasperation, 'was all over and done with before my time?'

'That explains why the General was so upset about your being a detective, sir, if you'll forgive my mentioning it.'

Sloan, who had been a detective for at least ten years without ever before feeling the fact to be unmentionable, looked at the faded gentleman's gentleman and said he would forgive him.

'I kept on telling him,' said Hirst, 'that it was all over and done with.' He took another sip of beer. 'But it wasn't any good. I had to get the doctor to him this morning, you know.'

'Hirst,' said Sloan dangerously, 'I need to know exactly what it was that was over and done with before my time and I need to know now.'

'The Hocklington-Garwell business. Before the last war, it was. And she is dead now, God rest her soul, so why drag it up again?'

'Who is dead?' Sloan was hanging on to his temper with an effort. A great effort.

'Her ladyship, like I told you. And Major Hocklington, too, for all I know.'

'Hirst, I think I am beginning to see daylight. Hocklington and Garwell are two different people, aren't they?'

'That's right, sir. Like I said. There's the General who you saw yesterday and then there was Major Hocklington – only it's all a long time ago now, sir, so can't you let the whole business alone?'

'Not as easily as you might think, Hirst.'

'For the sake of the General, sir . . .'

'Am I to understand, Hirst, that Lady Garwell and this Major Hocklington had an affair?'

Hirst plunged his face into the pint glass as far as it would go and was understood to say that that was about the long and the short of it.

Detective Inspector Sloan let out a great shout of laughter.

'Please, sir,' begged Hirst. 'Not here in a public bar. The General wouldn't like it.'

'No,' agreed Sloan. 'I can see now why he didn't like my asking him if he was called Hocklington-Garwell. In the circumstances, I'm not sure that I would have cared for it myself. Would a note of apology help.'

'It might, sir.' Hirst sounded grateful. 'But why did you do it, sir? It's all such a long time ago now. We never had any children in the family, sir, so we never had any nursemaids at all. And there's no call for a nursemaid without babies to look after, is there?'

'I asked him, Hirst, because a woman, who is also dead now, had a sense of humour.'

'Really, sir?' Hirst was polite but sounded unconvinced.

'Yes, Hirst, really. I never met her but I am coming to know her quite well. She misled me at first but I think I am beginning to understand her now.'

'Indeed, sir?'

'A very interesting woman. Give me your glass, will you?'

'Thank you, sir. I don't mind if I do.'

The Rector of Larking and Mrs Meyton joined Henrietta as soon as the inquest was over. She was standing talking to Bill Thorpe and Arbican.

'There is very little more you can do at this stage, Miss Jenkins,' the solicitor was saying. 'You must, of course, be available for the adjourned inquest.'

'I shan't run away.' Henrietta sounded as if she had had enough of life for one morning.

'Of course not,' pacifically. 'And then there will be the question of intestacy.'

'What does that mean?'

Mr Meyton coughed. 'I think that is the greatest virtue of education . . .'

Arbican turned politely to the Rector, who said:

'You learn the importance of admitting you don't know.'

'Quite so.' Arbican turned back to Henrietta. 'Grace Jenkins appears to have died without making a will. That is to say' – legal-fashion, he qualified the statement immediately – 'we cannot find one. It hasn't been deposited with the bank, nor presumably with any Berebury solicitor . . .'

'How do you know that?' asked Bill Thorpe.

'There is a fairly full account of the accident in yesterday's local newspaper. I think any Berebury firm holding such a will would have made themselves known by now.'

'The bureau,' said Henrietta heavily. 'I expect it was in the bureau.'

There was a little silence. They had nearly forgotten the bureau.

Arbican coughed. 'In the mean time, I think perhaps the best course of action would be . . .'

'I think,' Bill Thorpe interrupted firmly, 'that the best course of action would be for me to marry Henrietta as quickly as possible.'

14

Rooden Parva was really little more than a hamlet.

It lay in the farthest corner of the county, south of Calleford and south of the much more substantial village of Great Rooden. Sloan and Crosby got there at about half-past two when the calm of a country Saturday afternoon had descended on a scene that could never have been exactly lively.

'This is a dead-and-alive hole, all right,' said Crosby. They had pulled up at the only garage in Rooden Parva to ask the way and he had pushed a bell marked FOR SERVICE beside the solitary petrol pump.

Nothing whatsoever happened.

'Try the shop,' suggested Sloan tetchily.

They were luckier there. Crosby came out smelling faintly of paraffin and said Holly Tree Farm was about a mile and a half out in the country.

'This being Piccadilly Circus, I suppose,' said Sloan looking at all of twelve houses clustered together.

'They said we can't miss it,' said Crosby. 'There's only one road anyway.'

Holly Tree Farm lay at the end of it. It, too, had fallen into a sort of rural torpor, though this appeared to be a permanent state and in no way connected with its being Saturday afternoon. The front door, dimly visible behind a barricade of holly trees, looked as if it hadn't been opened in years. Knocking on the back one alerted a few hens which were pecking about in the yard but nothing and nobody else. The farmhouse was old, a long low building with windows designed to keep out the light and a back door built for small men.

They turned their attention to the yard. A long barn lay on the left, its thatched roof proving fertile ground for all manner of vegetation. Beyond was a sinister little shed about whose true function Sloan was in no doubt at all. Two elderly tractors stood in another corner beside a rusty implement whose nature was obscure to the two town-bred policemen.

'Is that a harrow?' asked Crosby uncertainly.

'I'd put it in the Chamber of Horrors if it was mine,' began Sloan when suddenly they were not alone any more.

A woman wearing an old raincoat emerged cautiously from behind the barn.

'Are you from the Milk Marketing Board?' she called, keeping her distance.

Sloan said they were not.

She advanced a little.

'The Ministry of Agriculture?'

Sloan shook his head and she came nearer still.

'No,' she said ambiguously, 'I can see you're not from them.' She had a weatherbeaten face, burnt by sun and wind, and she could have been almost any àge at all. Besides her old raincoat, she had on a serge skirt and black Wellington boots. 'We paid the rates . . .'

There were no visitors at Holly Tree Farm it seemed, save official ones. Sloan explained that he was looking for a man called Cyril Jenkins.

'Jenkins,' she repeated vaguely. 'Not here. There's just me and Walsh here.'

'Now,' agreed Sloan. 'But once there were Jenkinses here.'

Her face cleared. 'That's right. Afore us.'

'Splendid,' said Sloan warmly. 'Now, do you know what became of them?'

'The old chap died,' she said. 'Before our time. We've been here twenty years, you know.'

Sloan didn't doubt it. It was certainly twenty years since anyone repaired the barn roof.

'We got it off the old chap,' she said. 'The young 'un didn't seem to want it.'

'The young 'un?' Sloan strove to hide his interest.

'Yes.' She looked at him curiously. 'He didn't want it. He'd been away, you know, in the war.'

'That's right.'

'Didn't seem as if he could settle afterwards. Not here.'

Sloan could well believe it. Aloud he said, 'It isn't easy if you've been away for any time.'

'No.' She stood considering the two men. 'Times, it's a bit quiet at Holly Tree, you know. There's just Walsh and me. Still, we don't want for nothing and that's something.'

It wasn't strictly true. A bath wouldn't have been out of place as far as Mrs Walsh was concerned. Say, once a month . . .

'This young 'un,' said Sloan. 'Did he ever marry?'

She nodded her head. 'Yes, but I did hear tell his wife died.'

'Where did they go after you came here?' It was the question which counted and for a moment Sloan thought she was going to say she didn't know.

Instead she frowned. 'Cullingoak way, I think it was.'

'Just one more question, Mrs Walsh . . .'

She looked at him, inured to official questions.

'This old man, Jenkins . . .'

'Yes?'

'Did he just have the one son?'

She shook her head. 'I did hear there was a daughter too but I never met her myself.'

The Rector and Mrs Meyton had taken Henrietta out to luncheon in Berebury after the inquest. Bill Thorpe had declined the invitation on the grounds that there were cows to be milked and other work to be done. It was Saturday afternoon, he explained awkwardly, and the men would have gone home. Whether this was so, or whether it was because of the silence which had followed his mention of marriage, nobody knew. He had made his apologies and gone before they left the town hall.

Arbican had arranged for Henrietta to come to see him on Tuesday afternoon following the funeral in the morning. He had also enquired tactfully about her present finances.

There had been a lonely dignity about her reply, and Arbican had shaken hands all round and gone back to Calleford.

The mention of money, though, had provoked a memory on the Rector's part.

'This little matter of the medals,' he began over coffee.

'Yes,' she said politely. It wasn't a little matter but if Mr Meyton cared to put it like that . . .

'It solves one point which often puzzled me.' He took some sugar. 'Your mother . . .'

She wasn't her mother but Henrietta let that pass, too. She was beginning to be very tired now.

'Your mother was a very independent woman.'

'Yes.' That was absolutely true.

'Commendable, of course. Very. But not always the easiest sort of parishioner to help.'

'She didn't like being beholden to anyone.'

'Exactly.' He sipped his coffee. 'I well remember on one occasion I suggested that we approach the Calleshire Regimental Welfare Association . . .'

'Oh?'

'Yes. For a grant towards what is now, I believe, called "further education". In my day they called it . . .'

'After all,' put in Mrs Meyton kindly, 'that's what their funds are for, isn't it, dear?'

'Yes,' said Henrietta.

'But, of course,' went on Mrs Meyton, 'it was before you got the scholarship, and though they always thought you would get one, you can never be sure with scholarships, can you, dear?'

'Never,' said Henrietta fervently. She had never been certain herself, however often people had reassured her.

'Mrs Jenkins was quite sharp with me,' remembered the Rector ruefully. 'Polite, of course. She was always very polite, but firm.

Scholarship or no scholarship she didn't want anything to do with it.'

Mrs Meyton said some people always did feel that way about grants.

The Rector set his cup down. 'But, of course, it all makes sense now we know that Cyril Jenkins wasn't killed in the war.'

'No, it doesn't,' said Henrietta.

'No?' The Rector looked mildly enquiring.

'You see,' said Henrietta, 'she told me that the Regimental Welfare people did help.'

'How very curious.'

'I know,' she said quickly, 'that the scholarship is the main thing but it's not really enough to – well – do more than manage.'

The Rector nodded. 'Quite so.'

'Money,' concluded Henrietta bleakly, 'came from somewhere for me when I got there.'

'You mean literally while you were there?'

'Yes. The Bursar saw that I had some at the beginning of each term.' She flushed. 'I was told it was from the Calleshire Regiment otherwise . . .'

'Otherwise,' interposed Mrs Meyton tactfully, 'I'm sure you wouldn't have wanted it any more than your mother would have done.'

'No.'

The Rector coughed. 'I think this may well be pertinent to Inspector Sloan's inquiry. Tell me, did the Bursar himself tell you where it came from?'

Henrietta frowned. 'Just that it was from the Regimental Welfare Association.'

'How very odd,' said the Rector of Larking.

This information was one more small piece which, when fitted exactly together with dozens of other small pieces of truth (and lies), detail, immutable fact, routine enquiry, known evidence, witnesses' stories and a detective's deductions, would, one day, produce a picture instead of a jigsaw.

This particular segment was relayed to Inspector Sloan when

he made a routine telephone call to Berebury Police Station after leaving Rooden Parva. He and Crosby had called in at the Calleshire County Constabulary Headquarters to ascertain that the Calleford search for one Cyril Jenkins, wanted by the Berebury Division, had not yet widened as far as the villages.

'Have a heart,' said Calleford's Inspector on duty. He was an old friend of Sloan's called Blake. Rejecting – very vigorously – the obvious nickname of Sexton he was known instead throughout the county as 'Digger'. 'There's dozens of small villages round here.'

Sloan nodded. 'Each with its own separate small register, I suppose?'

'That's right.' Blake pushed some tea in Sloan's direction. 'Your superintendent as horrible as ever?'

'He doesn't change,' said Sloan.

'What with him and Happy Harry,' condoled Blake, 'I don't know how you manage, I really don't.'

For better or worse, Superintendent Leeyes was on duty for this weekend.

'Well, Sloan,' he barked down the telephone, 'how are you getting on?'

'Not too badly, sir. I've got a couple of promising lines of enquiry at the moment.'

'Hrrmph.' The Superintendent didn't like optimism in anyone, least of all in his subordinates. 'How promising?'

'Once upon a time, sir . . .'

'Is this a fairy story, Sloan?'

'A romance,' said Sloan shortly.

Leeyes grunted. 'Go on.'

'Once upon a time a certain Lady Garwell seems to have had an affair with a Major Hocklington.'

'Did she, by Jove?' mockingly.

'Yes, sir.'

'Got her name mentioned in the Mess?'

'I fear so, sir.'

'Things aren't what they were in my day, Sloan.'

'No, sir, except that this was all a long time ago.'

'That makes it worse,' retorted Leeyes promptly. 'Much worse. Morals were morals then. I don't know what they are now, I'm sure.'

'No, sir.' The Superintendent's views on vice were a byword in the Division.

'This Lady Garwell . . .'

'Yes, sir?'

'Are you trying to tell me that this girl who's the cause of all the trouble . . .'

That was a bit unfair. 'Henrietta, sir?' he said, putting as much injury into his tone as he dared.

'Henrietta.' He paused. 'Damn silly name for a girl, isn't it?'

'Old fashioned,' said Sloan. 'Almost historical, you might say.'

Leeyes grunted. 'You think she's the – er – natural outcome of this affair?'

'I shouldn't like to say, sir. Not without further investigation. The General's practically gaga.'

'Doesn't mean a thing,' replied Leeyes swiftly. 'Or rather, it helps the case.'

'In what way, sir?'

Leeyes gave a chuckle that could only be described as salacious. 'Suppose he's married to some young thing . . .'

'Well?'

'Then she's much more likely to dilly-dally with this young Major Somebody or Other.'

'Hocklington, sir.'

'Much more likely,' repeated the Superintendent, who was by now getting to like the theory.

'Yes, sir. I see what you're driving at.' That was an understatement. 'But we don't know for certain that she was young.'

'Then find out.'

'Yes, sir.' He swallowed. 'Any more than we know that Major Hocklington was young . . .'

'It stands to reason, Sloan, that they weren't old. Not if they had an affair.'

'No, sir.' Sloan didn't know Mrs Leeyes. Only that she was a little woman who bred cats. He wondered what it was like, being married to the Superintendent. He said inconsequentially, 'She's dead. Lady Garwell, I mean.'

'That doesn't stop her being Henrietta's mother,' snapped Leeyes.

'No, sir.'

'What about Major Hocklington?'

'Hirst – that's the General's man – didn't know.'

'Then find that out, Sloan, while you're about it.'

'Yes, sir.'

'After all, she could have been in early middle age twenty-two years ago.' The Superintendent himself had been in early middle age for as long as Sloan could remember. 'And then died herself comparatively early.'

'Dead and never called her mother, in fact,' misquoted Sloan, who had once seen the Berebury Amateur Dramatic Society play *East Lynne* – and never forgotten the searing experience.

Literary allusions were lost upon the Superintendent who, only said, 'And get Somerset House to turn up Hocklington-Garwell in the births for twenty-one years ago. Or just plain Hocklington, if it comes to that.'

'Or Garwell,' pointed out Sloan. 'An illegitimate child takes the mother's surname, doesn't it?'

Leeyes grunted. 'At least it's not Smith. That's something to be thankful for.'

'You don't suppose,' asked Sloan hopefully, 'that her ladyship – if she was, in fact, Henrietta's mother – would have taken out an affiliation order against the father?'

'I do not,' said Leeyes.

'Pity.'

'Those sort of people don't.' An eager note crept into the Superintendent's voice. 'What they do, Sloan, is to dig up a faithful nanny who knows them well and they park the nanny and the infant in a cottage in the depths of the country.'

Sloan had been afraid of that.

'And' – Leeyes was warming to his theme – 'they support the child and the nanny from a distance.'

In Lady Garwell's case the distance – either way – so to speak

– would be considerable, she being dead. Sloan presumed he meant Major Hocklington and said, 'Yes, sir, though I still can't see why Grace Jenkins should have to die just before the girl is twenty-one.'

'Ask Major Hocklington,' suggested Leeyes sepulchrally.

'Or, come to that, sir, why Grace Jenkins went to such enormous lengths to conceal the girl's true name and then talked quite happily about the Hocklington-Garwells. If Lady Garwell were the mother, it doesn't make sense.'

'Someone has been sending the girl money at college,' said Leeyes. 'She and the clergyman have just been in to say so.'

'Maintenance,' said Sloan.

'Via the Bursar.'

Sloan scribbled a note, his Sunday rest day vanishing into thin air. 'We could leave as soon as we've seen Cyril Jenkins . . .'

'And,' said Superintendent Leeyes nastily, 'you could see Cyril Jenkins as soon as you've had your tea and sympathy from Inspector Blake.'

Cullingoak was more certainly a village than Rooden Parva. It had all the customary prerequisites thereof – a church standing foursquare in the middle, an old manor house not very far away, shops, a post office, a row of almshouses down by the river, even a cricket ground.

'All we want,' observed Crosby, 'is a character called Jenkins.'

'Now,' said Sloan, 'if the civil register is correct, is called Cyril Edgar and should live at number twelve High Street.'

'Dead easy,' Crosby swung the car round by the church. 'That'll be the road the post office is in, for sure.'

'Stop short,' Sloan told him. 'Just in case.'

'Sir, do you reckon he's her father?'

'I'll tell you that, Crosby, when I've seen him.'

'Likeness?'

'No.' Sloan remembered Mrs Walsh with a shudder. 'Something called eugenics.'

They found number twelve easily enough. Most of the High

Street houses were old. They were small, too, but well cared for. Neither developers nor preservationists seemed to have got their hands on Cullingoak High Street. None of the houses were once 'wrong' ones now 'done up' for 'right' people. There was, too, a refreshing variety of coloured paint. The door of number twelve was a deep green. Sloan knocked on it.

There was no immediate reply.

'Just our luck,' said Crosby morosely, 'if he's gone to a football match.'

It was implied – but not stated – that had Detective Constable Crosby not had the misfortune to be a member of Her Majesty's Constabulary, that that was where he would have been this Saturday afternoon in early March.

'Berebury's playing Luston.'

'Really?'

'At home.'

That was the crowning injustice.

Next Saturday Crosby would have to spend good money travelling to Luston or Calleford or Kinnisport to see some play.

Sloan knocked again.

There was no reply.

He looked up and down the street. There would be a back way in somewhere. The two policemen set off and walked until they found it – a narrow uneven way, leading to back gates. Some as neatly painted as the front doors. Some not. None numbered.

Crosby counted the houses back from the beginning of the row. 'Nine, ten, eleven, twelve.' He stopped at a gate that was still hanging properly on both hinges. 'I reckon this is the one, sir.'

'Well done,' said Sloan, who had already noticed that that back door was painted the same deep green as they had seen in the front. 'Perhaps he's one of those who'll answer the back door but not the front.'

They never discovered if this was so.

When they got to the back door it was ever so slightly ajar.

It opened a little further at Sloan's knock, and when there was no reply to this, Sloan opened it a bit more still and put his head round.

'Anyone at home?' he called out.

Cyril Jenkins was at home all right.

There was just one snag. He was dead.

Very.

15

Superintendent Leeyes was inclined to take the whole thing as a personal insult.

'Dead?' he shouted in affronted tones.

'Dead, sir.'

'He can't be . . .'

'He is.'

'Not our Jenkins,' he howled. 'Not the one we wanted . . .'

'Cyril Edgar,' said Sloan tersely. That much, at least, he had established before leaving number twelve and a pale but resolute Crosby standing guard. 'As for him being ours . . .'

'Yes?'

'I should think the fact that he's had his brains blown out rather clinches it.'

Sarcasm was a waste of time with the Superintendent. 'Self-inflicted?' he inquired eagerly.

'Impossible to say, sir, at this stage.'

'Was there a note?'

'No.' Sloan paused. 'Just a revolver.'

He wasn't sitting in the comfort of Inspector Blake's office now. He was in the cramped public telephone kiosk in Cullingoak High Street hoping that the young woman with a pram who was waiting to use it after him couldn't lip-read. At least she couldn't hear the Superintendent.

Sloan could.

'What sort of revolver?' he was asking.

'Service.' Sloan sighed. 'Old Army issue.'

'Officers, for the use of, I suppose,' heavily.

'Yes, sir.'

Leeyes grunted. 'So it's still there?'

'Yes, sir. Silencer and all.'

'Not out of reach, I suppose?'

'No, sir.'

'I didn't think it would be.'

'By his right hand.'

'That's what I thought you were going to say. No hope of him being left handed?'

'None. I checked.' Sloan had searched high and low himself for signs which would reveal whether Cyril Edgar Jenkins had taken his own life or if someone had taken it for him.

'I don't like it, Sloan.'

'No, sir.' Sloan didn't either. There was nothing to like in what he had just seen. The recently shot are seldom an attractive sight and Cyril Edgar Jenkins was no exception. He had been sitting down when it had happened and the result was indescribably messy. Experienced – and hardened – as he was, Sloan hadn't relished his quick examination. At least there hadn't been the additional burden of breaking the news to anyone. 'He lived alone,' he told Leeyes. 'Mrs Walsh out at Holly Tree Farm was quite right about his wife. She did die about eight years ago.'

'Who says so?'

'The woman next door. Remembers her well.'

'Which wife?' demanded Leeyes contentiously.

Sloan paused. 'The one he had been living with ever since he came to Cullingoak.'

'Ah . . . that's different.' Sloan could almost hear the Superintendent fumbling for the word he wanted. 'She might have just been his concubine.'

'Yes, sir, except that we couldn't find any record of a marriage between Cyril Edgar Jenkins and Grace Edith Wright in the first place . . .'

'I hadn't forgotten,' said Leeyes coldly. 'Now I suppose you're going to set about finding out if he was really married to this second woman . . .'

What Sloan wanted to do – and that very badly – was to set about finding out who had killed Cyril Jenkins.

'Yes, sir. In the mean time, do you think Dr Dabbe would come over?'

'I don't see why not,' said Leeyes largely. When he himself was working through a weekend he was usually in favour of as many people doing so as possible. 'What do you want him for?'

'Inspector Blake is handling the routine side of this, seeing as it's in his Division,' said Sloan, 'but I want to talk to Dr Dabbe about blood.'

There was no shortage of this vital commodity in the living-room of number twelve Cullingoak High Street.

Sloan had vacated the telephone kiosk with a polite apology to the girl with the pram. In the manner of a generation brought up without courtesy, she had favoured him with a blank stare in return. Oddly disconcerted, but without time to wonder what things were coming to, he had hurried back to the house.

His friend, Inspector Blake, had just arrived from Calleford and was standing surveying the scene.

'Nasty.'

Sloan could only agree. Crosby, who had been surveying the same scene for rather longer and more consistently than either Blake or Sloan, was looking rather green at the gills.

'He got wind that you wanted a little chat, did he, then?' asked Digger Blake. He had brought his own photographer and fingerprint man with him and he motioned them now to go ahead with their gruesome work.

'Perhaps,' said Sloan slowly. 'Perhaps not.'

'Not a coincidence anyway,' said Blake.

'No. Someone knew.'

'Many people realize you wanted this word or two with him?' Digger's questions were usually obliquely phrased.

'Enough.' Sloan took a deep breath. 'A girl who said she saw him in Calleford yesterday afternoon.' Henrietta had probably been right about that, now he came to think of it, but how significant it was he couldn't sort out. Not for the moment. 'Her solicitor. He knew, of course. He's called Arbican.'

'That'll be Waind, Arbican & Waind, in Ox Lane,' said Blake. 'There's only him left in the firm now.'

'And a young man called Bill Thorpe . . .' He hesitated. 'I can't make up my mind about him.'

'What's the trouble?'

'Too ardent for my liking.'

'It's not whether you like it, old chap,' grinned Blake. 'It's if the lady likes it.'

'She's got quite enough on her plate as it is.' said Sloan primly. And he told Digger the whole story.

'A proper mix-up, isn't it?' Blake said appreciatively. 'Rather you than me.'

'Thank you. Crosby, if you want to be sick go outside.'

'Who else knew you wanted Jenkins?' asked Blake, who was nowhere near as casual as he sounded.

Sloan frowned. 'The Rector of Larking and his wife. Meyton's their name.'

'Lesson One,' quoted Blake. 'The cloth isn't always what it . . .'

'It is this time.'

'Oh, really? And who else is in the know?'

'No one that I know of. There's a James Heber Hibbs, Esquire . . .'

'Gent?'

'Landed gent,' said Sloan firmly, 'of The Hall, Larking, but he doesn't know about Jenkins. Not unless the girl's told him and I don't quite see when she would have done. Owns about half the village if you ask me.'

'For Hibbs read Nibs,' said Digger frivolously. 'Has he got a missus?'

'Yes, but you call her madam, my lad.'

'And their connection with this case?'

'Obscure,' said Sloan bitterly.

'Anyone else?'

Sloan hesitated. 'There's a certain Major Hocklington but . . .'

'But what?'

'He might be dead.'

'I see. Well, when you've made your mind up . . .'

'He might have had the MC and the DSO, too.'

'That'll be a great help in finding him,' murmured Digger affably, 'but I'd rather he had a scar on his left cheek, if it's all the same to you.'

'There's always the possibility,' said Sloan, 'that he had an agent.'

'If he's dead, for instance?' Blake moved out of the photographer's line of vision.

'That's right.'

Blake pointed the same way as the photographer's camera. 'He's not going to tell you. Not now.'

'No,' said Sloan morbidly, 'though, oddly enough, I'm after his blood too.'

It was something after eight o'clock that evening when Inspector Sloan, supported by a still rather wan-looking Constable Crosby, reported back to Superintendent Leeyes in person at the Berebury Police Station.

'As pretty a kettle of fish, sir,' Sloan said, 'as you'll find anywhere.'

'Suicide or murder?' demanded Leeyes.

But it wasn't as simple as that.

Dr Dabbe had got to Cullingoak at a speed which, as far as Sloan was concerned, didn't bear thinking about. He was well known as the fastest driver in Calleshire and nothing that his arch enemy, Inspector Harpe of Traffic Division, could do seemed to slow him down at all.

At the house Dr Dabbe had met his opposite number, the Consultant Pathologist for East Calleshire, Dr Sorley McPherson. The two doctors had treated each other with an elaborate and ritual courtesy which reminded Sloan of nothing so much as the courtship display of a pair of ducks at mating time.

With professional punctiliousness each had invited the other's opinion on every possible point.

The upshot – after, in Sloan's private opinion, a great deal of unnecessary billing and cooing – was that Cyril Edgar Jenkins had probably been shot in the head by someone sitting opposite him across the table, who had pulled out a revolver and leaned forward.

'We can't be certain, of courrrse' – Dr Sorley McPherson had rolled his 'r's' in an intimidating way – 'but it looks as if the rrevolver was placed in deceased's rright hand after death.'

'I see, doctor.'

'Suicide,' he went on, 'was doubtless meant to be inferrrred.'

Sloan thought the 'r's' were never going to stop.

'We'll be needing a wee look at the poor chap's fingerprints on the revolver handle. D'you not agree, Dabbe?'

Dr Dabbe had agreed. The powder burns, the position of the shot, the body, the revolver, all indicated murder made to look like suicide.

Sloan said all this to the Superintendent. 'But only inferred, sir. Not proved yet.'

Leeyes snorted in a dissatisfied way. 'Except, then, that he's dead, we're no further forward . . .'

Sloan said nothing. If Leeyes cared to regard that as progress there was nothing he could say.

'What about the blood?' said the Superintendent.

'Dr Dabbe's grouping it now. He's going to ring.'

Leeyes drummed a pencil on his desk. 'You say no one in Cullingoak saw or heard anything?'

'No one. The people in the house next door on one side were out and the woman in the other always has a lie down after her lunch. Anyone could walk in the back, just like we did. He did have a job in Calleford, by the way. She confirms that.'

'No other children?'

'No sir, not that she knew of.'

Leeyes grunted. 'And Major Hocklington – where have you got with him?'

'The Army are doing what they can, but . . .'

'I know, Sloan. Saturday night's not the best time.'

'No, sir. If he were a serving officer now it would be quite simple.'

'I presume' – coldly – 'you checked the Army List days ago.'

'Yes, sir.'

'So we have to wait.' Leeyes wasn't good at waiting.

'Yes, sir.'

'And our other friends?'

Sloan turned back the pages of his notebook though he knew well enough what was written there. 'Bill Thorpe excused himself pretty smartly after the inquest and went off just before Arbican went back to Calleford.'

'Went off where?'

'Larking, he says. He wouldn't have lunch in Berebury with the Meytons and Henrietta.'

'Why not?'

'Said he hadn't time. Had to get back to the farm.'

'And did he?'

Sloan said carefully, 'No one happened to see him at Shire Oak – which, of course, is not to say he wasn't there.'

'Did you get his background?'

'It seems all right, sir. Second son of middling-size farmers with quite a good name locally. Lived in Larking all his life. Known Henrietta ever since she was a child. Been home from agricultural college for about two years.'

'Found the body with the postman, could have knocked it down, stuck to the girl like a leech since it happened, wants to marry her quickly.' Leeyes's rasping tones supplanted Sloan's matter-of-fact report. 'Could have killed Cyril Jenkins. Could have known the whole story. Could have wanted money . . .'

'Why, sir?'

'He's the second son, Sloan. You've just said so.'

'Yes, sir.' It was futile to argue with the Superintendent.

Leeyes grunted. 'And this other fellow – the one with the money. What about him?'

'Hibbs?' said Sloan. The Superintendent was always suspicious of people with money, assuming it – in the absence of specific evidence to the contrary – to be ill gotten. Sloan cleared his throat uneasily. 'He and his wife went into Calleford for the day.'

'They did what?'

'Went into Calleford,' repeated Sloan, going on hastily, 'they had a meal at the Tabard. She went to a dress shop and he called in at a corn chandler's in the morning . . .'

'Whatever for?'

'He's hand-rearing some pheasants this year, sir.' Sloan himself had always wondered what you did at a corn chandler's. 'And he visited a wine merchant just after lunch.'

'When was Jenkins shot?'

'Roughly about three o'clock.' The two pathologists had been as agreed on this as on everything else.

'Could he have done it?'

'Easily. So could Bill Thorpe. Anyone could have done it. Even Arbican if he had had a mind to – to say nothing of Major Hocklington. Always supposing he exists.'

Leeyes was thinking, not listening. 'Sounds as if it could have been someone Jenkins knew fairly well – all this business of back doors and sitting down at the table together.'

'Yes, sir.' Inspector Blake had cottoned on to that fact, too, as he went methodically about his routine investigation. 'The only trouble is that we don't know who it was that Cyril Jenkins knew.'

'No.' Leeyes frowned. 'Or what.'

'The whole story, I expect,' said Sloan gloomily. 'That's why he had to go.'

The telephone rang. Leeyes answered it and handed it to Sloan. 'The hospital,' he said. 'Dr Dabbe.'

Sloan listened for a moment, thanked the pathologist, promised to let him know something later and then rang off.

'The late Cyril Jenkins's blood was group AB,' he announced.

'And the girl's?' asked Leeyes.

'We don't know yet. We're going to ask her if we can have some to see.'

'Tricky,' pronounced Leeyes. 'Be very careful . . .'

'Why, sir?'

'Because *if* this case ever gets to court' – he stressed the word 'if' heavily, and implied if it didn't it would be Sloan's fault – '*if* it does then you will probably find some clever young man arguing that you've committed a technical assault, that's why.'

'But if the putative father . . .'

'Get as many witnesses to her free consent as you can,' advised Leeyes sourly. 'That's all.'

'Yes, sir,' promised Sloan, 'and then we're going to Camford to see the bursar of her college.'

He and Crosby got up to go but Sloan turned short of the door.

'That AB blood group, sir . . .'

'What about it?'

'It's the same as Grace Jenkins's.'

'Well?'

'If the girl hadn't said the woman's maiden name was Wright, I could make out quite a good case for Grace Jenkins and Cyril Jenkins being brother and sister.'

16

'Dead?' said Henrietta dully.

'I'm afraid so.' Sloan wished her reaction could have been more like the Superintendent's. It couldn't be doing her any good sitting here in Boundary Cottage, hanging on to her self-control with an effort that was painful to watch.

'Inspector,' she whispered, 'I killed him, didn't I?'

'I don't think so, miss,' responded Sloan, surprised.

'I don't mean actually.' She twisted her hands together in her lap. 'But as good as . . .'

'I don't see quite how, miss, if you'll forgive my saying so . . .' It occurred to Sloan for the first time that this was what people meant by wringing their hands.

'By seeing him.' She swallowed. 'Don't you understand? If I hadn't seen him yesterday and recognized him, then he wouldn't be dead today.'

This, thought Sloan, might well be true.

'Perhaps, miss,' he said quietly, 'but that doesn't make it your fault.'

'I haven't got the evil eye, or anything like that, I know, but' – she sounded utterly shaken – 'but if he was my father and I've been the means of killing him . . . I don't think I could bear that.'

Sloan coughed. She had given him the opening he wanted. 'That's one of the reasons why we've come, miss. About the question of this Cyril Jenkins being your father.'

'Do you know, then?' directly.

'No, miss. We don't think he was but we can't prove it either way . . . yet.'

'Yet?' she asked quickly.

'Dr Dabbe – he's the hospital pathologist, miss – he says a blood test can prove something but not everything.'

'Anything,' she said fervently, 'would be better than this not knowing.'

'If you agreed to it,' he said carefully, 'and I must make it clear you don't have to, it might just prove Cyril Jenkins wasn't your father and never could have been.'

'Then,' said Henrietta in a perplexed way, 'who was he and what had he got to do with us?'

'We don't know . . .'

'Just that he's dead.'

'That's right, miss.'

She looked at him. 'How soon can you do this blood thing?'

'If you would come with me to the telephone and ring Mr Arbican – he's entitled to advise you against it, if he thinks fit – then I could ring Dr Dabbe now.' He grinned. 'It won't take him long to get here.'

It didn't.

A stranger would have noticed nothing out of the ordinary should he have chanced to visit the village of Larking the next morning. Not, of course, that there were any strangers there. Larking was not that sort of village. A Sunday calm had descended upon the place and the inhabitants were going about their usual avocations. About a quarter of them were in church. At Matins.

Henrietta was there.

She was staying at the Rectory now. She had been in that pleasant house on the green since late last night. Just before he had left, Inspector Sloan had said he would be greatly obliged if Miss Jenkins would take herself to the Rectory for the night.

'Otherwise, miss,' he had gone on, 'I shall have to spare a man to stay here and keep an eye on you.'

Mrs Meyton, bless her, had been only too happy to have her under the Rectory wing and Henrietta had been popped between clean sheets in the spare bed without fuss or botheration. The Rector presumably had been wrestling with his sermon because she hadn't seen him at all last night nor this morning when he had breakfasted alone between early service and Matins.

James Heber Hibbs read the first lesson.

Henrietta was devoutly thankful that today was one of the Sundays in Lent, which meant that she didn't have to listen while he fought his way through the genealogical tree of Abraham who begat Isaac who begat Jacob who begat . . .

She could listen to the Book of Numbers (chapter 14, verse 26) with equanimity but she didn't think she could bear to hear that unconscionable list of who begat whom when she was still no nearer knowing the father who had begat her. She sat, hands folded in front of her, while James Hibbs's neat unaccented voice retailed what the Lord spake unto Moses and unto Aaron.

She felt curiously detached. No doubt the events of the past week would fade into proportion in time just as those of the Old Testament had done but at the moment she wasn't sure.

'. . . save Caleb the son of Jephunneh, and Joshua the son of Nun,' said James Hibbs in those English upper-middle-class tones considered suitable for readings in church which would have greatly surprised both Caleb and Joshua, son of Nun, had they heard them.

That had been how a man was known in those far off days, of course. It mattered very much whose son you were, which tribe you belonged to . . . One day, perhaps, she, Henrietta, would be able once again to look into a mirror without wondering who it was she saw there, but not yet . . . definitely not yet.

A fragment of an almost forgotten newspaper article came back to her while she was sitting quietly in the pew. Somewhere she had read once that to undermine the resistance of prisoners in a concentration camp their captors first took away every single thing the poor unfortunates could call their own – papers, watches, rings, glasses, false teeth even. It was the first step towards the deliberate destruction of personality. After that the prisoners, utterly demoralized, began to doubt their very identity. Lacking reassurance in the matter, then surely existence itself would seem pointless, resistance became more meaningless still.

'. . . Here endeth the first lesson,' declared James Hibbs, leaving the lectern and going back to his wife in the pew which, abolition of pew rents or not, inalienably belonged to The Hall. He still walked like a soldier.

It didn't seem possible that last Sunday Henrietta had been at college in Camford, finals the biggest landmark in her immediate future, Bill Thorpe more nebulously beyond . . . her mother always in the background.

Only she wasn't her mother.

And the background had changed as suddenly as a theatre backdrop. The man in the photograph on the mantelpiece had come briefly alive – and mysteriously was now dead again.

Uncomforted by the Rector's blessing at the end of the service, she waited in her seat until the church emptied. That, at least, saved her from all but the most bare faced of the curious. Mrs Meyton insisted upon her lunching at the Rectory. Henrietta demurred.

'When, my dear child, have you had time to buy food?' Mrs Meyton asked.

Henrietta spoke vaguely of some cheese but was overruled by an indignant Mrs Meyton.

'Certainly not,' said that lady roundly.

It wasn't the happiest of meals. Henrietta ate her way through roast beef and Yorkshire pudding without appetite, one thing uppermost in her mind.

'They don't say very much in the newspapers,' she murmured. 'And the Inspector didn't tell me anything. Just that he was found dead . . .'

This was only partly true. The Sunday newspapers not available at the Rectory had covered the death of Cyril Jenkins fairly graphically (WIDOWER DIES . . . GUNSHOT DEATH . . . BLOOD-STAINED ROOM) but neither the Meytons nor Henrietta knew this.

The Rector nodded. 'I fear there is little doubt that his death is significant.'

'What I want to know,' demanded Henrietta almost angrily, 'is if he was my father or not.'

She didn't know yet if the little red bottle borne away last night by the pathologist – after a few mild stock jokes about vampires – was going to tell her that or not.

Mr Meyton nodded again. 'Quite so.'

And in an anguished whisper: 'And who killed him.'

'My dear,' began Mrs Meyton, 'should you concern yourself with . . .'

'Yes,' intervened the Rector firmly, 'she should.'

'I must know,' said Henrietta firmly, a tremulous note coming into her voice in spite of all her efforts to suppress it, 'whether I am misbegotten or not.'

Dr Dabbe could have told her something.

He telephoned Berebury Police Station.

'That you, Sloan? I've done a grouping.'

'Yes, doctor?'

'The girl's group O.'

Sloan wrote it down. 'Jenkins was AB, wasn't he?'

'That's right.'

'That means, doctor, that . . .'

'That he is not the girl's father,' said Dr Dabbe dogmatically. 'And that's conclusive and irrespective of the mother's blood group. A man with an AB group blood cannot have a child with O group blood.'

'Thank you, doctor. Thank you very much. That's a great help . . .'

'It's an indisputable fact,' said Dr Dabbe tartly, 'which is more to the point.'

Inspector Sloan and Constable Crosby reached the university town of Camford just before noon on the Sunday morning and drove straight to the centre of that many-tower'd Camelot. A friendly colleague directed them to Boleyn College.

'Funny person to call a ladies' college after,' muttered Constable Crosby, putting the car into gear again. 'Wasn't she one of Henry the Eighth's . . .'

'Yes,' said Sloan shortly, 'she was.'

They found the decorous brick building on the outskirts of the town and waited while the porter set about finding the bursar, Miss Wotherspoon. She did not keep them long. A petite birdlike figure came tripping down the corridor. Sloan explained that he had come about Henrietta Jenkins.

'Jenkins?' said Miss Wotherspoon. 'Nice girl.'

'Yes.'

'Not a First . . .'

'Oh?' said Sloan, who hadn't the faintest idea what she was talking about but wasn't prepared to say so.

'Perhaps a Second but I shouldn't count on it.'

'No . . .'

'And,' Miss Wotherspoon sighed, 'there'll be some young man waiting to marry her who doesn't care either way.'

'There is.'

Miss Wotherspoon shook her head. 'No use trying to stop them,' she said briskly. 'Take my advice about that. They hold it against you for ever afterwards.'

On that point Sloan was agreed with the Bursar, but before he could say anything further she went on.

'But I've just remembered, Henrietta Jenkins hasn't got a father.'

'That's right,' agreed Sloan.

'Then you must be . . .' began Miss Wotherspoon – and stopped.

'Who?' prompted Sloan gently.

But he wasn't catching the Bursar out that way.

'No,' she said. 'I think you must tell me.'

'The police,' admitted Sloan regretfully.

'You had better come to my study.'

She listened to Sloan's tale without interruption, waited until he was quite finished and then announced that she would have to take him to the Principal. He and Crosby tramped off after her and soon found themselves in a very gracious room indeed.

The Principal was an impressive woman by any standard save that of fashion. She had a calm, still authority, responsive yet unsurprised. Sloan and Crosby were invited to settle into chintz armchairs and to repeat their story.

'I see,' said the Principal when he had done – and not before. Both women exhibited a rare facility for listening. If this was the result of the education of women, then Sloan – for one – was all in favour.

'You will be able to see our difficulty, too,' said Sloan. 'You have this girl whom we have reason to believe is being maintained here beyond such scholarships and grants as she may have been awarded.'

'True,' said the Bursar, 'but we were given funds on the condition that she never knew the source.'

'I don't think she need,' replied Sloan seriously. 'I can't give you any sort of undertaking because this is a criminal case but unless such facts came out in open court I see no reason myself why she should be told.'

'In that case,' pronounced the Principal, 'I see no reason why Miss Wotherspoon should not divulge the – er – donor's name to you.'

'Thank you, madam.'

Miss Wotherspoon disappeared in the direction of her study and returned waving a piece of paper.

'It wasn't a lot,' she said. 'Just a small cheque each term to make things more . . . what is the word I'm looking for?'

The word Sloan was looking for – and that very badly – was on the paper the Bursar was holding. He retained his self-control with difficulty.

'Tolerable,' decided Miss Wotherspoon brightly. 'Grants and scholarships are all very well but a girl needs a bit more than that if she's going to get the most out of Camford.'

'The name,' pleaded Sloan.

Miss Wotherspoon looked at the paper in her hand.

'Would it,' she said rather doubtfully, 'be Hibbs? That's what it looks like to me. J. A. H. Hibbs.'

Sloan groaned aloud.

'The Hall, Larking, Calleshire,' said Miss Wotherspoon for good measure.

'He never said why, I suppose?' asked Sloan.

'Just a brief note with the first cheque saying he thought funds at home were rather low and the enclosed might help.' Miss Wotherspoon waved a hand vaguely. 'That sort of thing. The only condition was that the girl didn't know. I could tell her what I liked.'

'And what did you tell her?'

'A Service charity,' said the Bursar promptly. 'Plenty of girls receive money from them. There was no reason why she shouldn't.'

'There was,' said the Principal unexpectedly.

Sloan, Crosby and Miss Wotherspoon all turned in her direction.

'A very good reason,' said the Principal.

Sloan cleared his throat. It had suddenly seemed to go very dry.

'What was that, madam?' She looked the sort of person who could tell a good reason from a bad one. If she thought it a very good reason . . .

'She wasn't who she thought she was.'

'No. We have established that, madam, in Calleshire, but I should dearly like to know how you . . .'

'For entry to Boleyn College, Inspector, we require a sight of the candidate's birth certificate . . .'

'Of course!' Sloan brought his hand down on the arm of the chintz-covered chair with a mighty slap. 'We should have thought of that before.'

'Not, you understand, in order to confirm family details. We are not concerned' – here academic scruple raised its head – 'with the father's occupation but with the age of the candidate.'

'Quite so,' said Sloan, who was concerned about something quite different still. 'How very stupid we have been, madam. This would have saved us a great deal – might even have saved a life.'

As before, the Principal waited until he was quite finished before she continued. 'Naturally this also applied in the case of Henrietta Jenkins.'

'Yes . . .' eagerly.

'With her birth certificate came a letter from the woman whom she believed to be her mother . . .'

'Grace Jenkins . . .'

The Principal inclined her head. 'This letter, which was addressed to me personally, explained that the girl did not know the name of her real parents and was not to be told it until she was twenty-one.'

'Yes?' even more eagerly.

'This I felt was a most unwise procedure and one I would have counselled against most strongly. However . . .'

Sloan was sitting on the very edge of his chair. 'Yes?'

'However, her – er – guardian . . . is that who she was?'

'In a way,' said Sloan grimly.

'Her guardian's wishes were entitled to be respected.'

'And?'

'The birth certificate was returned to Mrs Jenkins and I have not mentioned the fact to anyone until today.'

'The name,' said Sloan. 'What was the name?'

The Principal paused. 'I don't think I can be absolutely certain . . .'

'Henrietta who?' said Sloan urgently.

'I am left with the impression that it was Mantriot.'

Bill Thorpe walked down from Shire Oak Farm about half past two and called for Henrietta at the Rectory. She went with him as much because the Meytons were obviously used to a post-prandial snooze on Sunday afternoons as for any other reason.

'I told you I'd seen Cyril Jenkins yesterday,' she said by way of greeting. Her feelings towards Bill Thorpe were decidedly ambivalent.

'You did,' agreed Thorpe.

'What price him being my father?'

'Perhaps,' diplomatically.

'Or do you still think it doesn't matter?'

Bill Thorpe grinned. 'A gooseberry bush would still do for me.'

'Well!' exploded Henrietta crossly, 'I think you're the . . .'

'Or a carpet bag. At Victoria Station.' He took a couple of paces back and raised an arm to ward off an imaginary blow. 'The Brighton line, of course.'

'The police,' said Henrietta, ignoring this, 'probably won't believe me, but . . .'

'The police,' declared Bill, 'are trained not to believe anybody. It is the secret of their success.'

They had passed the entrance gates to The Hall now and were walking down the road to Boundary Cottage.

'I've just thought of something,' said Henrietta suddenly.

'What's that?'

'If I'm not who I thought I was . . .'

'Yes?'

'I don't have to be an only child.'

'No,' agreed Bill Thorpe.

'I thought you were going to say that didn't matter either,' she said, a little deflated.

'But it does.' Bill Thorpe pushed open the gate of Boundary Cottage and stood back to let her go in first. 'Very much.'

'Very much?'

'Just in the one set of circumstances.' He turned to shut the gate behind him, farmer through and through. 'Unlikely, I know, but . . .'

'But what?'

'We must make absolutely sure,' he said gravely, 'that you and I are not brother and sister. I have every intention of marrying you and that's the only thing which could stop me.'

She laughed at last. 'Not allowed outside ancient Egypt?'

'The word is, I believe, taboo.'

Henrietta led the way up to the front door, still laughing.

She stopped as soon as she opened it.

'Whatever's the matter?' enquired Bill quickly. 'You've gone quite white.'

She stood stock-still on the doorstep.

'Someone's been in here,' she said, 'since I left last night.'

17

There was no question of either of them having a meal. It was offered by the Principal of Boleyn College and seconded by the Bursar. Even in the ordinary way Inspector Sloan (if not Detective Constable Crosby) would have refused an invitation to sit down with three hundred young ladies of academic bent. Today was not ordinary. Their one aim was to get back to Calleshire with all possible speed. They hurried away from the dreaming spires without so much as a backward glance and got out on the open road.

'Hibbs,' said Crosby glumly.

'Mantriot,' countered Sloan.

Crosby executed a driving manoeuvre between two lorries and an articulated trailer which he had not learnt at the police motoring school.

'It isn't going to help our investigations, Constable,' said Sloan testily, 'if we none of us live to find out Mantriot.'

'No, sir.' Crosby lifted his foot off the accelerator a fraction. 'I think I know something already.'

'You what?'

'The name, sir, it rings a bell.'

'In what way?'

'I don't know.'

'Then think.'

'Yes, sir.'

There was a short silence in the police car while Constable Crosby thought. This did not preclude him overtaking a sports car at a speed Sloan did not relish.

'If,' said Sloan, 'you would think any better away from the wheel, I will take it.'

'That's all right, sir, thank you. I don't have to think about my driving.'

'I noticed,' said Sloan sweetly.

There was another silence while they ate up the miles at a speed which was specifically forbidden at the police motoring school.

Crosby was observed to be frowning.

'Well?' said Sloan hopefully.

'It's in the past somewhere, sir.'

'I know that.'

'I mean what I remember.'

Sloan did not attempt to sort this out. He was now too busy wishing he had led a better life – time for reform having obviously run out.

The car swerved dangerously. 'I've got it, sir.'

'Have you?' muttered Sloan between clenched teeth. 'Then slow down.' He started to breathe again as the fields stopped flashing by quite so quickly. 'Now tell me.'

'I can't tell you anything, sir,' said Crosby helpfully, 'except that I remember the name.'

'Where?'

'The past.'

'I wish,' said Sloan, made irritable by fear, 'that you would stop saying that.'

'I mean, sir' – Crosby was never good at explanations – 'when I was trying to learn about the past.'

'Light is beginning to dawn, Crosby. Go on.'

'It all started when I didn't know who George Smith was, sir.'

'I'm not sure that I do either.'

'He drowned his wives,' said Crosby reproachfully. 'All of them.'

'Oh, him.'

'Yes, sir, but I didn't know at the time and they pulled my leg a bit at the station.'

'I'll bet they did.'

'Every time anyone mentioned the word "bath". So Sergeant Gelven – he said if I was ever going to get anywhere, I'd better read up famous cases.'

'The Tichborne Claimant,' remembered Sloan suddenly. 'That's how you knew about that . . .'

'Yes, sir.'

'But,' puzzled, 'how does Mantriot come in?'

'It's not a famous case, sir, I do know that.'

'Not yet it isn't,' retorted Sloan, 'but I shouldn't count on it staying that way.'

'So it must be a local one. After I'd done the others, sir, I went back through the Calleshire records. That's where I've seen the name, I'm sure.' Crosby spotted a rival county's radar trap and slowed down. 'But I don't remember when or where.'

'We'll soon find out,' said Sloan pleasantly. 'You can go through them again until you find it.'

Superintendent Leeyes's afternoon cups of tea were rather like American television shows which went from the late show to the late, late show to the late, late, late show thence merging imperceptibly into the early, early, early show, the early, early show and naturally enough the early show. His tea went on the same principle – the after lunch cup, the early afternoon cup, the middle of the afternoon one and so forth. It was impossible for Sloan and Crosby to guess which one he was at when they arrived back in Berebury.

'We've got him,' announced Leeyes triumphantly.

Sloan shook his head. 'I should say that gift lets Hibbs out.'

'And I should say,' retorted Leeyes robustly, 'that it lets himin.'

'I'll go down there at once, sir, and see.'

'There's one other thing, Sloan . . .'

'Sir?'

'This girl – I think she's starting to imagine things now . . .'

'I should very much doubt that.'

'You sent her away from home last night.'

'I tried to. I don't know if she went but I told PC Hepple he was to keep an eye on her if she didn't.'

'She did. To the Rectory. But she and the Thorpe boy went back to Boundary Cottage after lunch.'

'Yes?' said Sloan alertly.

'He rang up about an hour ago to say the girl swears someone's been in the cottage overnight.'

Sloan expired audibly. 'I thought they might. That's why . . .'

'Someone's got a key,' snapped Leeyes. 'We've known that all along. Why didn't you have the lock changed?'

'I wanted them to show their hand,' said Sloan simply. 'And they have.'

Sunday was Sunday as far as James Hibbs and his wife were concerned. It was late afternoon when Sloan and Crosby arrived at The Hall. This time, being Sunday, they were shown into the drawing-room. Tea at The Hall on Sundays would always be in the drawing-room. Tea this afternoon had been eaten but not cleared away. A beautiful Georgian silver teapot graced the tea tray, some sandwiches and a jar of Gentleman's Relish stood beside it. Sloan hankered after the sandwiches but not the tea. He had had some tea from a teapot like that once before – pale, straw-coloured stuff with a sinister taste. He had not been at all surprised to learn that it had come from China.

The two policemen were invited to sit on the large sofa in front of the fire. Their combined weights sank into it. Constable Crosby was the heavier of the two which gave Sloan's sitting position an odd list to starboard. No one could have described it as an advantageous situation from which to conduct an interview in what Sloan now knew to be a double murder case.

His tone was sharper than it had been earlier.

'You said before, sir, that you had never seen Mrs Grace Jenkins until she came to Larking.'

'Actually,' said Hibbs mildly, 'I don't think I saw her until quite a while afterwards. I was away myself, you know, at the time. I told you, if you remember, my old agent fixed up the tenancy.'

'Yes, sir, you did. You showed me a letter.'

'Ah, yes.'

'You showed me a letter,' said Sloan accusingly, 'but I don't think you told me the whole story.'

'No, Inspector? What else was it you wanted to know?'

'Why you sent money to be given to Henrietta at the university?' Sloan asked the question of James Hibbs but he was looking at Mrs Hibbs's face while he spoke.

It did not change.

'Come, now,' Hibbs smiled disarmingly. 'You surely can't expect me to have told you a thing like that.'

Mrs Hibbs nodded in agreement with her husband and said in her pleasant deep voice. 'It was a private benefaction, Inspector. Nothing to do with anyone but ourselves.'

'At the moment, madam, everything to do with Henrietta is to do with us.'

'We could see a need,' said Hibbs, embarrassed, 'that's all.'

'So you set about filling it?'

'That's right, Inspector. I don't hold with all these national appeals. I'd rather give on my own.'

'Charity beginning at home, sir?'

Hibbs flushed. 'If you care to put it like that.'

'I see, sir.' Sloan started to heave himself out of the sofa. 'I asked you earlier if the name Hocklington-Garwell conveyed anything to you and you said no . . .'

'I did.'

'I'm asking you now if you have ever heard the name of Mantriot before.'

'Hugo, you mean?'

'Perhaps. Or Michael. Michael was killed early on. Dunkirk.'

James Hibbs said very soberly, 'Yes, Inspector, of course I have . . .'

'Of course?'

'He was in the East Callies and I was in the West but . . . Good Lord . . . I never thought!'

'You never thought what, sir?'

'Of Henrietta being Hugo's.' Hibbs frowned into the distance. 'I must say, Inspector, in all the years I've been here it's never crossed my mind for an instant.'

'What hasn't, sir?'

'Inspector, are you trying to tell us that Henrietta Jenkins is the Mantriot baby?'

'I don't know, sir. Suppose you tell me.'

'You won't remember, of course . . .'

'No, sir.'

'It was all pretty ghastly,' said Hibbs. 'It was in the war, you know. Towards the end. Hugo had had a bad war one way and another . . .'

That, thought Sloan with mounting excitement, would explain the DSO and the MC.

'. . . but he got home for a spot of leave just after the baby was born. Everyone was delighted, naturally, but something went very wrong.'

'What?'

'I don't know.' Hibbs shrugged his well-tailored shoulders. 'They said afterwards that his mind must have been turned. Common enough thing to happen at the time, of course. He must have been through some rotten experiences before the end. Could have happened to any of us, I suppose.'

'What could, sir?' very quietly.

'Didn't you know, Inspector?'

'No, sir. Not yet.'

'One day he killed his wife and then he shot himself.' Hibbs shook his head sadly. 'It's all a long time ago now, of course. Some nanny took the baby . . .'

'Grace Jenkins!' cried Mrs Hibbs suddenly.

'Bless my soul,' said Hibbs.

Sloan started to move towards the door when Hibbs burst out laughing.

'It's a funny world, Inspector. Here's my wife and I sending money to Eleanor Leslie's daughter . . .'

'What's so odd about that, sir?'

Hibbs stopped laughing and said solemnly, 'Because Eleanor Leslie – that's who Hugo Mantriot married – was a great deal wealthier than you or I shall ever be. She was old Bruce Leslie's only daughter. You know – the shipping people.'

18

The next two hours were the busiest young Constable Crosby had ever known. First of all he was put down in front of a pile of dusty old records and told to get on with it. This was particularly difficult as Superintendent Leeyes and Detective Inspector Sloan were talking round him.

'So Hibbs realized you'd got on to the name and decided to play the surprised innocent,' said Leeyes triumphantly.

'I'm not sure, sir. If so, he did it very well . . .'

'He would,' snapped Leeyes. 'He's had plenty of time to get ready for it. Twenty-one years.'

'The important thing, of course,' said Sloan, 'is obviously the girl's twenty-first birthday. That'll be the day when she'll come into her mother's money for sure.'

'I should like to be quite certain that the young man at the farm didn't know that,' said Leeyes. 'His – er – wooing was a bit brisk.'

'But not until after Grace Jenkins died,' pointed out Sloan. 'He'd agreed to stay in the background until Henrietta finished at Boleyn College.'

'Then,' said Leeyes pouncing, 'he kills Grace Jenkins and goes ahead with Henrietta.'

Sloan shook his head. 'What I would like to know, sir, is where Cyril Jenkins comes in.'

'I think he committed just the one mistake,' said Leeyes

shrewdly. 'He knew who Henrietta was and he was probably the last person alive who did.'

'Bar one,' agreed Sloan ominously.

'Bar one,' agreed Leeyes. 'And what do you propose to do about it, Sloan?'

'Set a trap,' said that policeman, 'so deep that there'll be no getting out of it.'

It was half an hour later when Crosby gave a loud cry.

'Found something interesting, Constable?'

'A report of a road accident, sir.'

'When?'

Crosby glanced up to the top of the newspaper page. 'Almost six months ago.'

Sloan stepped over and read it.

'Do you believe in coincidence, Crosby?'

'No, sir.'

'Neither do I.'

'There's something I do believe in, sir.'

'What's that?'

'Practice making perfect.'

'You can say that again,' said Sloan warmly, 'we've just found this.'

Crosby read out the faded cutting which Inspector Sloan handed him. 'This bit, sir? "Deceased had apparently shot himself whilst sitting down. The weapon had fallen on to the table in front of him . . ." ' Crosby looked up. 'Just like Cyril Jenkins, sir . . .'

'Just like Cyril Jenkins,' agreed Sloan.

Later still.

'I've been a fool, Crosby.'

Crosby, no diplomat but still a career man, said guardedly, 'How come, sir?'

'We agreed a long, long time ago' (it was Wednesday actually) 'that where Grace Jenkins had gone in her Sunday best on Tuesday was relevant.'

'Yes, sir. Bound to have been. Someone who knew she would arrive at Berebury bus station too late to catch the five fifteen.'

'So she was bound to catch the seven five,' Sloan pointed to Crosby's notebook. 'She helped an old lady who fell getting off the bus, didn't she?'

'Yes, sir, but I don't see what . . .'

'The bus company will have the old lady's name and address. You can bet your sweet life on that. It'll be a rule of the house in case of an injury claim afterwards. Ten to one she came off the same bus.'

'Do you think so, sir?'

'It's worth a try.'

It was still Sunday.

That, to Henrietta, was the funniest part. It didn't seem like Sunday at all.

She was trying to explain to Inspector Sloan how it was she knew someone had been into the house during the night, but it didn't seem as if he wanted to know.

'That's all right, miss. I rather thought they might.'

'Inspector, were they looking for me?'

'I think so, miss.'

'You mean I'm in someone's way?'

'Let's say you're the stumbling block, miss.'

'What to?' Bewildered.

'A pretty penny, miss, though I'd say most of it's gone now.' He raised a hand to stem any more questions. 'Now that we know someone was here, would you mind just not mentioning it to anyone at all please.'

'Bill knows already. He was here . . .'

'To anyone else besides – er – Bill.'

'All right.' She didn't really care very much now whom she spoke to, still less what she said. 'The blood, Inspector, did it tell?'

'Yes, miss.' He paused. 'You're not Cyril Jenkins's daughter after all.'

'No.'

'You're not surprised?'

'No.' She hesitated. 'I think I would have felt it more.'

'Very probably, miss.'

'Affinity. That's the word, isn't it? I didn't feel that when I saw him. He was just a photograph, you see. Not like her.'

Sloan heard the warmth come flooding back into her voice and said as impersonally as he could, 'She really cared for you, miss. I expect that's what makes the difference, more than blood relationship.'

'Yes,' she turned her head away. 'Inspector, what about tonight? Do I go back to the Rectory?'

'Ah,' said Sloan. 'Tonight. Now listen very carefully. This is important.'

'No,' said Superintendent Leeyes flatly.

'But, sir . . .'

'Too risky. Suppose the girl gets hurt . . .'

'She won't be there to be hurt.'

'I still don't like it.'

'I can't think of a better way of making him show his hand.'

There was a long pause. It became evident that the Superintendent couldn't either.

Henrietta was standing in the telephone kiosk outside the post office. It was nearly ten o'clock in the evening.

The fact that the pile of small change feeding the coin box came from Inspector Sloan's pocket was highly significant.

'Is that you, Mr Hibbs? This is Henrietta Jenkins speaking.'

Sloan could hear his deep voice crackling over the line.

'It is.'

'I'm sorry to trouble you but I'd like some advice.'

'What's the trouble?' James Augustus Heber Hibbs, secular adviser to the village, did not sound particularly surprised. Just attentive.

'I was just going to bed,' said Henrietta, 'and I thought I'd like something to read. I . . . I haven't been sleeping all that well since . . .'

'Quite.'

'Well, I was getting a book out of the bookcase – one of my favourites actually – and I came across my mother's will. It's in an envelope – all sealed up. I just wondered what I should do.'

'Put it somewhere safe,' advised Hibbs sensibly, 'and ring your solicitor first thing in the morning.'

She had exactly the same conversation a few minutes later with Felix Arbican.

'Grace Jenkins's will?' echoed the solicitor. 'Are you sure?'

'Quite sure,' said Henrietta mendaciously. 'You said it would be a help.'

'It will,' said Arbican. 'I think you'd better bring it over to me first thing in the morning – just as you found it. In the mean time . . .'

'Yes?' said Henrietta meekly.

'Put it in the bureau.'

'But the lock's gone.'

'I don't suppose anyone would think to go back there a second time.'

Bill Thorpe might have been in when Henrietta rang the farm. He didn't say. He listened to her tale and said firmly, 'Before you leave the call box I should ring the police. Let them decide what to do. And then I should go straight back to the Rectory.'

'I'm not going back there tonight,' she said. 'I'll be all right on my own.'

'Now, listen to me, Henrietta Jenkins . . .'

'Not Jenkins,' said Henrietta sedately.

'Henrietta whoever you are, I won't have you . . .'

But Henrietta had rung off.

'I meant that,' she said to Sloan.

'What, miss?'

'That bit about not going back to the Rectory.'

'Oh, yes, you are.'

Henrietta smiled sweetly. 'Oh, no, I'm not, Inspector. What's more, you can't make me. I'm coming back to the cottage with you.'

*

For a long time nothing happened.

Henrietta switched lights on and off according to Sloan's bidding – kitchen first, then hall, ten minutes later the bathroom, and finally the bedroom one. Then, fully dressed, she crept downstairs again.

'Please, miss,' pleaded Sloan, 'won't you go and lie down in the spare room? If anything happens to you I shall be in for the high jump.'

'What's going to happen?' she asked.

'I don't know,' he said truthfully, 'but we're dealing with a confirmed murderer.'

'Inspector . . .' Henrietta found it easier to talk in the dark. She had the feeling that she was alone with Sloan though she knew Constable Crosby was in the next room and PC Hepple in the kitchen and Heaven knew who outside. 'Inspector, do you know now who I am?'

'Yes, miss, I think so. We'll have to check with Somerset House in the morning but . . .'

'Who?' she asked directly.

'Henrietta Mantriot.'

'Mantriot.' She tested out the sound, tentative as a bride with a new surname. 'Henrietta Eleanor Leslie Mantriot.'

'Your mother . . .' began Sloan.

'Yes?' There was a sudden constriction in her voice.

'We think she was called Eleanor Leslie. The spelling of Leslie ought to have given us a clue.'

'I've often wondered,' she remarked, 'where those names came from.'

'She's been dead a long time,' volunteered Sloan.

This did not seem to disturb the girl. 'I knew she must have been,' she said, 'otherwise Grace Jenkins wouldn't have . . .'

'No.'

'And my father, Inspector?'

'Your father, miss, we think was a certain Captain Hugo Mantriot.'

'Master Hugo!' she cried.

'Shhhhhsh, miss. We must be very quiet now.'

'I'm sorry,' she said contritely. 'I was always hearing about Master Hugo. I never dreamt that . . .'

'Now you know why, miss.' Sloan heard Crosby's whisper before Henrietta did and he was on his feet and out in the hall in a flash.

'Someone coming down the Belling road, sir.'

'Upstairs,' commanded Sloan. 'Quickly. You too, miss.'

In the end he went up with her and stood at the landing window. Together they watched someone approach the cottage on foot, slide open the gate and disappear behind some bushes in the garden.

'He's not coming in,' whispered Henrietta.

'Not yet,' murmured Sloan. 'Give him time. He's waiting to see if the coast's clear.' He withdrew from the window and passed the word down to Crosby and Hepple to be very quiet now.

It was quite still inside Boundary Cottage.

The next move was a complete surprise to everyone.

Constable Crosby's hoarse whisper reached Sloan and Henrietta on the front upstairs landing.

'There's someone else, sir.'

'Where?'

'Coming down the Belling road.'

The visitor did not pause in the garden. He came straight up to the front door.

'Inspector,' said Henrietta. 'Look! The man in the garden. He's following the other one in.'

Sloan did not stay to reply. He moved back to the head of the stairs and waited there, watching the front door open.

'He's got a key,' breathed Henrietta, hearing it being inserted into the lock.

'Shssshhhhh,' cautioned Sloan. 'Don't speak now.'

The front door opened soundlessly and someone came in. Whoever it was moved forward and then turned to shut the door behind him.

Only it wouldn't shut.

And it wouldn't shut for a time-honoured reason. There was someone else's foot in it.

Someone pushed from the inside and someone else pushed from the outside. The outside pusher must have been the stronger of the two for in the end the door opened wide enough to admit him.

Henrietta recognized the silhouette dimly outlined against the night sky and framed by the doorway. She clutched the banister rail for support. No wonder he had got the door opened in spite of the other man. Bill Thorpe was the strongest man she knew.

Bill Thorpe was apparently not content with having got the door open. He now advanced upon the other man, flinging himself against him. There was a surprised grunt, followed by a muffled oath. Then a different sound, the sudden ripping of cloth. In the darkness it sounded like a pistol shot.

It was enough for Detective Inspector Sloan.

He switched on the lights.

'The police!' cried a somewhat dishevelled Felix Arbican. 'Thank God for that. I caught this young man breaking into—'

'Felix Forrest Arbican,' said Sloan awefully from half-way up the stairs, 'I arrest you for the murder of Cyril Edgar Jenkins and must warn you that anything you say may be—'

'Thank you,' retorted the solicitor coldly, 'I am aware of the formula.'

19

'I thought it would be the solicitor,' said Superintendent Leeyes unfairly. 'Bound to be when you came to think about it.'

'Yes, sir.' Sloan was sitting in the Superintendent's office the next morning, turning in his report.

'What put you on to him in the beginning, Sloan?'

'It was the very first time we saw him, sir. I asked him if he knew of a client called Mrs G. E. Jenkins and he said no.'

'And?'

'And in the same interview he referred to her as Grace Jenkins though neither Crosby nor I had mentioned her Christian name, so I reckoned he knew her all right.'

Leeyes grunted. 'Stroke of bad luck that Hibbs fellow keeping his letter all those years.'

'Yes and no, sir. He'd written it a bit ambiguously at the time – it could indicate a settlement like he said if you cared to look at it that way, so it could have been said to have served his case as well.' He paused. 'I think he would know that an agent would file it, too. Besides . . .'

'Besides what?'

'It was a sort of insurance, sir. If we should get hold of it, it would bring him into the picture and keep him in touch in a rather privileged way, wouldn't it?'

Leeyes grunted again.

'That's why I told the girl about him early on,' said Sloan temerariously.

'You did what?'

'Sort of hinted that he was her mother's solicitor and so . . .' Sloan waved a hand and left the sentence unfinished.

'Suppose,' suggested Leeyes heavily, 'we go back to the very beginning.'

'The last war,' said Sloan promptly. 'A promising young officer in the East Calleshires called Hugo Mantriot of Great Rooden Manor . . .'

'Where's that?'

'Just south of Calleford.' Sloan resumed his narrative. 'This Hugo Mantriot marries the only daughter of the late Bruce Leslie . . .'

'Who's he?'

'The shipping magnate.'

'Money?'

'Lots.'

Leeyes nodded, satisfied.

'They have a baby girl,' went on Sloan.

'Henrietta?'

'Henrietta Eleanor Leslie Mantriot.' Sloan paused. 'When she's about six weeks old her father comes home on leave to Great Rooden and there's a terrible – er – incident.'

'What?' bluntly.

'According to the reports at the time Captain Hugo Mantriot went completely out of his mind, shot his wife and then himself. The Coroner was very kind – said some soothing sentences about the man's mind being turned by his wartime experiences and so forth. The whole thing played down as much as possible, of course.'

Leeyes grunted.

'Twenty-four people had been killed by a flying bomb in Calleford the same week – the police had more than enough to do – the Coroner hinted that the Mantriots were really casualties of war in very much the same way as the flying bomb victims . . .'

'Arbican kill them both?' suggested Leeyes briefly.

'I shouldn't wonder, sir, at all, though we're not likely to find out at this stage.' Sloan turned over a new page in his notebook. 'Mrs Mantriot had made a new will when the baby was born. I've had someone turn it up for me in Somerset House this morning and read it out. She created a trust for the baby should anything happen to either parent . . .'

'She being at risk as much as he was in those days,' put in Leeyes, who could remember them.

'Exactly, sir. Those were the days when things did happen to people, besides which her husband was on active service and there was a fair bit of money involved. So she created this trust with the trustees as . . .'

'Don't tell me,' groaned Leeyes.

'That's right, sir. Waind, Arbican & Waind. After all, of course, it's only guesswork on my part . . .'

'Well?'

'I reckon Grace Jenkins was already in the employment of the Mantriots as the baby's nanny. She was a daughter of Jenkins at Holly Tree Farm in Rooden Parva which isn't all that far away . . .'

'So?'

'I think Arbican suggested to her that she look after the baby. Probably put it into her mind that the infant shouldn't be told about the murder and suicide of her parents – that would seem a pretty disgraceful thing to a simple country girl like her.'

Leeyes grunted.

'From there,' said Sloan, 'it's a fairly easy step to getting her to pass the baby off as her own until the child was twenty-one. All done with the highest motives, of course.'

'Of course,' agreed Leeyes. 'And he keeps them both, I suppose?'

'That's right. Sets Grace Jenkins up in a remote cottage, maintains the household at a distance and not very generously at that . . .'

'Verisimilitude,' said Leeyes.

'Pardon, sir?'

'You wouldn't expect a widow and child to have a lot of money.'

'No, sir, of course not. Grace Jenkins falls for it like a lamb. Takes along a photograph of her own brother to forestall questions, and Hugo Mantriot's medals, and puts her back into bringing up Master Hugo's baby as if it's her own.'

'Then what?'

'Then nothing, sir, for nearly twenty-one years. During which time the Wainds in the firm die off, public memory dies down and Felix Arbican gets through a fair slice of what Bruce Leslie left his daughter.'

'The day of reckoning,' said Leeyes slowly, 'would be Henrietta's twenty-first birthday.'

'That's right. Grace Jenkins had no intention of carrying the pretence further than that. She was a loyal servant and an honest woman.'

'So?'

'She had to go,' said Sloan simply, 'and before Henrietta came back from University.'

'He just overlooked the one thing,' said Sloan.

It was the afternoon now and Sloan and Crosby were sitting in the Rectory drawing-room. In spite of all her protestations Henrietta had gone to the Rectory the previous night – or rather, in the early hours of the morning – after all. Bill Thorpe and PC Hepple had escorted her there to make – as Sloan said at the time – assurance doubly sure. Once there Mrs Meyton had taken it upon herself to protect her from all comers and she had been allowed to sleep on through the morning.

Now they were all foregathered in the Rectory again – bar the main consultant, so to speak. The case was nearly over, the Rectory china looked suitably unfragile and Mrs Meyton's teapot as if it contained tea of a properly dark brown hue – so Sloan had consented to a cup.

'Just one thing,' he repeated.

Nobody took a lot of notice. Henrietta and Bill Thorpe were looking at each other as if for the very first time. Mrs Meyton was counting cups. Constable Crosby seemed preoccupied with a large bruise that was coming up on his knuckle.

'What was that?' asked Mrs Meyton with Christian kindness.

'That a routine post-mortem would establish the fact of Grace Jenkins's childlessness.'

'Otherwise?'

'Otherwise I doubt if we would have looked further than a road traffic accident. We wouldn't have had any reason to . . .'

'Then what?' put in Bill Thorpe.

'Then nothing very much,' said Sloan. 'Inspector Harpe would have added it to his list of unsolved hit-and-runs and that would have been that. Miss Mantriot would—'

Henrietta looked quite startled. 'No one's ever called me that before.'

Sloan smiled and continued. 'Miss Mantriot would have gone back to university none the wiser. She's twenty-one next month. The only likely occasion for her to need a birth certificate after that would be for a passport.'

Bill Thorpe nodded. 'And if it wasn't forthcoming, she wouldn't even know where to begin to look.'

'Exactly.'

'Hamstrung,' said Bill Thorpe expressively.

'But,' said Henrietta, 'what about her telling me she had been a Miss Wright before she married?'

Sloan's expression relaxed a little. 'I never met Grace Jenkins, miss, but I've – well – come to respect her quite a bit in the last week. I think she had what you might call an ironic sense of humour. This Wright business . . .'

'Yes?'

'I expect you've all heard the expression about Mr Right coming along.'

Henrietta coloured. 'Yes.'

'Me,' said Bill Thorpe brightly.

'Perhaps,' said Sloan. 'In her case I think when she had to choose a maiden name so to speak – she chose Wright in reverse.'

'Well done, Grace Jenkins,' said Mr Meyton.

'That's what I think too, sir,' said Sloan. 'The same thing applies in a way with the Hocklington-Garwells who had us running round in circles for a bit.'

'What about it?'

'When she had to choose the name of a family she'd worked for – you know the sort of questions children ask, and she couldn't very well say Mantriot – I think she put together the names of two people involved in an old Calleshire scandal.'

'Hocklington and Garwell?'

'That's right. I gather it was a pretty well-known affair in the county in the old days.'

'That's how Mrs Hibbs knew about it!' said Crosby suddenly.

'I didn't know you'd noticed,' said his superior kindly, 'but you're quite right.'

'But it had nothing to do with the case at all?' said the Rector, anxious to get at least one thing quite clear.

'Nothing,' said Sloan.

'So there was a reason why she was older than I thought,' said Henrietta.

Sloan nodded. 'And for her having her hair dyed and for her not liking having her photograph taken.'

'And for Cyril Jenkins having to be killed,' said Bill Thorpe logically.

'He was her brother. And, of course, he knew the whole story. As far as Grace Jenkins was concerned there was no reason why he shouldn't.'

'So he had to die,' concluded Mr Meyton.

'Once I'd seen him,' cried Henrietta. 'He was quite safe until then.'

'Not really, miss. You see, he would have known about your going to be told the truth when you were twenty-one. He'd have smelt a rat about his sister's death before very long.' He paused. 'That's what put James Hibbs in the clear for once and for all.'

'What did?'

'He didn't know you'd seen Cyril Jenkins so there was no call for him to be killing him on Saturday afternoon.'

'I hadn't thought of that . . .'

'The only people who knew were young Mr Thorpe here, Arbican himself . . .'

'I told him,' said Henrietta, with a shudder.

'And Mr and Mrs Meyton here.'

'How did you know it wasn't me?' enquired Bill Thorpe with deep interest.

'I couldn't be quite sure. Especially when you turned up last night.'

'I wasn't going to come in,' said Thorpe somewhat bashfully. 'I just wanted to keep an eye on the place. Besides, I didn't have a key.'

'He had,' said Henrietta. She meant Arbican but didn't seem able to say the name.

'Yes, miss, he had. Had it for years, I expect. He used that when he came in on Tuesday. He had to make sure Grace Jenkins hadn't left anything incriminating around. He probably took your birth certificate away with him then and anything else that might have given the game away.'

'Inspector.' Henrietta pushed back a wayward strand of hair. 'What *did* happen on Tuesday?'

'We can't be quite sure but I should imagine Arbican summoned Grace Jenkins over to Calleford for a conference. You can imagine the sort of thing. "Henrietta's coming home – she's twenty-one next month – got to be told – modest celebration", and so forth.'

Henrietta winced.

'That -would explain the Sunday best that so puzzled Mrs Callows and Mrs Ricks,' said Sloan, 'and her catching the early bus into Berebury and the last bus back. Berebury to Calleford is a very slow run, you know. The bus calls at all the villages on the way.'

'He wouldn't have her to his office, surely?'

'No. I expect he took her out to lunch, then put her on the bus back which he knew would get her into Berebury after the five fifteen to Larking had left.'

'So he knew she would be on the seven five?'

'That's right. Then he drives himself cross country. It's a much shorter run. First he goes through the bureau and then waits in the pub car park until the bus gets in. He would be able to see her get off. All he has to do then is to time her walk until she's near enough to the bad corner for it to seem like a nasty accident.'

'Which it wasn't,' said Henrietta.

'No, miss.'

'Inspector.' The Rector spoke up. 'What was Arbican's motive in all this?'

'Gain,' said Sloan succinctly. 'Carefully calculated and very expertly carried out. Unless he confesses we shall never know whether he contrived the deaths of Henrietta's father and mother. It isn't impossible and they fell very smartly after the legal arrangements had been completed, but there is another death we do know something about now . . .'

'Cyril Jenkins, you mean?'

'Him, too, sir,' Sloan said to the Rector, 'but that was afterwards. This one was before Grace Jenkins was killed.'

It was very quiet in the Rectory drawing-room.

'Who was that, Inspector?'

'A certain Miss Winifred Lendry, sir.'

'I've never heard of her,' said Mr Meyton.

'I don't suppose any of you have.' Sloan looked round the room. 'It is her death that makes us realize that this was all a long-term plan. Miss Lendry was Arbican's confidential secretary until she was killed by a hit-and-run driver last autumn.'

It was on the Thursday morning that Constable Crosby picked up the telephone and handed the receiver to Detective Inspector Sloan.

'For you, sir. The Kinnisport police.'

'Good morning,' said Sloan.

'About this Major Hocklington,' began his opposite number in Kinnisport. 'Do you want us to watch him for ever? I've had a man posted outside his house for days now and the old boy hasn't stepped out of his wheelchair once . . .'

The Complete
Steel

For Munro – or Ornum – with love

What may this mean,
That thou, dead corse, again in complete steel
Revisit'st thus the glimpses of the moon . . .

Hamlet to Ghost

1

Ornum House was open to the public, which did not help the police one little bit.

On the contrary, in fact.

It was open every Wednesday, Saturday and Sunday from April to October, and to parties at other times by prior arrangement with the steward and comptroller.

It was also open – as all the guidebooks said – Bank Hols (Good Friday excepted). Henry Augustus Rudolfo Cremond Cremond, thirteenth Earl Ornum of Ornum in the County of Calleshire, drew the line at opening Ornum House on Good Friday.

'Religious holiday. Not a civil one. No beanfeasts in my house on Good Friday,' he had decreed, adding, as he always added when the subject came up, 'Don't know what m'father would have thought about having people in the house for money.'

There was usually someone on hand to make a sympathetic noise at this point.

'Guests, family and servants,' his Lordship would go on plaintively. 'That was all in his day. Now it's half Calleshire.'

This understandable repugnance at having his family home tramped over did not, however, prevent his taking a close interest in the daily tally of visitors. At the end of every open day, Charles Purvis, his steward, was summoned to give an account of the numbers – much as in Scotland on the days succeeding the Glorious Twelfth of August, the gamekeeper presented himself each evening with the game-bag totals.

Ornum House, attractive as it undoubtedly was, did not really compete in the Stately Home League Tables – it was too far off the beaten tourist track for that. Nevertheless it did have a respectable number of visitors each year. It was sufficiently near to Berebury to constitute a 'must' for people coming to that town, and sufficiently far from the industrial complex of Luston to be an 'outing' for people living there.

The outing was usually extended to cover visits to the thirteenth-century church of St Aidan or the twentieth-century roadhouse, the Fiddler's Delight – but seldom both.

On this particular Sunday in June the little church by the big house offered its own attractions. It was both quiet and cold and it was possible to sit down in a pew in peace and surreptitiously to slip off shoes grown too small on a hot afternoon. It had the edge – temporarily, at least – on the Fiddler's Delight which would not be open until six o'clock.

Mrs Pearl Fisher was a member of the public who had come to see over Ornum House and her feet hurt.

She hadn't even got as far as the house itself yet and they hurt already. This was partly because they were crammed into her best pair of shoes and partly because she had spent too long standing on them. In the ordinary way she spent her Sunday afternoons having a quiet nap but this Sunday was different.

Just how different it was going to be had not yet become apparent to Mrs Fisher when she and the twins and the rest of their party spilled out of the coach just before lunchtime.

The house and grounds were both fuller than usual. It had been wet for three weekends in a row, and now, suddenly, it was flaming June with a vengeance. There had been picnickers all over the park since noon disporting themselves among the trees in a manner not envisaged by Capability Brown when invited to lay out the great park in the then modern manner. (That had been after one of the Earls of Ornum had clapped a Palladian front on the south side of the medieval house. And *that* had been after he had got back from his first Grand Tour.)

The public, though, seemed to have got the idea of Capability's pleasances. They were positively full of people taking conscious pleasure from walking in them, enjoying their alternating sun and shade and the smooth grass underfoot, and, every now and then, exclaiming at an unexpected vista carefully planned by that master craftsman for them to exclaim at.

At least two people had entered into the spirit of the Folly which was set on a little rise some way from the House.

'No,' said Miss Mavis Palmer.

'Go on,' urged her ardent young man.

'No,' said Mavis, less firmly.

'Be a sport.'

Mavis giggled.

They had come to Ornum House for the day with a coach party from Luston, and there was no question but that they were enjoying themselves.

Mrs Pearl Fisher, who had come on the same coach, wasn't quite so sure she was. Apart from her feet, which were troubling her more than a little, there were the twins, Michael and Maureen, whom she had brought with her for the ample reason that Mr Fisher would never have forgiven her for leaving them at home. *His* Sunday was sacrosanct to the King's Arms and his own armchair.

Like Miss Mavis Palmer and her young man, Bernard, she came from Paradise Row, Luston. Any student of industrial philanthropy would immediately recognize this as a particularly grimy part of that particularly grimy town. By some Victorian quirk of self-righteousness the street names there varied in inverse proportion to their amenity.

The coach had been booked from door to door – which was one of the reasons why Mrs Fisher had put her best shoes on. What she had not reckoned with was the distance within the doors. There was no distance to speak of inside the house in Paradise Row, Luston, but there was a great deal of it once through the portals of Ornum House.

It had been an old house by the time Capability Brown saw it, and now it was an architectural nightmare. It was true to no one period, representational of nothing but a series of improvements by a series of owners. Behind the Palladian south front were Tudor bricks and behind those the remains of a donjon – a reminder that before the house there had been a castle with a great central keep.

Lord Ornum himself never forgot this.

'Those were the days,' he would sigh. 'Drawbridge, portcullis and broadsword in that order and you were all right. Keep all your enemies at bay. But now' – here he would open his hands expressively – 'now to keep out the enemy' (he was referring to Her Majesty's Commissioners of Inland Revenue) 'I have to lower the drawbridge and let everyone else in.'

Mrs Pearl Fisher and the twins didn't join the other picnickers in the park.

They had their sandwiches near the little church that was not far from the house. Churches were something that the utterly urban Mrs Fisher understood. She mistrusted large areas of grass and woodland. Grass other than corporation grass behind railings was outside her experience and such woodland as she knew in the ordinary way in Luston was no place to take thirteen-year-old twins.

'Let's go in them woods, Mum,' suggested Maureen.

'No.'

'Why not?'

Mrs Fisher set her lips. Like Disraeli, she never apologized, she never explained. She took a deep breath. 'You'll have your sandwiches over there by them graves.'

'I don't want to go near the mouldy old church,' protested Maureen, but both the twins recognized the note of flat command in their mother's voice and obediently settled themselves down among the headstones. Afterwards, while waiting for the next conducted tour of the house to begin, they went inside the church.

In view of what was to happen later, this was a pity.

True, Mrs Fisher promptly sat down in a pew and eased off her shoes but it was too early in what was to prove a very long day for her to have any real benefit from this short period of shoelessness. Besides, there was the discomfort of getting feet back into shoes now too small . . .

While she sat there Michael and Maureen scampered about the church in a singularly uninhibited fashion. Mrs Fisher had noticed before that there had been no wonder left in either twin since they had gone to a brand new comprehensive school in the middle of Luston which had everything – including showers which Mrs Fisher didn't think were quite nice. (This last opinion was in no wise influenced by the fact that there were no bathrooms in Paradise Row.)

Not unexpectedly, the chief objects of interest to the Fishers in the little church were connected with the Ornums. The family pew, for instance, with its coat of arms emblazoned on the wooden door. Strictly speaking both family pew and coat of arms should doubtless have gone with the abolition of pew rents but as the Earl of Ornum was patron of the living the question had – somehow – never arisen.

'Mum . . .' That was Michael.

'What is it now?'

'What does "atone" mean?'

'What do you want to know for?' temporized Mrs Fisher.

'It's on this picture thing.' Michael traced out the heraldic lettering on the coat of arms with a grubby finger. 'It says here "I will atone".'

'Does it?' said Mrs Fisher with genuine interest. 'I wonder what they got up to, then?'

But Michael Fisher had by then moved on to a tomb where a stone man lay in effigy, his stone wife by his side, his stone hands clasped round the hilt of a sword. A little stone dog lay at his feet – which Mrs Fisher thought silly – and his legs were crossed, which privately Mrs Fisher thought sillier still. Everyone knew you straightened out someone's legs when they died. Mrs Fisher, who had been in at nearly every death in Paradise Row since she married (marriage was the emotional coming-of-age in her part of Luston), lost interest in that particular Earl of Ornum who had gone to the Crusades.

Maureen was standing before a much later memorial. There was enough colour still to attract the eye to this one and a lot of gold lettering on black marble. Two figures – man and wife – were kneeling opposite each other. On either side of them was a row of smaller kneeling figures.

'Four, five, six . . . six girls,' Maureen called across to her mother.

'Don't shout,' said Mrs Fisher automatically.

'Mum, there's six little girls on this grave thing. Aren't they sweet? And four little boys.'

'Them's their children,' said Mrs Fisher. 'Big families they had then.' Mrs Fisher was one of nine herself. There was something very nice about big families. And as for the children in them – well, her own mother used to say children in big families were born with the corners rubbed off. Which was more than you could say for the twins.

Maureen wasn't listening. 'I've found some more children round the side, Mum, only you can't tell whether they're boys or girls . . .'

Mrs Fisher got to her feet. 'Time we was going,' she said decisively.

'What are they round the side like that for, Mum?' Maureen Fisher was nothing if not persistent. 'You can hardly see them.'

Mrs Pearl Fisher – without benefit of ecclesiology, so to speak – could guess. The tapestry of life in Paradise Row was every bit as colourful and interwoven as that of the aristocracy – only the middle classes were dull. Aloud she said, 'I couldn't say, I'm sure. Now, come along, do . . .'

They walked across from the church to the house.

Maureen sniffed. 'Lilac blossom everywhere,' she said with deep contentment.

'Only on the lilac trees,' her twin corrected her.

Mrs Fisher scolded them both with fine impartiality and they joined a small queue of people who were waiting to go inside the house. It was a queue which was turned into a party with one collective sweep of the guide's eye.

That was Mr Feathers.

He was a retired schoolmaster who lived in the neighbouring village of Petering. There were several guides at Ornum House and their work was done on the principle of one guide per public room rather than one guide per party. This was the fruit of experience. One guide per room ensured the safety of the room and contents. There had been lost – not to say, black – sheep in the days when it had been one guide per party.

'Is that the Earl, Mum?' asked Maureen loudly.

'No,' said Mrs Fisher, though for the life of her she couldn't have said why she was so sure. Perhaps it was because this man had glasses. Earls, she thought, didn't wear glasses.

Mr Feathers, having assembled his flock, led them into the Great Hall.

'Early Tudor,' he said without preamble, trying to assess the group and measure their interest in such things as king posts and hammer beams. He positioned himself in the centre of the floor. 'When they first built this room they used to have the fire where I'm standing now . . .'

'What about the smoke?' asked someone.

'The smoke,' continued Mr Feathers smoothly, 'was left to find its own way out as best it could. As you can see,' here he pointed upwards, past a substantial chandelier, towards the roof, 'it – er – kippered the beams very nicely.'

Thirty-five pairs of eyes obediently looked towards the roof. The thirty-sixth pair belonged to Michael Fisher who was taking a potentially dangerous interest in the inner workings of a very fine clock by Thomas Tompion. Fortunately the thirty-seventh pair was watching Michael Fisher. Mr Feathers had forty years' teaching experience behind him and was quite capable of pointing in one direction and looking in another. He also knew the vulnerable places in the Great Hall and bore down upon Michael at speed.

Michael's mother, who was usually the first person to stop Michael doing something, was perversely annoyed when Mr Feathers did so.

She was hotly defensive at once.

'He never touched it . . .' she said, though in fact she had been looking at the kippered beams at the time. 'Not a finger did that child . . .'

Mr Feathers' voice carried easily and clearly across the Great

Hall and above hers. 'After about a hundred years they got tired of choking from the smoke and in 1659 they put in the chimney at the far end.'

Everyone – including Michael Fisher this time – looked at the chimney and fireplace. It was a truly magnificent affair, running for half the width of the far end of the room. Inside it was space enough for a dozen people. There was a huge andiron there on which rested several young tree trunks by way of winter fuel. Behind was a fireback carrying the same heraldic message as did that on the family pew.

'What does it mean, Mum?' hissed Maureen, *sotto voce*.

'Property of the Earl of Ornum,' said Mrs Fisher smartly. 'Same as on the Corporation buses.'

Mr Feathers cleared his throat and resumed his hortatory address. 'The little cupboards on either side of the fire were for salt. That way it was always kept dry. Salt, you know, had quite some significance in olden days. It was by way of being a status symbol . . .'

'Below the salt,' put in a rather earnest-looking woman, who was clutching *A Guide to Calleshire*.

'Exactly.'

Mrs Fisher changed her not inconsiderable weight from one foot to the other and wished she could sit down. The only status symbol recognized in Paradise Row was a wedding ring – which served to remind her of Mavis Palmer, and her young man, Bernard. If she was any judge, Mavis would be needing one fairly soon.

Mr Feathers turned back to the centre of the hall and sketched a quick word picture for them. 'You can imagine what it must have been like here in the old days. The Earl and his family sat on that dais over there . . .'

'Above the salt,' chimed in the earnest one irritatingly.

'. . . and his servants and retainers below the salt in the main body of the hall. He would have had his own men-at-arms, you know, and one or two of them would always have been on guard.' Mr Feathers gave a pedantic chuckle. 'The floor wouldn't have been as clean then as it is just now . . .'

Pearl Fisher – Pearl Hipps, that was, before her marriage to Mr Fisher – was with him at once. As a girl she had seen the film where Charles Laughton had tossed his chicken leg over his shoulder with a fine abandon. Henry the Eighth, she thought, but Charles Laughton she was sure.

That had been in the days when she sat in the back row of the one and ninepennies at the flicks with Fred Carter. Actually they only paid ninepence and then used to creep backwards when the lights went out but it came to the same thing. Mrs Fisher came out of a reverie which included Fred Carter (he had been a lad, all right) and inflation (you couldn't get a cinema seat for ninepence these days) to see Mr Feathers, his back to the fireplace now, pointing to the opposite end of the room.

A Minstrels' Gallery ran across the entire width of the Great Hall.

'The music came from up there,' said Mr Feathers, 'though it was music of a somewhat different variety from that which you would hear today. They would have had lutes, and probably a virginal . . .'

'Mum,' Maureen Fisher tugged at her mother's sleeve. 'Mum, what's a virginal?'

Mrs Fisher, having no ready answer to this, slapped her daughter instead.

'. . . and,' continued Mr Feathers, 'they would have played up there, quite unseen, during the evening meal. Now, look up that way and a little to the left . . . Do you see up there – in the corner at the back of the Minstrels' Gallery . . .'

'A little window,' contributed someone helpfully.

'A little window,' agreed Mr Feathers. 'Behind it there is a small room. From there the Earl would keep an eye on what everyone was getting up to.' He spoke at large – but he looked at Michael Fisher.

'And they couldn't see him,' said a voice in the group.

'No,' Mr Feathers smiled a schoolmaster's smile. 'They couldn't see him.'

Several necks craned upwards towards the peephole but it was in shadow – as its Tudor creators had intended it should be. There was no light behind the window and it would be quite impossible to tell if there was anyone looking through it or not.

'For all we know,' said Mr Feathers in a mock-sinister voice, 'there may be someone there now, watching us.'

What the reaction of his listeners to this suggestion was, Mr Feathers never knew. At that very moment there was a terrible screech. It rang through the Great Hall and must have come from somewhere not far away. It was eldritch, hideous.

And utterly inhuman.

It was almost as if the sound had been deliberately laid on as a distraction because when it had died away Mrs Fisher became aware that Michael had completely disappeared.

2

Whatever else was in short supply in Paradise Row, emotion and drama were never stinted.

'Whatever's that?' gasped Mrs Fisher, clutching her heart and looking round wildly. 'And where's my Michael?' She pointed. 'Over there, that's where it came from.'

'Outside anyway,' said a thin woman in sensible shoes, as if this absolved her from any further action.

'Sounds to me as if someone was being murdered,' insisted Mrs Fisher.

Mr Feathers shook his head. 'Peacocks,' he explained briefly. 'On the terrace.'

Mrs Fisher was unconvinced. 'Peacocks?'

Maureen Fisher had already gone off in the direction of the noise and was starting to climb on a chair the better to see out of the window.

This galvanized Mr Feathers into near frenzy. 'Get down, girl,' he shouted. 'No one's stood on that chair since Chippendale made it and you're not going to be the first.'

Maureen backed down. 'I only wanted to see . . .'

'Gave me quite a turn, it did,' declared Mrs Fisher generally, looking round the party in a challenging fashion. Wherever she looked there was indubitably no sign of Michael.

The earnest woman – she who carried *A Guide to Calleshire*, and who had hardly done more than start at the noise – smiled distantly, and then the whole group began to move towards one of the doors leading off the Great Hall. Mr Feathers promised another guide upstairs, made absolutely sure Michael Fisher wasn't hiding anywhere, and then turned back to his next party.

Mrs Fisher, thinking about her feet and her Michael, shuffled along in the group towards the staircase. In Paradise Row a bare wooden staircase meant you couldn't afford a carpet. In Ornum House it obviously meant something quite different. For one fleeting moment it crossed Mrs Fisher's mind how wonderful it must have been to have swept down that staircase in a long dress – and then someone trod on her toe and instantly she was back in the present.

And there was still no sign of Michael.

There were pictures lining the staircase wall, small dark oil paintings in the Dutch style which did not appeal to Mrs Fisher though she liked the gold frames well enough, but there was a portrait on the landing at the head of the stairs which caught her eye.

Literally.

The sitter must have been looking at the artist because whichever way Mrs Pearl Fisher looked at the portrait, the portrait looked back at Mrs Pearl Fisher. It was of a woman, a woman in a deep red velvet dress, against which the pink of a perfect complexion stood out. But it was neither her clothes – which Mrs Fisher thought of as costume – nor her skin which attracted Mrs Fisher. It was her face.

It had a very lively look indeed.

And of one thing Mrs Fisher was quite sure. Oil painting or not, the woman in the portrait had been no better than she ought to have been.

'This way, please,' called the next guide. 'Now, this is the Long Gallery . . .'

Michael wasn't there.

By comparison with the lady on the landing Mrs Fisher found the portraits in the Long Gallery dull.

'Lely, Romney, Gainsborough . . .' chanted Miss Cleepe, a short-sighted maiden lady from Ornum village in charge of the Long Gallery, who recited her litany of fashionable portrait painters at half-hourly intervals throughout the season. By June she had lost any animation she might have had in April. 'That's the eleventh Earl and Countess on either side of the fireplace in their Coronation robes for Edward the Seventh . . .'

'Who's the one outside?' Mrs Fisher wanted to know. She jerked her finger over her shoulder. 'You know, on the landing . . .'

Miss Cleepe pursed her lips. 'That's the Lady Elizabeth Murton. She's dead now. Now, ladies and gentlemen, if you will look back at the Coronation paintings you will see a very good representation of the Earl's coronet . . .'

'This picture . . .' said Mrs Fisher.

'The coronet,' went on Miss Cleepe gamely, 'has eight balls on tall spikes alternating with eight strawberry leaves . . .'

Mrs Fisher, who did not in any case know what a coronet was, was not interested. 'This Lady Elizabeth . . .' she persisted.

Miss Cleepe gave in. 'Yes?'

'Who was she?'

Miss Cleepe turned back reluctantly, and said very slowly, 'She was a daughter of the house.'

'What did she do?'

'Do?'

'To be put out there?'

Miss Cleepe looked confused. 'She made rather an unfortunate marriage.'

'Ohoh,' said Mrs Fisher.

'With her groom.'

'They ran away together . . .' supplied Mrs Fisher intuitively.

'I believe so.'

Somewhere at the back of the party someone said lightly, 'Why didn't they just turn the picture to the wall?'

This had the effect of making Miss Cleepe more confused than ever. 'Her son, Mr William Murton, still comes here.'

Mrs Fisher gave a satisfied nod. 'That's why she's on the landing . . .'

'Yes.' Miss Cleepe paused, and then – surprisingly – ventured a piece of information quite outside her usual brief. 'She was known locally, I understand, as Bad Betty.'

Mrs Fisher looked round the rest of the party and said cheerfully, 'They're no different here reely, are they? Same as my cousin Alfred. No one's got any photographs of him any more. Or if they have, they don't put them in the front parlour.'

'The most valuable painting in the Long Gallery,' Miss Cleepe hastened to re-assert herself, 'is that one over there. In the middle of the right-hand wall.'

Everyone stared at a rather dark oil.

'It's by Holbein. Painted in 1532. It's of a member of the family who went in for law. Judge Cremond.'

The subject of the picture was fingering a small black cap.

'It's popularly known as *The Black Death*,' said Miss Cleepe.

The group looked suitably impressed. The only exception was an artistic-looking young man with long hair who held that the female form was the only subject worth painting.

Miss Cleepe paused for dramatic effect. 'And it's his ghost who still haunts the Great Hall . . .'

'I thought you'd have a ghost,' said someone with satisfaction.

Miss Cleepe nodded. She was absolutely sure of her audience now. 'He was a judge and he sentenced the wrong man to death. His soul can't rest, you see . . .'

The sightseeing party was almost equally divided into those who believed every word and the sceptics who believed nothing.

'That,' said Miss Cleepe, 'is where the family motto comes from.'

' "I will atone",' said Mrs Fisher promptly. She was, of course, numbered among the believers, her mother having hand-reared her on fable rather than fact.

'He doesn't look the sort of man to let something like that put him out,' observed a man in the party. A sceptic.

This was true. The thin lips which stretched across under the unmistakably Cremond nose, a nose common to all the family portraits, did not look as if their owner would have been unduly disturbed by the odd death or two in what were admittedly stirring times.

'Ah,' said Miss Cleepe melodramatically, 'but it was his own son who died. And now, whenever a member of the family is about to die, the Judge walks abroad.'

The sceptics continued to look sceptical and the believers, believing.

'And next to that is a portrait of the ninth Earl as a young man. That's a falcon on his wrist . . .' Miss Cleepe suddenly dived away from the party, showing a surprising fleetness of foot. She reached a priceless orrery just as Maureen Fisher was starting it spinning round.

'We got one at school anyway,' she said, 'and it's better than this.'

'No, you haven't,' retorted Miss Cleepe crisply. 'This is an orrery. What you have is a globe. That shows you the world. This is about space.'

Maureen Fisher looked sceptically at the antique inlaid wood. 'Space?'

'Space,' said Miss Cleepe. She raised her voice in the manner of all guides to include the whole party, and went on: 'In the olden days the ladies of the house would spend much of their time in this room. When it was wet they would take their exercise in here.' She pointed out of the far window. 'On fine days they would walk in the park – perhaps to the Folly.'

They all stared across towards the distant Folly. There was no sign whatever of Miss Mavis Palmer and her young man, Bernard. Mrs Fisher wished Miss Cleepe hadn't mentioned walking. For a few precious minutes – while thinking about the errant Lady Elizabeth Murton – she had managed to forget both her feet and the fact that Michael was still missing. Now they came into the forefront of her mind again.

'Who is the man in armour?' asked the earnest woman, indicating a painting near the far door. 'It looks like a Rembrandt.'

'No.' Miss Cleepe shook her head. 'It's quite modern, though it doesn't look it. The twelfth Earl – that is the father of the present Earl – was a great collector of medieval armour. You'll see the armoury presently, those of you who want to go down there.'

'Yes,' said Maureen Fisher simply.

'The Earl had himself painted in a suit of armour which used to belong to one of his ancestors.'

They all peered curiously at the painting of the helmeted figure.

'Sort of fancy dress?' said Mrs Fisher dubiously.

'You could say that,' said Miss Cleepe. 'Now if you'll all go through that door there and then round to the right . . .'

Mrs Fisher shuffled along with the crowd, uneasily aware that Maureen was getting bored and – which was worse – that Michael still wasn't anywhere to be seen.

'Perhaps,' suggested Maureen cheerfully, 'the ghost's got him.'

The next room was the solar.

'The what?' asked Mrs Fisher of the woman beside her.

'Solar,' said the woman.

'What's that?'

The next guide explained and then passed them along to the main bedroom. The lady in charge of the bedroom was a Mrs Nutting.

('Job for a married woman, that,' his Lordship had declared. 'No use putting Miss Cleepe there.'

Charles Purvis had agreed and had found Mrs Nutting.)

Mrs Nutting was well aware of the main points of interest in the bedroom.

No, the present Earl and Countess did not sleep in the four-poster.

Yes, four-posters were rather short.

And high.

The ceiling was very beautiful.

Yes, it was like lace work.

Or icing.

The bobble was the Tudor rose.

It was called pargeting.

Maureen Fisher tugged at her mother's sleeve. 'Them curtains round the bed, Mum, what are they for?'

'Warmth,' replied Mrs Fisher tersely, her eye for once on the guide.

For Mrs Nutting had moved across to a corner of the bedroom towards a great mahogany cupboard. More than half of the party expected a wardrobe full of robes – ermine at least. What was inside the cupboard was a miniature bathroom.

'The twelfth Earl had it put there,' said Mrs Nutting. 'Of

course, you can't lie down in the bath but it was as good as the old-fashioned hip bath of the day. You see the wash-hand basin first and then round to the right – the bath itself.'

Mrs Fisher was enchanted.

She wasn't one of those who was ambling through the rooms of the house in a pipe dream of vicarious ownership. She didn't see her own home as a miniature of what she saw in Ornum House. She didn't even have any reproduction furniture on whose quality she could now congratulate herself.

Nor was she seeking to reassure herself that the gap between the Fishers of this world and the Ornums was small – she knew it wasn't. And two minutes ago she would have sworn she wasn't going to go back to Paradise Row and change anything . . .

But a bathroom in a cupboard . . .

There was room for a cupboard in Paradise Row but not a bathroom. She moved closer.

'Before then,' expanded Mrs Nutting, 'hot water was brought up here in great copper jugs but the twelfth Earl designed this himself and had it fitted here. It hardly takes up any room at all . . .'

That was true.

The party, sheep-like, started to follow their leader towards the bedroom door. Mrs Fisher was the last to leave. She was studying the miniature bath.

There was still no sign of Michael. She hardly took in any of the drawing-room for thinking about him.

'Originally the with-drawing-room,' explained Mrs Mompson, the over-refined widow of a former doctor of Ornum who was graciously pleased – as she herself put it – to 'help out the Earl with the visitors'. 'Not, of course,' she added, 'a room in which actual drawing was done.'

Mrs Fisher did not listen. Gnawing anxiety about Michael had succeeded mild concern. Whereabouts in this vast house was he, and, more important, what was he up to?

After the drawing-room came another room, smaller but made infinitely charming by a most beautiful collection of china and porcelain. It lined the walls in cleverly illuminated glass cases.

Momentarily – only momentarily – Mrs Fisher was glad that Michael was out of the way of harming it.

Those members of the public who had come – whether they admitted it or not – hoping for a glimpse of 'the family' never knew – never even suspected – the woman in charge of the china.

'Very early Wedgwood mostly,' said Miss Gertrude Cremond, cousin to the present Earl. She had a gruff voice which carried well and, in spite of the heat, wore an old cardigan. 'Some Meissen and Sèvres brought back by the family from the Continent on their travels. Grand Tours and so forth . . .'

This was her private joke.

'And a little Ming bought in when they could afford it.'

This was her public joke.

She was a vigorous woman of indeterminate age. She had played hockey for Calleshire in her youth and still looked as if a distant cry of 'sticks' would distract her from the business in hand. She had never married and now her home was with her cousin, the Earl. She looked after the china and did the flowers and the myriad of other small inconsequential tasks that were at one and the same time above and beyond the housekeeper but too mundane for the Countess.

She did all the china herself and very occasionally in the crowd found a kindred spirit.

Not today.

'Lovely, isn't it?'

'We have a little Wedgwood bowl at home.'

'Glad I don't have to clean it all . . .'

'I do,' responded Miss Cremond, thus dispelling any suspicions in anyone's mind that she could possibly be other than hired help.

There were clucks of sympathy all round at the enormity of the task but soon they shuffled on. Like all such visitors they came, they saw, they fingered, they exclaimed, they went . . .

It was almost exactly an hour after leaving it that the party arrived back in the Great Hall.

The discomfort from her feet was vying in Mrs Fisher's mind with the constant fret about Michael – and with the interest of the bathroom. What she wanted more than anything else was a chair which didn't have a red cord stretched from arm to arm. It seemed, though, that the tour was not yet at an end. Mr Feathers was speaking to them again.

'Those of you who wish may now go down to the dungeons and armoury at no extra charge.' He paused. 'The twelfth Earl assembled one of the finest collections of medieval armour in the country. However, I must warn you that the stair is difficult . . .'

This last would have settled it for Mrs Fisher and her poor feet had Michael not been missing. Mr Feathers had not seen him. He was quite certain about this, declaring that he would know Michael anywhere.

'Like Maureen but a boy,' said Mrs Fisher by way of describing him.

Mr Feathers said with perfect truth that he remembered Michael only too well and he was sure he hadn't seen him since Mrs Fisher's party had left the Great Hall.

'The armoury,' he suggested. 'Perhaps he went down there.'

Mr Feathers had been right to winnow out the party. This was no staircase for the aged and infirm. It was not wood but stone and it wound its way down inside a turret. A hanging rope did duty as a banister but Mrs Fisher did not trust it. Instead she pressed herself against the outer wall invisibly helped by a force she did not recognize as centrifugal.

'We know one thing about the chap who built this,' called out Mr Feathers cheerfully from above. 'He was left handed. This staircase goes round the wrong way. That was so that his sword arm would be free.'

Mrs Fisher did not care.

The descending stair seemed interminable. She had no idea how many times it wound round. She concentrated on following the person ahead and trying to keep out of the way of the person behind. At long last the steps came to an end and she was on a level floor again. It was very gloomy.

'I don't like it down here, Mum,' complained Maureen. 'It's too dark.'

This was true: the only lighting came from two low-powered sconces on the wall.

('Don't overdo the electricity down there, Purvis.'

'Very well, my lord.'

'Got to get the right atmosphere.')

As far as Mrs Fisher was concerned they'd got it. She shivered and wished she was somewhere else. Just wait until she found Michael, that's all, she wouldn't half give him . . .

'This way for the dungeons.' That was Bert Hackle, one of the undergardeners at Ornum House. He was custodian of the dungeons and tackled the job with relish. 'This way, please.'

His voice boomed back from the bare stone walls and his boots grated on the floor much as those of a gaoler would have done. Mrs Fisher shivered again.

'This is the oldest part of the house,' he announced. 'Left over from when it was a castle. All the rest was built on top of this bit and lots more that's gone through the centuries.'

He waited for the echo to catch up with him.

'This bit here,' he put his hand on a stone wall that could only be called substantial, 'is what used to be a bastion.'

'Well I never,' murmured someone obligingly.

'And inside it is the donjon or dungeon,' said Bert Hackle, giving Mrs Fisher her first and last lesson in philology. 'Donjon – dungeon. See?'

He led the way round the wall, and, stooping, went through an arch where a door had been. They crowded in after him. 'This is where they kept the prisoners.'

His party were suitably impressed.

'Nasty, isn't it?'

'Glad I wasn't one.'

'Look at that damp. If they didn't have anything else they'd soon have rheumatism.'

This last was an unfair reflection on the original builders, whose stonework had, in fact, been perfect. The dampness could be laid entirely at Bert Hackle's door. The instinct of an undergardener is to sprinkle water everywhere and Bert Hackle had lent a touch of verisimilitude to the dungeon walls by the judicious application of a little water before visiting time.

His Lordship – who was not slow – had done nothing to stop

him. Indeed, on the last occasion he had been down there, the Earl had gone so far as to congratulate Bert on the fern species which was growing from a crack in the wall.

('Fine plant you have there, Hackle,' he had said.

'Thank you, my lord.')

Which Bert had taken as tacit approval.

'There'll be a well somewhere,' said someone in the party who knew about castles.

Bert Hackle pointed. 'Over there.'

The castle well was deep enough to need no faking and had been firmly boarded over on the advice of his Lordship's insurance company.

'Good water,' said the gardener. 'Nice and sweet.'

'Better than the piped stuff,' said a woman who had heard of – but knew nothing about – typhoid fever.

Hackle moved beyond the well head and took up a fresh stance in front of a low grating cut in one part of the floor. He cleared his throat impressively. The echo didn't quite know what to make of this and there was an appreciable pause before he began on what was obviously his *pièce de résistance*.

'If you was bad,' he said, 'you were thrown into the dungeons, but if you was really bad . . .'

Mrs Fisher was sure Michael must be about somewhere.

'. . . if you was really bad, they put you in here.' He bent his powerful arms down and pulled at the two iron bars of the grating. A great stone pivoted upwards, revealing a hole beyond. Three men might have stood in it.

'It's a n'oobliette,' announced Hackle. 'Where you put your prisoners and forgot them.'

'From the French,' translated the earnest woman.

Mrs Fisher craned her neck to make sure that Michael wasn't in it.

'They had it just here,' Hackle said in a macabre voice, 'so that the prisoners could hear the water being brought up from the well. Then they didn't give them none.'

It took everyone except Mrs Fisher a little time to sort out this double negative.

'They died of thirst,' she said at once, 'while they was listening to the water.'

Bert Hackle sucked his lips. 'That's right. Now, if you'll all come along here with me I'll show you the way to the armoury. It's been reconstitooted from part of the old curtain wall . . .'

But the oubliette – or perhaps the stone staircase – had been enough for some and the party which eventually entered the armoury was a very thin one. The earnest woman came – of course – and some three or four others . . .

'Michael Fisher!' Michael Fisher's mother gave a shriek of mingled anger and recognition. 'You naughty boy! You wait until I get you home . . .'

'It's lovely down here, Mum.'

'What ever do you mean by running away like that?'

'It's much more fun down here.' Michael remained undismayed by her anger.

Mrs Fisher took a quick look round. There was one thing about this part of the house which reassured her. The old things, having stood the test of so very much time, were more likely to stand the test of Michael Fisher. His mother did not think he could have got up to much in the armoury.

Wherein she was sadly wrong.

It was a truly fearsome collection. Weapons sprouted from the walls, antique swords lay about in glass cases, chain-mail hung from hooks and – as if this weren't enough – several suits of armour stood about on the floor.

'Whoopee,' shouted Michael. 'Look, Mum, this is what I've been doing . . .'

He darted off down the centre of the armoury, shadow boxing with the coat of war of some long-forgotten knight of a bygone age.

'Got you,' he said to one of them, landing a blow on the breastplate. It resounded across the hall.

'Mum . . .' This was Maureen, who had been studying the contents of one of the glass cases without real interest.

'What?'

'Mum, what's a belt of chastity?'

Mrs Fisher's answer to this was what the psychologists call a displacement activity. She shouted at her son.

'Michael, leave that suit of armour alone.'

'I just want to look inside.'

'Leave it alone, I tell you.'

The earnest woman looked up at the raised voice and politely looked away again.

Michael was struggling with the visor.

'Can't you hear what I say?'

There was at least no doubt about that. Mrs Fisher in full voice could be heard clearly from one end of Paradise Row to the other so the armoury presented no problem in audibility.

'Yes, I just want to . . .' Michael heaved at the visor with both hands.

'Mum . . .' It was a whine from Maureen. 'Mum, what's a belt of chastity?'

'Michael Fisher, you'll leave that suit of armour alone or else . . .'

What the alternative was no one ever knew. At that moment Michael Fisher managed to lift the visor.

He stared inside.

A face stared back at him.

It was human and it was dead.

3

The information was not exactly welcomed at the nearest police station. In fact, the Superintendent of Police in Berebury was inclined to be petulant when he was told. He glared across his desk at the Head of his Criminal Investigation Department and said:

'You sure it isn't a false alarm, malicious intent?'

'A body in a suit of armour,' repeated Detective Inspector C. D. Sloan, the bearer of the unhappy news.

'Perhaps it was a dummy,' said Superintendent Leeyes hopefully. 'False alarm, good intent.'

'In Ornum House,' went on Sloan.

'Ornum House?' The Superintendent sat up. He didn't like the sound of that at all. 'You mean the place where they have all those day trippers?'

'Yes, sir.' Sloan didn't suppose the people who paid their half crowns to go round Ornum House thought of themselves as day trippers but there was no good going into that with the Superintendent now.

'Whereabouts in Ornum House is this body?'

Sloan coughed. 'In the armoury, actually, sir.'

'I might have known,' grunted Leeyes. 'In that sort of set-up the armour is always in the armoury.'

'Yes, sir.'

'Who said so?'

Sloan started. 'The steward.'

'Not,' heavily sarcastic, 'not the butler?'

'No, sir. He's gone down to keep guard. The steward – his name's Purvis – came to telephone us.'

'And,' asked Leeyes pertinently, 'the name of the body in the armour?'

'He didn't say, sir. He just said his Lordship was sure we would wish to know.'

The Superintendent glared suspiciously at his subordinate. 'He did, did he?'

'Yes, sir.'

Leeyes took a deep breath. 'Then you'd better go and – what is it they say? – unravel the mystery, hadn't you, Sloan?'

'Yes, sir.'

'Though I don't want any touching of forelocks, kow-towing or what have you, Sloan. This is the twentieth century.'

'Yes, sir.'

'On the other hand,' very silkily, 'you would do well to remember that the Earl of Ornum is a Deputy Lieutenant for Calleshire.'

'I shan't forget, sir.' Even though it was the twentieth century?

'Now, who have you got to go with you?'

'Only Detective Constable Crosby,' apologetically.

Leeyes groaned. 'Crosby?'

'Sergeant Gelven's gone on that training course, if you remember, sir.'

The Criminal Investigation Department at Berebury was a very small affair, all matters of great criminal moment being referred to the County Constabulary Headquarters at Calleford.

The Superintendent snorted gently. 'I shouldn't have thought Crosby could unravel knitting let alone some masochistic nonsense like this.'

'No, sir.' But it would have to be Crosby because there wasn't anyone else.

'All right,' sighed Leeyes. 'Take him – but do try to see that he doesn't say "You can't do that there 'ere" to the Earl.'

*

Detective Constable Crosby – raw, but ambitious too – drove Inspector Sloan the odd fifteen miles or so from the police station at Berebury to the village of Ornum. The village itself was clustered about the entrance to the park – and it was a very imposing entrance indeed. Crosby turned the car in between two magnificent wrought-iron gates.

The gates were painted black with the finer points etched out in gold leaf. If the state of a man's gate was any guide to the man – and in Sloan's working experience it was – the Earl of Ornum maintained a high standard. Surmounting the pillars were two stone spheres and crouching on top of the spheres was a pair of gryphons.

Constable Crosby regarded them critically. 'They're funny looking birds, aren't they? Can't say I've ever seen anything like that flying around.'

'I'm glad to hear it, Constable. They don't exist.'

Crosby glanced up over his shoulder at the solid stone. 'I see, sir.'

'A myth,' amplified Sloan. 'Like unicorns.'

'Yes, sir.' Crosby slid the car between the gryphons and lowered his speed to a self-conscious fifteen miles an hour in deference to a notice which said just that. Then he cleared his throat. 'The house, sir, I can't see it.'

'Stately Homes aren't meant to be seen from the road, Constable. That's the whole idea. Carry on.'

Crosby subsided into silence – for perhaps half a minute. 'It's a long way, sir . . .'

Sloan grunted. 'The distance in this instance between the rich man in his castle and the poor man at his gate is about a mile.'

'A mile, sir?' Crosby digested this, dropping a gear the while. This particular police car wasn't used to a steady 15 m.p.h.

'A mile,' confirmed Sloan, whose own single latched gate led up a short straight path to a semi-detached house in suburban Berebury. In his view his own path had the edge – so to speak – on the Earl's inasmuch as it was flanked by prize rose bushes as opposed to great oak trees. Sloan favoured roses. He felt that there should be a moratorium on crime while they were in bloom.

'Sir, if we were to go over fifteen m.p.h. would a prosecution hold under the Road Traffic Acts?' Crosby was young still and anxious for promotion. 'They'd have to bring a private prosecution, wouldn't they? I mean we couldn't bring one or could we?'

Sloan, who was watching keenly for a first glimpse of Ornum House, said, 'Couldn't do what?'

'Bring a prosecution for speeding on private land.' Crosby kept his eye on the speedometer. 'Traffic Division wouldn't be able to do a thing, would they?'

Sloan grunted. Traffic Division were never ones for being interested in the finer academic points of law. Their line of demarcation was a simple one.

Fatals and non-fatals.

However, if Crosby wanted to split hairs . . .

'Going over the limit any time, anywhere, Constable, isn't the same thing as proving it.'

'No, sir, but if you had two independent witnesses . . .'

'Ah,' said Sloan drily. 'I agree that would be different.' He peered forward, thinking he saw a building. 'I don't know when I last saw two independent witnesses. Rare birds, independent witnesses. I'd put them in the same category as gryphons myself.'

Crosby persisted. 'But if you had them, sir, then what? I could ask Traffic, I suppose . . .'

Sloan happened to know that Inspector Harpe of Traffic Division wouldn't thank anybody for asking him anything else just at this moment. Superintendent Leeyes had today posed him about the most awkward question a police officer could ever be asked. It was: why were all the damaged cars from the accident jobs attended by his three crews finding their way into the same garage for repair? If anyone was getting a rake off there would be hell to pay . . .

'Sir,' Crosby pointed suddenly. 'Something moved over there between the trees. I saw it.'

Sloan turned and caught a glimpse of brown. 'Deer. And there's the house coming up now. Keep going.'

There was a young woman sitting by a baize-covered table near the front door. She had on a pretty summer frock and she was all for charging Sloan and Crosby half a crown before she would let them in.

'Half a crown, did you say, miss?' Sloan was torn between a natural reluctance to tell anyone who didn't already know that the police had been sent for – and the certain knowledge of the difficulty he would have in retrieving five shillings from the County Council No. 2 Imprest Account, police officers, for the use of.

'Half a crown if you want to go into the house,' she said firmly. 'Gardens and park only, a shilling.'

They were rescued – just in time – by a competent-looking young man who introduced himself as Charles Purvis, steward and comptroller to the Earl of Ornum.

'That's all right, Lady Eleanor,' he said. 'These two gentlemen have come to see me. They're not visitors.'

She nodded and turned to give change to the next arrivals.

The steward led the two policemen through the Great Hall – Mr Feathers was saying his piece there to a fresh party – and then down the spiral staircase.

'We closed the armoury at once, Inspector – you'll watch your step here, won't you . . .'

Sloan was going to watch his step in Ornum House all right. He had his pension to think of.

'Shall I go first, Inspector?' offered Purvis. 'It's a bit tricky on the downward flight . . .'

It wasn't only the staircase that was going to be tricky either. Sloan could see that already.

'Hang on to the rope,' advised Charles Purvis. 'As I was saying, we closed the armoury at once but didn't tell more people than was absolutely necessary.'

'Not Lady Eleanor?' said Sloan.

'No, she doesn't know yet.' Purvis turned left at the bottom of the staircase and led the way down the dim corridor. 'We felt it would only cause comment to close the entire house at this stage.'

A body in the armoury of a Stately Home was going to do more than cause comment, but Sloan did not say so. Instead, he murmured something about not letting those who were in the house out.

'The earlier parties will have gone by now,' said Purvis regretfully. 'The armoury is the last of the rooms on exhibition because relatively few people are interested. They mostly don't come down here at all, but go into the park next.'

They passed the dungeon and the well head and found Bert Hackle standing guard at the armoury door.

'There's nobody here now, Mr Purvis, but me. Mr Dillow . . .'

'The butler,' put in Purvis.

'That's right,' said Bert Hackle. 'He's taken all those that were in here along to the kitchen with Mrs Morley.'

'Thank you, Hackle.' Purvis opened the armoury door and walked in, the two policemen at his heels.

At first glance it did not seem as if anything was amiss.

All was still and the room resembled a museum gallery as much as anything. There were eight suits of armour, each standing attentively facing the centre of the room as if alert for some fresh call to arms. Sloan regarded them closely. The visors were down on all of them but one at least was more than a mere shell.

'Which . . .' he began.

'The second on the right,' said Charles Purvis.

Sloan and Crosby advanced. A little plaque on the floor in front of it read 'Armour with tilt pieces, *circa* 1595.'

Sloan lifted the visor very, very carefully. There might be more fingerprints than those of Michael Fisher here. The visor was heavier than he expected but, just as the boy had done, he got it up at last.

Inside was the face of a man verging on the elderly and more than a little dead. Inspector Sloan touched his cheek though he knew there was no need. It was quite cold. He looked back at the steward.

'Do you know who . . .'

'Mr Meredith,' supplied Charles Purvis, adding by way of explanation. 'Our Mr Meredith.'

'Our Mr Meredith?'

'Librarian and archivist to his Lordship.'

'You knew him well, then?'

'Oh, yes,' said the steward readily. 'He comes – came – to the house most days. He was writing a history of the family.'

'Was he?' Sloan tucked the fact away in his mind. 'Where did he live? Here?'

'No. In Ornum village. With his sister.'

Sloan lowered the visor. It was just like banishing an unpleasant fact to the back of one's mind. At once the room seemed normal again.

Crosby got out a notebook.

'Mr Osborne Meredith,' said Purvis, 'and his address was the Old Forge, Ornum.'

'If he came here every day,' said Sloan, 'perhaps you could tell me the last day you saw him here.'

The steward frowned slightly. 'Not today, I know . . .'

Sloan knew that too. That cheek had been too chill to the touch.

'I don't recall seeing him yesterday either, now I come to think of it,' went on Purvis, 'but he might well have been here without my seeing him. He came and went very much as he wished.'

Sloan waved a hand in a gesture which took in the whole house. 'Whereabouts in here would you expect to see him?'

'He spent most of his time in the library and in the muniments room.'

'Did he?' said Sloan, adding ambiguously, 'I'll be checking up on that later.'

Purvis nodded. 'But how he came to be down here in the armoury, and in this, Inspector, I couldn't begin to say at all.'

'And dead,' added Sloan.

'And dead,' agreed Purvis sombrely. 'His Lordship was most distressed when he was told and said that I was to give you every possible assistance . . .'

'He came and went,' observed the egregious Detective Constable Crosby, 'and now he's gone.'

If anything, Dr Dabbe, the Consultant Pathologist to the Berebury Group of Hospitals, was more put out by the news than the Superintendent had been.

But for a different reason. Because it was Sunday afternoon and he was sailing his Albacore at Kinnisport.

'Send him along to the mortuary, Sloan,' he said from the yacht club telephone, 'and I'll take a look at him when I get back.'

The tide must be just right, thought Sloan. Aloud he said, 'It's not quite like that, doctor. The body's at Ornum House . . .'

The medical voice sounded amused. 'What are you expecting, Sloan? True blue blood? Because I can assure you that . . .'

'No, doctor. It's not like that at all.' The telephone that the steward had led him to was in a hallway and rather less private than a public kiosk. 'We're treating it as a sudden death . . .'

The sands of time having run out for one more soul.

'Well, then . . .' said the doctor reasonably.

'He's in a suit of armour for the tilt, *circa* 1595,' said Sloan, 'and I not only don't know that we ought to move him, but I'm not at all sure that we can.'

Then, duty bound, Sloan telephoned Superintendent Leeyes at Berebury.

'I've been wondering what kept you,' said that official pleasantly. 'And how did you find the man in the iron mask?'

'Dead,' said Sloan.

'Ah!'

'Dead these last couple of days, I should say – though there's not a lot of him visible to go by, if you take my meaning, sir.'

Leeyes grunted. 'I should have said a good look at the face should have been enough for any really experienced police officer, Sloan.'

'Yes, sir.' If the deceased had happened to have been shot between the eyes, for instance . . .

'So?'

'I've sent for Dr Dabbe, sir, and I'd be obliged if I might have a couple of photographers and a fingerprint man . . .'

'The lot?'

'Yes, please, sir. And if they'll ask Lady Eleanor to tell the steward when they arrive . . .'

'Lady who?'

'Lady Eleanor, sir. His Lordship's daughter. She's on duty at the door.'

'Is she? Then she'll probably send them round the back anyway,' said the Superintendent, 'when she's taken a good look at them.'

'Yes, sir,' dutifully. Then, 'The deceased is a Mr Osborne Meredith, librarian to the Earl . . .'

'Ha!' Triumphantly. 'What did I tell you, Sloan? Librarian. He got the idea from a book, I'll be bound. Mark my words, he'll be one of these suicides that's got to be different . . .'

'Different,' conceded Sloan, at once. 'This is different all right, but as to the other, sir, I couldn't say. Not yet.'

4

Detective Constable Crosby was still keeping watch in the armoury when Charles Purvis and Inspector Sloan got back there.

'I've just checked up on the other seven suits of armour, sir,' he said virtuously.

'Good.'

'All empty.'

'Good,' said Sloan again, slightly startled this time. Honest as always, even with himself, Sloan admitted that this was something he wouldn't have considered. He'd got a real eager beaver on his hands in young Crosby. Surely Grand Guignol himself wouldn't have thought of seven more men in seven more suits . . .

'And,' went on Crosby, 'on the ways into here.'

'There's just the one, isn't there?' said Sloan.

'That's right, sir. The door.'

Purvis, the steward, seemed inclined to apologize for this. 'That's because we're below ground level here, Inspector, and so we can't very well have windows. Nor even borrowed light. It's all artificial, the lighting down here.'

Sloan looked round. In a fine imitation of medieval times, flaming-torch style lighting had been fixed into basket type brackets high up on the walls.

'The lighting's not very good,' said Purvis.

'Effective, though.'

Purvis nodded. 'Most people are glad to get back upstairs again.'

Sloan went back to the second suit of armour on the right. 'Tell me, had anyone mentioned to you that Mr Meredith was missing?'

'No, Inspector. We – that is, I – had no idea at all that everything was not as usual. We shouldn't have opened the house at all today had there been any suggestion that . . .' His voice trailed away.

'Quite so,' said Sloan.

'Complete surprise to us all.' He ran his hand through his hair. 'Nasty shock, actually.'

'You said he lived with his sister . . .'

'That's right. His Lordship has gone down to Ornum to break the news.'

'Himself?'

Purvis looked surprised and a bit embarrassed. 'Not the sort of job to delegate, you know. Come better from him anyway, don't you think? Take it as a gesture perhaps.'

'Perhaps.'

'Then get the Vicar to go round afterwards. Helpful sort of chap, the Vicar.'

'Good,' said Sloan, content that the ground was also being prepared for him. A visit from a humble policeman shouldn't come amiss after all that.

'Though, as to the rest' – the steward waved a hand to embrace the armour – 'I can't understand it at all. It's not as if it was even his subject. It's Mr Ames who's the expert.'

'Ames?'

'The Vicar. Bit of an enthusiast about armour. If we get any visitors who're really keen we ring him up at the Vicarage and he comes in.'

Sloan looked round the armoury. 'There's never a full-time guide here, then?'

'No. Hackle brings people as far as the door when he's finished showing the dungeons and so forth – you need a man there because of the oubliette – and then they find their own way out in their own time.'

'I see.'

Purvis pointed to an arquebus hanging on the wall. 'Not everyone's subject.'

'No.'

'But Mr Ames catalogued this collection years ago, and he always comes in if special parties come.'

'Special parties?'

Purvis nodded. 'As well as the ordinary visitors we have what you might call specialist groups. People who are interested in just one facet of Ornum House. Parties come to see the armour and I tell Mr Ames. It's the same with the pictures and books and manuscript records. Take next week, for instance. I've got a party who call themselves 'The Young Masters' coming down to see the pictures on Monday. Arranged it with Mr Meredith so that he could—' Purvis came to a stop when he saw where his sentence was getting him. 'Oh, dear, I'd forgotten all about that.'

Sloan looked at the suit of armour that contained the late Mr Meredith and said, 'What other – er – speciality of the house do you have?'

'The Ornum collection of china,' replied the steward, not without pride, 'is thought to be one of the finest still in private hands.'

'I see.' Sloan scratched his chin. 'Before I see his Lordship, do you think you could just give me some idea of the set-up here?'

'Set-up?' said Purvis distantly.

'Who all live here, then . . .'

'Well, there's the family, of course . . .'

Constable Crosby got out his notebook and started writing.

'There's his Lordship,' said Purvis, 'and the Countess and their children.'

'Lady Eleanor?' said Sloan.

'Lady Eleanor is their only daughter,' said Charles Purvis, a curiously strangled note creeping into his voice.

'And who else?'

'Lord Cremond, his Lordship's son.'

'And heir?' enquired Sloan.

Purvis nodded. 'His only son.'

'I see. That all?'

The steward smiled faintly. 'By no means.'

'Oh?'

'Then there's his Lordship's cousin, Miss Gertrude Cremond.'

'Quite a family.'

'And,' went on Purvis, 'his Lordship's aunts, Lady Alice and Lady Maude. They are, of course, rather – er – elderly now.'

Sloan sighed. That, being translated, meant eccentric.

Purvis hadn't finished. 'His Lordship's nephew, Mr Miles Cremond, is staying in the house just now, with his wife, Mrs Laura Cremond, and then, of course, there are the indoor staff . . . Dillow, the butler, and so on.'

Sloan sighed again.

'Do you want me to go on?' asked Purvis.

'Oh, yes,' said Sloan grimly, pointing to the suit of armour. 'No man could have got into this contraption on his own. I can work that much out from here.'

'I know,' said Purvis flatly. 'That's why we sent for you.'

Mrs Pearl Fisher was sitting in the biggest kitchen Sloan had ever seen in his life.

She was by no means the only person in the room but she contrived – by some subtle alchemy which would have done credit to a first lady of the stage – to give the impression that she was.

She was sitting at a vast deal table and she was drinking tea. Teas (2/- per head) were available to visitors in the Old Stables but this pot was obviously on the house. It was being administered by the housekeeper, Mrs Morley, a lady who looked as if she had only just stopped wearing bombasine. A personage whom Sloan took to be Mr Dillow, the butler, hovered at an appropriate distance.

'I don't know that I'll ever get over the shock,' Mrs Fisher was announcing as Inspector Sloan and Crosby went in.

'The tea will help,' Mrs Morley said drily.

Mrs Fisher ignored this. 'Sent me heart all pitter-patter, it did.'

'Dear, dear,' said Mrs Morley.

Histrionically, Mrs Fisher laid her hand on her left breast. 'It's still galloping away.'

'Another cup of tea?' suggested Mrs Morley.

Both ladies knew that there would be brandy and to spare in a house like this but one of them, at least, was not prepared for it to be dispensed.

'It can bring on a nasty turn, can a sight like that,' offered Mrs Fisher.

Mrs Morley advised a quiet sit.

Mrs Fisher said she thought it would be quite a while before her heart steadied down again.

Mrs Morley said she wasn't to think of hurrying. She was very welcome. Besides the Police Inspector would want to hear all about it, wouldn't he, sir?

Sloan nodded. Crosby got out his notebook.

'I shall never sleep again,' declared Mrs Fisher. 'That face! I tell you, it'll come between me and my sleep for the rest of my born days.'

'Tell me, madam . . .'

'Them eyes,' she moaned. 'Staring like that.'

'Quite so. Now . . .'

'He didn't die today, did he?' she said. 'I know that much . . .'

'How do you know that?' Sharply.

'He was the same colour as poor old Mr Wilkins in our street, that's why . . .'

'Mr Wilkins?'

'Putty, that's what he looked like when they found him.'

'Indeed?'

'Three days' milk there was outside his house before they broke the door down,' said Mrs Fisher reminiscently. 'And he looked just like him.'

'I see.'

'In fact,' said Mrs Fisher, seeing an advantage and taking it all in the same breath, 'if it hadn't been for my Michael there's no knowing when you might have found the poor gentleman, is there?' She looked round her audience in a challenging manner. 'It's not as if there was any milk bottles.'

Sloan nodded. It was a good point. There had been no milk bottles outside the armoury door. Nothing that he knew of to lead to that particular suit of armour. There was indeed no knowing . . .

Where was Michael now?

Michael Fisher, it presently transpired, was somewhere else being sick.

'I don't know what he'll be like in the coach going home, I'm sure,' said Mrs Fisher with satisfaction. 'I shouldn't wonder if we don't have to stop.'

Maureen was dispatched to retrieve Michael.

Finding the dead face had had its effect on the boy. His complexion was chalky white still, and there was a thin line of perspiration along the edge of his hair line. He looked Sloan up and down warily.

'I didn't touch him, mister. I just lifted that front piece thing, that's all.'

'Why?' asked Sloan mildly.

'I wanted to see inside.'

'But why that particular one? There are eight there.'

'Tell the Inspector,' intruded Mrs Fisher unnecessarily.

'I dunno why that one.'

'Had you touched any of the others?'

Michael licked his lips. 'I sort of touched them all.'

'Sort of?'

'I'm learning to box at school.'

'I see.'

'I tried to get under their guards.'

'Not too difficult surely?'

'More difficult than you'd think.' Michael Fisher's spirit was coming back. 'Those arms got in the way.'

'But you got round them in the end?'

'That's right.'

'And this particular one – the one with the man inside . . .'

'It sounded different when I hit it,' admitted Michael. 'Less hollow.'

'That's why you looked?'

'Yes.'

'No other reason?'

Michael shook his head.

It was the first time in Sloan's police career that he had ever been conducted anywhere by a butler.

'Mr Purvis said I was to take you straight to his Lordship,' said Dillow, 'as soon as his Lordship got back from the village.'

'Thank you,' murmured Sloan politely.

He couldn't place the man's voice. It wasn't a Calleshire one, that was certain. While that didn't make him a foreigner, at least he knew he wasn't local. The Earl might have lived in Ornum for centuries. Dillow hadn't.

There was no denying that the butler was a man of considerable presence. As tall as the two policemen and graver. Sloan, who had subconsciously expected him to be old, saw that he was no more than middle-aged. He had a curious way of walking, and the sort of pseudo-portentous bearing that would have served him well in politics or the Church.

'If you would be so good as to follow me, gentlemen . . .'

Sloan and Crosby obediently fell in behind Dillow of the stately mien and set off on the long journey from the kitchen to what the butler referred to as the Private Apartments.

'You would have known Mr Meredith, of course,' began Sloan as they rounded their first corridor.

'Certainly, sir. A very quiet gentleman. Always very pleasant, he was. And no trouble.'

'Really?' responded Sloan as noncommittally as he could. Mr Osborne Meredith might not have been any trouble to a butler. He was going to be a great deal of trouble to a police inspector.

This police inspector.

'He usually went home to luncheon,' said the butler. 'Ah, through this way, I think, sir, if you don't mind.'

He changed direction abruptly at the distant sound of voices. Sloan had almost forgotten the house was still full of people who had paid to see some – but by no means all – of the sights of Ornum House.

'Sometimes,' went on the butler, whose mind seemed to be totally concerned with meals, 'he would take tea with the family but more often than not he would be – ah – absorbed in his work and I would take him a pot to himself in the library.'

'I shall want to see the library presently.'

'Very good, sir.'

'And the – er – muniments room.'

'Certainly, sir.' Dillow had at last reached the door he wanted. He moved forward ahead of them, coughed discreetly and announced:

'Two members of the County Constabulary to see you, my lord.'

As a way of introducing a country police inspector and his constable, Sloan couldn't have improved on it.

There were two people in the room: a middle-aged man with a long drooping moustache and a pretty woman with fair hair and wide-open eyes of china blue. There was grey now among the fair hair and a rather vague look. The two had obviously just finished afternoon tea and the scene reminded Sloan of a picture he had once seen called *Conversation Piece*. The only difference as he remembered it was that in the picture the tea had not been drunk. Here, the meal was over, a fact appreciated by Dillow, who immediately began to clear away.

'Bad business,' said the Earl of Ornum.

'Yes, sir – my lord,' Sloan amended hastily. In the nature of things interviews with the titled did not often come his way.

'Poor, poor Mr Meredith,' said the Countess. 'Such a nice man.'

Not being altogether certain of how to address a Countess, Sloan turned back to the Earl. 'You've seen his sister I understand, my lord?'

'No. Tried to. Not at home.'

'Oh?'

'House shut up.' The Earl pulled gently at one side of his drooping moustache. 'She must be away. Accounts for one thing though, doesn't it?'

'What's that, sir – my lord?'

'No hue and cry for the man. General alarm not raised. Just

chance that the boy – you've got his name, haven't you?'

'Michael Fisher, Paradise Row, Luston,' said Constable Crosby, reading aloud from his notebook.

'Just chance that he opened the visor. Otherwise,' the Earl gave another tug at his moustache, 'otherwise we might never have found him, what?'

'Possibly not, my lord,' said Sloan. In fact the late Mr Meredith might very well have begun to smell very soon but in a medieval castle there was no knowing to what an unusual noisome aroma might not have been attributed.

Drains, suspected Sloan.

'Of course,' went on his Lordship, 'that suit might have acted like one of those Egyptian things . . .'

'Mummy cases?'

'That's it. He might have – er – dried up.'

'He might,' agreed Sloan cautiously. He would ask the pathologist about that. A mummified corpse was certainly one which stood the least risk of being found.

'Should never have thought of looking there for him anyway. Not in a hundred years.'

'Quite so,' said Sloan. 'Now when did you last see Mr Meredith yourself, my lord?'

'Just been talking to m'wife about that. Friday, I thought,' he said, adding, 'Millicent thinks it was Thursday.'

The Countess of Ornum had a high, bell-like voice. 'Days are so alike, aren't they, Inspector?'

Sloan said nothing. They might very well be for the aristocracy. They weren't for police inspectors.

'I thought it was Thursday but it may have been Friday.' The Countess looked appealingly round the room as if one or other of the numerous pieces of furniture could tell her.

'I see – er . . .' Sooner or later the nettle of how to address this vague doll-like woman would have to be grasped. He added firmly, 'My lady.'

He doubted if she even heard him.

'It isn't,' she said, fluttering her eyes at him, 'as if anything happened on either day.'

'No, my lady?'

She smiled. 'Then I might have remembered.'

It was rather like interviewing cotton wool or blotting paper.

'It would be very helpful, my lady,' said Sloan formally, 'if you could remember.'

'I know.' She gave him a sweet smile. 'I will try. Such a nice man.'

'Indeed?' said Sloan, unmoved. It was no great help to him that the deceased had been a nice man.

'Everyone liked him,' said the Countess vaguely.

Someone patently hadn't but Sloan did not say so. Instead he turned back to the Earl. It was easier.

'The pathologist will be here presently, my lord, and the police photographers and so forth, after which we will be removing Mr Meredith to the police mortuary at Berebury.'

'Quite so, Inspector.' Another tug at the moustache. 'Purvis will give you all the help you need. Unless it's a bearer party you want. Then there's Hackle and Dillow and m'nephew.'

'Your nephew?'

'Miles. M'brother's boy. Staying with us. Hefty chap.'

'And where would I find him?' Sloan would want to interview everybody in time – but especially the hefty.

His Lordship withdrew a watch and chain from his vest pocket. 'Silly mid on.'

Sloan could hear Crosby snorting by his side. 'Where?' he said hastily.

'The cricket field. Playing for Ornum against Petering.'

'I see, sir.'

'Blood match, you know. Meredith would never have dreamt of missing it in the ordinary way.'

'Keen on the game, was he, my lord?'

'Very. That's how he got the job here in the first place.'

'Really?'

'Team needed a bowler. M'father took on Meredith.'

'As librarian?'

The Earl looked at Sloan. 'As a bowler, Inspector. By the time he got past being a bowler no one else knew where to find anything in the library.'

'I see, sir.' Sloan himself had started as a constable and worked his way up but things were obviously done differently here. He cleared his throat. 'And Lord Cremond, my lord? I shall have to have a word with him in due course.'

'Henry? He's at the match, too. Scoring.'

'Scoring?' That didn't sound right for the son and heir.

'Cut his hand on Friday,' said the Earl, 'so he couldn't play.'

'It was Thursday, I think,' said the Countess.

Detective Constable Crosby, who had made a note, crossed it out and then – audibly – reinstated it.

'I'm sorry to hear that,' intervened Sloan quickly. 'Nothing serious, I hope.'

'No, no.' The Earl stroked his moustache. 'Caught it on some metal somewhere, he said.'

'I see, sir. Thank you . . .'

'I blame myself about Meredith,' said the Earl unexpectedly. He had a deep, unaccented staccato voice. 'This is what comes of having the house "open". I knew no good would come of it in the long run but, you know, Inspector, there's a limit to the amount of retrenchment . . .'

'Quite so, my lord.'

'Though what my father would have said about having people in the house for money . . .'

Sloan prepared to go. 'For the record then, Mr Osborne Meredith was your librarian and archivist, my lord?'

'That's right.'

The Countess waved a hand vaguely. 'He was writing a history of the family, wasn't he, Harry? Such a pity he won't be able to finish it now.'

'Yes,' said the Earl of Ornum rather shortly.

'My brother's called Harry, too,' said Detective Constable Crosby chattily.

Inspector Sloan shot him a ferocious look.

'Mr Meredith had just made such an interesting discovery,' said the Countess of Ornum, undeflected. 'He told us all about it last week.'

'What was that, my lady?' asked Sloan.

The pretty, vague face turned towards him. 'He'd just found some papers that he said proved that Harry wasn't Earl of Ornum after all.'

5

'What was that you said, Sloan?'

Inspector Sloan said louder and more clearly into the telephone, '*Burke's Peerage*, sir. Please.'

Superintendent Leeyes, still at Berebury Police Station, grunted. 'That's what I thought you said. And is that all you want?'

'For the time being, sir, thank you. I'm expecting Dyson for the photographs any minute now and Dr Dabbe is on his way over from Kinnisport.'

Leeyes grunted again. 'And all you want is a *Peerage*?'

'That's right, sir. No . . .' Sloan paused. 'There is something else, please, now you ask.'

'And what may that be?'

'A dictionary.'

'A dictionary?'

'Yes, sir. Unless you can tell me what muniments are.'

He couldn't.

The two policemen had made their way to where the telephone stood only with difficulty. Without the aid of the butler, Dillow, the way had seemed long and tortuous.

And, at one point, doubtful.

That had been when they had turned left and not right by the largest Chinese vase Sloan had ever seen.

'Can't think why they didn't pop the body into that, sir,' said Crosby gloomily. 'Saved us a lot of trouble, that would.'

'There'll have been a reason,' murmured Sloan.

That was one thing experience had taught him. There was a reason behind most human actions. Not necessarily sound, of course, but a reason all the same.

'This chap with the cut hand,' said Crosby, 'we'll have to have a word with him, sir.'

'We shall have to have a great many words with a great many people before we're out of here,' said Sloan prophetically. 'This way, I think . . .'

He was wrong. By the time they had taken two more turnings they were lost.

They were in part of the house where the chairs were not roped off with thick red cord, where no drugget lay over the carpet. And on the various pieces of furniture which lined the corridors were small, easily removed ornamental items . . .

'Do you mind telling me what you are doing here?' It was a thin voice, which seemed to materialize out of the air behind them.

Constable Crosby jumped palpably, and they both spun round.

A very old lady whose skirt practically reached her ankles was regarding them from a doorway. She was hung about with beads which swung as she talked. Round her sparse grey hair and forehead was a bandeau and her hands were covered in the brown petechiae of arteriosclerotic old age. In her hand was the receiver of a hearing aid which she held before her in the manner of a radio interviewer.

'You may have paid your half crown, my man, but that does not give you the run of the house.'

'Lady Alice?' divined Inspector Sloan.

The thin figure peered a little further out of the doorway. 'Do I know you?'

'No,' said Sloan.

'I thought not,' triumphantly, 'because I'm not Alice. She's in there.'

'Lady Maude?' hazarded Sloan.

She looked him up and down. 'That's right. Who are you? And what are you doing here?'

'We've come about Mr Meredith,' said Sloan truthfully.

The beads – by now confused with the wire from the hearing aid to her ear – gave a dangerous lurch to starboard as she shook her head vigorously. 'That man! Don't mention his name to me.'

'Why not?'

But Lady Maude was not to be drawn.

She retreated into the doorway again. 'I never want to see him again . . .'

'You aren't going to,' muttered Crosby, *sotto voce*.

'Not after the things he said.' Lady Maude's voice had the variable register of the very deaf. 'My sister and I are most upset. He used to take tea with us. We do not propose to invite him again.'

The door closed and Sloan and Crosby were left standing in the corridor.

'Dear, dear,' said Crosby. 'Not to be invited to tea. That would have upset the deceased a lot, I'm sure.'

'But not, I fancy, enough to drive him to suicide,' murmured Sloan, trying to take his bearings from the corridor.

'It means something though, sir, doesn't it?'

'Oh, yes, Constable, it means something all right, but what, I couldn't begin to say. Yet.'

'No, sir.'

'Now to find our way out of here.'

'Yes, sir.'

'Lead on, Crosby,' he said unfairly. 'After all, you are a detective constable.'

Charles Purvis, steward to the thirteenth Earl of Ornum, had no difficulty in finding his way about the great house and in his turn reported to his superior in much the same way as Sloan had done to his.

'I've arranged for the postmistress to ring us as soon as Miss Meredith gets back to the Old Forge, sir.'

His Lordship nodded. 'And the boy?'

'Michael Fisher? I took the liberty of slipping him a pound, sir.'

'Good. Don't like to think of a man lying dead in the house and us not knowing.'

Purvis said, 'We'd never have found him . . .'

'No.' The Earl waved a hand. 'The boy's mother – what happened to her?'

'Mrs Morley gave her tea and the Inspector can see no reason why they shouldn't all go back in the charabanc with the rest of the party.'

'Thank God for that,' said his Lordship fervently. 'The boy sounds a terror.'

'He is,' said Purvis briefly. 'I've just been talking to the coach driver. He's all ready to go but he's two short.'

'Not the boy and his mother?'

'No. A Miss Mavis Palmer and her boyfriend. Last seen three hours ago in the Folly . . .'

'Were they?' said the Earl thoughtfully. 'Well, get them found, Charles. And quickly. The sooner that particular coachload is off the premises the better. And then come back here. There are one or two other matters which need attending to.'

'Yes, sir.'

'And when Henry and Miles get back from that cricket match send them to me, will you?'

'Yes, sir.'

The Earl tugged his left-hand whiskers. 'Charles . . .'

'Sir?'

'You'll have the Press here by morning . . .'

The young man nodded. 'I'd thought of that. Dillow is going to put them in the morning-room and then get hold of me as quickly as he can.'

'Then there's my cousin and Eleanor.'

'Miss Gertrude is still in the China Room, sir. I don't think the last of the visitors have quite gone yet. And Lady Eleanor is – er – cashing up at the front door.'

'They'll both have to be told.' The Earl waved a hand. 'The house is full of police . . .'

This last was an exaggeration. Inspector Sloan and Constable Crosby had already been swallowed up by the house. And there would, in any case, have been room for the entire Berebury Division in the Great Hall alone.

'Yes, sir,' murmured Purvis who was not paid to contradict the Earl.

'And my aunts.'

'We're all right for the moment there, sir. They won't have been out yet. The visitors have hardly gone.'

'If I know them,' declared Lord Ornum, 'they'll be abroad any minute now. On the war path. Looking for damage.'

Purvis moved over towards the window. 'We've got a little time anyway, sir. They'll wait until that coach has gone.'

The Earl sighed heavily. 'And then, Charles, you'd better find out exactly where my nephew William has been all this week.'

Purvis hesitated. 'I think he's down, sir . . .'

The Earl sighed again. 'I thought he might be.'

'Someone told me that he was in the Ornum Arms last night,' said Purvis uneasily.

'Bad news travels fast.'

'Yes, sir.'

'Then slip down to his cottage and tell him I want to see him, will you, there's a good chap. I think we'd better keep him in the picture in spite of everything.'

'Very well, sir.'

The Earl lifted an eyebrow. 'You don't agree?'

Charles Purvis said carefully, 'He's a very talkative young man, sir.'

'He gets that from his father.'

'Yes, sir, but it might do some harm . . .'

'He's my sister's boy, Charles. I can't have him kept in ignorance of trouble here.'

'No, sir.'

'After all,' a gleam of humour crept into the Earl's melancholy countenance, 'we always hear when there's trouble there, don't we?'

'We do indeed,' agreed Charles Purvis grimly.

*

The first of the experts in death had arrived at Ornum House by the time Inspector Sloan and Constable Crosby got back to the armoury. They were the two police photographers, Dyson and his assistant, Williams.

Dyson was standing by the door lumbered about with his equipment.

'Nice little place you have here, Inspector.'

'And a nice little mystery,' rejoined Sloan tartly.

Dyson looked up and down the two rows of armoured figures. 'Make quite a pretty picture, this will . . .'

'I'm glad to hear it.'

'The lab boys will think I've been to the waxworks or something.' Dyson walked forward. 'Which is the one that didn't get away?'

'Second on the right,' said Sloan, 'but we'll want some of the total setting too.'

'A pleasure.' Dyson assembled his camera and tripod with a rapidity which belied his flippant approach. His assistant handed him something, there was a pause, and then a quick flash. 'Don't suppose these chaps have seen anything brighter than that since Agincourt or something.'

Sloan was inclined to agree with him. There was an overall gloom about the armoury that had got nothing to do with the presence of the dead.

Williams, Dyson's assistant, was rigging up some sort of white sheet to one side of the suit of armour for the tilt, *circa* 1595. He had persuaded Crosby to stand holding one end.

'Need the reflected light,' explained Dyson.

Sloan nodded. Dyson never complained about his conditions of work. If he needed anything he brought it with him. He and Williams were self-sufficient members of the police team.

They moved their tripod in front of the suit.

'Inspector . . .'

'Well?'

'Open or shut?'

'Open *and* shut,' said Sloan. 'Crosby's done the headpiece for fingerprints.'

'Close-helmet,' said Dyson.

'What?'

'Close-helmet,' repeated Dyson. 'That's what it's called. Not headpiece.'

'Oh, is it?' said Sloan in neutral tones. 'I must remember that.'

There was another bright flash. Then Williams moved forward and lifted the visor. Inspector Sloan was surprised again at the sight of the dead face.

'I remember,' said Dyson improbably, 'when I was an apprentice photographer on the beach at Blackpool, people used to put their faces into a round hole like this . . .'

'Oh?'

'And we'd take a picture and they'd come up riding on the back of a sea-lion.'

'They did, did they?' said Sloan. 'Well, let me tell you . . .'

'Or a camel, sir,' interposed Constable Crosby suddenly. He was still holding one end of the sheet. 'I've been done riding on the back of a camel.'

Sloan snapped. 'That's enough of . . .'

'This chap reminds me of that,' said Dyson unperturbed. 'Sort of stepping into a set piece, if you know what I mean, Inspector. Just the round face visible.'

'I know what you mean. Now get on with it.'

'Right-oh.'

But for the fact that their subject was dead, the pair of them might have been taking a studio portrait.

'Back a little.'

'A bit more to your right, I think.'

'What about an inferior angle?'

'Good idea.'

'Hold it.'

Quite unnecessarily.

'Now a close-up.'

'Just one more, don't you think?' Dyson turned. 'Anything else, Inspector?'

Sloan grimaced. 'I should think the only thing you two haven't done is to ask him to say "cheese".'

'No need,' said Dyson ghoulishly. 'The face muscles contract anyway when you're dead, and you get your facial rictus without asking.'

'I see.' It was perhaps as well that Dyson had gone in for photography. Knowing all the answers as he did would have got him nowhere on the police ladder of promotion.

Nowhere at all.

'He looks peaceful enough to me,' commented Dyson. 'Any idea what hit him?'

'Not yet.'

'Plenty of weapons to choose from.' Dyson made a sweeping gesture which took in the whole collection. 'Perhaps it was that one.'

'That's a spetum,' announced Constable Crosby who was close enough to read the label.

'A what?' said Sloan.

'Spetum. Honestly, sir.'

'Is it indeed?' said Sloan.

' "Often confused with a ranseur",' added Crosby, straight from the label.

'Well,' said Dyson, 'I'd rather have that for my money than that nasty-looking piece over there . . .' He indicated a heavy-headed weapon studded with vicious-looking spikes. 'What in the name of goodness is that?'

Crosby leaned over and read aloud, 'That's a "holy water sprinkler".'

'Well, I'm blessed,' said Dyson, for once strangely appropriate in the phraseology of his reaction. 'And the one next to it?'

Crosby moved a step towards a ferocious iron ball on the end of a short chain. 'That's called a "morning star",' he said, 'similar to a "military flail".'

Dyson grinned. 'Queer sense of humour the ancients had, didn't they?'

'They did,' said Sloan shortly.

Dyson swung his camera back on his shoulder, and took the hint. 'We'd better be going then.' He picked up the heavy tripod. 'Williams . . .'

'Coming.'

'Williams . . .' Dyson pointed towards the suit of armour with the wrong end of the tripod. 'Williams, it's closing time.'

Williams obediently moved forward and lowered the visor and they went.

Dillow put down the heavy silver tea tray.

Presently he would take away the silver teapot (Ann and Paul Bateman, 1792), the hot water jug (Paul Storr, 1816) and the tray (unknown craftsman, 1807), clean them and stow them away in green baize in his pantry. For the time being he laid the tray on the kitchen table. Mrs Morley, the housekeeper, would see to the china (Copeland) and the housemaid would deal with everything else.

Mrs Morley looked at the butler. 'I expect you could do with a cup of tea yourself, Mr Dillow, after all that fuss and to-do.'

He sank into a chair. 'That I could, Mrs Morley, thank you. It's bad enough as it is on open days but finding Mr Meredith like that . . . oh, dear, oh dear.'

'It's not very nice, I must say.' Mrs Morley pursed her lips. 'Dying is one thing – we've all got to go sometime, Mr Dillow – but dying in a suit of armour . . .'

Dillow shook his head. Seen close to, he was not as old as he seemed at first sight. It was simply that his occupation and bearing gave the impression of age. 'I don't like it at all,' he said.

'The Press will,' forecast Mrs Morley, herself an avid reader of the more sensational Sunday newspapers.

The butler said, 'I got quite accustomed to the Press in my last position. My late employer – er – almost encouraged them. Always offered them a glass of something.'

'Ah, Mr Dillow, but then he was in business.'

'Baggles Bearings,' said the butler promptly. ' "All industry runs on Baggles Bearings" – that was their advertising slogan. I think they did, too. No money troubles there.'

'Business is different,' insisted Mrs Morley.

'Free advertising, that's what he called it every time there was anything in the papers. He used to say even having his art collection mentioned did the bearings a bit of good.'

'Well I never,' said Mrs Morley, who could not have said off-hand what a bearing was and who knew still less about advertising.

'Mind you,' said Dillow ominously, 'once they got hold of a story there was no stopping them . . .'

Mrs Morley looked disapproving. 'I don't think his Lordship will favour them mentioning Ornum House.'

'They'll rake up everything they can lay their hands on,' warned Dillow.

'I'm sure,' stoutly, 'there would be nothing that Mr Meredith would need to hide. There couldn't have been a pleasanter gentleman.'

'I wasn't thinking of Mr Meredith, Mrs Morley.'

The housekeeper looked up quickly. 'Master William hasn't been in trouble again, has he?'

'I couldn't say, I'm sure, Mrs Morley.'

Butler and housekeeper exchanged meaningful glances.

Mrs Morley poured out two cups of tea.

The butler took a sip. 'He's down, that's all I know.'

'When?'

'I heard he was in the Ornum Arms last night.'

Mrs Morley clucked her disapprobation. 'No good ever came out of his going there.'

'The police,' said Dillow carefully, 'are going to want to know when Mr Meredith was last seen alive.'

'Friday,' said Mrs Morley. 'You did a tea tray for him in the library.'

'So I did,' concurred Dillow. 'Just after four o'clock.'

'Hot buttered toast,' said Mrs Morley, 'if you remember. And fruit cake and *petit beurre* biscuits.'

'He ate the lot,' said Dillow. 'There was nothing left when I took his tray.'

'When would that have been, Mr Dillow?'

'About five o'clock.'

'And who saw him after that?'
'I couldn't say, Mrs Morley. I couldn't say at all.'

6

Charles Purvis hurried away from the Private Apartments and slipped easily through the complex layout of the house until he reached the entrance courtyard. Still parked there was a coach. It was painted a particularly raucous blue and, by some irony too deep for words, it was drawn up by the mounting block used by all thirteen Earls of Ornum in the sweep of carriageway where coaches of an entirely different sort had been wont to go into that wide arc of drive which brought them to the front door.

Michael Fisher was standing on the mounting block and the coach driver was sitting peacefully at the wheel of his vehicle with the infinite patience of his tribe. Sooner or later the missing passengers would turn up, lost time could always be made up on the open road and in any case there was very little point in starting off before opening time. Rather wait here than outside the Fiddler's Delight.

Charles Purvis walked across to the coach to be greeted with excited waves of recognition from Mrs Fisher.

'Ever so nice, isn't he?' she announced to the assembled coach load, friends and neighbours all, which Purvis was surprised to find annoyed and embarrassed him far more than the deepest insult could have done. 'He's what they call the stooward . . .'

He was saved by Michael Fisher doing a sort of war dance on the mounting block.

'Here they come.'

Purvis turned and everyone in the coach craned their necks to see a slightly dishevelled and more than a little flushed Miss Mavis Palmer appear, her boyfriend a few paces behind. There were encouraging shrieks from the entire coachload.

'Come on, Mavis . . .'

'Good old Bernard . . .'

'Attaboy!'

The driver started up the engine by way of reprimand to the late-comers – who immediately put on a spurt. Miss Palmer, noted Charles Purvis, outpaced Bernard with ease. He did not begin to contemplate the dance she had doubtless been leading the young man through the park all afternoon, but stood back to let them climb aboard.

With a final burst of cheering and an utterly misplaced fanfare on the coach horn – tally-ho on another sort of coach horn would have been more bearable – the party from Paradise Row, Luston, finally moved away.

Charles Purvis watched for a moment and then walked across to the doorway.

'Lady Eleanor . . .'

'Seventeen, eighteen, nineteen . . .' She turned. 'How much is nineteen threepenny pieces?'

'Four and ninepence.'

'Are you sure?'

'Er . . . yes . . . I think so.' Normally a very sure young man, Lady Eleanor Cremond was able – with one appealing glance – to convert him into a very uncertain creature indeed.

'That comes right then,' she said.

'I don't see how it can,' ventured Charles Purvis, greatly daring. 'You shouldn't have ninepence at all if you're charging a shilling and half a crown.'

She smiled sweetly. 'There was a man with one leg . . .'

'Cut rates?'

'I let him into the park for ninepence. I didn't think he could walk far.'

Charles Purvis sat down beside her at the baize-covered table. 'I've really come to tell you something rather unpleasant. Mr Meredith's been found dead.'

'Not Ossy?' she said, distressed. 'Oh, the poor little man. I am sorry. When?'

'We don't know when,' said Charles Purvis, and told her about the armour.

'But,' she protested in bewildered tones, 'he didn't even like armour. It was the books and pictures that he loved. And all the old documents.'

'I know.'

'In fact,' spiritedly, 'he wouldn't even show people the armoury unless Mr Ames couldn't come up from the Vicarage.'

'I know that too.' He began toying with a wad of unused tickets. 'When did you last see him yourself?'

She frowned. 'Friday afternoon, I think it was.'

'You'd better be certain,' he warned her. 'The police will want to know.'

'The police?'

He nodded.

'It was Friday,' she said slowly. 'Just before tea. I went along to the library and he was there on his own.' She hesitated. 'He seemed all right then . . . no . . . more than all right. Almost exuberant. On top of the world. You know the sort of feeling . . . excited, that's it.'

'Did he say anything?'

'Say anything? Oh, no. I just said I thought he usually took tea with the great aunts on Fridays and he said . . .' She paused.

'What did he say?'

'He said he thought he had upset them by his discoveries about the earldom.'

'And that,' said Charles Purvis wryly, 'is putting it mildly.'

To say that Dillow waylaid those returning from the village cricket match would be an exaggeration and tantamount to unsubtlety on the butler's part.

He simply happened to be hovering, soft footed, in the entrance hall when they happened to return.

'We won,' announced Lord Henry as he entered. He was a

physical parody of his father, seasoned by his mother's vagueness. 'Good match, though.'

'I'm very glad to hear it, sir, but . . .'

'It's a help, of course,' chimed in Miles Cremond, close on his heels, 'having Henry scoring for us.'

'Indeed, sir?'

'Rather.' Miles was a square, thickset man with only some of the Cremond family characteristics. His features would blunt badly with time. Already there was a blur where his chin had been. In contrast, his wife, Laura, was a sharp-featured angular woman, accustomed to command.

'Miles, you should go straight up to change now.'

'Yes, dear . . .'

Dillow coughed. 'His Lordship has asked to see you all as soon as you came back . . .'

The Earl and Countess were still in their sitting-room. The Earl got to his feet as the three of them trooped in.

'Something wrong, Father?' That was Lord Henry.

'Yes.'

Laura Cremond said urgently: 'What?'

'Mr Meredith has met with an accident here . . .'

'Good Lord. Poor chap,' said Henry. 'I'd no idea he was even in the house.'

'Neither,' said the Earl of Ornum drily, 'had anyone else.'

'Didn't think he usually came in at the weekend anyway.'

'He didn't.'

'Thought it funny he wasn't at the match though,' went on Henry. 'Haven't known him miss a match in years.'

'Especially the Petering one,' put in Miles, fresh from victory.

The Earl of Ornum, aided by several tugs at his moustache, told them about the body in the armour.

Laura Cremond sat down rather suddenly in the nearest chair. 'But when did he die?'

'That, Laura, I can't tell you.'

Lord Henry said thoughtfully, 'Someone wasn't expecting him to be found . . .'

'No,' agreed the Earl.

'You couldn't know that that little stinker – what did you say his name was . . .?'

'Michael Fisher.'

'Michael Fisher was going to open up Grumpy like that.'

'To open up who?'

'Grumpy.' Lord Henry gave an engaging smile. 'You did say the second suit of armour on the right, didn't you, Father?'

'I did.' Heavily.

'That,' said his son and heir, 'was Grumpy. We called all the suits of armour after Snow White and the Seven Dwarfs, you know, when we were small.'

'Did you?'

'Snow White was the puffed and slashed suit,' ventured Miles. 'Had a feminine touch about it, we thought.'

'Indeed?' said the Earl.

'That was the Decadence,' said Lord Henry. 'We all used to play down there a lot, didn't we, Miles?'

'Oh, yes,' affirmed Miles. 'Cut our milk teeth on the armour, you might say.'

'It was Mr Ames, really,' said Lord Henry. 'He was such an enthusiast he didn't seem to mind how much we hung about. Taught us a lot.'

'All the names for the parts,' agreed Miles. 'I've forgotten most of them. I expect Henry and William have, too, by now.'

'William,' the Earl sighed. 'I was forgetting William played with you.'

Lord Henry frowned in recollection. 'There was Dopey, Sleepy, Sneezy – that was the one with the long nose piece . . .'

'I dare say,' said the Earl, 'but I don't see . . .'

'Bascinet!' said Miles Cremond suddenly. 'I've just remembered . . .'

'I thought that was something you put a baby in.' The Countess of Ornum, silent until now, came to life like an actress on cue.

'Bascinet,' repeated Miles. 'That was what Sneezy's helmet was called. A visored bascinet.'

'That's right,' agreed Lord Henry. 'And Dopey's was called a burgonet.'

'A closed burgonet,' added Miles. 'That's what made him look so simple. See, we haven't forgotten after all.'

'You do seem to have forgotten that this isn't a nursery game,' said his wife sharply.

Miles subsided. 'Er – no. Rather not.'

'There were seven without Snow White,' said Lord Henry consideringly. 'I wonder why he ended up in Grumpy?'

'That's easy,' said Miles. 'Don't you remember, Henry? Grumpy came to pieces easiest.'

The Earl's head came up as he said sharply: 'Who knew that?'

'Everyone,' said Miles helpfully.

Laura Cremond looked round. 'Someone put him in there who didn't mean him to be found, I suppose?'

The Earl nodded. 'I think so, Laura. And the police want to talk to you all as soon as they can.'

After his encounter with Lady Maude, Inspector Sloan found it a positive relief to be talking to a trained specialist.

He met Dr Dabbe and his assistant, Burns, in the Great Hall. It hadn't taken the fastest (living) driver in Calleshire long to get from Kinnisport on the coast to Ornum, veering into Berebury to pick up his assistant. His black bag went with him everywhere.

'The weather was just right for sailing,' said the doctor reproachfully. 'Sunday, too.'

Sloan said, 'If it had been as warm down there as it is up here, I fancy our chap would have been found a bit sooner.'

'Like that, is it?' The pathologist took in the Great Hall at a glance and followed Sloan down the spiral staircase. Burns brought up the rear.

Dabbe waved his free hand. 'Did he walk down here or was he carried?'

'I couldn't say, doctor. Not yet. I've only seen his face so far.'

'I see.' Dabbe reached the bottom step. 'This the basement?'

'Dungeon level,' Sloan corrected him gloomily. After all, this was not a department store. 'I don't know if they go lower than this.'

'Moat?' suggested Dabbe. 'They usually had moats.'

Constable Crosby let them into the armoury.

'Ah . . .' said Dabbe, looking round appreciatively. 'Do I take my pick?'

'Second on the right,' said Sloan, and not for the first time.

Perhaps he should have put a fresh notice beside the one that was already there. ('Man in Armour', perhaps, or 'Human Remains, *circa* Now'.)

Aloud he said only, 'We've put a chalk ring on the floor, doctor, round him – er – it . . .'

' "Armour for the tilt, *circa* 1595",' read out the pathologist. 'Well, well, well . . .'

It wasn't well at all, though Sloan forbore to say so.

'I don't think I've ever seen a corpse – er – girded before,' said Dabbe.

'No.' Neither had Sloan.

The pathologist advanced and looked the armour over. That was one of the things Sloan admired in him. He came, he looked, he examined – then he spoke.

'The deceased . . .'

'Mr Osborne Meredith.'

'Wasn't a very tall man.'

'No,' agreed Sloan. The suits of armour – though intimidating – were not large. Both policemen looked down on them without difficulty.

'Too much school milk, that's what it is,' said Dr Dabbe.

'Pardon, doctor?'

'We're all taller now. People were smaller then.' He walked round behind the armour. 'It's a pretty complete job. He didn't intend to be stabbed in the back.'

Sloan nodded in agreement. From where he was standing it looked as if the man in armour hadn't intended to be stabbed anywhere at all.

'No chinks,' said Detective Constable Crosby.

Sloan favoured him with a withering stare, and the pathologist's assistant, Burns, who rarely spoke, got out a large thermometer.

'Cold but not damp,' observed Dabbe generally.

'Yes,' agreed Sloan. It was one of the hottest days of the summer outside but the heat hadn't penetrated down here. All in all, a good place to park a body if you didn't want it found too quickly.

Dabbe was still circling the armour rather as a terrier spoiling for a fight will go round and round his adversary.

'Either, Sloan, they popped him in here pretty smartly after death or else they waited until rigor mortis passed off.'

'Oh?'

'Regard the angle of the arms.'

Sloan took a fresh look at the man in armour. The boy, Michael Fisher, had said something about the arms.

Dr Dabbe pointed to – but did not touch – the right arm. It was bent at the elbow in a half defensive position. 'He's still on guard.'

'Yes, doctor.'

'Before rigor mortis or after. Not during.'

'I see.'

'After, I expect,' said Dabbe mordantly. 'By the time you got all this – er – clobber on, it would have begun to set in.'

That was another thing to think about. Sloan mentally added it to a very long list of matters already requiring thinking about. Some of them required action, too, but not until the pathologist had finished. Sloan had been at the game too long not to know that the medical evidence was always of primary importance . . .

'That's another thing,' said Dabbe.

'What is?' Inspector Sloan came back to the present with a jerk.

'How he got into all this.'

'Quite so, doctor.'

'And how we're going to get him out.' The pathologist gave a fiendish grin. 'I can't do a post-mortem with a tin opener.'

'No, doctor.'

'Of course,' went on Dabbe, 'you had an armour-bearer in the old days . . .'

'So you did.' Sloan had forgotten that.

'What you might call a body servant, eh, Sloan?' The pathologist's morbid sense of humour was a byword throughout the Berebury Force.

'Quite so.' Weakly.

'I shouldn't have said he'd got into this on his own though, even in this servant-less day and age,' said Dabbe.

'No.'

'And I think,' said the pathologist, 'that we can rule out natural causes too. Unless coincidence is stretching out a particularly long arm.'

'Yes.'

'That,' said Dabbe cheerfully, 'leaves us the usual Coroner's trio. Misadventure, suicide or murder.'

'Misadventure?' said Sloan.

'Commonly known, Inspector, as pure bad luck.'

'I don't quite see how . . .'

'The trap for the unwary pathologist, that's what misadventure is,' said the doctor feelingly. 'Suppose this chap got into this rigout for some perfectly sound reason and then found he was trapped in it . . .'

'Well?'

'He could have shouted his head off and no one would have heard him through the visor let alone through the twelve-foot walls they seem to go in for down here.'

'That's true, but I don't think he did get in to it himself and then call for help, doctor.'

'Oh? Why not?'

'You see, we've checked the floor for footprints. It's all been swept perfectly clean round the armour. Too clean.'

'Has it indeed? And what about fingerprints?'

'None of them either. Crosby's been over the lot. The armour's been handled all right – but with gloves on.'

The pathologist nodded swiftly. 'In that case we can't do a lot of harm by going inside.'

He didn't touch the visor but went straight to the helmet, lifting it with both hands from behind.

There was – after all that – no doubt about how Mr Osborne Meredith had died.

The back of his skull had been staved in.

7

After he left Lady Eleanor, Charles Purvis went to his car. Ornum House was too far from any of its neighbours to visit them on foot – especially if time was short.

He drove the mile to the village, went through the ornamental gates and out into the High Street. All of the properties there were in good condition, most belonged to the Earl. He nosed his car gently past the usual Sunday afternoon village traffic and stopped outside the last cottage in a row not far from the post office. Most of the village would be watching the cricket, the rest getting ready for Evensong. He was quite sure the occupant of number 4 Cremond Cottages would be doing neither.

The man who came to the door was older than both Lord Henry Cremond and Charles Purvis and already running to over-weight. He was dressed in old corduroy trousers that were none too clean and a shirt so open-necked as to be undone.

No one could have called his manner agreeable.

'Well, well, if it isn't Charlie-boy.'

Purvis stiffened. 'Good afternoon, William. Your uncle has sent me down . . .'

'I didn't think you'd come on your own.'

Purvis tightened his lips. 'No, I don't think I would.'

Suddenly the man grinned. It changed his face completely. 'Fifteen all. Your serve.'

'Your uncle sent me down,' repeated Purvis stolidly, 'to say he wants to see you.'

'That's a pleasant change, I must say,' drawled William Murton. 'I've never known him actually want to see me before.'

'Well, he does now,' shortly.

'Why?'

The steward hesitated. 'There's been a spot of trouble up at the house.'

'Has there? I'm sorry to hear that.' William Murton did not sound particularly sorry. He squinted across the doorway at Charles Purvis. 'Someone run off with the family plate, then, or something?'

'Not that sort of trouble.'

Murton raised his hands in mock horror. 'You don't mean to tell me that some cad has asked for my cousin Eleanor's hand in marriage?'

Charles Purvis flushed to the roots of his hair. 'No.'

'Not that sort of trouble either?' Offensively.

'No.'

'Well, well, how interesting. I shall come at once.' He paused on the threshold. 'Tell me, does this invitation include a meal, do you suppose?'

'He wants to see you,' repeated Purvis.

'I see. What you might call a general summons rather than an invitation.'

What Detective Inspector Sloan could have done with was a ball of string.

That was what pot-holers used when they were in dark caves and wanted to be sure of their way back. It was not unlike that in Ornum House. What he was looking for was the door behind which Lady Maude had retreated earlier on. If he could find a large Chinese vase he thought he would be all right from then on.

He could, of course, easily have asked someone to take him there but there were risks inherent in the way in which he was announced which might very well disturb the two old ladies with whom he wanted a quiet chat. With whom he wanted a quiet chat before anyone else got to them – which was why he had slipped away from the armoury for a few moments.

He was unlucky with the Chinese vase. He found it all right. Vast, well proportioned and delicately coloured, there was no mistaking it.

Except for one thing.

Its twin.

It wasn't until he had opened a whole series of the wrong doors that he realized the gigantic vase he and Crosby had seen had been one of a matching pair. He found the other – the right one – at the far end of the same long corridor. From then on it should have been plain sailing.

He knocked on Lady Maude's door.

A thin old lady – the same one as he had seen earlier – appeared. Fortunately she recognized him.

'I've seen you before . . .'

'That's right, Lady Maude. I wanted to see you again. You and Lady Alice.'

'You did?' Sloan felt himself being scrutinized. 'Why?'

'Someone has killed Mr Meredith.'

She stared at him for a moment. 'Have they indeed? You'd better come in. This way.' She turned abruptly on her heel and went back into the room. 'Alice, Alice, where are you?'

Lady Alice was – if that were possible – even older than her sister. Old age, however, had not altered the outline of the Cremond nose which was planted firmly in the middle of a face that in its time must have been striking. Say about the year the old Queen died . . .

He stood in front of her. 'Good afternoon, your ladyship.'

A claw-like hand lifted a lorgnette and examined him through it in a silence that soon became unnerving. Sloan hadn't felt like that since his early days as a very jejune constable – when he was being checked over by his station sergeant before he was allowed out on the beat. Pencil, notebook, whistle . . . subconsciously he wanted to make sure that they were all there now.

'Who are you, my man?'

'My name is Sloan, Lady Alice . . .'

'Well?'

Perhaps, conceded Sloan to himself, that hadn't been such a good beginning after all. Circumlocution was a device for handling the middle-aged – not the very old.

'Someone has killed Mr Meredith.'

'Ha!' said Lady Alice enigmatically.

Perhaps, he thought, to the very old death was such a near and constant companion that they minded less . . .

'And I,' he went on, 'am a police officer who has come to find out all about it.'

Of course, there was always the possibility that she would have expected him to have been in red. 'The Scarlet Runners', that was what the Bow Street people had been called in their day.

Or should he have just said he was Sir Robert Peel?

'Good riddance,' said the old lady vigorously.

He had been wrong to worry about upsetting her, then.

'Tryin' to make out that great-great-great-grandfather Cremond was a bastard.'

'Dear me,' said Sloan, conscious of the inadequacy of his response.

'Thought the title should have gone to someone else.'

'No!'

'Yes,' countered Lady Alice firmly. 'Said it was all in the archives.'

The sooner Superintendent Leeyes sent him that dictionary the better. Then he could find out if archives were the same thing as muniments.

'Always knew it was dangerous to meddle in papers,' went on the old lady. 'Told m'brother so.'

That disposed of the world of scholarship.

'He should have sacked Meredith when he got past cricket.'

And sport.

'Always wanted to die in the saddle myself . . .' said the old lady.

Sloan took a second look at Lady Alice. The days of cavalry charges were over, he knew, but in any case surely women had never . . .

'A good way to go,' she said.

Light dawned. Sloan said, 'The hunting field . . .'

'That's right. Now, my man, tell me, who killed him?'

The lorgnette was back again, hovering above the Cremond nose.

'I don't know, Lady Alice.'

'He didn't break his neck, did he?'

'No.'

'Seen a lot of men go that way. Takin' fences.'

Lady Alice had obviously taken her own fences well. At the gallop probably.

Full tilt.

Which brought him back to Osborne Meredith.

Full circle.

'What can you tell me about Friday?' he asked.

Lady Alice might be older but she was less vague than Millicent, her nephew's wife. 'On Fridays Maude and I prepare for Saturday and Sunday.'

'Saturday and Sunday?'

'We do not leave our rooms until the evening on Saturdays and Sundays and Wednesdays.'

Sloan blinked. He had heard that Mohammedans observed certain rules of behaviour between sun-up and sun-down – but not elderly English spinsters of the Christian persuasion.

'All the year round?' he said tentatively.

With the Mohammedans he understood it was during Ramadan.

'April to October,' said Lady Alice.

'And Bank Holidays,' said her sister.

'Except Good Fridays,' added Lady Alice.

'I see,' said Sloan who was beginning to . . .

'My nephew is, of course, head of the family now but . . .'

'But what?' prompted Sloan.

'But neither my sister nor I approve of the house being "open". What our late brother would have thought we do not like to contemplate.'

'Quite,' murmured Sloan diplomatically. 'So when the house is – er – "open", you both remain in your apartments?'

'Always.'

It was a pity, that, he thought. Lady Alice and Lady Maude were good value at half a crown.

'Now, about Friday . . .'

'Yes?'

'Did you see Mr Meredith at all?'

'No.'

'What did you do after tea?'

'What we always do after tea – play ombre.'

'Ombre?' One thing was absolutely certain about ombre, whatever it was. You didn't play it for money any more. Inspector Sloan had been a policeman long enough to know all the games you could play for money.

The old lady nodded. 'A game our mother taught us.'

That took you right back to the nineteenth century for a start. It was the twentieth that Sloan was concerned about.

'Who won?' he asked casually. That was as good a memory test as anything.

He was wrong there.

'Maude,' said Lady Alice promptly. 'She always wins on Fridays.' She waved a thin hand. 'It's so much easier that way.'

'I see.'

'I win on Tuesdays, Thursdays and Saturdays.'

'Friday afternoon,' he said desperately. 'Did you see anyone about on Friday afternoon?'

Lady Alice shook her head. 'Just the Judge. And that was much later. As I was going along to dress for dinner.'

'The Judge?' Sloan sat up. He really would have to watch his step if there were judges about.

'Judge Cremond,' said Lady Alice.

Sloan sighed. Surely there couldn't be more Cremonds still? Purvis hadn't mentioned him in his list of those in the house.

He said, 'He's a member of the family, too, I take it?'

'Oh, yes,' the old lady laughed, 'he's a member of the family all right.'

'I shall have to interview him in due course, then. I'll make a note of the . . .'

The old lady's laugh was a cackle now, and not without malice. 'I doubt if you'll be able to do that, Mr Sloan, whoever you are. You wouldn't even see him.'

'No?'

'He's been dead these two hundred and fifty years.'

'A ghost?' Sloan sighed. There would have had to have been a ghost, he supposed, in a house like this, but Superintendent Leeyes wouldn't like it all the same.

The lorgnette described an arc in the air on its way towards the Cremond nose. 'That's right. Mark my words, young man, someone's going to die soon.'

Lady Maude chimed in like a Greek chorus of doom. 'The Judge always gets uneasy when someone in the family is going to die.'

The Reverend Walter Ames, Vicar of Ornum and Perpetual Curate of Maple-juxta-Handling, was not a preacher of long sermons at any time.

On this particular evening in June he took as his text 'unto him that hath shall be given' (a point on which in any case he could seldom think of much to say), said it with celerity and hurried across from the church to Ornum House.

He reached the armoury just as Inspector Sloan got back there.

'I've just heard the sad news,' said the Vicar somewhat breathlessly. 'Terrible. Quite terrible.'

'Yes, sir.' Inspector Sloan took a quick look round the armoury. Dr Dabbe was engaged in contemplating the armour rather as an inexperienced diner pauses before he makes his first foray into a lobster. Detective Constable Crosby was still prowling round the walls looking at the weaponry.

'I thought something was odd,' went on the Vicar, who was grey haired and patently unused to hurrying.

'You did, sir? Why was that?' asked Sloan.

'I blame myself now for not doing more at the time though I don't see what more . . .'

'For not doing what?' asked Sloan patiently.

Mr Ames took a deep breath. 'It's like this, Inspector. Meredith sent me a message asking me to come to see him . . .'

'When would that have been, sir?'

'Friday afternoon. He rang my wife – I was out at the time – and told her that he'd made an important discovery and he wanted my opinion on it.'

Sloan looked up quickly. 'What sort of discovery, sir?'

The clergyman shook his head. 'Ah, he wouldn't say. Not to my wife. And not over the telephone. We – er – still have a – er – manual exchange here in Ornum, you know. Er – a womanual exchange, Inspector, if you take the point . . .'

Sloan did.

'He just left a message with my wife,' went on the Vicar, 'asking me to come up to the house . . .'

'And did you, sir?'

'Oh, yes, Inspector. That was what was so odd.'

'What was so odd?'

'When I got here I couldn't find him.'

'What time would that have been, sir?' It was, Sloan thought, for all the world like a catechism.

'About half-past five. He told my wife he would be working in the muniments room after tea, and that I would find him there. But I didn't.'

'What did you do then?'

'Glanced in the library – I didn't see him there either – and came away again.'

'Then what?'

'I decided I'd missed him after all and that I'd call at the Old Forge on my way back to the Vicarage. Which I did.'

'But he wasn't there,' agreed Sloan.

'Quite so. No reply at the Old Forge.' The Vicar averted his eyes from the armour. 'At the time I thought I would be seeing him at the cricket on Saturday and Sunday – a two-day match, you know, the Ornum versus Petering one – so I didn't go back to his house again.'

'But he wasn't at the cricket,' persisted Sloan.

'No,' admitted Mr Ames. 'I must confess I was surprised about that – though it is now painfully clear why he wasn't there.'

'Did you do anything more?'

The Vicar shook his head. 'I'm afraid not. I realize now that I should have done but it rather slipped my mind . . .' He looked round at Dr Dabbe, his silent assistant Burns and Constable Crosby and said apologetically, 'I fear that I underestimated the importance of poor Meredith's discovery – whatever it was.'

Sloan nodded. 'I dare say you did, sir.'

'Meredith often got excited about his work you know, Inspector . . .' Clearly this was going to take a good deal of expiation on the Vicar's part.

'I understand, sir. You thought he was crying wolf . . .'

'I think,' very fairly, 'that we all tend to exaggerate what is important to us and to diminish what others regard as important.'

But it was after all that that Mr Ames really began to assist the police in their enquiries.

Not in the usual sense.

'I thought that this would be the particular suit of armour,' he said, 'as soon as I heard about the tragedy.'

'Why?' demanded Sloan sharply.

'It disarticulates more easily than the others.'

'You don't say,' murmured Dr Dabbe, who hadn't yet been able to disarticulate it at all.

'Who all would know that?' asked Sloan.

'Everyone,' said the Vicar blithely. 'It's the one I demonstrate on when people come. A most interesting piece if I may say so. Poor Meredith. A real expert in his own field, you know.'

'It's a question of the post-mortem, Vicar,' intervened Dr Dabbe, anxious to get on in his own line of country.

'Quite so. Now, you've got the skull off, I see . . .'

Someone had also almost got Meredith's skull off too, and Mr Ames winced visibly at the sight.

'Yes,' agreed Dabbe, 'but that's not enough for the Coroner.'

'Of course not.' Mr Ames nodded rapidly. 'What you want to do is to get down to the – er – ah – um . . .'

'Body,' said Dabbe.

'Er – quite so. Well, it's not difficult.'

'Can I get this off for a start?' asked the doctor.

'The pauldron? Only if you remove the besaque . . .'

Detective Inspector Sloan motioned to Crosby and they both stood aside for a few moments, the better to relish the edifying situation of someone using long words which the doctor did not understand.

Dr Dabbe leaned forward and caught his sleeve on a protruding hook as he did so. He swore under his breath.

'Ah, you've found the lance rest then, doctor.' That was Mr Ames.

'Let us say,' murmured the pathologist pleasantly, 'rather that it found me.'

'Perhaps it might be as well to start with the gauntlets and couters. Then we can get the vambraces off.'

'That will be a great help, I'm sure.'

'Well, you'll be able to see the hands and forearms,' said the Vicar practically, 'but the breast-plate and the corsets are really what . . .'

'I beg your pardon?'

'The breast-plate and corsets . . .'

'Corsets?'

'That's right.'

'So that's where it all began . . .'

'The corselet was a sort of half-armour,' explained Mr Ames academically, 'but these are true corsets.'

'Well, well, well . . .'

'Made in pairs, usually hinged, and tailored to fit.'

'You don't say. And that?'

The Vicar coughed. 'The cod-piece, and now,' hastily, 'to get the gorget off . . .'

The figure of an elderly man in a dark grey suit was beginning to emerge.

Blood had run down the back of the neck and on to the collar and suit, and had dried there.

As the Vicar deftly loosened the corset the body started to keel over . . .'

8

Drawn together by the unexpected, the family had stayed together in a group in the sitting-room of the Private Apartments. They were still there when Charles Purvis got back from Ornum village with William Murton.

Murton made a little mock bow towards them.

'You wanted to see me?' he said. There was the faintest of ironic stresses on the word 'wanted'.

'Thought we'd better put you in the picture, William,' the Earl said gruffly. 'Something of a mishap . . .'

'Yes?'

'Meredith's been found dead in the armoury . . .'

'In a suit of armour, actually,' added Lord Henry quickly. 'In the suit we called Grumpy. Do you remember Grumpy?'

William Murton nodded. 'I remember Grumpy all right.' He frowned. 'Second on the right on the way in.'

'That's right,' said the Earl heavily.

There was a slight pause.

'Poor Ossy,' said William. William Murton was a strange admixture of physical characteristics. He was heavier than the Cremonds but he too had the Cremond nose. With it, though, he had a flamboyance of manner missing in the others. 'Somebody put him there, I take it?'

'Quite so,' said the Earl.

'When?'

'Nobody seems to have seen him since Friday.'

'I came down on Friday,' said William, 'seeing as you probably don't like to ask.'

'When on Friday?' said Laura Cremond harshly.

William turned towards her with an expressionless face. 'In the afternoon, Laura. When did you come down?'

She flushed. 'Thursday.'

'We came down for the match,' mumbled Miles.

'Match?' said William Murton, looking round at everybody. 'Match?'

'You know,' said Miles eagerly. 'Ornum versus Petering.'

'Tiddleywinks?'

'Cricket.'

Laura Cremond said, 'He's teasing you, Miles.'

'Cricket,' said William, slapping his thigh. 'Of course. That reminds me – I had some money on that.'

Miles stared at him. 'Money on a cricket match?'

'That's right, old boy.'

'But people never . . .'

'Gents don't,' said William. 'People do. Who won?'

'We did.'

'Good. Thought you would. Old Lambert owes me a fiver then.'

'Ebeneezer Lambert never backed a winner in his life,' observed the Earl sadly. 'Same in my father's day. Poor judge of horses.'

'And men,' said William.

'Men?'

'He was a friend of my father's, you know.'

'Quite so,' said the Earl.

'You could have almost called them colleagues,' went on William bitterly, 'seeing how Lambert was a saddler and my father was a groom.'

'Quite so,' said the Earl again.

'Only colleague isn't quite the right word when it comes to following a trade, is it?'

'Craft,' said the Earl mildly. 'You worry too much about the past, William. It's all over now.'

'Me worry about the past? I like that! You've all got a full-time man here doing nothing much else except poke about into family history. And if that isn't worrying about the past I don't know what is.'

'Only we haven't got him any more,' said Lord Henry diffidently, 'have we?'

William turned towards his cousin. 'No more you have. Met with a nasty accident, did he?'

'So it would seem,' said Henry. 'The police are down in the armoury now. Then they want to see us all.'

'It's a pity,' observed William to no one in particular, 'that it should happen just when Ossy was getting on so well, isn't it . . .'

'Very.'

'Or was I misinformed?'

'No.'

'There are those,' added Murton meaningfully, 'who might say that meddling with the past is downright dangerous, aren't there?'

'There are,' agreed Lord Henry, 'and who's to say they aren't right?'

Alone of the rest of the family Miss Gertrude Cremond was not in the sitting-room. She was still presiding over the room devoted to the display of fine china.

Detective Inspector Sloan found her there by the simple process of following the route which the public took through the house. It was, he decided, rather like playing one of those games based on the maze principle. Each time he came to a dead end – in this case either a locked door or a thick looped cord – he went back two paces and cast about in another direction.

Eventually he came to the china. It looked very beautiful in the long light of an early summer evening – which was more than could have been said for Miss Gertrude Cremond. She was shorter and squarer than the Earl, but still unmistakably a Cremond.

She had the nose.

She could not remember when she had last seen Osborne Meredith alive.

'He wasn't really interested in the china, Inspector. Not as an expert, I mean.'

'I see, miss, thank you.' Some unmarried ladies Sloan called 'miss', some he called 'madam'. There was a fine distinction between the two which he wouldn't have cared to have to put into words and was nothing to do with age.

'But if I can help you at all in any other way . . .' said Miss Cremond.

'You deal with the china yourself, do you?'

'All of it,' she agreed. 'And the flowers. Lady Eleanor helps me with the flowers when she is at home. As a rule we do those on Tuesdays and Fridays. We have fresh flowers in all the public rooms when the house is "open" . . .'

'Fridays you'll be busy,' he said.

'Always.'

'This last Friday, can you remember what you did in the afternoon?'

'The Great Hall Chandelier,' responded Miss Cremond promptly. 'It took a long time – in fact I came back after tea to finish it off. You must have it hung back if the public are to be admitted. It would soon get broken if not.'

'Quite so, miss. And afterwards?'

She frowned. 'It took me until it was time to change. Dillow hung it after dinner.'

'I see, miss, thank you.' He paused. 'If you should remember noticing anything at all unusual about Friday evening I should be glad to be told.'

'Of course, Inspector.'

Sloan began to go. 'Lady Alice tells me that she saw Judge Cremond on Friday evening . . .'

Subconsciously he had expected a light laugh and an apology for an eccentric old lady. What he got was:

'Oh, dear.' And a worried look came over Miss Gertrude Cremond's plain face. 'That's a bad sign, I must say.'

*

'Well, Sloan?'

Sloan was back on the telephone to Berebury Police Headquarters.

'Dr Dabbe has had a look at the body now, sir.'

Superintendent Leeyes grunted. 'Well?'

'Depressed fracture, back of skull.'

'Not suicide, then.'

'No, sir. Not accident either. Not unless someone popped the lid – I mean, the helmet – back on again afterwards, stood him in the right place and dusted the floor all round.'

'Murder, then.'

'I'm afraid so. Hit,' said Sloan pithily, 'very hard on the back of the head with an instrument which may or may not have been blunt.'

'I suppose,' rejoined Superintendent Leeyes, 'that we could have expected the traditional at Ornum.'

'Yes, sir. As to what did it . . .'

'If you mean weapon, Sloan, for Heaven's sake say so.'

Sloan coughed. 'We're a bit spoilt by choice for weapons, sir.'

'Are you?'

'There are one hundred and seventy-seven, sir, not counting two small cannon at the front door.'

'I don't think,' nastily, 'we need count the cannon, do you, Sloan?'

'No, sir.'

'What other sort of weapons do you have – er – on hand?'

Sloan took a deep breath. 'What you might call assorted, sir. Very. Everything from a poleaxe to a partisan.'

'A what?'

'A partisan, sir. Of blued steel.' Sloan hesitated. Offering information to the Superintendent could be a tricky business. 'It's like a halberd.'

'Is it, Sloan?' Dangerously. The only partisans known to the Superintendent were his enemies on the Watch Committee. (The only place, if it came to that, where there was a Resistance Movement.) 'I take it that a halberd is like a partisan?'

'No, sir – I mean, yes, sir.'

'Then you'd better find out exactly which one it was that killed him, hadn't you?'

'Yes, sir.' He cleared his throat. 'Constable Crosby's started going through the catalogue now . . .'

'Catalogue?' echoed Leeyes. 'And do you propose, Sloan, looking the murderer up in *Who's Who* or some such similar publication?'

'No, sir.' Patiently. 'A catalogue of the weapons was made by the Vicar, a Mr Walter Ames, who's something of an authority on arms and armour . . .'

'Is he indeed?'

'And Crosby's going through it now.'

'I see.'

'The trouble, sir, is that the family's been armigerous . . .'

'Been what?'

'Armigerous.'

'Where did you get that word?'

'The doctor used it, sir.'

'That,' said Leeyes severely, 'doesn't mean you should.'

'It's a heraldic term, sir, not a medical one. It means the Ornums have been entitled to bear arms for a very long time. Like,' suddenly, 'like police are allowed to carry truncheons.'

It was not a happy simile.

'Truncheons,' said Leeyes trenchantly. 'What have truncheons got to do with it?'

'They are weapons we're entitled to carry, sir. In the same way the Ornums were entitled to bear arms in the old days. That's why there is so much of it about in the armoury – to say nothing of the fact that the twelfth earl was a great collector.'

'It seems to me,' said his superior officer pontifically, 'that you are confusing arms with weapons. It's a weapon you want, Sloan. And quickly.'

'Yes, sir.'

'What other long words did the doctor use?'

'He said he thought the deceased had been dead for roughly forty-eight hours . . .'

'Friday . . .'

'Yes, sir.'

'No one saw him alive on Saturday, I suppose?' The Superintendent had no more faith in medical than in any other considered opinion.

'Not that I've heard about,' said Sloan carefully. 'Tea time on Friday seems to have been the last occasion he was seen.'

'And how long had he been in the armour?'

'Dr Dabbe couldn't say, sir, but he thought he hadn't been put into it until after rigor mortis had passed off.'

'That means the body must have been parked somewhere, Sloan . . .'

'Or just left, sir, where it was killed.'

'Where was that?'

'I don't know, sir. Not yet. It's a big house.'

'Not,' sarcastically, 'a room for every day of the year?'

'Not quite, sir, but . . .'

'But you haven't quite mastered the geography yet, eh, Sloan? Is that it?'

That was one way of putting it.

Not a way Sloan himself would have chosen but Superintendent Leeyes was not a man with whom to argue.

Instead of arguing Sloan said formally, 'I have already interviewed some of those persons present in the house and warned them that I shall wish to talk to them again . . .'

A noncommittal grunt came down the line.

'I have also instigated enquiries about the present whereabouts of the deceased's sister and am endeavouring to establish who was the last person to see him alive . . .'

'The last but one will do nicely for the time being, Sloan.'

'Yes, sir.'

'These people in the house . . .'

'The Ornums and their servants, sir.'

'I see. That's the Earl . . .'

'And his wife, his cousin, his two aunts on his father's side, his son and his daughter, his nephew and his nephew's wife.'

'Ha! The extended family, Sloan.' The Superintendent had once read a book on sociology and felt he had mastered that tricky discipline.

'I beg your pardon, sir?'

'Nothing, Sloan. Just a technical term.'

'I see, sir. There is also an additional nephew.'

'Oh?'

'A Mr William Murton.'

'Makes a change from Ornum, I suppose,' observed Leeyes.

'His mother was an Ornum. She married a groom.'

'She did what?' The Superintendent, who dealt daily with sudden death, larceny, road traffic accidents and generally saw the seamy side of human nature, was not easily shocked but there were some things . . .

'She ran away with her groom,' said Sloan. 'Mr William Murton, the Earl's nephew, is the outcome of the union.'

'And where does he come in?'

'I couldn't say, sir. Not yet. He has a cottage in Ornum village which he uses – mostly at weekends. The rest of the time he lives in London. I understand he paints.'

The Superintendent didn't like that.

'And,' pursued Sloan, 'there is also the Earl's steward, a man called Charles Purvis. He lives in a little house in the Park and comes all over a twitter whenever he looks at young Lady Eleanor.'

'Like that, is she?'

'No, sir,' repressively, 'she is not. Apart,' he went on, 'from this – er – one big happy family' – Sloan didn't know if this was the same thing as an extended one or not – 'there are the servants.'

'Loyal to the core, I suppose?'

'Well . . .'

'Above suspicion?'

That was not a term Sloan had been taught to use.

'Trusted to the hilt, then,' suggested Leeyes, who in his youth had been grounded in heroic fiction.

'No . . .'

'Been with them all their lives?' The Superintendent was rapidly running out of phrases associated with family servants.

'No, sir. Oddly enough, not. The cook has. Started as a tweeny at twelve and worked her way up but the housekeeper has only been there a couple of years and the butler rather less. About eighteen months. The other girl – I don't know what you'd call her . . .'

'I'd call her maid-of-all-work,' said Leeyes promptly.

'She's been with them about three years. That's the indoor staff. Outside there are two men and a boy looking after the Park and gardens. One of them – Albert Hackle – comes in on open days to show off the dungeons.'

'Perhaps,' said Leeyes, 'there'll be someone in them soon.'

Sloan said sedately that he would see what he could do and rang off.

What he wanted to do next was to find the parts of the house where Osborne Meredith had spent his working time. The library and the muniments room.

Stepping away from the telephone the first person he met was Lord Henry. He asked that young man to lead him to them.

He wished he had gone there sooner.

The library was apparently in perfect order.

The muniments room looked as if it had been hit by a tornado.

9

Detective Inspector Sloan didn't step very far into the muniments room.

Just far enough to see that the disarray was not that left by an exceptionally untidy scholar.

It was not.

From where he stood he could see that it had been carefully calculated. Sheets of manuscripts lay disarranged on the floor, documents of every sort were strewn all over the place. A great chest lay open, its contents distributed far and wide.

'Phew!' whistled Lord Henry over Sloan's shoulder.

'Don't come any further, my lord,' warned Sloan. 'I'll need to take a proper look round the room first.'

'It's a bit of a mess.'

'Quite so.'

Typical English understatement, that was. Sloan's gaze swept the room and noted that the disturbance had every appearance of being systematic. It looked as if every drawer had been opened, every deed unrolled. Long scrolls of paper covered all the surfaces, and, sprinkled over everything like some monstrous oversize confetti, were dozens and dozens of filing cards.

'Poor Ossy,' murmured Lord Henry quietly. 'I hope he didn't see this. A more orderly man didn't exist.'

'Those filing cards . . .'

'All the deeds, documents and depositions,' said Lord Henry, 'recorded and cross referenced. It took him years.'

Sloan nodded. 'The room was never locked?'

'No. This part of the house isn't ever shown to the public.' Lord Henry was still looking at the room as best he could round the police inspector. 'That's a funny thing, though.'

'What is, my lord?'

'The room isn't kept locked but the document chests always are.'

Together they peered at the iron-banded chests. Keys were clearly visible from where they stood, still in the locks.

'Who had the keys to them?' asked Sloan automatically.

'Just my father and Ossy.'

'I see.' Sloan made a mental note about that. The contents of the deceased's pockets would be recorded by the police in due course. Just at the moment they were inviolate behind a portion of armour called a tasset.

Lord Henry frowned. 'Ossy would never have left them open like that – or even with the keys in. They're much too important for that.'

'He might not have had the choice,' Sloan reminded him.

'No, of course not. I was forgetting.' Lord Henry's gaze rested on the dishevelled room. 'There's another extraordinary thing, Inspector, isn't there . . .'

'What, my lord?'

'All this confusion . . .'

'But no actual damage.'

This was quite true. Disorder reigned supreme but none of the papers appeared to be torn or defaced.

'Just as if someone only wanted a muddle,' said his Lordship perceptively.

'These documents must have value,' began Sloan. 'It stands to reason . . .'

'To an antiquarian perhaps, Inspector. But not an intrinsic value like the pictures or the books or the china.'

Sloan shifted his weight from one foot to the other. 'If there was anything missing . . .'

Lord Henry said carefully, 'Then only Ossy would be able to tell you.'

'And he can't do that now.'

'No.' The younger man paused. 'Moreover, Inspector, if he were here to tell us, it would take him a very long time indeed to put this room to rights – even though we may think nothing's been damaged. Months. Years, perhaps.'

Sloan could see that for himself.

'Presumably,' he said, going on from there in his mind and thinking aloud, 'this room would otherwise have told us something useful.'

'But what?' asked Lord Henry, surveying the muddled muniments from the door.

Sloan decided that their message – if any – would have to wait for the time being.

He turned his scrutiny to the floor. There was no blood immediately visible. Mr Osborne Meredith did not appear to have been killed here. And whoever had created this disturbance had been careful not to stand on any of the papers.

Or had they?

Sloan dropped to his knees and looked along at ground level. There was an imprint of sorts on one piece of paper.

A heel mark.

A heel mark so small and square that it must have come from a woman's shoe.

Detective Constable Crosby was asking Charles Purvis the Earl's name.

He did not know it but this – like matrimony – was not something to be taken in hand lightly.

'It's for the Coroner,' he began. 'I need to know the full name of the occupier of the premises in which the deceased is presumed to have met his death.'

'The full name?' said Charles Purvis dubiously.

'The full name.'

'Henry,' said the steward. 'The eldest son is always called Henry.'

Crosby wrote that down.

'Augustus.' After the Duke of Cumberland – or was it the Roman General?

Crosby wrote that down too.

'Rudolfo.'

'Rudolfo?'

'The tenth Earl was invested with a foreign order. He was the English ambassador to the country at an awkward time diplomatically and – er – carried it off well. Saved the situation, you might say. He called his own son after their reigning monarch of the day – that went down well, too. The name has been kept.'

'I see,' said Constable Crosby laconically. 'That the lot?'

Purvis stiffened. 'By no means. There's Cremond too.'

'That's the surname, isn't it?'

'As well.'

'As well as what?'

'As well as being a Christian name.'

Crosby wasn't sure what Purvis meant and said so.

'Twice,' said Charles Purvis.

'You mean he was christened Cremond as well as having it as a surname.'

'That's right.'

'Cremond,' Crosby looked incredulous, 'and Cremond?'

The steward coughed. 'That dates back to the middle of the eighteenth century when . . .'

Crosby wasn't listening. 'William Edward Crosby Crosby,' he said under his breath, for size.

'I beg your pardon, Constable?'

Crosby turned back to his notebook, and read aloud 'Henry Augustus Rudolfo Cremond Cremond?'

Name of a name of a name, that was . . .

'That's right,' agreed the steward and comptroller. 'Thirteenth Earl Ornum of Ornum in the County of Calleshire, Baron Cremond of Petering . . .'

'There isn't,' said Detective Constable William Edward Crosby of 24 Hillview Terrace, Berebury, with tremendous dignity, 'any room on the form for that.'

*

Sloan methodically sealed the door of the muniments room and went back next door to the library. This was a very fine room.

It was divided into six small bays all lined with books – three bays on either side of the centre. The right-hand three each ended in a window and a window seat with a view over the park. The left-hand three consisted entirely of bookshelves with a sliver of table down the middle. At the far end was a head and shoulders bust of Lord Henry.

'My great-great-grandfather,' murmured Lord Henry.

Sloan shot a swift glance from the bust of Lord Henry and back again. There was no discernible difference between the two.

'Army,' said Lord Henry by way of explanation. 'Too young for Waterloo. Too old for the Crimea.'

Sloan advanced. Apart from the neckwear, the bust might just as well have been Lord Henry. It was as near a replica as he'd seen.

'Mr Meredith worked here too, I take it,' he said generally.

Lord Henry nodded. 'Spent nearly all his time between the library and the muniments, though he was always popping down to have a look at the pictures, too.'

'As to Friday,' said Sloan, 'if he'd been working here then, what sort of traces would you have expected to find?'

'None,' said his Lordship promptly. 'He wasn't that sort of scholar. When he'd finished with a book, he'd put it back in its right place.'

Sloan wasn't surprised. From what little he'd seen of the body that had emerged pupa-like from the chrysalis of the armour, he'd have said Meredith was a neat, dapper little man.

Lord Henry carried on: 'He was quite mild about everything else but it was as much as your life was worth to spoil the order on the bookshelves . . .'

This wasn't perhaps the happiest of comparisons and Lord Henry's voice trailed away.

'I see,' said Sloan, moving down the three bays.

Everything was utterly neat and tidy. At the end by the door a small stack of papers on the table there was the only testimony that the room had ever been used at all. The first two bays seemed normal enough. Sloan paused at the third.

The casual observer – the untrained eye – would probably have seen nothing.

Sloan did.

What he saw was on the spine of Volume XXIV of *The Transactions of the Calleshire Society*.

Blood.

This, then, was in all probability where the librarian and archivist to the Ornum family had met his death.

Sloan stepped carefully round the thin table and measured a few distances with his eye. The photographers would have to come back and bring the lab boys with them. In the meantime . . .

At a quick guess the deceased could have been sitting at the inside end of the table which ran the length of the bay. He had been hit from behind – the pathologist had told him that much – and from above. The height of the book with the blood on it confirmed that.

Lord Henry cleared his throat. 'This the spot, then?'

'I think so,' said Sloan. There was nothing much else to point to it. The table might have had blood on it and been wiped clean. There might be drops on the floor. The library carpet was Turkey red which didn't help . . . And any derangement of chair and table had long ago been made good. And marks of scuffed heels on the pile of the carpet would have . . .

'The cleaning arrangements in here . . .' began Sloan.

But he had asked the wrong man.

'Not really my department,' said his young Lordship frankly. 'Dillow will know.'

'I see,' said Sloan. He wouldn't mind another word with the butler. 'Where would I find him now?'

'It's easier than that.' Lord Henry drifted across the library and tugged at a green silk sash. 'He'll find us.'

It was, in fact, simplicity itself.

'Thank you.' Sloan wasn't sure about the paths of righteousness but those of some people could be made very smooth indeed. He cleared his throat. 'By the way, my lord, your injury . . .'

'Silly thing to do.' Lord Henry's bandaged hand was still drooping down like a limping dog's paw. 'I cut it on Friday morning fiddling about with my car.'

'Were you alone at the time?' enquired Sloan pertinently.

'Oh, yes, Inspector. Nobody else here really cares about cars. I caught it between the fan blade and the engine.'

'I see.'

'Trying to tune her up a bit and all that . . .'

The library door opened. 'You rang, my lord?'

'Ah, Dillow, the Inspector wants another word with you.'

The butler, professionally expressionless, turned expectantly to Sloan.

'Friday,' said Sloan. 'Friday afternoon. You said you brought Mr Meredith his tea here.'

'That is correct, sir. At four o'clock. I collected the empty tray a few minutes before five.'

'Did you see Mr Meredith then?'

'Not the second time, sir. The tray was on the table by the door and I just collected it . . .' The man hesitated. 'In fact, sir, I'm afraid I assumed Mr Meredith had gone home because the Vicar called about half an hour later, asking for him, and he said he'd tried the muniments room and he wasn't there. I took the liberty of telling him that Mr Meredith must have gone home then, though of course I realize now that . . .'

'Quite so,' said Sloan. 'And after that?'

'After, sir?'

'When did you next come in here?'

Dillow frowned. 'Yesterday morning sometime, sir, it would have been. Just to see that the room had been put to rights. Though Mr Meredith was such a tidy gentleman that I knew nothing would need doing.'

'And did it?'

'No, sir, not that I recollect.'

'Whose job is it to see that the room has been tidied?'

'Mine, sir, to see it had been done. Edith's to – er – do it.'

'Edith?' The nuances of the division of labour among domestic staff were lost on Sloan. Now if it had been police work . . .

'She's the housemaid, sir, but . . .'

'Yes?'

'On open days, sir, we all tend to devote ourselves to the rooms which are "shown".'

'I see. And the muniments room?'

'I didn't go in there, sir, at all. Mr Meredith liked to deal with that himself. It's a small room and when any cleaning was done in there Mr Meredith always arranged to be present himself so that nothing was disturbed.'

'The muniments room? Turned upside-down? Look out, Dillow, you're spilling that soup . . .'

'I beg your pardon, my lord.'

'I should think so. Henry, who the devil would want to play about in the muniments room, of all places? Nobody ever goes in there.'

'Couldn't say,' said his son and heir. 'But somebody has – er – did. And you can't go and see because the Inspector has sealed it up. And the library.'

The dining-room at Ornum House that evening was scarcely more festive than the armoury. The Earl of Ornum sat at one end of the table, the Countess at the other. Ranged round the table were the rest of the family.

Dillow hovered.

William Murton, whose summons to Ornum House had, in fact, gone on to include a meal, took an immediate interest. 'That means something, doesn't it? I mean, you wouldn't go to the bother of stirring up the papers without a reason, would you?'

'I wouldn't,' responded Henry.

'But,' asked Laura Cremond, 'what was there in there that mattered anyway?'

'Search me,' said Lord Henry frankly. 'Never could make head nor tail of those papers myself. All that cramped writing. In Latin, too, most of it. Still, I expect it meant something . . .'

'Your inheritance,' said his father drily.

'It must have meant something to somebody else too,' pointed out Miles Cremond who always followed his wife's conversational leads. 'Else they wouldn't have messed it about.'

Cousin Gertrude, who was a considerable trencherwoman, looked up from a bit of steady eating and said, 'Does that mean that now no one can prove that Harry here isn't Earl of Ornum?'

There was a small silence.

The Earl of Ornum crumbled some bread and wondered why it was that plain women so often went in for plain speaking.

'Well,' demanded Gertrude Cremond, 'can they or can't they?'

Millicent, Countess of Ornum, was always equal to a straight question.

'Poor Mr Meredith,' she said tangently, 'to be killed *and* to have his work spoilt like that . . .'

'Ossa on Pelion,' murmured Lord Henry, upon whose education a great deal of money had been expended.

'Too terrible,' said the Countess.

'To be killed by someone he knew,' observed her daughter quietly.

'Eleanor! Surely not.'

'Unless some total stranger happened to walk in, take a dislike to his face and kill him.'

'But,' protested Millicent Ornum, 'he had a nice face. Crinkled but pleasant. Not the sort of face you'd take a sudden dislike to at all.'

Eleanor sighed. 'Exactly, Mother.'

'So it wasn't his face,' drawled William Murton.

'It must have been something else then, what?' said Miles Cremond with the air of one reaching a studied conclusion.

'Yes, Miles,' said Lord Henry kindly. 'We think it was.'

'So if Ossy's dead and the papers are all messed up then no one can prove anything?'

'A veritable nutshell, old chap. There's just the one small point . . .'

'What's that?'

'Who did for Ossy?'

A baffled look came over Miles Cremond's face. 'Yes, of course.'

'It's no use our pretending,' said Cousin Gertrude bluntly, 'that it doesn't make any difference to any of us whether Harry here is

Earl of Ornum because it does.' She looked round the table. 'To every single one of us.'

There was a chorus of protest.

'Yes, it does,' insisted Gertrude. 'Henry here'll kill himself one day in that sports car of his. Always trying to make it go faster and faster.'

'I say, Cousin Gertrude, steady on . . .'

'That means Miles would come into the title and you can't tell me that wouldn't please Laura.'

Laura Cremond's thin face went a sudden pink. 'Really, Gertrude, I don't think that remark is in the best of taste.'

'Neither is murder.'

'Are you suggesting that Miles and I killed Mr Meredith?'

Gertrude Cremond was equal to a frontal attack. Not for nothing had she stood foursquare against the opposing centre-forward on the hockey field. 'No,' she said, 'but you were both late for dinner on Friday evening, weren't you?'

'Well, I must say that sounds remarkably like an insinuation to me.'

'Merely an observation,' remarked Cousin Gertrude, unper-turbed. 'Why were you both so late?'

'Miles went for a walk and I waited for him to get back before I came down. That's why.'

'Did you go for a walk, Miles?'

'What? Oh, me? Yes, rather.'

'Where?'

'Where? Oh – in the park, you know. Actually I went round the ha-ha. To get in training for the match, what? No exercise to speak of in town, don't you know.'

'Never touch it myself,' said William Murton, looking with close interest from one flushed face to the next.

'Touch what?' said Miles.

'Exercise.' William patted his tummy. 'Went to seed early myself. Less trouble.'

Cousin Gertrude rounded on him as if he'd been a wing-half coming up fast on the outside. 'There's no need for you to talk, William. You'd miss your Uncle Harry here more than anyone.'

'True.'

'You may not touch exercise,' she went on tartly, 'but you're certainly not above touching him for money when you need it.'

'Granted.' He made a mock bow in her direction. 'But you will be pleased to hear I've turned over a new leaf. My – er – touching days are gone.'

This produced total silence. The Earl and his son exchanged a quick glance.

'Truly,' said William. 'I haven't asked you for a loan this trip, Uncle Harry, now have I?'

'Not yet,' said that peer cautiously.

Cousin Gertrude was inexorable. 'Moreover,' she went on, 'there's the Judge taking to walking about again. I hear that Aunt Alice saw him on Friday evening. You all know what that means.'

There was an immediate chorus from Eleanor, Henry, Miles and William. 'Someone's going to go!'

Laura Cremond turned on her husband. 'Really, Miles . . .'

'Sorry, dear, learnt the responses as a child.'

'You are now a grown-up.'

'Yes, dear.'

'I don't think,' said Gertrude astringently, 'that Laura quite appreciates that the Judge being seen always means that someone is going to die.'

'He's dead,' insisted Laura. 'You've all been saying so.'

'Not Ossy. He doesn't count. It's got to be a member of the family,' declared Gertrude.

'It's a family legend . . .' said William Murton, adding ironically, 'You needn't worry, Laura. It only applies to blood relations.'

'Like the two black owls and the Duke of Dorset in *Zuleika Dobson*,' explained Lord Henry swiftly. Laura was looking cross . . .

'And the dying gooseberry bush in the walls of Kilravock Castle,' added Lady Eleanor.

'And just as true,' insisted Miss Cremond.

'Never mind, Cousin Gertrude,' said Lord Henry helpfully. 'Perhaps it's one of the great-aunts. After all, they are knocking ninety and they can't live for ever, you know . . .'

'Talking of the aunts,' said Eleanor suddenly, 'where are they tonight?'

'They've taken umbrage,' said her brother.

'Why?'

'Mother used Great-Aunt Maude's hearing aid as a pepper pot last night.'

'No!'

'It's a fact,' said Lord Henry. 'Poor old Maude. She stood it on the table all the better to hear with and Mother started shaking it all over her soup.'

'It is a bit like one, you know,' murmured Millicent Ornum defensively, 'until you look at it closely.'

But Cousin Gertrude had not done.

Heated and anxious she said, 'Don't you all realize that somebody we know killed poor Ossy?'

There was silence.

'Someone here in Ornum House,' she said. 'Perhaps someone in this very room now.'

The Earl of Ornum cleared his throat, and said in a low rumble, ''Fraid you're probably right, Gertrude.'

Laura Cremond said spitefully, 'What about you, Gertrude? You've got more to lose than any of us, haven't you?'

10

Monday morning dawned with its customary inevitability.

With it came the news that there had been a road traffic accident at Tappett's Corner on the main Berebury to Luston road the night before. Superintendent Leeyes was not pleased about this.

'A ruddy great pile-up,' he moaned, flinging down the report in front of Inspector Sloan as soon as he arrived on duty. 'One woman driver who wouldn't have been safe out with a pram, one commercial vehicle with no business to be on the road at all on a Sunday . . .'

Inspector Sloan picked up the paper and began to read.

'. . . and a family saloon,' said Leeyes, 'driven by two old women.'

The report said that it had been driven by a husband with his wife sitting beside him but Sloan knew what the Superintendent meant. He had been speaking figuratively. There were some real figures, too.

Two people had been taken to hospital and three vehicles to the suspect garage.

'If there's anybody in my division getting a kickback out of this, Sloan,' threatened Leeyes, 'there's going to be real trouble.'

'Yes, sir.' He looked at the report. 'It is the nearest garage to Tappett's Corner.'

'I know that.'

'And they're the only people with heavy lifting gear for this van.'

'I know that, too, and it doesn't help, does it?'

'No, sir.'

It didn't.

If there was something wrong there was something wrong and explanations were neither here nor there.

'This other business, Sloan . . .' Only a true policeman, jealous in honour, would have such an order of priority. 'How far have you got? We can't hang on to a case like this, you know.'

'Some of the way, sir.' Sloan knew Superintendent Leeyes wouldn't want anyone else here while he was worried about Inspector Harpe's men. 'I think the deceased was killed in the library between four o'clock and half-past five on Friday afternoon.'

Leeyes grunted.

'He was last seen alive,' went on Sloan, 'by Lady Eleanor, the Earl's daughter, just before four and by the butler, Dillow, immediately after that.'

'But by five thirty . . .'

'By five thirty. That was when the Vicar, Mr Walter Ames, arrived at Ornum House in response to a message . . .'

'A message?'

'A message to the effect that his friend, Mr Meredith, had made an important discovery.'

'What?'

'I'm afraid so, sir.'

'What sort of discovery?'

'We don't know, sir. Yet. All we know is that he telephoned the Vicar's house during that afternoon and left a message with the Vicar's wife asking Mr Ames to step around to the house as soon as he could.' Sloan paused. 'I think that by the time he got there Mr Meredith was dead.'

'Someone else knew about his discovery?'

'Yes, sir. I think so.' He coughed. 'The telephone at Ornum House is somewhat public, sir. It's in the entrance hall. Anyone could have heard him.'

'Someone did?'

'I'm very much afraid so, sir.'

Leeyes grunted again. 'Go on . . .'

'There are bloodstains at the far end of the last bay in the library. I'm having them analysed this morning. He could well have been killed there and left there until the opportunity arose to take his body to the armoury.'

'Without being seen?'

'It was a chance that would have to be taken. I should not imagine that the library was used all that often and the blood stains are at the far end of the last bay. In fact Mr Ames did look in the library for the deceased and called out his name – but when he did not appear or answer he went away.'

'Beyond call,' observed Leeyes succinctly, 'and recall.'

'Exactly, sir. Then there are the muniments . . .'

'Documents,' supplied Leeyes, 'kept as evidence of rights or privilege.'

'Thank you, sir. I thought they might be. Well, at some time after five thirty on Friday afternoon when the Vicar looked in the muniments room and noticed nothing amiss, and at some time before I got there myself yesterday afternoon, some person or persons unknown had played havoc with them.'

The Superintendent's eyebrows shot up. 'Ho ho!'

'Yes, sir. All we know at present about who did it was that they were wearing a size six and a half lady's shoe.'

'A woman, eh?'

'Someone wearing a lady's shoe,' said Sloan more precisely. 'There are three ladies in the house who take that size in foot-wear. Mrs Laura Cremond, Miss Gertrude Cremond and the housekeeper, Mrs Morley.' He paused. 'It's a popular size.'

The Superintendent stroked his chin. 'So there was something that mattered in the muniments room . . .'

'Something they thought mattered,' Sloan corrected him obliquely.

'Motive?'

'Perhaps, sir,' said Sloan, and told him about the threatened earldom.

'Ah, Sloan, kind hearts may be more than coronets but when it comes to the crunch . . .'

'Quite so, sir. If it – er – should turn out to be that sort of crunch then there are a fair number of people with a vested interest in the status quo, I agree, but . . .'

'But what?'

'That particular discovery was relatively old hat by last Friday.'

'How relatively?'

'The immediate family and the steward had known all about it for nearly a week . . .'

'Stewards,' interrupted the Superintendent didactically, 'are notoriously untrustworthy.'

'Unjust,' murmured Sloan, whose Sunday schooling had been impeccable. 'I don't know if this one is or not yet. Anyway, if the Ornums and their steward had known about it for so long what I don't quite see is why the deceased should suddenly get excited on Friday afternoon. If it's the same discovery, that is.'

'How soon did the nephews get to hear about it?' The Superintendent's own theory of relativity was more simply stated than Einstein's.

The nearer the degree of relationship, the greater the likelihood of murder.

'Miles Cremond and his wife were told when they arrived on Thursday for the weekend.'

'The weekend?' echoed Leeyes. 'Thursday?' Police weekends began at noon on Saturdays.

'Yes, sir. He works in London.'

'That explains it. What at?'

'For a shipping company,' said Sloan carefully, 'as a figurehead, I should imagine.'

'No head for figures though?'

'I shouldn't think he would go much beyond a batting average, sir. He's with the Pedes Line.'

'They're in deep water,' said Leeyes, unconsciously apposite. 'Everyone knows that.'

'Yes, sir.'

'And the other nephew? The artist one . . .'

'I don't know when he found out, sir.' Sloan paused. 'He's a bit of a puzzle.'

'I'm tired of crazy mixed-up kids, Sloan.'

'I don't quite know what to make of him, sir,' he said seriously. 'I think he could well be one of those. I've put in some enquiries about both nephews to London.'

'Good. The deceased's sister,' went on Leeyes. 'Has she turned up yet?'

Sloan shook his head. 'There's no sign of her. The postmistress thinks she's visiting a friend but doesn't know for sure. Crosby's been round the outside of the house to make certain she's not hanging in the woodshed or anything like that but I hardly like to ask for a warrant to break in for a better look.'

Superintendent Leeyes' grunt indicated that he wouldn't get one if he asked.

'What now, Sloan? I can't keep Headquarters out of the case for ever.'

'I'm just waiting for the post-mortem report on the deceased from Dr Dabbe and then I'm going back to Ornum House . . .'

'Gadzooks,' observed the Superintendent sardonically, 'stapping his vitals, is he?'

Detective Constable Crosby was in Sloan's office struggling with the small print in the *Peerage*. 'A telephone message from London, sir. Just come through . . .'

'The nephews?'

Crosby shook his head. 'Firm of solicitors, name of Oaten, Oaten and Cossington – representing the Earl of Ornum. The senior partner is on his way down now.'

Sloan was not surprised. He pointed to the book. 'Have you got the succession sorted out?'

'Yes, sir. Sir, did you know that once everyone was either an earl or a churl?' Crosby had obviously begun at the very beginning. 'They were all divided into those two groups.'

'People have always been divided into two groups, Constable, and the sooner you get that into your head the better.' At school he had learnt about patricians and plebeians, as a young man about proletarians and . . . proletarians and . . . Sloan couldn't think now who the others had been but he could still remember getting very excited about it at the time. It had seemed so important. Now that he was older he knew the grouping was simpler than that.

Oneself versus The Rest.

'And,' went on Crosby industriously, 'they made men earls when they didn't want to make them marquesses or dukes.'

'You don't say,' remarked Sloan. 'Status rearing its ugly head again.'

'Beg pardon, sir?'

'Nothing. The Ornums . . .'

'Yes, sir. It's all down here.' He paused. 'Everything.'

'Everything?'

'Well, sir, they don't half say what they mean . . .'

Sloan regarded the heavy tome with respect. That wasn't always the case with big books. 'Good.'

'Very clear,' said Crosby primly.

'Oh?'

The Constable squinted down at the page and read aloud, ' "The succession is limited to heirs of the body male," sir, that's what it says here.'

'Indeed,' said Sloan gravely.

'And something about lords of creation.'

'Are you sure?'

Crosby took another look. 'Lords of the first creation.'

'Ornum isn't one of those, surely?' Not with a Norman Keep and a Tudor Great Hall.

'No, sir, I don't think so. Henry the Eighth gave them extra land after some battle or other . . .'

'England, Home and Booty,' murmured Sloan.

'. . . and they seem to have been Hereditary Beacon Keepers to the Crown for the County of Calleshire since the reign of Queen Elizabeth the First.'

'Very useful thing to know,' agreed Sloan, 'but what about now?'

'Lord Henry inherits.'

'And if anything happens to Lord Henry?'

'Miles Cremond, eldest son of the younger brother of the twelfth earl, is next in succession.'

'I thought he might be,' said Sloan.

'I can't find Miss Gertrude Cremond anywhere . . .'

'Too far from the main line.'

'. . . but the two old ladies are here. Daughters of the eleventh Earl.'

'That's going back a bit.'

'And I've found William Murton. At least,' Crosby put a large forefinger on a tiny line of print, 'I think so. It says here after Lady Elizabeth . . . married W. Murton of Ornum, "one s" '.

'That,' said Sloan solemnly, 'is what happens when you run away with your groom. We will make a point of seeing William Murton again very soon. Now, this business of the Earl not being the Earl . . .'

Crosby slapped the book. 'Not here . . . There's just a bit about their escutcheon . . .'

'No blot?' Deadpan.

'Not yet, sir.' Crosby grinned. 'There's quite a long piece about their coat of arms but I didn't think you'd want to go into that.'

'You never can tell,' said Sloan. 'The Bordens had a lion, rampant, on their crest, bearing a battle-axe, proper. Let me have a look . . .'

Whatever doubts existed about the title to the Earldom of Ornum there could be none about the parentage of Lord Henry Cremond.

Seen together, the Earl and his son were absurdly alike. Seen sitting between his father and mother Lord Henry would have done for an illustration for one of Mr Mendel's textbooks on hereditary characteristics. He had her skin, his colouring, the Cremond nose, her vague manner, his mannerisms.

Lady Eleanor, their daughter, who was there too, was less certainly a Cremond in appearance. More definite than her mother, less pessimistic than her father, more practical than either, she had been leavened by a vein of common sense in sheer reaction to a mother as *distrait* as hers.

The four of them were in the sitting-room of the Private Apartments. They looked like a *tableau vivant* of a family.

Until the Earl spoke.

'I don't like it,' he said. 'It's not like William not to be short of money.'

'No,' agreed Lord Henry.

'Always has been.'

'Yes.'

'Should have thought he always would be.'

'Yes.'

'After all, there's no reason for him to change.' The Earl pulled his moustache and corrected himself. 'There's no reason that we know of for him to change.'

'No.'

'His father was the same. Never a bean.'

Henry nodded.

'My father,' went on the Earl gloomily, 'had to support his father or else see m'sister starve. Couldn't do that.'

'No.'

'And you, my boy, will probably have to support his children.'

'Yes.'

'Can't let them starve either. Not family.'

'Course not,' murmured Lord Henry.

'But William isn't married yet, dear,' said the Countess.

'He should be,' retorted her husband cryptically.

The Countess looked blank.

'More than once,' added her husband.

'Harry, what do you mean?'

'A roving eye,' said the Earl warmly, 'that's what that young man's got. And no money to go with it.'

'But he hasn't got any children, dear, surely . . .'

'Their mothers say he has . . .'

'No!'

'I understand,' said the Earl drily, 'that there have been several unsuccessful attempts to get him as far as the altar.'

'You mean . . .' A wave of comprehension swept over Millicent Ornum's face.

'I do. Paternity and maintenance.'

'Well, really, Harry, I do think that's the . . .'

'Mother, there's no use making a fuss now,' Eleanor interrupted her realistically. 'After all it comes from our side of the family.'

'Eleanor!'

'Well, it does. Aunt Elizabeth wasn't known as Bad Betty for nothing.'

This was too much for the Countess. She appealed to her husband.

'Harry, I don't need to remind you that your father would never have her name mentioned in this house as long as he lived.'

'True, my dear, very true.' The Earl's hand sought solace by his moustache. 'Perhaps he was wiser than we knew. It does seem to lead to trouble. Shall I apply a similar interdiction?'

But by then his wife had caught up with an earlier imputation. 'Eleanor . . .'

'Yes, Mother?'

'William's mother was not on our side of the family.'

'She was . . .'

'She was on your father's side, which is different.'

This being true of all families, noble and otherwise, Eleanor did not debate it. 'Yes, Mother,' she said obediently.

'I must say it's not like William not to be on his beam ends by the time he comes down to Ornum.' Lord Henry changed the subject with the deftness of long experience.

'I don't like it,' reiterated the Earl. 'I don't like it at all.'

Lord Henry, who lacked a moustache to tug, instead fondled the tassel of the chair cushion. 'Laura and Gertrude don't exactly hit it off, do they?'

'Never have,' said his father. 'Difficult woman, Gertrude.'

'Laura's no peacemaker either,' said Eleanor.

'Rather not,' agreed Henry. He cleared his throat. 'She and Miles were late for dinner on Friday.'

'I noticed,' said the Earl heavily.

'And she went to bed uncommonly early.'

'I know.' A permanent air of melancholy seemed to have settled on the Earl of Ornum.

'They're staying on – Miles and Laura, I mean,' said the Countess, 'because of this business about poor Mr Meredith, and Dillow's not having his day off today because of all the reporters coming.'

There was a moment's gloomy silence, and then:

'There's something else, isn't there?' said Lady Eleanor.

Her brother looked up. 'What's that?'

'Something that no one seems to have thought about,' said Lady Eleanor. 'We all think poor Ossy was murdered because he knew something.'

'Yes . . .'

'What we don't know is why someone went to all that trouble to put him in the armour.'

'To stop him being found,' said Lord Henry promptly. 'His sister is away. He wasn't going to be really missed for ages.'

'Exactly.' Eleanor waved a hand. 'That's what I mean. He might not have been found for days.'

'So?'

'So the delay was important. That's right, Father, isn't it?'

The Earl sighed. 'I'm afraid so, my dear.'

'Why?' asked Lord Henry immediately.

'I don't know.'

Every now and then Millicent Ornum came into the conversation with a remark that proved she had been listening.

She did so now.

'I expect,' she said brightly, 'it's because of something that hasn't happened yet.'

11

Inspector Sloan telephoned Charles Purvis, the steward, at Ornum as soon as he could.

'You'll be having some visitors at the house today,' he said.

'If you mean the Press,' responded Purvis promptly, 'they're here now.'

Sloan hadn't meant the Press. 'No, the Vicar. I want him to be there when we open up the armoury again, and some people from our Forensic Laboratory. They'll want to examine the library and the muniments room and so on.'

'Very well, Inspector. I'll see that they are allowed in.'

'And the county archivist . . .'

'Ah . . .'

'With the Earl's permission, that is. We've asked him to come over from the County Record Office at Calleford to examine the muniments for us.'

'He'll come all right,' said Charles Purvis cheerfully. 'Like a shot . . .'

'Oh?'

'He's been trying to get a really good look at them for years only Meredith would never let him.'

'Really?' Sloan tucked that fact away in his mind, too. 'And I would like to see the four regular guides to the house, please. The ones who took people round this weekend.'

Purvis promised to arrange this with them straightaway.

'About eleven o'clock suit you for that, then, Inspector?'

Sloan said that would do very nicely and rang off.

Then for the second time Detective Constable Crosby drove him out to Ornum. On this occasion they stopped first in the village itself.

Cremond Cottages were a neat little row of four dwellings, with the initials 'H.C.' carved into a small tablet in the middle over the date 1822. Though it was by no means early by the time they knocked on the door of number four, William Murton had not yet shaved.

'Ah, gentlemen, good morning, and welcome to my humble home.' There was the faintest of ironic stresses on the word 'humble'. He ushered them in. 'I thought you'd be along sooner or later.'

The downstairs rooms of the cottage had been knocked together into one and decorated in a manner more redolent of town than country. There was a painting hanging over the fireplace which Sloan took to be an abstract. There was a large eye in one corner of it; the rest was an unidentifiable mixture of colour and design.

Constable Crosby saw the picture as he entered the room and took a deep breath . . .

Sloan said swiftly, 'Is that your own work, Mr Murton?'

The artist nodded. 'My grandmother – my paternal grandmother, needless to say – was fond of texts on walls. She had this one hanging over her bed.'

'This one?' Faintly.

'Well, the same thing in words. I prefer to express the idea in paint, that's all.'

'I see,' said Sloan cautiously. He took a second look at the painting.

'You've recognized it, of course,' said Murton ironically.

Sloan, who only knew what he didn't like in modern art, said, 'I don't know that I have, sir.'

' "Thou God Seest Me." ' There was no mistaking the mocking tone now. 'Reaction against all that traditional stuff up at the house, you know.'

'Quite so.' If the painting was anything to go by, it was a pretty violent reaction.

'And over there . . .' Murton pointed to where an excessively modern wall bracket in the shape of a nude female figure – just this side of actionable – supported a light fitting.

Constable Crosby's eyes bulged and his lips started to move.

'Over there,' continued Murton, 'my grandmother had "There's No Place Like Home" worked in embroidery.'

'Did she?'

'Set tastefully in a ring of roses.'

Inspector Sloan, whose own hobby was growing roses – rather than growing girls – said, 'That must have been very nice, sir.'

'Pure Victoriana, of course.'

'Naturally, sir.' He coughed. 'This *is* your home, I take it?'

'Well, now, Inspector, that's a good question.' William Murton's eyes danced mischievously. 'It's like this. By virtue of long residence I'm a protected tenant here . . .'

That, decided Sloan privately, must have caused a certain amount of chagrin in some quarters.

'. . . so,' went on Murton, 'it would be downright foolish of me to leave, wouldn't it?'

'I see what you mean, sir.'

'So I stay. After all,' gravely, 'my family have lived here a very long time.'

'Quite so.'

'And there's nothing wrong with being a cottager, you know. My father was a cottager.'

'So,' said Sloan impassively, 'you use this for a weekend cottage.'

'Got it in one, Inspector.'

'You come down every weekend?'

'Not quite . . .' tantalizingly, '. . . every weekend. Just – er – every now and then.'

'Why this particular one?'

Murton shrugged a pair of surprisingly broad shoulders. 'The spirit moved me. I didn't come down to do poor Ossy in, if that's what you mean.'

'You knew him, of course?'

'Oh, yes. We were all brought up together as children, you know. Like puppies. Miles' parents were abroad a lot and mine couldn't provide for me properly,' he grimaced, 'so . . .'

'So,' concluded Sloan for him, 'you had the worst of both worlds.'

Murton looked at him curiously. 'That's right, Inspector. I was brought up half a gentleman. You think as children that the world's an equal place. It's later when you realize that Henry gets the lot.'

'Disturbing,' agreed Sloan.

'Especially when you're older than he is and you can see his father had the lot, too. And all your father had was this.'

'Quite so, sir.'

'That's what's made me into a sponger.'

'A sponger?'

'A sponger, Inspector, that's what I said. I don't earn my keep like Cousin Gertrude cleaning chandeliers for dear life and I don't stay on the fringes like Laura, hoping for pickings . . .'

'I see, sir.'

'And I don't stand around praying for miracles like that efficient ass, Charles Purvis. I'm a plain hanger-on.'

'I see, sir. And for the rest of the time you do what?'

'This and that,' he said easily.

Sloan could find the proper answer by picking up the telephone. He said instead, 'Now, as to Friday . . .'

William Murton hadn't a great deal to tell him about Friday.

Yes, he had originally intended to come only for the weekend.

Yes, he had come down on Friday afternoon.

By train.

About half-past five.

He had spent Friday evening at the cottage.

Alone.

Saturday he had stayed in bed until tea time and the evening he had spent in the Ornum Arms.

At least twenty people would confirm this, including Ebeneezer Lambert down the road.

If the Inspector should by any remote chance happen to see old Lambert he might tell him that he had lost his bet and owed him, William Murton, Esquire, a fiver.

And not to forget the esquire. We might not all be earls but there was no law yet against us all being esquires, was there?

And if the Inspector wanted to know who he thought had done it . . .

The great-aunts.

'In fact, sir,' said Crosby, as he drove Inspector Sloan from the cottage up to the house, 'we aren't short of suspects, are we?'

'No.'

'That chap ran right through the lot of us. Did you notice, sir?'

'He didn't mention Dillow,' said Sloan, 'and he didn't mention Mr Ames.'

'The Vicar?' said Crosby. 'I hadn't thought of him.'

'You should think of everyone, Constable. That's what you're here for.'

'Yes, sir.'

'He came to the house at about the right time on Friday afternoon,' said Sloan. 'He told us so.'

'Yes, sir.'

'And he knows about armour.'

'He doesn't look like a murderer.'

'Neither did Crippen.'

This profound observation kept Constable Crosby quiet until they reached Ornum House.

Dillow was at hand as ever. Ubiquitous, that was the word for him. Whenever someone came in or went out Dillow seemed to be there.

'The Vicar is in the Great Hall, gentlemen, waiting your arrival, Mr Purvis is in the morning room interviewing the Press . . .'

'The Queen is in the parlour eating bread and honey,' muttered the incorrigible Crosby, irritated by all this formality.

'Very good, sir,' murmured the butler smoothly, not at all put out.

Sloan reflected that an irrepressible police constable must be child's play to a man who had worked for that eccentric million-aire, Baggles.

'And, sir, Edith, the housemaid – you indicated you wished to speak to her – is available whenever you wish.'

'Now,' suggested Sloan. 'I just wanted to know when she last went into the library.'

Dillow produced Edith immediately. She was willing and cheerful but not bright.

'Yeth, sir,' (she was slightly adenoidal too) 'Saturday morning, sir. There was nobody there then.'

This was clarified by Sloan into 'No body'.

'That's right,' agreed Edith. 'Nobody at all.'

'Did you go right into the library – to the very far end?'

'Oh, yeth, sir.'

'Past the furthest bay?'

'Yeth, sir. Because of the General.'

'The General?'

'Yeth, sir. He gets very dusty if you leave him over the day.'

'Ah, you mean the bust . . .'

Edith looked as if she hadn't liked to mention the word in front of three gentlemen. She nodded.

'And what time would that have been?'

'Nine o'clock, sir. After I cleared the breakfasts.'

'Thank you, Edith. That's all.'

Edith looked relieved and went. In the distance at the top of the great balustraded staircase they caught a glimpse of Cousin Gertrude tramping across the upper landing.

Mr Ames was waiting for them in the Great Hall. He looked older in broad daylight.

'We've just been checking a few facts,' said Sloan truthfully. 'The family and so forth.'

'One of the oldest in the county,' said the Vicar. 'Hereditary Beacon Keepers to the Crown for Calleshire since the reign of Queen Elizabeth the First . . .'

Sloan hadn't meant that sort of fact.

'She was afraid of the Spanish coming, you know, Inspector.'

'Really?'

'The old Norman tower above the keep has a flat roof.' The Vicar smiled a clerical smile. 'The Norman invasion, you remember, had been a successful one. A highly successful one.'

'Yes, sir.' Stolidly.

'A beacon fire lit there could be seen from the roof of Calle Castle which is some way inland. They in turn would light a beacon fire there and so on.'

'I see, sir, thank you.'

'And then there was James the Second.'

Sloan was not interested in James the Second.

'He,' said Mr Ames, 'was afraid of the Dutch. Now George the Third . . .'

Sloan had come about murder not history.

'He was worried about the French. Napoleon, you know.'

'I don't think the historical side concerns us, Vicar.' It was, after all, as Superintendent Leeyes had said, the twentieth century.

'And then,' said Mr Ames, unheeding, 'there was 1940 and the Germans. We had a really big beacon all ready for firing then. Bert Hackle's father – old Hackle – he used to keep look-out . . .'

'Quite so, sir. Now if we might come back to the more immediate past – like Friday.'

With police-like patience he set about taking the Vicar through all the details of his abortive visit to the house following Osborne Meredith's message. Mr Ames obediently retailed his story for the second time.

He had had a message, he had come up to the house, he had not seen Meredith in the muniments room or anywhere else . . .

'The document chests,' said Sloan suddenly. 'Were they shut or open?'

The Vicar screwed up his eyes the better to remember. 'Open,' he said eventually. 'That's what made me think Meredith would still be about somewhere.'

'Did you see anyone else while you were here?'

'Dillow – he said he thought Meredith had gone home as he wasn't about – and Miss Cremond – Miss Gertrude Cremond, you know. She was cleaning the chandelier in here.'

They all looked upwards.

'A very lovely piece,' said Mr Ames. 'French crystal.'

'Was she alone?' asked Sloan.

The Vicar nodded. 'Miss Cremond,' he murmured diplomatically, 'is in total charge of all the Ornum china and glass. Lady Eleanor helps her with the flowers but Miss Cremond handles all the rest herself.'

'I see, sir.'

'It was all still down on the table when I saw her,' said Mr Ames. 'Hundreds of pieces.'

'A day's work,' agreed Sloan, turning to go.

As he did so he stopped in his tracks.

Sloan would not have described himself as a sensitive man. If he thought of himself at all it was as an ordinary policeman – warts and all. But at that moment – as he stood with Crosby and the Vicar in the Great Hall – the atavistic sensation came to him that they were being watched.

It was a very primitive feeling.

The hairs on the back of his neck erected themselves and an involuntary little shiver passed down his spine. Primeval reactions that were established long before man built himself his first shelter – let alone medieval castles.

Sloan let his gaze run casually round the Great Hall. It was not long before he spotted the peephole up near the roof in the dim corner behind and beyond the Minstrels' Gallery. He drifted slowly towards the door under the gallery and so out of sight of the peephole.

Once there, he changed to a swift run, going up the vast staircase as quickly as he could, his sense of direction working full blast.

He kept right at the top of the stair and chose the furthest door. He flung it open on a small panelled room.

There was nobody there.

But in the opposite wall, low down, was a little window giving not to the out of doors but to another room. He stepped across and peered through it.

He was looking down at the Great Hall. From where he stood

he could see the Vicar still talking to Crosby. The Constable was standing listening in an attitude of patient resignation. Sloan straightened up again, and stepped back into the corridor.

And somewhere not very far away he heard a door closing gently.

12

Charles Purvis was being put through his paces by the Press and he was not enjoying it.

For one thing, though, he was deeply thankful. With the help of Dillow he had at least managed to bottle up all the reporters in the same room. The thought of a stray one happening upon Lady Alice was too terrible to contemplate.

'Gentlemen,' he began, 'I can give you very little information . . .'

'Can we see the Earl?' asked one of them immediately, mentioning a newspaper which Purvis had only seen wrapped round fish.

'The Earl is Not At Home.'

'You mean he isn't here?'

'No,' said Purvis, 'just Not At Home.'

'You mean he won't see us?'

'His Lordship is not available,' insisted Charles Purvis. He had a fleeting vision of a sub-heading 'No Comment from Earl of Ornum'. (What the reporters wrote, in fact, was 'Earl Silent'.)

'Do we understand, steward, that the body was in the armour all day on Saturday and Sunday while visitors were being shown round?'

'I believe so,' said Purvis unhappily as the reporters scribbled away. ('Little did those who paid their half-crowns at the weekend know that . . .')

'How do you spell "archivist"?' said somebody.

The man from the oldest established newspaper told him.

'When are you open again?' asked another man.

'Wednesday,' said Purvis cautiously, 'I think.'

'That your usual day?'

'Yes.' (They wrote 'Business as Usual, says Steward'.)

'That means you won't actually have closed at all?'

'Yes.' ('We Never Close, says Earl's Steward.')

'I reckon this is the first "Stately Home Murder", boys.'

Purvis winced and the others nodded.

'This Earl of yours . . .' The voice came from a man at the back.

'Yes?'

'He's not much of a talker, is he?'

'A talker?' Charles Purvis was discovering the hard way that stone-walling is an under-rated art – not only on the cricket pitch but everywhere else too.

'That's right,' said the reporter, who had been doing his homework. 'He's been a member of the House of Lords for thirty years . . .'

'Yes?'

'I've looked him up.'

'Oh?'

'He's only spoken twice. On red deer.'

'That's right.'

'Both times.'

'It's his subject.'

There were hoots of merry laughter at this.

Purvis flushed. 'He has his own herd, you know, and . . .'

But the reporters were already on to their next questions.

'Our Art man,' said a crime reporter, 'our Old Art man, this is, tells me you've got a Holbein here.'

'That's right,' confirmed Purvis.

'What's the Earl doing taking in washing when he's got a Holbein?'

Purvis hadn't expected the interview to go like this. 'It's of a member of the family,' he retorted, stung. 'That's why.'

('Steward says Holbein would have been sold long ago but for sentimental reasons' they wrote.)

'Our New Art man,' said another newspaper man, 'says the Earl's nephew has just had an exhibition. Murton's the name. William Murton.'

'Oh?' This was news to Charles Purvis. 'I didn't know that.'

'One of the smaller galleries,' said the man, 'but quite well written up.'

'The other nephew,' a bald man informed them gratuitously, 'Miles Cremond, is with the Pedes Shipping Line.'

'Is he now?'

'And our City Editor,' he went on, 'says they're pretty ropey these days.'

'Now is the time for all share-holding rats to leave the sinking ship?' suggested an amiably cynical man near the door.

'Pretty well,' admitted the bald chap.

'Has he got any other good tips, Curly?'

'Buy the rag and see,' suggested the bald man. 'Money well spent, they tell me.'

They were surprisingly well informed.

They had already sucked the reference books dry. They had taken in a visit to a gratified Mrs Pearl Fisher at Paradise Row, Luston, on their way to Ornum. (The whole street had ordered copies of tomorrow's papers.) They had attempted to suborn Edith, the housemaid, at the back door of Ornum House before coming round to the front, and they had got nowhere at all with Superintendent Leeyes – and all before breakfast, so to speak.

'The family,' said a man with a disillusioned face, whose paper specialized in what it was pleased to call 'human interest'. 'Can we have some pictures?'

'No,' said Purvis.

'They've got a son and a daughter, haven't they?'

'Yes.' Tightly.

'Some pictures would be nice. Family group and so forth.'

'No.'

'I think we've got one of Lady Eleanor on the files anyway.'

Purvis blanched.

'Some charity performance somewhere.'

Charles Purvis breathed again.

'She's not engaged?' suggested the reporter hopefully.

'No.'

'Nor opened a boutique or an antique shop or anything like that?'

'No.'

'No family secrets passed down from father to son on his twenty-first birthday?'

'No.'

'No secret rooms?'

'I'm afraid not.' Purvis was genuinely regretful. If there had been a secret room in Ornum House he would willingly have taken them to see it. Anything to divert their questioning.

'Sure?'

'The Rating people would have found it,' said the steward bitterly.

'The victim's sister,' said a young man with long hair and a red tie. 'What's happened to her?'

Purvis relaxed a little. 'We don't know. We think she's visiting friends but we don't know where.' He looked round the assembled company. 'That's really where we could do with your co-operation, gentlemen. She probably doesn't know about this terrible business' – out of the corner of his eye he saw the 'human interest' man writing rapidly – 'and the police hope that she will read about the death and get in touch with them.'

'Will do.'

Charles Purvis doubted very much if Miss Meredith ever read either the 'human interest' paper or the one with which the young man with the long hair and the red tie was associated but sooner or later she would hear . . .

To Purvis' distress the newspaper of which his Lordship had been a loyal reader all his life had also sent a reporter. He, too, had a question . . . It was like treachery.

'The weapon, Mr Purvis, can you tell us what it was?'

He shook his head. 'I understand the weapon has not yet been found.'

*

He was wrong.

The weapon had been found.

On the upstairs landing Inspector Sloan had met up with the team from the Forensic Laboratory. A taciturn pair of men who knew a bloodstain when they saw one. They had seen one on the spine of a book in the library and now they were looking at another.

They were all in the armoury. One suit of armour had gone – *the* suit of armour – and the gap stood out like a missing tooth. The armoury itself looked like a gigantic game of chess after a good opening move.

Detective Constable Crosby had begun by working from quite a different premiss – that one of the hundred and seventy weapons listed in the catalogue would be missing. So he and Mr Ames had been conducting a bizarre roll-call.

'One anelace.'

'Present.'

'One voulge.'

'Yes. A very early piece,' said the Vicar with satisfaction. 'Not many of them about.'

'A tschinke?'

'That's right. The tenth Earl brought that back with him from abroad. It's a sort of sporting gun.'

Crosby eyed it warily. If that was the sort of souvenir that came from foreign parts he would stay at home.

'He was an ambassador,' said the Vicar.

'I know.' Crosby moved his finger down the list and said cautiously, 'A pair of dolphins.'

'Both here. Lifting tackle, you know, for guns.'

Crosby didn't know. 'Three bastard swords,' he continued.

'All here.'

At the third attempt . . . 'A guardapolvo.'

'Yes.'

'A Lucerne hammer.'

'Yes.'

Crosby hesitated. 'A spontoon.'

'Yes.'

'A brandistock.' Crosby looked up from the list. 'What's that?'

'A weapon with a tubular shaft concealing a blade . . .'

Crosby lost interest.

The Vicar pointed. 'You can jerk the blade forward.'

'We call it a flick knife,' said Crosby laconically. 'Next. A godentag. What's that?'

'A club thickening towards the head,' said Mr Ames indicating it with his hand, 'and topped with an iron spike. Hullo, it's not hanging quite straight – someone must have . . .'

'Don't touch it,' shouted Crosby, dropping the list and making for the wall.

Mr Ames' hands fell back to his side but he went on looking.

So did the pair from the Forensic Laboratory – only they looked through a powerful pocket lens and they looked long and hard.

'Blood,' said the more senior of the two, 'and a couple of hairs.'

Inspector Sloan turned to the Vicar. 'What did you say it was called, sir?'

'A godentag,' said Mr Ames. 'Taken literally it means "good morning".'

Detective Constable Crosby caught the affirmative nod from the laboratory technician to Inspector Sloan and interpreted it correctly. 'If that's what did it, sir, shouldn't it be "good night"?'

Charles Purvis had been as good as his word. He came down to the armoury to tell Sloan that the four guides were waiting for him in the oriel room.

'They're all there except Hackle and he's working in the knot garden if you want to see him too.'

Inspector Sloan hesitated. A knot garden sounded like a *noh* play. 'Where's that?' he asked cautiously.

'Just this side of the belvedere,' said the steward, trying to be helpful. 'By the gazebo.'

'And the oriel room?' said Sloan, giving up. It was like learning a new language.

'I'll take you there,' said Purvis. He hadn't finished with the Press – he didn't suppose you ever finished with the Press – but he had done what he could.

The oriel room had been a felicitous choice on the part of Purvis. It was a room that was never shown to the public while still not being quite the same as the Private Apartments. Mrs Mompson, Miss Cleepe, Mrs Nutting and Mr Feathers were there and Dillow was plying them with coffee.

Pseudo-privilege for pseudo-guests.

The thin Miss Cleepe declined sugar, the tubby Mrs Nutting took two spoonfuls.

'I know I shouldn't,' she said, 'but I do like it.'

As usual, Mrs Mompson remained a trifle aloof. 'Poor little Miss Meredith,' she said with condescension. Mrs Mompson called other women 'little' irrespective of their size. 'I do feel so sorry for her . . .'

'I feel more sorry for Meredith myself,' said Mr Feathers practically. 'Not the sort of end I'd fancy.'

Mrs Nutting shivered. 'Nor me. We must help the Inspector all we can.'

It wasn't very much.

Sloan took them through the previous Saturday and Sunday – not so many people on the Saturday but then there never are – but Sunday was crowded. They wouldn't be surprised if Sunday had been a record. (It wouldn't stay that way for long if it had been, thought Sloan. Not after tomorrow's papers came out.)

Mr Feathers had noticed nothing out of the ordinary in the great hall. Miss Gertrude Cremond had been along to see the chandelier in daylight, and expressed herself pleased with it. It wouldn't need doing again for the season, otherwise all had been as usual.

Mrs Nutting reported that one small child had got under the four-poster while her back was turned but had been extricated (and spanked) without difficulty.

'Otherwise,' she said cheerfully, 'just as usual. Same sort of people. Same questions.'

Miss Cleepe, as angular as Mrs Nutting was curved, twisted her hands together. The long gallery had been much the same. The usual difficulty of parties made up of people who really cared about painting and those who neither knew nor cared.

'It's so trying if you sense that they're bored,' she said, 'but the Holbein always interests them.'

'After you've told them what it's worth,' said Mr Feathers brutally.

She sighed. 'That's so. They always take a second look then.' She put down her coffee cup. 'And of course they always ask about the ghost. Always.'

Mrs Mompson, who had for some time been trying to engineer an exchange of pictures between the long gallery and the drawing-room, said, 'That picture doesn't get the light it should in the long gallery.'

'It is rather dark,' agreed Miss Cleepe. 'It's such a long, narrow room, and the bulb in its own little light was broken. Dillow's getting another for me.'

'I've always said that over the fireplace in the drawing-room is where that picture should be,' declared Mrs Mompson. 'Where everyone could really see it properly.'

'I don't know about that, I'm sure,' said Miss Cleepe nervously. 'After all, too much light might be bad for the picture.'

'It's practically in the half dark in the long gallery where it is. Half way from each window and not very good windows at that.' Mrs Mompson had over the fireplace in the drawing-room at present an eighteenth-century portrayal of the goddess of plenty, Ceres, that she had long wanted to be rid of. The goddess had been depicted somewhat fulsomely and Mrs Mompson did not think the artist's conception of that bountiful creature quite nice.

'I think,' she went on, 'the Holbein would be seen to real advantage over my fireplace.'

Miss Cleepe flushed. To lose from her showing ground the most valuable item in the house and the ghost at one fell swoop was more than she could bear.

'Oh, dear!' she fluttered. 'Do you really? I should be very sorry to lose the Judge. Very sorry. I always feel he's a real interest to those to whom the other pictures mean nothing.'

Inspector Sloan made no move to stop them talking. The policeman's art was to listen and to watch. Not to do. At least not when witnesses were talking to each other, almost oblivious of an alien presence in their midst. Almost but not quite.

Mrs Mompson, who had no wish for an immediate ruling on the subject of the Holbein from Charles Purvis, said firmly, 'Nothing, I assure you, Inspector, out of the ordinary happened in the drawing-room while I was in charge.'

Sloan, who would have been surprised if it had, nodded.

'One young woman went so far as to finger the epergne,' she went on imperiously, 'but I soon put a stop to that.'

'Quite so, madam. Thank you all very . . .'

Miss Cleepe had not done.

In a voice which trembled slightly she said, 'I really don't think I could possibly manage the long gallery without the Holbein.'

Sloan was ringing back to base. Base wasn't very pleased at his news.

'Someone,' declared Sloan, 'has tried to get into the muniments room since we sealed it up yesterday.'

'They have, have they? What for?'

'I don't know, sir. I'd arranged for the county archivist to come over and start going through the records. When Crosby went up there with him he found someone had had a go at the lock.'

'There's something in there,' said Leeyes.

'Yes, sir.'

'And someone's still after it.'

'Yes, sir. They haven't got it though. The locks held.'

'Just as well,' grunted Leeyes. 'By the way, Sloan, I've just had the Ornums' lawyer here. He's on his way out to you now. Watch him.'

'Yes, sir.'

'One of those clever chaps,' said Leeyes resentfully. 'Said he was representing the Earl's interests. Representing them!' Leeyes snorted. 'Guarding them like a hawk, I'd say.'

Sloan was not surprised. People like the Ornums went straight to the top and got the very best. He said gloomily, 'I suppose the

Earl will be another of those who know the Chief Constable personally too . . .'

They were the bane of his existence, those sort of people, assuming that acquaintanceship was an absolution.

'Be your age, Sloan.'

'I beg your pardon, sir?'

'The Earl wouldn't be bothered with people like the Chief Constable.'

'Not be bothered with the Chief Constable?' echoed Sloan faintly.

'That's what I said. The Home Secretary, Sloan, was his fag at school, and the Attorney-General's his wife's third cousin, twice removed.'

'Oh, dear.'

'Exactly.' Sloan heard the Superintendent bring his hand down on his desk with a bang just as he did when he was standing in front of him. 'So if there's any arresting to be done . . .'

'Yes, sir.' Sloan took the unspoken point and tried to check on something else. 'The rules, sir, aren't they different for peers of the realm?'

'I don't know about the written ones, Sloan,' said Leeyes ominously, 'but the unwritten ones are.'

'Yes, sir.' Absently. He was thinking about the Tower of London. He and his wife, Margaret, had gone there on their honeymoon. Was it just a museum still or were there dark corners where extra-special prisoners lay?

'You could call it a case,' said Leeyes judicially, 'where a wrongful arrest isn't going to help the career of the police officer making it.'

'Quite so, sir.' He cleared his throat. 'I'm nowhere near that stage yet, sir, but we think we've found the murder weapon. A club called "good morning".'

'A club called "good morning",' said Leeyes heavily. 'You wouldn't by any chance be trying to take the mickey out of a police superintendent called Leeyes, would you, Sloan, because if you are . . .'

'No, sir.' Hastily. 'It's number forty-nine in the catalogue and its other name is a godentag. The forensic boys have found blood and hair on it but no fingerprints. Dr Dabbe hasn't seen it yet, of course, to confirm that . . .'

'That reminds me,' interrupted Leeyes. 'Dr Dabbe. He's been on the phone with his report.'

'Oh?'

'Those pathologists,' grumbled the Superintendent. 'They upset everything.'

'Why?'

'You said, Sloan, that the butler took Meredith his tea at four o'clock and collected the empty tray at five.'

'That's right, sir. He saw him at four but not at five. And Lady Eleanor saw him just before tea time.'

'Tea time, perhaps,' said Leeyes, 'but not tea.'

'Not tea?'

'Nothing had passed deceased's lips for three hours before death. Dr Dabbe says so. Killed on an empty stomach, in fact.'

'Somebody ate Meredith's tea,' said Sloan, turning back the pages of his notebook.

'Very likely, but not Meredith,' pointed out the Superintendent with finality. 'Dr Dabbe says so.'

13

'So somebody got him in between Dillow taking him his tea and him getting his teeth into it?' concluded Constable Crosby succinctly. He was still in the armoury though the Vicar and the laboratory people had gone.

'That's right.' There were more elegant ways of putting it but in essence Crosby was right. 'Though, after Meredith had made his celebrated discovery and telephoned the Vicarage in Ornum.'

'Do we know when that was, sir?'

'Mrs Ames thinks it must have been about half-past three.'

'Then we're getting nowhere fast,' Crosby said, disappointed, slinging his notebook down on the table that Dillow had provided for them in a corner of the armoury. (It was of inlaid walnut and quite unsuitable.)

'Oh?'

'William Murton was seen to get off the 5.27 p.m. Luston to Berebury slow train at Ornum Station on Friday afternoon and I still think he did it,' said Crosby all in one breath.

Sloan regarded his constable with interest. 'You do, do you? Why?'

'He's a painter for one thing . . .'

'That's not a crime. Yet.'

'What I mean, sir, is that he's a bit of an oddity . . .'

'Nor is that.'

'Suddenly he isn't short of money any more.'

'Meredith wasn't a rich man,' countered Sloan, 'and the connection with this case and money is – to say the least – obscure.' It would be there, of course – it nearly always was once you'd ruled out lust – but Sloan couldn't see where it lay.

'Yes, sir.'

'Did you arrange for him to be watched?'

'Yes, sir. PC Bloggs is tailing him.' He paused. 'London came through on the blower.'

'Well?'

Crosby sucked his lips. 'From what they can make out he's in dead trouble with a woman.'

The nearest Constable Crosby himself had ever come to being in trouble with a woman was being late off duty, thus missing the start of the big picture.

There was something almost paternal in Sloan's tone. 'If every man who was that, Crosby, committed a murder, we'd never get a rest day.'

Crosby played his last card. 'The Earl thinks he did it.'

'I know. It's the best circumstantial evidence we've got that the Earl didn't do it himself. Not that William Murton didn't.'

'The Earl?' echoed Crosby, shocked. 'You don't think he did it, do you, sir?'

'No, as it happens, I don't, but he's a suspect like everyone else.'

All people being equal but some being more equal than others. Especially earls.

It was a natural step from there to Lord Henry.

'That's another thing I've checked,' said Crosby, 'without any joy.'

'What is?'

'His young Lordship's car. There is some blood down between the fan blade and the radiator. I've told those two vampire chaps . . .'

'Laboratory technicians.' Mildly.

'Them. They're going to have a look when they've finished with the "good morning".'

'He could have put it there,' pointed out Sloan.

'Yes, sir,' briefly. Crosby flicked back the pages of his notebook.

'There are no fingerprints on the "good morning" by the way . . .'

'I hadn't expected there would be.'

'And Mrs Morley, the housekeeper, said she bandaged Lord Henry's hand for him after he cut it. Friday, it was. In the morning.'

'I see.'

'She saw the wound.'

'Doubting Thomases,' said Sloan bitterly, his mind darting back to his Sunday School days. 'That's what we should be called, isn't it? Not coppers.'

'I couldn't say, I'm sure, sir,' murmured Crosby. 'Anyway, Mrs Morley said it was quite a nasty cut. He couldn't have held a cricket bat.'

'Or a godentag?'

'Not according to Mrs Morley, he couldn't. She wanted him to have the doctor. Right across the palm, it was, and the index finger.'

'And he got it from a motor car, not from squeezing a dead man into a metal suit of armour?'

Crosby's case rested on Mrs Morley and he said so.

'I see,' said Sloan. 'So you think Lord Henry is out as a suspect but William Murton still in?'

'Except that he got off the 5.27 all right,' repeated Crosby, 'because the station master saw him himself.'

'And have you checked that he didn't nip up the line and get on at the station before?'

'Not yet,' replied Crosby in a nicely shaded manner which implied he had been about to do so.

'I should,' advised Sloan. 'What size shoes does he take?'

Crosby stared. 'I didn't notice, sir.'

'I did. A nine, at least.'

'He's a big chap,' agreed Crosby cautiously.

'Too big for a lady's shoe, size six and a half, anyway,' observed Sloan, turning back the pages of his own notebook. 'And the Countess and Lady Eleanor both take a five.'

'Handy, that.'

'Handy?'

'They can share,' said Crosby. 'Like my sister does.'

'Crosby, people like this do not share shoes.'

'No, sir.'

'Assuming,' severely, 'that the person who left a heel mark in the muniments room did so inadvertently, and I think they did . . .'

'Yes . . .'

'That means Miss Gertrude Cremond, Mrs Laura Cremond or Mrs Morley went in there and turned everything upside-down.'

'Unless it was an outside job, sir.'

'Crosby,' Sloan controlled a sigh. 'We both know this wasn't an outside job.'

'Yes, sir.'

'So one of the three went in there . . .'

'After Meredith was killed, sir, or before?'

'Well, he's hardly likely to have stood by and watched, is he now?'

'No, sir.' Crosby scratched his forehead. 'Miss Gertrude Cremond's big enough to have dotted a small man who was sitting down at the time for all that she's not young.'

'True.'

'Mrs Laura Cremond isn't.'

'No. Neither was Lady Macbeth.'

'Pardon, sir?'

'Lady Macbeth. Another small woman. She got someone killed.'

'Secondhand, you mean, sir.'

'Precisely.'

'You think she might have egged on the Honourable Miles, sir?'

'Goaded would be a better word, Crosby.'

'Yes, sir.' He paused and said carefully, 'I don't think he would have thought of it on his own.'

'No.'

'Mrs Morley would have had to have got Dillow to do it for her,' went on Crosby. 'For all that she's got biggish feet for a woman she doesn't look the club-swinging sort.'

'There is another possibility . . .'

Crosby sighed. He wasn't good at assimilating more than two or three at a time.

Inspector Sloan tapped his notebook. 'That the attack on the muniments had nothing to do with the murder of Meredith.'

Crosby had not thought of this. 'Coincidence?' he said doubtfully.

'Not exactly. Just two things happening on the same day.'

'Matching up with the two separate discoveries, sir?' suggested Crosby brightly. 'The one about the earldom . . .'

'Which may or may not be true . . .'

'And the one Meredith made on the Friday afternoon . . .'

'Which we know nothing whatsoever about . . .'

'That he tried to get in touch with the Vicar to tell him?'

'Well done, Constable. Now, can you tell me the only significant thing that we know about Friday afternoon so far?'

'No,' said Crosby promptly. 'Nothing else happened apart from Meredith finding out something . . .'

'Let's put it another way,' said Sloan patiently. At this rate they'd have to call in outside help, whether Superintendent Leeyes wanted it or not. 'What change in routine was there on Friday afternoon that we already know about?'

Crosby gave a short laugh. 'The only thing that was different that we know about for certain sure . . .'

'Yes?'

'The two old birds upstairs . . .'

'Lady Alice and Lady Maude.' There were moments when he would have welcomed more sophisticated assistance too. This was one of them.

'Lady Alice and Lady Maude,' Crosby tacitly accepted the emendation. 'They didn't ask the deceased to tea like they usually did on Fridays . . .'

'Exactly, Crosby.'

'You mean that is important, sir?'

'I mean,' grimly, 'that that's the only positive pointer we have so far. That and the fact that William Murton has been in Ornum for all of forty-eight hours without asking his uncle for money which I understand practically constitutes a record.'

*

'That is unusual,' admitted the Earl of Ornum. He was in the Private Apartments regaling a tall thin individual with something from a decanter and thin biscuits. 'I think it is – er – pretty well accepted that William only retreats to Ornum when his – er – other commitments become very pressing.'

The Earl had introduced Sloan and Crosby to the bleak-looking man. He was, it transpired, Mr Adrian Cossington, the senior partner in the old established law firm of Oaten, Oaten and Cossington, and if his ascetic appearance was anything to go by, he had long ago done with all human desire and feeling. His pleasures, if any, looked as if they were confined to wrestling with 'nice' legal points, or perhaps advising against the indulgences proposed by his clients.

He was obviously opposed to the Earl of Ornum saying anything to anyone at all at this stage – but especially to Inspector Sloan.

'Don't be silly, Cossington,' said the Earl testily, showing more courage in dealing with the solicitor than Sloan would have dared to have done. 'The fellow's got to find out who killed Meredith, hasn't he?'

'Certainly, my lord, nevertheless your own responsibilities in the matter are confined to . . .'

'Dammit, man, there's such a thing as justice.' He turned. 'Isn't there, Inspector?'

'I think so,' said Sloan cautiously. Asked point-blank like that he wasn't sure that there was.

'In your own interest, my lord,' protested Cossington.

'We are not considering my interest, Cossington, we are considering law and order.'

That was different.

Sloan, who wasn't sure about justice, was absolutely certain about law and order. You'd got to have it or you were barbarian.

The Earl was taking his stance. 'I can't have my own librarian and archivist killed in m'own house, Cossington, now, can I?'

That was what rankled, thought Sloan irrelevantly. From the Earl's point of view it was 'touch my servant and you touch me'. That was how it would have been in the old days. The first Earl would have had his own following, half servant, half army.

Vassals, obedient to him unto death. And the Earl would have been obedient to the King, would have taken an oath of obedience at the King's coronation.

Every Earl at every Coronation.

Even now.

It had a name, that oath. He would remember it in a moment. An odd word . . . fealty, that was it.

The solicitor had started to explain to the Earl that narrow line between obstructing the police in the execution of their duty and those tenuous circumstances in which no man need offer evidence that might incriminate himself.

Sloan wasn't listening. He was looking across at the thirteenth Earl of Ornum with new eyes. He, Charles Dennis Sloan, Detective Inspector in Her Majesty's County Constabulary of Calleshire, was the natural heir and successor to the Earl in this matter of law and order. Where once the Earl had kept unruly villeins obedient so now did he. Sloan, too, had taken an oath of allegiance. And he hadn't realized until now how ancient was his duty . . .

The Earl of Ornum hadn't been listening to the solicitor either. 'Purvis tells me you've asked the county archivist in, Inspector . . .'

'Yes, my lord. With your permission . . .'

His Lordship nodded. 'Meredith wouldn't have liked it but that can't be helped. Not now. Possessive lot, these archivists. Always wanting to build their own empires. Never prepared to lend a hand with anyone else's.'

'Was there anything that anyone hankered after, then?' asked Sloan suddenly. It was something he should have asked before.

The Earl thought for a moment. 'Some items are always being asked for on loan.'

'Which are they, my lord?'

The Earl waved a hand. 'Some very early Court stuff which seems to have survived. Records of Oyer, Terminer and Assize. That sort of thing.'

One lecture, that's all they'd had when Sloan joined the Force, on the history of the legal system in England. And he hadn't listened anyway.

'The old Courts of Gaol Delivery, you know,' said his Lordship. 'Going back a good bit now, of course. Not many of them about these days. Things have changed since then.' A faint gleam of humour crept into the melancholy countenance. 'Now we have you, Inspector, and Cossington over there instead of just me.'

Justice instead of rough justice?

Sloan wasn't sure. He cleared his throat and came back to the point. 'These records, my lord, are they worth stealing?'

'Nothing is worth stealing, Inspector.'

Sloan flushed. 'I'm sorry, my lord. I meant . . .'

The whole atmosphere in the Private Apartments had changed subtly. 'They have a value, Inspector . . .'

'Yes, my lord, I'm sure . . .'

'But too high a value to have a price.'

'I see, my lord.'

'No, Inspector, you do not see. The county archivist would like them for his empire. He sees himself as the true representative of the common man – to whom he probably thinks they should belong anyway. The ratepayer incarnate.'

'Quite so . . .'

'What was it that French fellow said . . .'

'I couldn't say, my lord . . .'

'Property is theft.'

It was not a police point of view. Nor an English one, if it came to that. Property was respectable in the police world. Men without property were like gamblers without a stake, a rootless, drifting menace. Men with nothing to lose.

'The Inns of Court would like them for their empire,' went on his Lordship, 'because they see themselves as a profession and they think a profession can have a body. It can't. It's only as good as the worst of its members.'

'Yes, my lord.' As far as the aristocracy was concerned professions were doubtless new jumped-up callings.

'One of the universities wants them for their empire because they think they represent the intellectual man and that that is sufficient reason. It isn't.'

'No, my lord.'

'The intellectual man can be swayed by intellect . . .'

'Yes, my lord.' Sloan had thought that was the whole idea.

'Dangerous, that.'

'Very possibly, my lord.' Was that the aristocrat pronouncing on the meritocrat?

'Brains,' pronounced his Lordship oracularly, 'are all very well in their way. That right, Cossington?'

Mr Adrian Cossington was far too clever to admit to having any at all and merely murmured, 'A point of view, my lord, a point of view.'

In a moment, thought Sloan, he's going to say 'my country, right or wrong'.

But he didn't.

Instead the Earl said, 'That's when you get political arithmetic creeping in, Inspector.'

'Do you, my lord?' Sloan didn't know about political arithmetic but he did know that the Earl was trying to convey a philosophy to him, a philosophy which did not encompass murder.

'The greatest good of the greatest number.'

'I see, sir.' Wasn't that known as 'the common weal', or was that something different?

'And, Inspector, because they are of historical value I may not sell them to the highest bidder.'

'No, my lord?'

'My country which bleeds me white does not allow me the freedom of the market place.'

Sloan was more aware now of Cossington stirring in the background.

'All I may do, Inspector, is to retrench against a taxation system whose only aim is to deprive me of my inheritance.'

'Those Court records,' said Sloan, policeman not politician, 'would they have been in the muniments chests?'

'In the ordinary way,' agreed the Earl.

'But not on Friday?' Sloan's view of Ornum was blinkered to Friday.

The Earl shook his head. 'They've been on loan to the Great-orex Library since the beginning of June.'

'Who knew all this?'

'Anyone who cared to read the papers,' said his Lordship blandly.

'Cor,' said Constable Crosby expressively as they left the Private Apartments, 'he's agin the government if you like.'

Inspector Sloan's mind was elsewhere. He was wondering if hounds felt the same sense of disappointment as he did now when they had been following a scent which turned out to be false. For a moment he had thought he had been on to something.

Crosby waved a hand. 'And he calls this being bled white.'

'All things are relative, Crosby.'

Just how relative, though, was all this to a handful of police constables getting a few shillings' palm oil from a greedy garage proprietor every now and then?

'I'd like to have his sort of money all the same,' persisted Crosby.

'No, you wouldn't.' The mental dichotomy between this investigation and the other was almost too much. They were at the extreme opposite ends of the scale.

But it was the same scale.

He knew that.

And so did Superintendent Leeyes.

'Try me,' said the Constable cheerfully, 'that's all I ask, sir.'

Sloan looked across at Crosby, trying to see in him the lineal descendant of those early Earls of Ornum. Crosby suppressing tearaways on motorcycles or calming over-excited yobbos on a Saturday night or pounding the beat mid-week, but that image, too, had faded now.

'I want to see Lady Alice again,' he said abruptly.

As before Lady Maude opened the door and led the way to her sister.

'Just one more question, your ladyship,' he began.

The lorgnette hovered above the Cremond beak again. 'Well?'

'Who all knew you hadn't invited Mr Meredith to tea on Friday?'

From where Sloan was standing the lorgnette magnified the beady eyes.

'Just,' said her Ladyship balefully, 'Mr Meredith.'

14

Miles Cremond looked as if he could have eaten any number of extra teas at any time. His overweight was of the solid, long-standing variety. He was very willing to talk to Inspector Sloan and Constable Crosby. He didn't often get an audience who hung on his every word like they did.

'Came down for the cricket,' said Miles, sounding faintly aggrieved. 'Not for all this business. Always come for this match. 'Stradition.'

Sloan listened carefully. What he was listening for was a clue as to why the murder had happened exactly when it did.

'I mean to say,' Miles went on, 'the poor old chap never did anyone any harm, did he?'

'Not that I know of, sir.' Sloan went on to establish that Thursday was the first time Miles and Laura had heard about the archivist's doubts about the earldom.

'A lot of nonsense, I'm sure, Inspector,' said Miles warmly. 'Course Uncle Harry's the right chap. It stands to reason . . .'

Sloan didn't know if primogeniture was reason.

'The rest's history, isn't it?' said Miles.

'I couldn't say, sir, I'm sure.'

'A lot of families chop and change in the succession, I know, but we've been luckier than most.'

'Really, sir?'

'Because of this thing about battles, what?'

'What thing?'

'Never getting there,' said Miles. 'Whenever there's been a war the Cremonds always seem to have been either too old or too young to fight, what?'

'The General . . .' said Sloan suddenly, remembering the bust in the library.

'That's right. Him, too. I think one of them got to Blenheim but his gout held him back from the actual fighting, what?'

'Quite so, sir.' Where Sloan came from the word 'what' was a simple interrogative. This man used it like a full stop. 'Now, about Friday, sir . . .'

'Yes?'

'Where were you at the material . . . at tea time on Friday?'

'Had a quick cup with the others.'

'The others?'

'Uncle Harry, Aunt Millicent, Henry and Eleanor, Cousin Gertrude and m'wife. I didn't stay with them more than five minutes. I wanted to get out of doors and Cousin Gertrude wanted to get back to her chandelier so we went.'

'What sort of time would this have been, sir?'

He frowned. 'I must have been heading for the ha-ha by ten past four.'

'I beg your pardon, sir?'

'The ha-ha.'

'That's what I thought you said.' Sloan tried it out for himself. Tentatively. 'The ha-ha?'

'That's right, Inspector.'

'And what,' cautiously, 'did you do when you got there?'

'Walked round it.'

'I see, sir.' It was like one of those radio parlour games where everyone else knew the object. He suppressed an urge to say: Can you eat it? Instead he murmured, 'Did you see anyone while you were there?'

Miles Cremond frowned again. 'Purvis. He was talking to Bert Hackle by the orangery.'

Sloan sighed. It was altogether too simple to suppose that you kept oranges there. 'Anyone else?'

'No, Inspector.'

'And when did you get back?'

'Late.'

'Late? Late for what?'

'Dinner, Inspector. I'd hardly left myself time to change. M'wife was waiting for me and we went down together a bit late.'

'And you were walking all the time, sir?'

'Yes, Inspector.'

'Round the ha-ha?'

'Yes.'

'Very funny,' said Crosby not quite inaudibly enough.

'What's that?' Miles Cremond jerked forward.

'Nothing, sir,' interposed Sloan smoothly. 'Now, was there anything else you can tell us about Friday?'

But the Honourable Miles Cremond couldn't think of anything out of the ordinary that had happened on Friday or any other day for that matter.

The whole business was a complete mystery to him, what?

So it was too, apparently, to his wife Laura.

She did, however, think any discoveries of Osborne Meredith's about the earldom were perfectly absurd.

'Perfectly absurd,' she repeated for good measure.

'You didn't take them seriously, you mean, madam?'

'I didn't, Inspector.'

'It seems,' said Sloan mildly, 'as if someone did.'

There was no denying that someone – someone wearing a woman's shoe, size six and a half – had taken them seriously enough to have a real go at disturbing the muniments.

He said so.

'But,' protested Laura, 'but you couldn't take all this away and give it to someone else.' She waved a hand in a comprehensive gesture which included house, park, and – somehow – earldom.

'I couldn't,' agreed Sloan. 'There would have to be a successful claimant through the Law Courts.'

'But,' she wailed, 'we don't even know who the claimant would be . . .'

'No?' Sloan would have to try to work out the significance of that later. 'Mr Meredith would presumably have known.'

It seemed Laura Cremond had not thought of this.

'He might,' suggested Sloan, 'have been the only person who did know . . .'

She lifted her head sharply at this. There was nothing Cremond about her at all, noted Sloan. Just the touch of fast-fading handsomeness and a good hairdresser.

'You mean,' she ventured cautiously, 'that now he's dead we may never know?'

'I couldn't say, madam, at this stage. He may have left a written note.'

'No.' Quickly.

Too quickly.

'No, madam?'

'I mean,' she flushed, 'not that anyone knew about.'

'He might have communicated the result of his researches to someone outside the family.' Sloan's eyes drifted downwards in the direction of her shoes. He said austerely, 'Tell me again about Friday afternoon, madam, please.'

She was beginning to look flustered. 'There's nothing to tell, Inspector. I went to my room after tea – there wasn't anything else to do really. Cousin Gertrude had gone off to finish her chandelier, Uncle Harry always has a little sleep just about then and my husband had gone for a walk . . .'

'Lord Henry and Lady Eleanor?'

'They went down to Ornum village to see their old nanny – she's not been well.'

'And the Countess?' It was like a roll call.

'Aunt Millicent?' Laura Cremond said waspishly. 'You can't really have a conversation with Aunt Millicent.'

'No.' Sloan supposed you couldn't. Any more than you could talk to a butterfly. He murmured, 'I see, madam. So you went to your room?'

'That's right, Inspector.'

'And stayed there?'

'Yes, Inspector.'

Sloan looked down at her for a long moment and then said

soberly, 'I think you have had a lucky escape, madam. A very lucky escape indeed.'

Talking to Lady Eleanor Cremond was a refreshing change. Sloan could quite understand why Charles Purvis was smitten.

She was all that a good witness should be.

Simple, direct, sure without being categoric.

'I saw Ossy just before four o'clock,' she repeated.

'Alive and well?'

'Very well, Inspector, if you know what I mean. Almost excited.'

'About what?'

'He didn't tell me. We just chatted for a moment or two, then I took a book and went away.' She paused. 'He was a real enthusiast, you know . . .'

'Yes.' That hadn't saved him. Almost the reverse, you might say. He watched her closely. 'His tea?'

'No, I didn't stay for that. I asked him to join us as he wasn't going up to the great-aunts but he said he had something he wanted to do and he was expecting Mr Ames any minute.'

Tea time on Friday had suddenly become immensely important.

Lady Eleanor, though, was thinking about luncheon today.

'You must be famished,' she said, looking at her watch. 'I'll get Dillow to bring you something. Where will you be?'

'Thank you, that would be kind, your ladyship. The armoury . . .'

'You don't want to eat there, Inspector.' She thought for a moment. 'I know the very place. The gun room.'

The gun room it was. As appropriate a murder headquarters as anyone could meet.

'They've got weapons on the brain here, that's their trouble,' grumbled Crosby, looking round the small room which was literally lined with guns. 'Look at 'em. I should have thought they'd have got enough downstairs without this little lot.'

'With one notable exception,' Sloan reminded him, 'those downstairs are ornamental. These are for use.'

The guns showed every sign of having as much loving care expended on them as did the china.

'Those deer that the Earl's so keen about,' said Crosby.

'Yes?'

'Does he shoot them?'

'He breeds them first,' said Sloan.

'Then he shoots them?'

'I expect so.'

Crosby scratched his forehead. 'Funny lot, the aristocracy, sir, aren't they?'

'Government by the best citizens, constable, that's what it means.' Sloan took out his pen and got back to business. 'It's one weapon on one brain that's our trouble, you know.'

Dillow brought them welcome beer and sandwiches, and was word perfect about what he'd said before.

'No, sir, I was not aware until I took tea to their Ladyships upstairs that Mr Meredith was not taking tea with them as usual on Fridays.'

'What time would that have been?' Sloan discovered there was one exception to the rule that policemen called all other men 'sir'. That was when the other chap got it in first.

'About half-past three, sir. They like it early on account of their taking a short nap after luncheon.'

'Thank you, Dillow.'

The phrase constituted dismissal to a butler and Dillow left them.

They went on working while they ate. Inspector Sloan turned over a fresh sheet in his notebook. Outside the window a peacock shrilled harshly.

'Why doesn't he shoot them instead?' muttered Crosby indistinctly.

'They're another sort of ornament, that's why.'

'Give me the gryphons any day.' Crosby took another sandwich. 'At least they don't make a noise.'

Sloan stared at the blank page in front of him. 'Now then, how far have we got?'

'Nowhere,' said Crosby.

'We know who the victim is,' said Sloan patiently. That was a head start on some of the cases he'd been on. 'And we know where we think he was killed.'

'Sitting down at the table at the far end of the library,' agreed Crosby. 'Confirmed as probable by the forensic people.'

'How nearly do we know when?' The inductive method, that's what this was called. Crosby didn't seem much good at the deductive sort.

'After Lady Eleanor and Dillow saw him about four o'clock.'

'But before he'd had time to eat his tea.'

'Unless they're both lying, sir,' said Crosby assiduously.

'True.'

'We don't know why he was killed.' Crosby was making good headway with the sandwiches.

'Half-why,' said Sloan, taking one himself while they were still there to take. 'He'd found out something somebody didn't want him to know. Mrs Ames confirms the telephone call, by the way, but you must check on the Vicar's movements before five thirty.'

'I have,' said Crosby unexpectedly. 'I had a word with the postmistress. She knows everything. He was in the village until just before half-past five. She saw him going in and out of houses.'

Sloan nodded. 'So we know when – within limits.'

'But we don't really know why, sir, do we?' Pessimistically.

'We know where.'

'But we don't know who.' Crosby took the last sandwich. 'These are jolly good, sir, aren't they?'

'They were,' said Sloan sarcastically. He was wasting his time.

'We know who it wasn't though, sir, don't we?' mumbled Crosby, undeterred by a mouthful of sandwich.

'Oh?'

'It wasn't the Earl and Countess because they were together in the drawing-room from tea time onwards.'

'There might have been collusion between them. They're husband and wife, remember . . .'

Crosby frowned. 'I shouldn't care to collude – colluse – what you said, sir – with the Countess myself. Too risky. Anyway, their son and daughter didn't leave them until about twenty past four and I bet old Meredith would have got his teeth into his tea by then if he'd been alive to do it.'

'Like you fell upon your lunch just now?'

'Well, sir, he wouldn't have just sat looking at it, would he?'

'I agree it's unlikely.'

'And if the Hon. Miles is speaking the truth . . .'

'If . . .'

'Purvis and Hackle were together completely outside the house.'

'That leaves . . .' Sloan started to write.

'Cousin Gertrude, who was on the loose.'

That was one way of putting it.

'Miles himself,' said Crosby. 'He could have seen the two others from a window.'

Sloan nodded. 'Make a note to ask them if they saw him.'

'William Murton, who may or who may not have been in Ornum.'

'And Dillow,' said Sloan.

'Four suspects,' concluded Crosby, recapping. 'Cousin Gertrude, Miles, William and Dillow.'

'While we're reconstructing the crime,' said Sloan, 'let's go on with what happened after.'

'After, sir?'

'It can't have escaped your notice, Crosby, that the body wasn't found in the library.'

'No, sir.'

'Well, then . . .'

'Somebody removed it from the library.'

'Well done. The murderer, would you think? Or did someone come along and tidy it away just to be helpful?'

'Unlikely, that, sir.'

'Of course it's unlikely,' snapped Sloan. Sarcasm was a real boomerang of a weapon. He should have remembered that. He went on more peaceably: 'The murderer moved it to the armoury . . .'

'Yes, sir, but they didn't put it straight into the armour, did they, because of rigor mortis. The doctor said so.'

Sloan tapped his notebook. 'Now I wonder when he did that . . .'

'Dead of night?' suggested Crosby brightly.

'Leaving the body from four o'clock onwards in the library.'

'Risky,' agreed Crosby.

'But not desperately risky. They don't strike one as great readers here. Crosby . . .'

Crosby was engaged in draining the beer bottle to the very last drop. 'Sir?'

'Think.'

'Yes, sir.'

'The muniments come into this somewhere. I wish I knew how.'

'Whoever did the muniments,' offered Crosby after a little thought, 'did them after Meredith had been – er – done.'

'I grant you that,' said Sloan immediately. 'Meredith wouldn't have stood for that. When were the muniments disturbed?'

'We don't know, sir.' There was positively no beer left now.

Sloan dropped his pen on to his notebook. 'There's no end to the things we don't know. What we want, Crosby, is someone who went into the library that evening.'

'Or someone who saw the murderer carrying the body to the armoury,' said Crosby helpfully.

Sloan looked at him for a minute and slowly picked up his pen again. 'We've got that, haven't we, Constable?'

'Have we, sir?'

'Don't you remember?'

Crosby stared. 'No, sir.'

'Someone saw somebody in the Great Hall, don't you remember?'

'No, sir.'

'Just before dinner, Crosby, on Friday,' with mounting excitement. 'After the dressing bell had gone. While everyone in the house could reasonably be expected to be dressing for dinner in their own rooms.'

Light began to dawn on Crosby's face. 'You don't mean . . .'

'I do. Lady Alice Cremond saw . . .'

'Judge Cremond.'

'Exactly.'

'But he's a ghost.'

Sloan sighed. 'Do you believe in ghosts, Constable?'

'No, sir.'

'Neither do I. I'm prepared to bet that what the old lady saw – without her lorgnette, mind you – was not a sixteenth-century ghost at all but a twentieth-century murderer carrying the body of a small man.'

It was Police Constable Albert Bloggs who disturbed them.

Dillow brought him to the gun room.

'He said you were here, sir,' said Bloggs, jerking a thumb at Dillow's departing back. 'I didn't know whether to come straight here or to ring through to the station.'

'What about, Bloggs?' asked Sloan warily.

'That young chap, Murton, sir, who I was watching.'

'Go on.'

'He's gone and given me the slip.'

15

'Find him,' commanded Superintendent Leeyes briefly over the telephone.

'Yes, sir,' said Sloan.

'And quickly.'

'Yes, sir.'

'Where did he go missing?'

'Here,' said Sloan miserably.

'What!' exploded Leeyes. 'You mean he's on the loose somewhere in that ruddy great house and you don't know where?'

'Yes, sir. Bloggs tailed him after lunch from his cottage in the village up here to the house and then Murton went round the back somewhere and Bloggs lost him.'

'Bloggs lost him,' repeated Leeyes nastily. 'Just like that. A child of ten could probably have kept him in sight. It's very nearly Midsummer's Day, Sloan, it's not even dusk let alone dark and he lost him.'

'Yes, sir.'

'So I suppose Bloggs went round to the front door and rang the bell.'

'More or less,' admitted Sloan unhappily. He didn't really see what else Bloggs could have done but that.

'And what has Murton come up to the house for, Sloan? Have you thought about that?'

'Yes, sir.' Sloan had in fact been thinking about very little else since Bloggs had arrived at the gun room. 'I don't know, sir, but I'm worried.'

'So am I,' said Superintendent Leeyes from the detached comfort of his own office in Berebury Police Station. 'Very.'

The Countess of Ornum poured a second cup of coffee for Mr Adrian Cossington. It was practically cold and he hadn't asked for it anyway but he didn't complain. Luncheon had been over for some time and a general move away from the drawing-room was in the air.

'I'd like you to take a look at the herd, Cossington,' said the Earl. 'A good year, I think, after all. You sometimes get it after a bad winter.'

'Certainly, my lord. I shall look forward to that.' The very last thing the City solicitor wanted to do was to plod across the park after the Earl hoping to catch a glimpse of the fleeting shy creatures. Legally speaking – and Mr Cossington rarely spoke or thought otherwise – deer were not particularly interesting to him. Being *ferae naturae*, there was no private property in them or common law crime in killing them.

'Just the thing after a meal, a good walk in the park,' observed the Earl.

'Very pleasant, my lord.' Cossington was still automatically considering the legal aspects of deer. The only remedy against having your own deer killed was to prevent trespass in pursuit of them or to punish the trespasser . . .

The Earl rose. 'When you've finished your coffee, then, Cossington . . .'

The solicitor hastily swallowed the tepid fluid. In the ordinary way he liked a certain amount of *sang froid* in his clients, but the aristocracy were inclined to carry things a little too far.

'Are you coming too, Henry?' asked his father.

'Er – no. 'Fraid not. Got to get the car straightened out, you know. Thanks all the same.'

'Eleanor?'

'All right, I'll come.'

Cousin Gertrude got to her feet and said heavily, 'Well, this won't do. I've got work to do.'

'Poor Gertrude,' said the Countess sympathetically, 'you're always so busy.'

'Someone's got to do the flowers,' she said. 'They haven't been touched since Friday what with one thing and another.'

'Mostly one thing, what?' blurted Miles.

She ignored him. 'Hackle brought some fresh flowers in this morning. That's one thing you can say for the month of June. There's no shortage of flowers.'

'And no shortage of vases,' observed the Countess, 'so that's all right.'

'Quite,' said Gertrude stiffly. 'Quite.'

Mr Adrian Cossington felt constrained to say something about the murder. 'Are you making any changes in – er – routine since – er – yesterday's discovery, my lord?'

The Earl stared. 'Changes? Here?'

'Yes, my lord.'

'No.'

Cossington tried again. 'The public, my lord. Are they still to be admitted as usual?'

'Certainly.'

'Is that wise, my lord?'

'Wise?'

'The murder . . .'

'If they want their vicarious bread and circuses, Cossington, I see no reason to stop them.'

'You'll have a great crowd . . .'

'You think so? Good.'

'Culture vultures in the long gallery,' said Lord Henry.

'Eager beavers in the great hall,' chimed in Lady Eleanor.

'And aesthete's foot by the time they get to Cousin Gertrude in the china room,' added Lord Henry.

'How disgusting that sounds,' said the Countess. She turned to a hitherto rather silent Miles and Laura. 'What are you two going to do?'

Laura said that she had a splitting headache and was going to lie down, and that Miles was going out for a walk.

'He needs some air,' she said.

'Just like Friday,' observed Cousin Gertrude.

'Not like Friday at all,' retorted Laura.

Gertrude grunted. 'No, of course not. That was exercise he wanted then, wasn't it?'

'He got it,' said Laura pointedly, 'but not by killing old Mr Meredith.'

'Just by walking in the park, what?' said Miles.

The Countess made a vague gesture in the direction of the coffee pot but no one took her up on this. 'Has anyone remembered to feed the little man from County Hall?'

Lady Eleanor said, 'I told Dillow, Mother. And about the police.'

Mention of the police started Adrian Cossington off again. 'My lord, are you sure that it is prudent to open the house again so soon . . .'

'I think,' said the Earl, encompassing a whole philosophy, 'one should always carry on as usual.'

'A few changes might well be indicated, my lord. As your legal adviser . . .'

'When it is not necessary to change,' quoted the Earl sententiously, 'it is necessary not to change. I think you may take it, Cossington, that things are back to normal now.'

They weren't.

Not from the point of view of Sloan and Crosby and the luckless Bloggs.

Sloan had barely got back from the gun room when a police motor cyclist arrived from Berebury with a sheaf of reports.

The pathologist's official one, marked 'Copy to H.M. Coroner': the facts of death in the language of Academe. Brutality smoothed down to detached observation.

A note from aforementioned H.M. Coroner appointing Thursday for the inquest.

A dry comment from the Forensic Laboratory: the blood from

the spine of the book in the library complied with all the accepted tests with that of the deceased. The hairs on the instrument known as exhibit B . . .

'What's exhibit A?' said Sloan suddenly.

'A for armour,' said Crosby who had done the labelling.

And B for blunt instrument? Sloan didn't ask.

. . . Exhibit B resembled that of deceased under all the known comparison indices. So did the blood on exhibit B. An attempt had been made to wipe it clean. There were no fingerprints.

Two reports from London whence enquiries had been put in hand about Miles Cremond and William Murton.

The Pedes Shipping Line was nearly on the rocks. It was suspected that the name of the Honourable Miles Cremond was included on the Board of Directors solely to lend an air of credibility to the operations of the company. If, the writer of the report put it graphically, the Inspector was thinking of making an investment the South Sea Bubble would be a better bet.

William Murton lived at the address stated, which was a bedsitter-cum-studio, and apparently possessed two characteristics unfortunate in combination – expensive tastes and a low income.

'Living it up without having anything to live on,' said Crosby, who wouldn't have dared.

'Except his uncle,' said Sloan. 'I reckon he lives on him.'

'I don't know why he lets him, sir, honestly I don't. My uncle . . .'

'It's called *noblesse oblige*.'

It would seem, went on the compiler of the report, a man with a taste for a good phrase, that William Murton pursues his career in fits and starts and nubile young ladies all of the time.

Near the bottom of the sheaf was a scribbled note from Inspector Harpe of Traffic Division begging Sloan to come to see him as soon as he possibly could.

Sloan slipped that one into his inside jacket pocket. If there was anything approaching natural selection in troubles it was their tendency to multiply at the wrong time.

There was also a communication from the policeman who had

interviewed the executors of the late Mr Beresford Baggles to the effect that Michael Joseph Dillow had worked for Mr Baggles until the latter's death from apoplexy. Dillow had been left the sum of five hundred pounds by Mr Baggles being in his employ and not under notice at the time of his death.

The legacy had not yet been paid out owing to the difficulties encountered by the executors on the discovery that Mr Baggles' considerable collection of the works of the artist Van Gogh were fakes (which discovery had occasioned the apoplexy) but that Dillow would be receiving it as soon as the estate was wound up.

'Van Gogh,' murmured Sloan. 'That's the chap who cut off his ear, isn't it?'

PC Bloggs, who in another day and age would doubtless have had both his ears chopped off for him, remained silent.

Crosby sniffed. 'Funny fellows, painters.'

Which brought them back to William Murton.

'It'd take an army to find him in this place,' said Crosby, thinking aloud. 'There's I don't know how many rooms . . .'

'Just under the three hundred,' said Sloan.

'And what's to stop him dashing from one to the other while you're searching?'

'Nothing,' agreed Sloan wearily. 'Nothing at all. However, reinforcements are on the way.'

On the terrace outside the gun room window a peacock shrieked derisively.

Bert Hackle was carrying a wooden board. 'Will this do, Mr Purvis?'

The steward measured it with his eye. 'That's about right, Bert, thank you. Now let's see if it'll fit.'

Charles Purvis had in his hand a stout sheet of white card on which he had been labouring for a tidy effect. On it had been printed as neatly as possible 'Armoury 2/6d extra'.

'Very nice,' said Hackle, who was a great admirer of the Earl.

'It's not the same as a printed notice, of course,' murmured Purvis, standing back to see the effect, 'but there isn't time to have it done properly by Wednesday.'

Hackle jerked his shoulder towards the top of the armoury stairs. 'Reckon they'll let us in there again b'Wednesday?'

'His Lordship does.' Charles Purvis looked round. 'Now to find something to put the board on.'

'What we want,' said Bert, 'is a proper stand.' By rights Bert Hackle shouldn't have been in the great hall at all in his gardening boots but as there had been Hackles in Ornum village almost as long as there had been Cremonds in Ornum House – though not so well documented – he was privileged in his own right. He creaked across the floor looking for something suitable. 'If we was to lean it up against this we'd be all right.'

'Not if Mr Feathers saw us,' retorted Purvis smartly. 'That's his best piece of ormulu on malachite, that is.'

Hackle, whose interest in minerals was confined to the rocks in the rockery, tried again. 'What about that box thing?'

That box thing was satinwood inlaid with ivory and contained the ceremonial trowel with which his Lordship the eleventh Earl had cut the first turf for the first railway line to link Luston and Berebury. (It had been a singularly happy occasion as his Lordship, being the owner of all the suitable land in between these two places, had been able to name his own price. And had.)

'Much better,' said Purvis. 'Now, if you'll just heave that table a bit nearer the doorway . . .'

Standing on the table and propped against the satinwood box the notice was now eminently readable.

Mr Robert Hamilton did not accord with Inspector Sloan's conception of the common man.

The county archivist was exceedingly spry, erudite and helpful.

Inspector Sloan, being in the position of having a force too meagre to be worth deploying, had taken it with him to the muniments room. Insofar as the murder of Osborne Meredith had a focal point it was in this part of the house.

'Ah, Inspector . . .' Mr Hamilton looked up. 'Come in. I don't think we can say you'll disturb anything any more than it's been disturbed already.'

'No. Have you had any visitors here, sir, so far?'

'Yes, indeed, Inspector. A Miss Gertrude Cremond came along to see if she could help, a Mrs Laura Cremond who thought something of hers might be in here and the butler.'

'Dillow?'

'Is that his name? He left me something to eat in the library but I asked him to bring it here instead.'

'Not William Murton?' Sloan described the missing man. 'You haven't seen him?'

Hamilton shook his head, while Sloan glanced round the room.

'Someone,' observed Mr Hamilton profoundly, 'was wanting to impede research here.'

'Yes.'

'It'll take a week or more to go through' – Robert Hamilton waved a hand at the chaotic papers – 'and restore even the semblance of order – quite apart from finding whatever it is I'm supposed to be looking for in here.' He cocked his head alertly. 'You can't give me even a small clue as to what that can be?'

Sloan shook his head. 'All we know is that someone stirred them up and that someone tried to get in here last night after we'd sealed the door.'

'Ah. Well, there's no wilful damage that I can see, and that's something – for there's as pretty a collection of documents here as you could hope to find. Nor theft, I should say at a quick guess . . .'

'No.'

'Someone ignorant,' added Mr Hamilton. 'Someone plain ignorant.'

'A woman,' said Sloan. 'We have reason to believe it was a woman.'

'Ah,' said the archivist, 'that explains it. They seemed to be aiming at mayhem.'

'I think,' said Sloan slowly, 'that they were aiming at making it difficult for anyone to prove that the Earl of Ornum wasn't the Earl.'

'Yes,' said the archivist unexpectedly. 'The poor fellow wrote me about that a week or so back.'

'He did?' Sloan sat up.

'He was mistaken, of course,' declared Mr Hamilton. 'I can assure you, Inspector, the succession is perfectly sound. Perfectly.'

'But Mr Meredith thought . . .'

'He made a common mistake. He was misled by a case of *mort d'ancestre* in the family. Tricky, of course.'

'You mean . . .'

'And he was also a wee bit confused about socage.'

Sloan was aware of Crosby's head coming up like a pointer.

'Socage,' repeated Sloan carefully.

'That's right, Inspector. Common socage. Meredith was all right in his facts but a bit out in his inferences. He was,' said the utterly professional Robert Hamilton, 'an amateur. A good amateur, mind you, I will say that, but not a trained man.'

'He hadn't told anyone he had been mistaken,' said Sloan, trying to assimilate the news and place it in the pattern of the crime.

'Now, Inspector,' Hamilton smiled faintly, 'there's not many people in a hurry to do that, is there?'

'True,' agreed Sloan. Better though, perhaps, to admit a mistake and keep your skull intact . . . 'This socage, Mr Hamilton . . .'

'The tenure of land other than by knight-service.'

Why was it, thought Sloan, that no one would explain things to him in words that he understood?

'Knight-service?' he echoed wearily.

'That's right,' said the amiable Mr Hamilton. 'Estates like these came directly from the crown in the beginning in return for services rendered . . . usually men at arms in times of war . . .'

That explained the armoury if not the gun room.

'You see, Inspector, in theory all land belongs to the King or Queen as the case may be.'

'Not still?' said Sloan, thinking of his roses, and his neat semi-detached house in suburban Berebury.

'Yes.' The archivist chuckled. 'I dare say you're of an age to have done your own knight-service yourself, Inspector.'

Sloan hadn't thought of it in that light before but . . .

'Not quite the same thing,' admitted Hamilton, 'but not all

that far away. That's where the earldom came in. Men who brought their armies with them to the King's wars. They were made earls—'

'The rest,' interrupted the unconscionable Constable Crosby triumphantly, 'were churls.'

It was not often that Charles Purvis was caught on the wrong foot. He was a naturally competent man, unobtrusively given to attending to detail. Even the distraction of admiring the adorable Lady Eleanor from afar did not normally cause his work to suffer.

But, as it was subsequently agreed, a murder in the house was enough to put any man off his stroke, to drive less important matters out of mind.

So it was that when a coach drew up at the front door of Ornum House at exactly three o'clock he was all prepared to send it away. True, it was not quite the same as the sort of coach which usually came to the house on open days. It was infinitely more luxurious: and it did not proclaim the fact in letters a foot high.

Charles Purvis saw the coach from the great hall and as Dillow for once did not seem to be about he went himself to the door.

'I'm very sorry,' he began firmly, 'but the house is not open today . . .'

'Mr Purvis?'

Charles Purvis found his hand being crushed in a vice-like grip.

'I'm Fortescue, Mr Purvis. Cromwell T. Fortescue. You wrote me . . .'

'I did?' Purvis blinked.

'You sure did. You wrote me, Mr Purvis, to say we might see the Earl's pictures today. We're the Young Masters Art Society . . .'

Hot on the wheels of this coach came another one.

Nothing like as luxurious as the first, it had been commandeered by Superintendent Leeyes to convey as many of his Force as he could drum up to Ornum House to assist Inspector Sloan in the hunt for William Murton.

It took their concerted efforts, directed by Inspector Sloan and aided by Constables Crosby and Bloggs, about an hour to find him.

In the oubliette.

Dead.

16

'He can't be,' bellowed Superintendent Leeyes.

'He is, sir. I'm very sorry . . .'

'I should think so, Sloan. You haven't heard the last of this. If Bloggs hadn't lost him . . .'

Sloan forbore to point out that Constable Bloggs had been watching William Murton for a totally different reason.

'And, Sloan, if you had got on to him quicker then this wouldn't have happened . . .'

'No, sir. Dr Dabbe says that's not so. He thinks he was killed as soon as he got to the house.'

'Just after Bloggs lost him,' pointed out Leeyes inexorably.

'It means, sir, that someone was ready for him.'

'I know that, Sloan. You don't have to tell me.'

'No, sir.'

'Ready and waiting,' snapped Leeyes.

'Yes, sir.'

'With' – on a rising note – 'three able-bodied policemen actually in the house at the time.'

'Yes, sir.' It was no good explaining that Ornum wasn't a house but a 'House', that it wasn't a two up and two down jerry-builder's delight. Or that medieval dungeons were sound-proofed as a careless in-built extra.

'That doesn't make it look any better on paper either,' grumbled Leeyes.

'No, sir.' Nothing could make that poor distorted face look any better now either, Sloan knew that. William Murton, half gentleman, half painter, father but not husband, nephew but never heir, penniless but never properly penurious, had gone to another world where presumably all things were wholly good or wholly bad.

'And who killed him, Sloan? Tell me that . . .'

Sloan back tracked. 'Up until this afternoon, sir, we had four suspects for the murder of Mr Osborne Meredith. William Murton was one of them . . .'

'We are not, I hope,' remarked Leeyes coldly, 'playing elimination games.'

'No, sir. Leaving out Murton . . .'

'Suicides don't strangle themselves as a rule.'

'Quite so, sir,' hastily. 'As you say, leaving out Murton we would have had three suspects for the first murder.'

Sloan wasn't a bardolator – wouldn't even have known the meaning of the word – but he had once been to see a performance of *Macbeth*. It had been the insouciant irony of the cast list which he had remembered, could quote to this day: 'Lords, Gentlemen, Officers, Soldiers, Murderers, Attendants and Messengers.'

Give or take a soldier or two he reckoned they'd got the lot at Ornum today.

First and Second Murderers, there had been in the play. Was there going to prove to have been a First Murderer for Osborne Meredith and a Second Murderer for William Murton?

Doubtful.

Or a First and Second Murderer for each as in the play?

A husband and wife? That most committing of all partnerships at law. My wife and I are one and I am he, the books said. With Miles and Laura Cremond it would be the other way round. There was no doubt there who wore the kilt . . .

Three suspects were two too many for Superintendent Leeyes and he said so.

'Can't you do better than that, Sloan?'

'Not at the moment, sir. Miss Gertrude Cremond, Mr and

Mrs Miles Cremond and Dillow could all have committed the first murder . . .'

'And which did?'

'I don't know, sir. Of course, the second murder puts a different complexion on things . . .'

As soon as the word was out of his mouth Sloan wished he had chosen another one instead.

Any word but complexion.

William Murton's had been hideous. A mottled reddish-blue with swollen tongue protuberant between discoloured lips.

Dr Dabbe, recalled at great speed from Berebury, had been terse.

'Strangulation,' he had said at his first glance. 'Not more than two hours ago at the outside. Something thin pulled over his head from behind and then tightened. I don't know what. I'll have to tell you later.'

Sloan didn't know what either. The instrument of death had disappeared between swollen engorged folds of skin. He hadn't realized the frightening vulnerability of the human neck. That a large and powerful young man like William Murton could be done to death with a quick twist of something thin round the throat seemed all wrong.

After luncheon.

Everyone in the house had dispersed after luncheon. Sloan had established that easily enough.

Then what?

Enter First Murderer for Second Murder?

'Why kill him anyway?' The Superintendent's question came charging into his train of thought.

'I don't know . . .' began Sloan – and stopped.

He did know.

Something at the back of his mind told him.

It teased his subconscious. Still nominally listening to Superintendent Leeyes, he flipped back the pages of his notebook. Somewhere this morning – it couldn't only have been this morning surely – it seemed aeons ago – William Murton had said something to him which . . .

He found the place in his notebook.

'I don't,' William Murton had said and he, Sloan, had written down, 'earn my keep like Cousin Gertrude cleaning chandeliers for dear life. I'm a sponger.'

How did William Murton, who was supposed not to have come up to Ornum House at all on Friday, know that Cousin Gertrude had been cleaning a chandelier all day? Something must have put it into his mind.

Not just 'a chandelier', of course, but the great hall chandelier.

That same great hall where towards evening the ancient and ageing Lady Alice Cremond had seen what she fondly took to be the ghost of her long departed ancestor, Judge Cremond.

To know that Cousin Gertrude had been cleaning the chandelier one would have had either to see her doing it or see the pieces of crystal on the table and know that this was one of the duties arrogated to herself by the formidable Miss Cremond. Or, perhaps, as a very long shot, have talked to someone who had mentioned it.

But if William Murton had been in the house on Friday after all, why hadn't he said so?

There was one simple and very sinister answer to that question. Was it because William Murton had seen that same figure and not only known it not to have been Judge Cremond but had – dangerously – recognized it?

'A pikestaff . . .' Superintendent Leeyes was saying.

'I beg your pardon, sir?' Cousin Gertrude was as plain as a pikestaff: was that what he meant?

'A pikestaff,' repeated Leeyes irritably. 'Was he killed with something fancy from the armoury?'

'No, sir,' dully. 'The armoury's locked. It'll have been something more modern than that.'

Dr Dabbe still hadn't established what by the time Sloan got back to the oubliette.

It was a macabre setting for murder. Death went well with bare stone and it was the little crowd of modern men who looked incongruous.

Crosby was there and a considerably shaken Bert Hackle. He

it had been who had led the police search party to this part of the house, who had given a quick jerk at the oubliette grating without considering for a single second that there might be anything at all within – still less the crumpled heap that had been William Murton.

The Reverend Walter Ames was somehow also of the party. Sloan didn't know whether he hadn't gone home after this morning or had gone and come back again and he was too busy to care.

Dr Dabbe was still the central figure in the drama with the others playing supporting roles. Doctors, realized Sloan, were like that.

All three professions had something to tell the police inspector.

Rather like 'The Ballad of Reading Gaol', thought Sloan, who in his day had been what is known as 'good at school'. His schooling had been of a vintage that had included – nay insisted – on the learning of verse by rote.

'Murton . . .' began Detective Constable Crosby, 'shouldn't have been in the house at all by rights . . .'

> (The Governor was strong upon
> The Regulations Act.)

'If he'd stayed at home,' said the Law flatly, 'he'd have been all right.'

'The deceased,' pronounced Dr Dabbe, 'was attacked from behind and died very quickly.'

> (The Doctor said that Death was but
> A Scientific Fact.)

'He struggled,' observed Medicine, 'but it didn't do him any good.'

'God rest his soul,' murmured the Reverend Walter Ames.

> (And twice a day the Chaplain called,
> And left a little tract.)

'Perhaps,' suggested the Church gently, 'in the fullness of time we shall be better able to see his life in true perspective.'

Was this man of God comforting him, too, wondered Sloan? PC Bloggs couldn't properly be blamed for this death, but could he, Sloan? The Superintendent would blame everybody, he always did, so that, working for him, you had yourself to work out where real responsibility lay.

As for perspective it was like looking down the wrong end of a telescope. Far away lay a greatly diminished figure . . . Dr Dabbe was going now. 'I've seen all I need here, Inspector. Send him back to Berebury and I'll be getting on with the post-mortem for you.' 'Thank you, doctor . . .' The pathologist poked a bony finger towards the oubliette. 'Forgotten,' he said pungently, 'but not gone.'

He should have worked all this out before now.

Before William Murton died.

Sloan took Crosby with him to see their Ladyships upstairs. Now that the house really was full of police he thought he could leave the oubliette for a while.

Lady Maude answered his knock and the two policemen trooped in. It was quite impossible to tell if any hasty harbinger of bad tidings had told the two old ladies about their great nephew William. Sloan himself had broken the news to the Earl and Countess first and then to the rest of the family. As he had expected, Lord Henry and Lady Eleanor had been most upset . . .

With the two old ladies though it was as if a lifetime of keeping the upper lip stiff meant that it could no longer bend.

'William . . .' he began tentatively.

Lady Alice inclined her head. 'Millicent has told us. We expected something, you know. The Judge was about.'

The chair Sloan had been given was hard and straight backed. He twisted on it uncomfortably, unsure of what to say next. 'He shouldn't have died . . .'

The old, old face was inscrutable. 'We've all got to die, Mr Sloan . . . some of us sooner than others.'

'Yes, your ladyship,' he agreed readily, 'but he was young.'

Sloan was struck by a sadder thought still. Perhaps, seen from Lady Alice's vantage point, a lost middle age was not something to mourn and that, as for old age – you could keep it.

'Poor boy,' said Lady Maude. She, Sloan was sure, would have a lace-edged handkerchief somewhere and would shed a private tear for the dead William. ·

Lady Alice was made of sterner stuff.

She leaned forward. 'Tell me, Mr Sloan, do you read Boccaccio?'

'No, your ladyship.' He had a vague recollection that that was the name of one of the authors that some public libraries did not stock but he was probably mistaken.

'He put it very well for us all.'

Sloan waited.

' "Many valiant men and many fine ladies",' she rumbled, ' "breakfasted with their kinsfolk and that same night supped with their ancestors in the other world." '

Sloan cleared his throat. In a way, that wasn't so very far removed from what he had come about.

'Your ladyship, can you remember Friday afternoon?'

'Of course.'

'Tea time?'

'Yes?'

'How many cups were there on the tea tray?'

But in the end it was Lady Maude who remembered, not Lady Alice at all.

'Only two, Mr Sloan, because we hadn't invited Mr Meredith, you see.'

Sloan and Crosby were walking down the great staircase together.

'We know when, Crosby.'

'Yes, sir.'

'We know where, Crosby.'

'Yes, sir.'

'And now we know who, Crosby.'

'Yes, sir.'

The dialogue was as rhythmical as their steps down the stair treads.

'We still don't know why.'

'No, sir. Murton . . .'

'William Murton had to die.'

'Yes, sir.'

'He came up to the house on Friday evening though he told us he didn't . . .'

'Yes, sir.'

'And saw something.'

'It didn't do him any good.'

'Ah, but he thought it was going to, though,' said Sloan sadly. 'He made the mistake of thinking he was on to a good thing.'

'And so he came up to the house today . . .'

'Tricky business, blackmail,' murmured Sloan ruminatively. 'I don't think our William can have been quite up to it. He should have stuck to the Earl. He would have seen him through.'

There was somebody coming along the upper landing behind them and hurrying down the stairs after them. A man's voice called out: 'Inspector . . .'

Sloan turned.

Charles Purvis was descending on them as quickly as he could. 'Inspector . . .'

'Yes?'

'I've just been taking the Young Masters Art Society round. They'd arranged to come and I forgot to cancel them what with one thing and another . . .'

'Yes?' prompted Sloan.

'So when they came just now rather than send them away I took them round myself . . .'

Quite obviously Charles Purvis hadn't heard about the dead William Murton yet.

'. . . They'd come all the way from London and anyway they didn't know about Mr Meredith . . .'

'Well?' expectantly.

'They've just got to the Holbein – the picture called *The Black Death* . . .'

'Of Judge Cremond?'

'That's right.'

'Well?'

'They say it's not a Holbein at all.'

17

Sloan would have given a great deal not to have been interrupted at that precise moment.

The very last thing that he wanted to do at this minute was to talk to his colleague Inspector Harpe of Berebury's Traffic Division.

Inspector Harpe who was known throughout Calleshire Constabulary as Happy Harry because he had never been seen to smile – he maintained that there had so far never been anything to smile at in Traffic Division – had actually telephoned him at Ornum House and was asking for him urgently.

One of Sloan's own constables brought him the message. One of the first acts of the police posse from Berebury had been to take over the telephone. Another had been to encircle the house. Lady Alice Cremond would have had a phrase for that.

Stoppin' the earths.

That was what he was trying to do now. Now he had got on to the right scent at last.

Inspector Harpe soon drove all huntin', shootin' and fishin' analogies out of his mind.

'That you, Sloan?' he asked guardedly. 'About this other business – you know . . .'

'I know.'

'There was an accident just before dinner time today at the foot of Lockett Hill – near the bottom by the bend – you know . . .'

'It's a bad corner.'

'You're telling me. We've been trying to get the County Council to put a better camber on it for years but you know what they're like . . .'

'I do.'

'They say it's the Ministry but then they always do . . .'

'And the Ministry say it's the County,' condoled Sloan.

'That's right – how did you know? And everyone blames the police. It was a fatal, by the way . . .'

So someone had died while 'they' were fighting about improving the road.

'And what happened?' Sloan prompted him. Happy Harry wasn't the only one with a fatal on his hands today.

'We had this call and my nearest car was practically at Cullingoak – it couldn't have been farther away, Sloan, if it had tried.'

'That's how it goes,' agreed Sloan. He hadn't time to be standing here commiserating with his colleagues. 'So . . .'

'By the time it got from Cullingoak to Lockett Hill . . .'

With blue tower light flashing, two-tone horn blaring and every child on the route shouting encouragement.

'By the time it arrived,' said Harpe, 'the garage – *the* garage – if you know what I mean . . .'

'I know.'

'They were there.'

'Damn.'

'Sloan. I trust those boys, they're good lads for all that I shout at them.'

'Quite, but that doesn't help, does it?' It might hinder but Sloan didn't say so.

'They must find out some other way,' insisted Harpe.

'How?' said Sloan automatically.

In a case like this it was not enough just to prove – or have events prove for you – that someone was guiltless. Oh, it might be all right in a court of law . . . what was it called in England? The accusatorial system: has this person been proved by the prosecution beyond reasonable doubt to have committed whatever it was you were accusing him of?

Or her?

But as far as he, Sloan, was concerned, give him the other approach – the Continental one – any day of the week.

The inquisitorial outlook.

Who committed the crime? Just as with Inspector Harpe's traffic crews, so it was here at Ornum now. Events had proved that William Murton was not likely to have been guilty of the murder of Osborne Meredith but those same events had not revealed the true sequence of events.

Yet.

'How?' he repeated. 'Someone must have told the garage where to go. Someone must have been telling them each time or they couldn't have been getting there so quickly.'

'I know,' mourned Harpe. 'I've done my best. I've been reading up all those incidents.'

Incidents was a good word.

Even in his present hurry Sloan could appreciate it. It covered everything from a flying bomb to an allegation of conduct unbecoming to a police officer and a . . . With an effort he brought his mind back to what Happy Harry was saying.

Before he mixed his metaphors.

'And one thing struck me,' went on Harpe, 'as common to them all. Until now.'

'Oh?' Only long training kept Sloan's ear to the telephone. He wanted so badly to throw it down and bring his mind back to Ornum.

'Each time the breakdown van got on to one of those accident jobs so mysteriously . . .'

'Yes?'

'It was out of working hours. Take last night, for instance, at Tappett's Corner . . .'

'But not today surely,' said Sloan. 'Today's Monday. Isn't it?'

He wouldn't have been unbearably surprised to learn that they had run over into Tuesday – Sunday seemed so long ago.

'That's right. Today spoils it.'

'It'll have to wait,' said Sloan pointedly. He would ring off in a minute and pretend afterwards that he'd lost the connection.

'I'll have to tell the Old Man . . .' said Harpe unhappily.

'I'm afraid so.'

'You don't think it'll stop him screaming for help over your business?'

'He's probably doing it already,' said Sloan.

Charles Purvis took him along to the long gallery as soon as he put the telephone down.

'I'd clean forgotten about them,' admitted the steward. 'I never gave them another thought.'

'Who are they?'

'They call themselves the Young Masters Art Society and they're doing a European picture tour taking in as many . . .'

'Old Masters?'

'That's right. As many Old Masters as they can. They've already done one trip doing the public collections, galleries and so forth.'

'It's not the same,' said Sloan promptly. If he had learnt anything from his twenty-four hours in Ornum House it was that.

'No,' agreed Charles Purvis. 'That's what they say.'

They went back up the stairs, Constable Crosby two paces behind them.

'I was just taking them round the long gallery,' went on Purvis, 'telling them what little I did know about the pictures – it's not very much actually because that's not my line. I'd told them about Mr Meredith though and explained that they'd have to make do with me, when we got round to the Holbein . . .'

'Halfway down on the right-hand wall in a bad light?'

'That's right. It doesn't do to put your best picture in full sunlight.' Charles Purvis might not know as much about the paintings as Osborne Meredith but he had been trained in how to care for them. 'You keep it away from daylight as much as you can. Certain sorts of artificial lights are better . . .'

Inspector Sloan halted suddenly on the staircase.

Constable Crosby didn't and all but cannoned into him from behind and below.

'Miss Cleepe,' cried Sloan, bringing his hand down on the banister in a great smack. 'She told us this morning . . .'

'Miss Cleepe?' Purvis merely looked bewildered. 'Miss Cleepe didn't tell us anything.'

'A walloping great clue,' declared Sloan solemnly, 'and we none of us spotted it. Did we?'

'No, sir,' said Constable Crosby.

'No, Inspector,' said Purvis wonderingly. 'Miss Cleepe? Are you sure you mean Miss Cleepe?'

'Miss Cleepe. Crosby, it's in your book what she said.'

Crosby obediently turned back the pages in his notebook, licking his thumb as he did so. 'Would it be the bit about the Holbein, sir?'

'Of course it's about the Holbein,' snapped Sloan testily. 'Can't you see, Crosby, that all of this is about the Holbein? It always has been. Right from the very beginning only we didn't know.'

'No, sir.' Staidly. Crosby ran his finger down the page. 'Where do you want me to start?'

'They were talking about the long gallery being rather dark,' said Sloan, 'and then Miss Cleepe said something about . . .'

'I've got it, sir. Here. It was after that bit about the ghost. Miss Cleepe said, "It's such a long, narrow room, and the bulb in its own little light was broken. Dillow's getting another for me." '

'The light over the picture was broken,' breathed Purvis. 'Of course.'

'I should have spotted that,' said Sloan. 'It was a break with normality and so it was significant.'

'There is this special light over the picture,' agreed Purvis. 'It's meant to show it up without injuring it. It doesn't get a lot of light otherwise.'

Constable Crosby made a credible attempt at imitating the refined tones of Mrs Mompson by raising his voice to an affected squeak and reading from his notebook: ' "It's practically in the half dark in the long gallery where it is. Halfway from each window and not very good windows at that." '

Sloan said, 'Are you feeling all right, Crosby?'

'Yes, sir. Thank you, sir.'

Charles Purvis said slowly, 'Someone put a broken light bulb in so people shouldn't get a good view of the picture . . .'

'That's right.'

'Most people wouldn't know the difference between the one that's hanging there and the real thing. I wouldn't for one – you'd have to be a real expert.'

'We aren't concerned about most people,' said Sloan, 'are we? We're concerned with one person . . .'

'Osborne Meredith.'

'Precisely.'

'The real expert,' agreed Purvis. 'The only person who would know . . .'

'Other than the Young Masters,' said Sloan softly.

'You mean they come into this too?'

'I shouldn't be surprised.'

Charles Purvis grasped the balustrade of the staircase. 'This is all getting very complicated, Inspector.'

'On the contrary,' said Sloan. 'It's getting simpler and simpler all the time. I now know what Mr Hamilton should be looking for in the muniments room. Crosby . . .'

'Sir?'

'Assemble everyone in the Private Apartments, please, while I see the Young Masters and the archivist.'

Though it was tea time there was nothing of the drawing-room tea party about the gathering in the Private Apartments now. True, people were drinking tea but they were drinking it thirstily because they needed it. They were not eating at all because they were not hungry.

The only person, in fact, to touch the food, noted Sloan, had been Cousin Gertrude. With her, the shock over William Murton's death had taken a different form. She had forgotten to take off the gardening apron in which she had been doing the flowers. A pair of scissors poked out of the apron pocket and a piece of twine drooled down the front.

William Murton's death had driven the Countess to even

greater heights of absentmindedness. She was pouring tea as if her life depended on it but the hand that held the teapot shook so much that as much tea went in the saucer as in the cup. Dillow made one or two deft attempts to field the wavering stream but in the end he went away for more hot water and clean saucers.

Mr Adrian Cossington was very much taking a back seat but Laura Cremond had been badly affected by the news. She was sitting – unusually docile – beside Miles on a small couch. Her face had a pinched frightened look and she never took her eyes off Inspector Sloan's face.

He and Crosby were seated near the door. If he leaned a fraction to his right, Sloan could see through the window and down to the main door of the house. There were two figures in blue standing where once footmen in powder had waited – only these two figures were policemen and their different duty was to let no one pass. There were other figures, too, at all the other exits from Ornum House, but only Sloan and Crosby knew this.

Mr Ames had gone across to the church, otherwise everyone was in the house.

Lady Eleanor looked as if she had been crying and Lord Henry as if his hand was hurting him. Dillow came back with more hot water for the Countess.

'I knew someone was going to die what with the Judge walking and everything,' said Cousin Gertrude gruffly. 'Didn't think it would be William, though.'

'But why did it have to be William?' asked Lady Eleanor, a husky catch in her voice. 'I know he was difficult and odd but he wouldn't have really harmed anyone . . .'

Inspector Sloan shuffled his notes. 'I think, your ladyship, that he came up to the house on Friday evening.'

'I didn't see him.'

'Nobody saw him.'

'Well, then, how do you know . . .'

'I don't know,' said Sloan, 'but I think. I think he came up quietly round about the time you were all dressing for dinner.'

'Nobody much about then,' grunted the Earl.

'Exactly. It's the one time when you could all be expected to be in your rooms.' He paused significantly. 'A fact, incidentally, also appreciated by Osborne Meredith's murderer.'

There was total silence in the room. The Countess stopped pouring tea and the silver teapot hovered, precariously suspended over a cup. Dillow was going to be lucky to escape scalding.

'But why did he come up like that in the first place?' Lord Henry wanted to know. 'He was always welcome, you know. He wasn't as bad a chap as you might think from talking to him. Didn't do himself justice . . .'

'He might,' said Sloan cautiously, 'have been in the habit – the bad habit – of coming up here without any of you knowing.'

The Earl cleared his throat. 'Very true, Inspector. I think he did. Suspected it myself before now.'

'Harry!' That was the Countess. 'You never told me.'

'No need, my dear. As Eleanor says, he was quite harmless.'

'But what did he do here?'

'Nothing, probably. Just have a look round.'

'And where did he go?'

The Earl gave his moustache a tug. 'I expect the Inspector has guessed . . .'

Sloan nodded. 'I think so, my Lord. I think William Murton was in the habit – the bad habit – of slipping up into the room behind the peephole.'

'To see what he could see,' said Lord Henry slowly.

Sloan turned. 'Yes, my lord. Somebody watched me from there this morning but when I got up to the room they'd gone.'

'Not William surely?'

'No,' said Sloan. 'That was somebody else watching me.' Now he knew who that had been, too. There had been two people in the vicinity to choose from . . .

'William saw something on Friday,' concluded Lady Eleanor shakily.

'Something nasty,' put in Cousin Gertrude, winding twine round her finger.

'Something very nasty,' agreed Sloan. 'I think he saw someone carrying the body of Osborne Meredith across the great hall to the armoury staircase.'

'How very clever,' observed the Countess inconsequentially.
Her husband turned. 'Clever, m'dear?'

'To choose the only time when we would none of us be about.'
She smiled sweetly. 'That means it must be someone who knows
us really well, doesn't it?'

Perhaps, thought Sloan, one could redefine an aristocrat as a
man or woman to whom a fact held no terror.

'I think,' murmured the Earl, 'we are already agreed on that.'

'It stands to reason anyway,' said Cousin Gertrude, that firmly
entrenched spinster, who, having long ago abandoned feeling,
was left only with logic.

Over on the couch Laura Cremond stirred. 'I don't know how
you can all just sit here without knowing.'

'Difficult, what?' agreed Miles.

'Perhaps,' said Lord Henry acutely, 'the Inspector wants a
little suspense.'

What, in fact, Sloan was waiting for was a message from the
county archivist, Mr Robert Hamilton.

He got it quite soon.

PC Bloggs knocked on the door and handed him a note.

It was all he needed now . . .'

18

Whether Sloan wanted any extra suspense or not he got it with the arrival at the door of the Private Apartments a moment or two later of Charles Purvis and a large genial man who introduced himself as Fortescue.

'Cromwell T. Fortescue of the Young Masters Art Society,' he said, 'visiting your house by courtesy of Earl Ornum to see your beautiful pictures.'

The Countess seized another cup and began to pour wildly.

Charles Purvis followed him in and, noticed Sloan, manoeuvred himself into a position exactly opposite Lady Eleanor. It was obvious that he had long ago learned the lesson of the lovelorn that you can sit opposite someone without seeming to stare whereas if you sit beside them you have to keep turning your head.

Which is noticeable.

The Earl grunted: 'You've told him about Meredith, have you, Purvis?'

'Indeed, he has, my lord,' responded Mr Fortescue before Purvis could speak. 'I am deeply sorry. The whole of our Society would wish to be associated with these sentiments, I know . . .'

'A message has arrived from Miss Meredith too,' said Charles Purvis. 'She's seen an early edition of an evening paper and she's coming back straightaway.'

'Poor dear,' said the Countess. 'Charles, will you meet her at the station and see that she doesn't need anything? She might like to come up here for the night . . .'

Sloan doubted it but did not say so. In Miss Meredith's position he'd have opted for his own little house, where you could at least count the rooms.

'We'll have to see about the vault, too,' said the Earl.

Death might be the great leveller, noted Sloan silently, but William Murton was wholly family now.

Cromwell T. Fortescue wasn't used to being overlooked. He said loudly and clearly, 'We're sorry to have arrived at a time like this, my lord . . .'

The Earl inclined his head.

'. . . and also to be the bearers of such sad news but Cyrus Phillimore is quite sure of his facts.'

'More bad news?' said Laura Cremond faintly. 'I don't believe it. There can't be any more.'

'It may not be news, of course,' said Fortescue more tentatively, 'but I hardly think the Earl here would subscribe to a deception.'

'Certainly not,' said Adrian Cossington, the solicitor, upon the instant, 'and should you be implying this . . .'

'What,' asked the Earl of Ornum mildly, 'is Mr Fortescue trying to tell us?'

'Among your paintings, Earl,' said Mr Fortescue, 'you have a painting said to be by Hans Holbein the Younger.'

'We have.'

'It's one of the lesser-known ones because it's been here since he painted it. One owner, you might say.'

'That is so. My ancestor, the Judge, had it painted in 1532 the year before . . . before the family tragedy. Holbein was in London then . . . just beginning to make his name.'

'Cyrus Phillimore agrees with all that,' said Fortescue. 'The only thing he doesn't agree with is that Holbein painted this particular picture. He says it's a fake.' Dillow pressed a cup and saucer into his hand and the courtly Mr Fortescue bowed in the direction of the Countess. 'I guess it's not the sort of news that any of you wanted to hear . . .'

The Countess hadn't yet remembered to put the teapot back on the tray but it didn't stop her talking.

'Tell me, Mr Fortescue, how long hasn't it been a Holbein?'

'I couldn't begin to tell you that, Countess. Only that Cyrus Phillimore says . . .'

Lord Henry said quietly, 'Not very long, Mother.' He turned slightly. 'That right, Inspector?'

'Yes, my lord. Not very long.'

'Friday?' suggested Lord Henry.

'Very possibly, my lord.'

'Friday afternoon perhaps . . .'

'Perhaps, my lord.'

'Ossy's discovery!' cried Lady Eleanor. 'That must have been what Ossy discovered! That the Holbein was a fake . . .

'We think so, your Ladyship.'

The Countess of Ornum lowered the teapot on to the large silver tray with a clatter. 'You mean the picture was actually changed over on Friday afternoon?'

'Yes, your Ladyship.'

'And that little Mr Meredith knew about the change?'

'We think he spotted it by accident . . .'

Cromwell T. Fortescue began: 'Cyrus Phillimore says it's a very good fake . . .'

Nobody took any notice of him.

'And having spotted it,' said Lord Henry, 'he dashed to the telephone to ring up his pal the Vicar to ask him to pop along and confirm his worst suspicions . . .'

'That's what we think, my lord,' agreed Sloan. 'It would be the natural thing to do before he told your father. After all, it is a pretty serious allegation . . .'

'I'll say,' said his young Lordship inelegantly. 'He's worth a pretty packet, is the old Judge.'

'And where is he now?' demanded Cousin Gertrude.

Laura Cremond said unsteadily, 'I know where the picture is.'

Everyone looked towards the sharp-faced woman who sat beside Miles.

'I say,' said Miles. 'Do you? Good.'

She ignored him. 'It's lying under a pile of old maps in the muniments room. It's not damaged at all.'

There was an expectant silence.

'I'm afraid,' went on Laura Cremond, not without dignity, 'that I have a confession to make, and it's very kind of the Inspector to give me the chance.'

Miles looked as if he couldn't believe his eyes and ears. 'I say, old girl, steady on. This isn't a revivalist meeting, you know.'

'I'm sorry to have to tell you,' said Laura, 'that on Friday evening I behaved rather badly . . .'

'Not as badly as somebody else,' said the Countess sadly.

'Nearly,' insisted Laura. 'I'm afraid I disturbed the muniments.'

'Good Lord!' said Miles.

'I'm very sorry. I just couldn't bear the thought of Uncle Harry not being Earl any more . . .'

Cousin Gertrude had finished winding up the twine. 'If Laura saw it there,' she said bluntly, 'why didn't she tell us and save all this trouble?'

Laura flushed and her voice was so low as to be nearly inaudible. 'I didn't like to say . . .'

'You didn't like to say!' exclaimed Cousin Gertrude scornfully; Gertrude who had herself never left anything unsaid.

'I thought perhaps Uncle Harry had arranged to . . .' Laura faltered and began again. 'Owners do change pictures over themselves sometimes, you know, and sell the original without saying anything to anyone . . .'

'I expect,' murmured the Countess serenely, 'he will one day.'

Laura was getting to her feet. 'I know I did something I shouldn't, Uncle Harry and Aunt Millicent, and I'm very sorry. Miles and I are going now and we shan't be expecting any more invitations to stay at Ornum . . .'

The Earl was keeping to a more important train of thought. 'So Meredith was killed because he knew about the fake picture . . .'

'And to prevent him telling anyone else, my lord.' A steel-like quality crept into Sloan's voice. He cleared his throat and everyone turned in his direction. If you cleared your throat in the Berebury Police Station they thought you had a cold coming but it was different here.

Everything was different here.

'It all happened,' he said, 'because he wasn't invited to tea with your lordship's aunts like he usually was on Fridays.'

'You're joking, Inspector,' Gertrude Cremond said.

'Indeed I'm not, madam. I'm perfectly serious. As a rule, Mr Osborne Meredith always took tea with their Ladyships upstairs on Fridays.'

'You could count on it,' said Lady Eleanor.

'Someone did,' said Sloan soberly, 'and it was their undoing.'

The Countess of Ornum picked up the teapot again. Dillow peered into the hot water jug and apparently finding it empty, picked it up . . .

'Don't go, Dillow.'

'Very well, sir.' He stood with the jug in his hand.

'Friday,' said Sloan, 'was an exception. Their Ladyships upstairs did not invite Mr Meredith to tea as he had offended them by his historical researches. They did not, however, tell anyone they hadn't done so . . .'

'So poor old Ossy turns up in the long gallery just after the Holbein had been changed over,' concluded Lord Henry, 'when by right he should have been pinned between Great-Aunt Alice and Great-Aunt Maude while they told him how things ain't what they used to be.'

'Quite so.'

'Then what, Inspector?'

'Then,' said Sloan in a voice devoid of emphasis, 'he goes to the telephone where he is overheard ringing the Vicar's wife.' He turned towards Lord Ornum. 'Your telephone isn't exactly private, your lordship.'

'It's the draughtiest place in the house,' responded the Earl. 'My father wouldn't have it anywhere else. Didn't like it.'

'After that,' said Sloan, 'I reckon the murderer had about a quarter of an hour in hand. A quarter of an hour in which to decide what to do and to go down to the armoury and pick his weapon.'

Lady Eleanor shivered. 'If only I'd stayed talking to Ossy . . .'

'No, your ladyship, that wouldn't have made any difference. He'd have just waited until you'd gone.'

A thought had penetrated Miles Cremond's brain. 'I say, Inspector, you couldn't go walking through the house with a club, what? Look very odd.'

'Yes, sir, I quite agree. There is one way though in which it could be carried quite easily without being seen . . .'

Miles Cremond, having had one thought, wasn't immediately up to another. He frowned but said nothing.

'. . . and don't forget,' went on Sloan smoothly, 'that Mr Meredith wouldn't have known who to suspect of changing the picture. Dillow, I think her Ladyship has finished with the tea tray now. Would you like to take it away?'

'Certainly, sir.' With an expressionless face the butler put the hot water jug back beside the teapot and picked up the tray.

He was halfway across the room with it when Sloan said to him conversationally, 'Did you have any trouble hiding the godentag under Mr Meredith's tea tray, Dillow?'

In the end it wasn't the Countess of Ornum at all who dropped the silver teapot.

It was Dillow.

'That you, Sloan?' Superintendent Leeyes didn't wait for an answer. 'I think it's high time we got some help in this case . . .'

'There's no need now, sir, thank you.'

'Can't have the Earl thinking we aren't efficient. I'm going to ring the Chief Constable now and tell him that . . .'

'I've just made an arrest, sir.'

'. . . I think we should ask him to call in Scotland Yard. After all, you've had nearly twenty-four hours and . . .'

'I've just arrested Michael Joseph Dillow, sir.'

'Who?'

'The butler.'

'What for?'

'The murder of Osborne Meredith.'

'Are you sure?'

'Yes, sir. It all fits in.'

'What does?'

'Motive, means, opportunity . . .' Sloan couldn't think offhand what else constituted a murder case.

'Motive?'

'Theft, sir. Of a very valuable picture. I think,' added Sloan judiciously, 'that he had a bit of really bad luck there.'

'Where?'

'In Osborne Meredith spotting the switch-over just when he did.'

'So,' astringently, 'did Meredith.'

'Quite so, sir. Otherwise Dillow had timed things quite well. Meredith was sure to be at the two-day cricket match on the Saturday and Sunday – he would never have missed that if he was alive – and it was highly unlikely that anyone but Meredith would have spotted that the Holbein was a fake. The forgery's a really expert job . . .'

'Who did it?'

'Dillow won't tell us but I strongly suspect the same hand that did the pseudo Van Goghs which his last employer found he owned.'

Superintendent Leeyes grunted.

'But to lessen the risk,' pursued Sloan, 'Dillow put a dud electric light bulb in the fitting over the picture. It's in a bad light as it is and Miss Cleepe is short-sighted anyway and isn't an expert.'

'Then what?' demanded Leeyes.

'I think he killed him when he took his tea tray in, ate the tea himself and left the body in the library.'

'Sloan,' irritably, 'there's something very old-fashioned about all this – butlers and bodies in the library.'

'Traditional, sir,' Sloan reminded him. 'You said we could expect the traditional at Ornum.'

Leeyes grunted again.

'He left him in the library, sir, while he deflected the Vicar. It's not the sort of library anyone uses much in the ordinary way. Then after he sounded the dressing bell,' the only dressing bell Sloan knew was that on his own alarm clock which went off every morning at seven o'clock, not every evening at seven thirty, but he was prepared to believe that there were others, 'while all those in the house were changing he carried the body down to the armoury . . .'

'Quite a good time to choose.'

'Very. Except for one thing. William Murton was watching him from the spyhole above the great hall. As well as seeing Dillow carrying Mr Meredith's body he also saw the chandelier lying on the table – which was what put us on to him having been there.' Sloan discreetly omitted Lady Alice from the narrative. Ghosts were all very well in Ornum House; in the stark scrubbed police office in Berebury they became too insubstantial to mention.

'What put you on to Dillow?' enquired Leeyes. 'That's more important.'

'Teacups,' said Sloan. 'There should have been three on their Ladyships' tray.'

'Teacups?'

'There were only two,' explained Sloan, 'which meant that by the time he took them their tea Dillow must have already over-heard Meredith telling the Vicar's wife that he would be waiting for her husband in the library and guessed exactly what discovery Meredith had made.'

'Meredith could have told him himself that he wasn't going up to the two old birds,' objected Leeyes.

'If he did, sir, then Dillow was lying when he said he hadn't seen him earlier. Six of one half a dozen of the other . . .'

'And Murton?'

'William Murton decided that in future Dillow could subsidize his pleasures – he therefore didn't ask his uncle for a loan this weekend – which I gather was something so unusual as to be remarkable.'

'So he got what was coming to him . . .'

'I'm afraid so, sir. As soon as he tried it on, probably. He was dealing with a tougher nut than he knew. Than we knew,' Sloan added honestly. Dillow hadn't gone quietly but there had been policemen everywhere.

'Hrrrrrrrmph,' said Leeyes. 'And what stopped Dillow just clearing off with the picture?'

'Michael Fisher, Mrs Laura Cremond and me,' said Sloan.

'The boy found Mr Meredith too soon, Mrs Cremond stirred up the muniments and I sealed the door. If I hadn't I think it would have gone out today under Dillow's arm.'

'Today?'

'His day off. Bad luck, really. He parked it in the safest place he knew. He tried to break the door down in the night and to lure the archivist out with food today.'

'Hrrrrrmph,' said Leeyes again. 'And Murton?'

'I expect,' said Sloan, 'Dillow suggested he and Murton go somewhere for a nice, quiet chat – like the dungeons.'

Inspector Sloan had left Constable Crosby and Constable Bloggs on duty outside the door of the Private Apartments with firm instructions about the Ornum family remaining undisturbed.

The door, therefore, in theory should not have opened at all at this juncture, still less should an incredibly old lady in black have got past them armed with nothing more intimidating than a lorgnette.

But she had.

'Why,' demanded the querulous voice of Lady Alice Cremond, 'has Dillow not brought us our tea?'

Detective Constable Crosby turned the police car in that wide sweep of carriageway in front of Ornum House where the coaches of the Earls of Ornum had been wont to go into that wide arc of drive which brought them to the front door.

There was room to have paraded the entire County Force and to spare – but there were only two members of it present: Inspector Sloan and Constable Crosby.

'Home, James, and don't spare the horses,' commanded Sloan, climbing in.

'Beg pardon, sir?'

Sloan sighed. 'Headquarters, Crosby, please.'

'Yes, sir.'

They drove through the park, past the Folly and ignoring the

Earl's prize deer. Crosby steered the car between the gryphons on the gate finials without a sidelong glance.

Sloan looked at his watch and thought that – with a bit of luck – he'd be home in time to nip round his garden before the light went. Yesterday – was it only yesterday? – there had been a rose, a new rose, nearly out. It might not be good enough for showing but he thought he would try.

You could never tell with judges.

They left the copybook village of Ornum behind and got on the open road.

They were on the outskirts of Berebury when they saw the ambulance.

It was in a hurry. Crosby slowed down and eased to the side of the road as it flashed by in the opposite direction. The sound of its siren was nearly extinguished by the roar of the motorcycle which was following the ambulance at speed.

'That's Pete Bellamy, that is,' observed Crosby inconsequentially.

'Well I hope Traffic pick him up . . .'

'Always follows the blood wagon, does Pete.'

'Say that again, Crosby.'

'About Pete Bellamy, sir? He lives opposite the ambulance station . . .'

'Where does he work?'

'Some garage in the town, sir. He's just got himself the bike.'

'So that each time the bell goes down he chases the ambulance . . .'

'That's right.'

'Only when he's not at work of course.'

'That's right, sir.'

'When's his dinner time?'

'I couldn't say, sir. Is it important?'

'And if it's a smash-up he rings his boss.'

'I expect so, sir. They don't pay them a lot you know. Not apprentices.'

'And his boss comes out with the breakdown truck on the off-chance.'

'They do it in other places,' said Crosby defensively. 'Big main road counties. Near black spots and so forth. The truck just follows the ambulance.'

'Maternity cases,' said Sloan sarcastically, 'must be a big disappointment to them.'

'It's probably worth it,' said Crosby. 'One good roundabout's worth a lot of swings in the car trade.' He said anxiously, 'Is it important, sir? Shall I have to tell him to stop?'

Sloan breathed very deeply. 'No, Crosby. Just to drive more carefully.'

He reached into his briefcase for the formal charge sheet.

Presently he read it out to a sullen silent prisoner.

'Michael Joseph Dillow, you are charged that on Friday, June 20th, last, you did feloniously cause the death of one Osborne Meredith against the Peace of Our Sovereign Lady the Queen, her Crown and Dignity . . .'

Sloan paused.

He hadn't thought of it like that before either.